A DOCKLANDS WENDIGO

A DOCKLANDS WENDIGO

Clarke Buvelot

2011

Fastnet Books
227 Donnelly Street
Armidale, New South Wales, 2350
Australia

www.fastnetbooks.net

publishing@fastnetbooks.net

First published 2011

National Library of Australia
Cataloguing-in-Publication entry:

Buvelot, Clarke, 1964 —
A Docklands Wendigo

ISBN-13: 978-0987171214
ISBN-10: 0987171216

To Bill, who shared with me many adventures in London — but none quite like this.

PRELUDE

North West Territories, Canada, late autumn, 1926.

The short autumn day has faded into a short twilight. Low-hanging clouds prevent any aurora borealis this night. Instead a susurration of snow floating lightly earthwards adds to accumulated drifts and loads further the boughs of the fir trees. Pale grey smoke from the chimney of the log cabin mingles with the miasma of snowflakes. A few rays from oil lamps force their way through a chinks in curtains punctuating the blanketing darkness and catching the occasional snowflake, turning it into a flicker of gold.

The cabin that belongs to the Stillwaters is a simple design, mainly of wood and stone, much more like a European dwelling than anything the generations of their ancestors may have once lived in. Inside the decor, such as it is, reflects the indigenous rather than the imported and Mary Stillwaters, her Anglicised name notwithstanding, cannot be mistaken for anything except the descendent of a long line of those Asiatic ancestors who crossed the land-bridge over the Bering Straits ten or twenty thousand years before. Her hair is raven black and long, tied in a tight single plait, her face is crevassed and lined, but even if she is a grandmother she is not all that old – families are started young among the Algonquin. As seems to be invariably the case, Mary is engaged in cooking something, not as her forebears would have done over an open fire but on a large cast-iron stove.

The room is vaguely smoky, the light yellow from the stove as much as the oil lamps scattered about. George Stillwaters sleeps in a chair at the other end of the single large room, which is almost the totality of the house. The third person in the cabin is a child, the first of the many grandchildren of George and Mary have and will have but the only one living with them now. To little Johnny, just seven years-old, Mary and George are and would always remain Granny and Grandpa. Granny cooking, Grandpa sleeping were to become fixed images for Johnny, not the only such images of his childhood, of course. Even in his later years, he would draw up memories of spending time with his grandfather in outdoor activities, especially hunting trips, of being encouraged to develop the skills with gun and knife which led to Private John J. Stillwaters, Royal Canadian Army, surviving the ill-fated Dieppe Raid in 1942 and the later advance through France and Holland to the surrender at Luneberg Heath in 1945, all the while taking potshots, usually terminal ones, at Germans.

Now, however, it is as little Johnny at play on a buffalo rug on the floor that he hears for the first time the word 'wendigo.' As he plays, he is only vaguely aware of the background sound of the wind blowing outside the lodge, and then abruptly above this, an uncanny howling that is not the wind nor anything else he has heard before in his young life. He stops his play and looks up, frightened. Another howl. Granny stops stirring the cooking pot and turns to him, notices how scared he is.

'What is that, Granny?' he asks.

Granny pauses in thought for a moment, then beckons him across to her. She puts an Indian blanket around his shoulder.

'They are the lost children of the tribe. The sad ones of the deep snows.'

'Why can't they come inside and be warm, Granny?'

'We cannot invite them inside, my grandson, because they have lost to right to sit at the fires of people.'

'They must be cold, Granny.'

'It is the way of the wendigo, to be cold and yet burn with longing for what they once were, eternally. Listen to me, it is time you knew of such things.'

She glances at Grandfather but he just continues dozing. 'In the old days, when our people still hunted for food, young men would go searching for deer and moose right up until the snows became too deep. Now and then it would happen that the snows would come early or that a sudden blizzard would catch hunting bands far from the lodges and tepees. And unable to get back or to shelter, many braves would die. Some would fall to eating their companions to stay alive, often long after their friends had died of the cold for the snows kept them fresh. But if no thaw came and rescue was impossible, once the meat was gone those who survived by eating others would have to crack the bones and eat the marrow inside. Once they did that, these poor lost souls would change, change into creatures who were doomed to roam the wilderness, eating only human flesh. These are the wendigoes. And when the first snows come, they are reminded of what they once were and they seek the homes and fires of their tribes. But they must never be let in, and you must never go out to them because their desire for human flesh overpowers their memory of being men and they will eat you.'

The howling stops and only the sound is of the wind.

II

London, May 10, 1941.

'It's the dogs what hear 'em first,' said Tommy Robinson. 'And it's you that hears the dogs first,' said Ted Worthington, emphasizing the *that*. Not for the first time, Ted wondered how it was that Robinson could have such acute hearing when he was a physical wreck in every other respect. The nightly climb to the roof of Selwyn's warehouse left Tommy gasping for air and shaking for the first five minutes, even when most of it was via the goods elevator. As Ted knew, the real reason that Robinson had taken the task of fire-watching during air-raids was that he was afraid of going down into the tube station, had a phobia of being buried alive. Ironically, if the blast hadn't killed him, Tommy's paranoia would have been fully justified.

In confirmation of Tommy's claim, a swelling chorus of howling dogs arose, spreading in both Ted's imagination and in reality across London, from dog to dog, street to street. A few seconds behind this and overpowering it came the deeper moaning howl of the air raid sirens. The dogs always reacted to the first subsonic whispers as the sirens 'fired up.'

Not that there were as many dogs as there had been before the war. Long before the first bomb fell on London in September 1940 (probably an accident in the first place but Churchill's reaction in demanding the bombing of Berlin set off the Blitz, maybe Hitler would have bombed London anyway), much fearful nonsense, helped on its way by H.G. Wells' *The Shape of Things to Come*, was mooted abroad about the consequences of both animals and humans (of the criminal and insane type) being let loose by the bombing. Hysterical owners put their dogs down, panicked by the exaggerated claims that dogs rendered ownerless in the mass bombing so apocalyptically predicted would revert to wild states, roaming the rubble of the cities in fearsome packs. (A mere 150 years earlier, this was a normal situation for dogs in London, anyway, but cultural memories are short.) Despite the similar predictions about lunatics and mental patients, nobody had openly advocated *their* destruction in the interests of the safety of the wider community, at least not in England, or not in public.

A short time after the bombing entered popular parlance as 'the Blitz,' there were very few individuals who did not know someone who had heard of someone who was related to someone who lived in the same street as someone who had been trapped in the rubble of their collapsed home, buried alive (or dead) with their pet dog (very much alive) which had then taken to eating its owner to survive itself. Less common were stories about owners, who finding themselves with the situation reversed, ate their pets. As with most folk tales, the accuracy of these stories was not the issue – although arguments about the veracity added greatly to their telling in pub, shelter and rationing queue. The stories were of course used for the thrilling effect of their telling and, as an added benefit, scaring the pants off those hardy, sentimental or careless citizens who had ignored the government warnings or the dire predictions of their neighbours and had not destroyed their dogs at the outbreak of hostilities. (Cats, parrots and hamsters seemed exempt from these parables.) The repeaters of such stories would have been astonished to learn that their accounts were, in one instance, quite true and accurate except in one small detail. The eating of dead and dying bombing victims was not done by a member of the species *canis*. It would be some forty years before the fact became known – and then less than a handful of people hear of it, let alone would believe it.

The siren above Salmon Lane, Limehouse was attached to the corner of Selwyn's warehouse, a Victorian pile of grime-encrusted brick and taped and boarded windows. With the U-boat attacks starting to take effect and with greatly reduced imports anyway, its massive floors and halls were no more than half full. The army had considered requisitioning the space for its own purposes, but then nothing had happened. That was the army, perfectly capable of turning up without notice and simply taking over a warehouse, or a stately home, and equally as capable of giving months of warning and never turning up at all. Nonetheless, a fire watch was maintained on the roof each night by those employees who because of their age had not joined up or had not been conscripted.

Ted lent on the parapet, as far from the screaming siren as he could get, and gazed at his neighbours as they responded to the warning. He looked for his old lady, who would soon step out the front door of number 35, carefully lock it, and give him a wave before joining the stream of neighbours heading for the Limehouse underground station two blocks away towards the river.

But first came what Ted called 'the scurriers'; those who shot out of their doors, front or back, and scuttled to the station entrance, shooting down it like rabbits into their bolt holes. These speedsters were of two types. Those who were scared and didn't care who noticed or knew it. And those who wanted to get onto the platform first, to get the best positions. Ted looked with distaste at the hurrying figure of Oliver Gray. *Sciving git*, thought Ted and would have gobbed a lump of phlegm on him if he could have been reasonably sure of hitting him from this height.

Gray was hurrying because he stood to earn his usual five bob by grabbing a place by the wall and holding on to it. Not that he was averse to just taking one from someone else if he had to but it caused fewer problems if he got it by arriving first. Later Madge Hastings, would wend her way through the crowded platform and give him five bob for the spot. If she was sufficiently schickered, she might allow him a swig of her gin, but usually she wasn't that far gone this early in the evening.

And the sirens were early this evening. This was still a lingering glow of twilight west, far beyond Tower Bridge but allowing its monumental Victoria Towers to stand out in fading silhouette. The bridge was raised as, raid or no raid, a freighter was making its way out of the Pool of London. It was darker on the ground in Salmon Lane. The sun hardly ever penetrated even in daytime thanks to the warehouse occupying most of the south side of the street. Certainly dark enough for three drunks staggering out of *The Waterman's Arms* to be shouted at by an ARP warden for letting a momentary shaft of light out. 'You daft buggers! Shut that door!'

'Go plait yer shit, mate,' said one of them. But he quickly pulled the door closed.

Now, like ants from a nest a child has poked a stick into, people were pouring out of the houses of Salmon Lane, Conder Street, Brenton Street and the other small streets, lanes and alleyways that connected with it. Women and children mainly, with old men and a sprinkling of younger, most carrying some items or other – gas masks and bedding rolls, food wrapped in newspaper, bottles of beer, flasks, torches by those who had managed to obtain batteries. One woman carried a canary in a cage.

From number 17, Ernie Darlington stepped out with a gramophone in his hands. His wife, arms full of 78 records, struggled to shut the door behind her. His complaint that she needed to be careful of the records because he predicted a shellac shortage only prompted her to wonder aloud if Churchill was going to drop Victor Sylvester foxtrot records on Hitler and let him and Goering dance themselves to death.

In Yorkshire Road, where it met Salmon Lane at an oblique angle just near the station entrance, a young mother pushed a baby in a wicker pram out of her front door, causing an old Chinese man to execute a dainty but hurried sidestep to save his shins.

'Mind legs, missy,' he smiled, 'You hit Chinaman with baby, you have to marry, yes.'

'Cheeky yellow sod,' the mother muttered, wondering for a moment how he knew she wasn't married.

Kids, having gravitated to each other, were playing games, dodging in and out of the crowd. A harassed mother grabbed at a passing child and gave him a clip across the ear then realised he was not one of hers. The boy, too used to clips and slaps to care who they came from, tagged a slightly older girl who chased him off into a bombed house.

The sirens began to fall silent, their staggered muting across the metropolis sounding like a fading echo. With the loss of the sirens and with people disappearing into the dark maw of the tube station, the noise of voices, feet, doors, began to dwindle. Just faintly, noticed at first by the most acute of hearing or the most fearful, was the murmur of aircraft, no more than a hum as yet.

A woman's voice screamed, 'Margaret Hilda! Margaret Hilda!'

Knowing grins and nods passed between those nearest to the shouting woman. Margaret Hilda, barely fifteen (if that), emerged unseen by her mother from a small brick air raid shelter, the type no one in their right mind would use to escape the bombs except in the last and most dire circumstance. She ran her fingers through her shock of disarrayed red hair and smoothed down her dress, as red as her hair.

'Can't stop now, Johnny,' she said, speaking back into the shelter. 'I must get down the tube. Mum'll be fretting. I'll meet you tomorrow same time, same sandbag.'

As she spoke, a soldier with Canadian flashes on his uniform, stepped out of the shelter, doing up his trousers. Although not the only uniformed figure to have surged past in the last few minutes, he stood out because he was clearly a native American, an 'Injun' he would be called hereabouts. He made a last minute attempt to grab Margaret Hilda but she was off, skipping through the people to her mother.

'Hello, Mum,' she said.

'Where you been?' demanded her mother, pushing her towards the station entrance.

A woman listening nearby turned to her companion. 'Don't matter where that one's been. It's who's been with her.' Laughing, they walked into the station.

Although some stragglers still made their way to the station, the streets were becoming eerily silent, except for the sound of approaching planes. Bombs began to fall some distance away even as the last few were swallowed up by the darkness of the tube station. Beyond the docks, a searchlight thrust its phallic beam into the sky and seconds later an anti-aircraft battery opened up. Then planes were overhead.

A weird light enveloped the street as a parachute flair floated down. Shadows never cast by the sun in Salmon Lane danced as the flare floated down to splutter out somewhere in the maze of slums beyond Commercial Road. It had been dropped prematurely or maybe too late for no bombs followed immediately close by.

Darkness returned. Then the sounds of voices in argument. At the corner of Barnes Street, an Air Raid Warden, conspicuous because of an eye patch that covered an empty eye-socket, the result not, as he liked to boast, the result of enemy action but of disease as a malnourished child in the Depression, was trying to drag an old lady out of her front door.

'Come on, Grannie Ricketts. You got to take shelter,' he said as he pulled.

An ancient crone was putting up a good show of resistance. 'I ain't going down that hole the ground, yer one-eyed devil.'

'It's a tube station. People go down it every day. Your neighbours are all down there.'

'More fool them then. They ain't got the sense god gived a dormouse. I ain't going down no one's grave.'

'There's only trains down there. It's a tube station,' the warden repeated.

'What would you know? They stuck them all down there. All them poor souls. Some of them were me own family. Round the time of the jubilee.'

Another warden hurried up.' What's going on, Sam. Oh it's her again is it?'

As the combined efforts of two men were now carrying her reluctant feet down the steps, Granny Ricketts continued, 'All of London done up like Christmas and half this street and the next and the next all pegging out. And getting stuck in one big hole and covered up and forgotten about.'

'Come on, Gran,' said Sam, 'You've been down the Odeon again.'

'You think I don't know. I was about to drop me last that

year. I ain't afraid of no Hitler but I was afraid for me kids and I was afraid for me then. I seen them.'

She gave up the unequal struggle and allowed the warden to simply hold her arms. She turned to the second. 'That bleeding Hitler can have my house. It's the sodding landlord's anyway. But he ain't having my chops. Not after I queued for 'em. So you just bloody nip back and bring me 'em. They're still in the pan.'

Sam nodded to his fellow warden, who shrugged and walked back to the house.

'And I know how many there is,' shouted Granny, 'So don't you go nicking any, see.' She turned to Sam. 'And I know who you are, Sam Rooney. I knowed you when you had two eyes. You was a little bugger even then.'

The whine and blast of bombs was now too close for comfort and once again the street was lit, this time from falling incendiaries.

'For god's sake,' said Sam and hurried Granny Ricketts the remaining yards into Limehouse Underground Station.

Sergeant Billy Leggett, although a regular soldier since before the war, was still unhappy at having to work with an upper-class twit like Major Thomas Parrington. Okay, Parrington was a major, despite his young age, but Leggett assumed that was down to string-pulling or a sweetener to get Parrington to take on the job of unexploded bomb disposal or both. A shrewd man, Leggett was quite right. He glanced with only passing curiosity at the ARP warden running past with a frying pan of smoking chops and turned his attention back to the side entrance of the Limehouse Station where Parrington was talking with a young man who Leggett definitely disapproved of. Errol Gray was well on his way to earning the epithet 'wide boy.' Having somehow dodged the draft,

Errol and his twin brother, Oliver, had begun to quickly exploit the absence of older, more established criminals in the area and now had fingers in nearly everything shifty that went on around here. At the moment, 'here' was clearly in supplying Parrington with black market cigarettes as Parrington handed him some money and started filling his cigarette case. Gray noticed Leggett's approach and moved away rather quickly. Leggett wondered for a moment where the other twin was but dismissed both from his mind as minor irritants. Standing with the major was a scruffy street urchin, a kid who seemed to have attached himself to Parrington. Leggett knew that the kid was more than just a street brat; he was one of an increasing number of orphans created by the bombing and other exigencies of the war but one cunning enough to have avoid being taken in hand by the authorities. Quite how and where he lived was a mystery but there were enough abandoned houses, and certainly more than enough partially damaged ones for a shrewd kid to hole up in.

The kid had just turned up one day and attached himself to them – to Parrington actually. Leggett didn't like the kid, Not that Leggett didn't like kids in general. He and his missus had three of their own but there was something about this kid that was, as Leggett tried to tell his wife, 'spooky.' It was mainly his eyes, he reckoned. The pupils were so light as to be almost colourless. The kid was also, again in Leggett's terms, 'as cunning as a shit house rat.' Parrington seemed to tolerate the kid who had an uncanny ability to turn up almost as soon as Parrington and Leggett arrived in Limehouse from their depot in a requisitioned school near Dulwich. Until they received a message about an unexploded bomb, Parrington and Leggett usually sat in the Limehouse Town Hall, which also served as the Air Raid Precaution centre for the district.

The kid would hang around all night. Occasionally, Parrington even let him tag along when they went out to the site of a bomb but mostly he did not. The kid was no doubt useful; he was always able to scrounge cigarettes for Parrington when the Gray brothers weren't around. Whether he stole them or bought them on the black market was not clear. Where the kid went in daytime, Leggett didn't know, not that he really cared. He would be just as happy if the little blighter disappeared altogether.

To Parrington, it was a bit like having a fag such as he had in his senior years at his public school. But, just as in those years he had never had any type of physical intimacy with his fags (that sort of thing was reserved to being mainly between the older boys themselves; any senior boy who did – or was rumoured to do – that sort of thing with juniors was openly designated a 'queer' in the confused sexual milieu of an upper-class all boys boarding school), so Parrington never considered, at least consciously, anything of that nature with the kid, Nicky. Not that he necessarily found the idea distasteful in principle; he would certainly have found it distasteful on class grounds. One simply did not shag the lower orders. It wasn't a question of personal hygiene – boys at public schools in Parrington's time were no more interested in personal hygiene than were the working-class (except for the a few 'dandies,' most of whom were designated 'queers' on those grounds alone) – and appearance had nothing to do with either. Even if Nick had been pretty, which he wasn't, Parrington would never have been able to overcome that entrenched class prejudice.

Leggett, only too aware of Parrington's class attitudes (which from his own class perspective he endorsed), still wondered, not for the first time, about Parrington's interest in the boy but as he had never seen anything untoward, he decided it was probably harmless. For someone who had been a professional soldier since his own teens, Leggett was surprisingly unworldly. But then Leggett had not been to a public school. Whatever the situation, as long as Parrington slipped the kid a few bob, well, the kid was probably better off by it.

Leggett looked away again, watching a stray incendiary being leaped upon by an alert warden with a bucket of sand. The first immediate wave of bombers seemed to have gone across and missed its target, if its target was the East End and the docks, as bombs were dropping much further west. *Not our bleeding area, thank god,* he thought.

The drone of planes and the frantic flailing of the searchlights suggested there was much more to come, so it was a fair bet that he and the major would be hard at it before the night was out. He wondered for the first time if as many British bombs that were dropped on Germany failed to explode as German bombs on London: was some silly prick of a *feldwehr* somewhere in Germany standing around waiting for his officer to get on with it like he was?

'I ain't scared of old Hitler,' the kid was boasting. 'Or his bombs. I want to stay up here and help you.'

Parrington's toffee-nosed accent contrasted with the surprisingly deep timbre of his voice. 'Well, of course, you do, Nick old man. And you do, fetching tea and I appreciate you getting me cigarettes for this.'

Parrington extracted again his silver Dunhill cigarette case from his tunic pocket, and looked at the Parrington Arms engraved on it – a gift from his father, Sir Arbuthnot Parrington, baronet, on his graduation from Sandhurst. He was two older brothers away from the title but the family's long connection with the army had at least got him faster promotion than he deserved. He opened the case and extracted a black-market cigarette. He did not offer one to Nick or to Sergeant Leggett. Nor did he notice Nick's shrewd glance as he put the case into his trouser pocket.

'I can't have you up here, old chap, while the Boche is unloading these fireworks, now can I?' he continued. 'What would your old mum say, what?'

Leggett winced. 'Sir, the brat's parents are dead. The very first raid, sir.'

Parrington dismissed any consideration of lower-class sensibilities over dead parents and lit his cigarette. As he flicked the match away, he noted that the next lot of bombs were falling, down to the east and therefore probably on the docks.

'You said I was a member of your squad,' whined Nick, and paused as Margaret Hilda slipped out of the station behind Parrington. She winked at Nick and skipped away to a soldier waiting in an archway a few yards from the entrance. *Bloody skirts*, thought Nick. 'I am too, a member of your squad. Ain't I, sergeant?'

Leggett was too busy watching Margaret Hilda, wondering how he could manage to get a chance with her.

'If that's so, old chap,' Parrington responded to Nick, 'Then I am your superior officer, am I not? This is wartime and you follow your superior officers orders – to the letter, to the letter. Do you have any idea what happens if orders are not obeyed in wartime, Nicky?'

'All I want to do...,' Nicky tried to explain.

Parrington continued, 'I would be perfectly within my rights to shoot you, right here on the spot. In fact it would be my duty. Insubordination. That's the big word for it. And the perpetrators get shot. That's what happens in wartime.'

He released his service revolver from its leather holster and brandished it in a mock-serious fashion. The movement brought Leggett back from his revery about Margaret Hilda. For a moment he was startled. Parrington winked in his direction. He put the revolver back and pushed back the long uncut fringe of Nick's hair that fell down over the boy's eyes, an action he immediately regretted. In reaching for his handkerchief to wipe his hand, he touched the cigarette case, and this time offered Nick a cigarette from it. Nick's greasy fringe flopped down again as he took a cigarette.

'There's a good chap,' Parrington said, closing the case again 'Now you pop down here where you'll be nice and cosy and safe, and the sergeant and I will nip off and defuse the odd bomb or two.'

He placed the cigarette case in his great coat pocket and again wiped his hands on his silk handkerchief. He turned away. 'Sergeant. Collect the gear. I expect it won't be long before we'll need it.'

As if in answer, a fresh stick of bombs whined down much closer. Nick took a quick step forward, briskly removed the cigarette case from Parrington's pocket and was away into the underground station. Totally unaware of his loss, Parrington strolled off towards a small army truck parked nearby.

'That boy's hair... We really must do something about the state of these people after the war, Leggett. Well, not you, Leggett. Me and people like me.'

'Sir,' said Leggett, thinking, *I hope the little shit has nits, sir*.

Inside the underground station, the ticket hall was dimly lit by faint blue lights and by light seeping up from the platforms deep below. The drone of the aeroplane engines was muted in here and overpowered by the grinding of the escalators. Bombs and anti-aircraft fire were largely indistinguishable from each other as odd, unsyncopated thumps. Nick made his way towards the down escalator, paying no attention to the ticket booth attendant, who in turn paid no attention to him. All the people who had streamed through since the sirens went off were planning to stay not travel, and if they were planning to travel, well, that would be the problem of the ticket collector at the place they got off. Even so, the ticket seller figured there was less possible future strife if he stayed where he was. You never knew when some officious inspector might front up and besides, he didn't fancy having to worry about hanging onto the money from his cash drawer down on the platform with all those people crushed in together. He thought that once he was happy everybody was in who was coming in, he'd nip out and put up some of the new posters that had just arrived. At least these were getting a bit more comical. The first ones, still up on the walls and down the side of the escalator were a bit too bossy for him. 'Is This Journey Necessary?' one of them read. And then there was the one which exhorted 'Your Courage. Your Cheerfulness. Your Resolution. Will Bring Us Victory.' The stick he got about that one: *Who's you? Who's us?* ticket buyers asked, as if he was responsible for anything more than pasting them to the walls. Still, it was a good question. But this latest one was quite witty, he thought: 'Be Like Dad. Keep Mum.'

Nick stepped on to the escalator. He was in no hurry and he was thinking about what use he could make of the major's precious cigarette case. The engraved coat of arms worried him. Being so identifiable made it tough to flog. A drunken woman suddenly staggered onto the escalator and, more as a result of drink and the downward movement of the escalator than intention, pushed past him, almost running down the steps.

'Bloody old cow,' Nick said, tempted to jump down after her and give her an extra shove.

A bomb blast nearby saved him the trouble. The shock wave reverberated down the escalator and sent the woman tumbling the last few yards to the bottom, where a combination of drink and fall laid her out, unhurt but unconscious. Nick stepped over her recumbent body, uninterested in the amount of bare fat thigh and underwear she was revealing.

A middle-aged man dragged himself up from where he had been sitting near where the escalator debouched onto the platform. 'Blimey, that was a close un. Is she alright?'

'Course she is,' a nearby woman replied, recognising the recumbent woman. 'She's just Mozart-and-Liszt, as usual.'

The man walked over and pulled the unconscious woman's dress across her legs.

Another woman piped up. 'I would be too, if I could afford the booze every night. Lucky cow.'

'Leave it out, she's all right, she is.' said the man, straightening up. 'Now, how about it, Doris?'

The woman named Doris laughed. 'You'd be so lucky, Bert Hardcastle. I should cocoa.'

Nick ignored the sexual banter and moved along the crowded platform, a tight-rope balancing act stepping along the thin space left at the edge of the tracks. An officious London transport attendant proceeding in the same direction tried to stop people spilling over the first of two white lines painted parallel to the platform edge. 'Stay behind the white line till 7.30.' he repeated, occasionally giving an obtruding limb a shove with his boot. A middle-aged man, squirming uncomfortably between two women – wife and mother-in-law – squinted up at the attendant. 'Yeah, yeah, we know, mate. Can't inconvenience the bloody passengers.'

'Who'd be coming here at this time of night in the middle of a bleeding air raid, that's what I want to know,' the mother-in-law said. Nobody bothered to answer her.

Towards the far end of the platform, the tide of people had petered out and slightly more space existed between groups. Nick passed without interest a family of Hasidic Jews, huddled against the wall. The father was deeply engrossed in reading the *Torah*, the mother braided her daughter's hair, the teenage son watched surreptitiously a young woman dancing an eccentric jitter-bug to the music from Ernie Darlington's gramophone. A tough-looking adolescent was less interested in the dancing woman than in the Jews. He stared at them with hatred. 'Bleeding hebes,' he muttered loud enough to be heard by those closest to him, 'Look at 'em. All their bloody fault.'

A one-legged man trying to sell copies of *The Daily Worker* from a satchel slung under one arm, turned quickly. 'It's your boss Moseley's mates what are dropping them bombs you're hiding from, comrade, not the rabbi and his family. They're dodging 'em too, only they ain't making a song-and-dance about it like you.' The few nods and grins from others around him were enough to prevent the adolescent from wanting to make more of it. 'Fucking bolshie,' he muttered.

Dust and bits of rubbish suddenly began to be blown along the track and the platform. A warm wind pushed along the tunnel. The attendant doubled his efforts. 'Come along now,' he shouted, 'Get behind the line. London Transport is good enough to let you down here. A bit o' give and take. Behind the line, then, eh?'

The imminent arrival of train caused those closest to the white lines to push back a little. 'I'll give you give and take, mate,' muttered someone. 'Right little Hitler, him' said a woman. Any other comments were lost as an underground train roared out of the tunnel and screeched to a stop. Its windows were criss-crossed with tape to prevent flying glass in case of a bomb blast. A brief moment and the doors slid open. In the carriage opposite where Nick stood was a group of well-dressed elegant men and women, resplendent in dinner suits, evening dresses, jewellery. They languidly surveyed the scene in front of them. Nick stared back, not sure this wasn't a hallucination, these splendid creatures, groomed, impeccable, transcendent. The doors closed. The train pulled away, stirring the barely settled detritus again.

'There's your true class enemy, brother,' said the one-legged paper-seller, 'Sodding upper class coming down to see how the oppressed masses are doing, for something to do before dining at the Ritz.' He spat onto the tracks.

Nick followed a man anxious to relief himself to the very end of the platform but stopped as the man clambered down into the dimness of the tunnel beyond. Grandma Ricketts had made her own space and was warming her chops over a tiny spirit stove. The man she borrowed the stove from was complaining about how long she was taking. 'Terrible fings happens if your meat ain't cooked proper,' she replied, peering myopically at the chops.

'Go on with you,' a woman laughed. 'He only wants to make sure there's some left so he can drink it.'

Grandma turned the tap off and the blue flame died. She pushed the stove back to the man. Nick watched as the fat stopped sizzling and Grandma plunged a fork into one of the chops and lifted it from the pan. 'Giz a chop, Gran. I'm starving.'

'Get out of it, you scrounging little git,' she replied, blowing on the chop.

'Garn you miserable old sinner. I'll swap youse. Here, look a coupla ciggies for one of them chops. What'd you reckon to that?'

'Show us then.'

20

Nick pulled Parrington's cigarette case from his pocket and opened it, revealing it was full.

'Four, if'n they're Virginia mind,' said Grandma, 'Six if'n they're Turkish.'

'Course they're Virginia. Here.'

Nick carefully removed four cigarettes. Grandma dropped the chop she had speared, picked the smallest of the others and speared that instead, thrusting it at Nick. He grabbed it and juggled it, it was hot.

Oliver Gray sitting against the wall a few yards away, watched the transaction, his eye on the cigarette case. 'Here, son, sell us that cigarette case. There's two bob in it for yer.'

Nick glanced at him. He know Oliver for what he was, a spiv, a draft-dodger.

'Two bob! Go boil your sodding head.'

'Maybe I'll just bust yours, you little turd. And have it anyhow,' Oliver spat.

Nick laughed. 'Yeah. I just see you getting out of your comfy spot. Leaving it empty while you try and catch me, you fat bag of wind. You wouldn't get your half-crown for keeping if you did.'

Oliver started to get up but the close attention he was receiving from people far less comfortable nearby caused him to change his mind. He was stymied, at least until his client turned up and paid him for saving the spot. 'You'll keep, sunshine,' he muttered. 'When me brother gets here.'

Nick laughed and turned to Granny. 'I don't think his brother's coming. I seen him just now and he reckoned he had fatter fish to fry.'

Grandma farted. The man whose stove she had borrowed complained about it ponging enough already without her contribution. 'Garn, better an empty house than a bad tenant,' laughed Grandma. She farted again to confirm the point.

'Chrise, nobody wants to hear from brother round mouth down here,' Oliver joined in. 'Specially as you stink already, you old bat.' He was seconded by another man. 'Yeah, why don't you nick orf right down the end?'

'Leave her alone,' said Nick.

'Who asked you?' said the Spiv. 'Now Granny, just bugger off down the far end and let us breathe a little bit better, eh.'

Several others supported the motion.

'And take the midget toe-rag with you before I sort him,' added Oliver now the others seemed to be on his side for once.

'You couldn't sort your own shit, mate,' Nick retorted.

Grandma had already started to move and she muttered as much to herself as to those who objected to her presence. 'I don't want to mix with you lot. I don't even want to be down here. Youse made me. I warned youse but. Don't say I didn't.'

Nick followed, his thoughts on maybe getting another chop if he showed he was on her side.

'That flash git's going to sit on his gazoo all night for sod-all, but. The bint he's keeping the spot for is sewed up and flat on her kisser way back there.' He added hopefully, 'Giz another chop, eh?'

Grandma stopped at the very point the platform petered out. 'Gerroutofit.'

The area was greasy with spilled oil and splattered with rubbish that had blown in eddies into the stains. She lowered herself gingerly to the platform, more worried about her joints than the filth.

'I stuck up for you,' Nick cajoled.

'You wanna eat something, suck the marrow out of the bone you got. Good scoff inside a bone. Probably best bit. You know that, eh?'

'You're mad, you old bat.' Nick sent the chop bone

spinning into the blackness of the tunnel.

'Hey, watch it.' A voice from the blackness. The man who had gone to relieve himself clambered back onto the platform.

'And you do pong, you old shitbag,' Nick said and looked back to see if he could find a space further away. But he had no chance to find out. The explosion threw him off the platform and into the tunnel beyond.

Untouched and unconcerned by the raining bombs and incendiaries, unilluminated by the questing searchlights, unmolested by the impotent barrage of anti-aircraft fire, a huge landmine drifted slowly down on its parachute. It touched the earth, or the road surface at least, next to the entrance to the underground station, seemed to hesitate, then rolled inexorably into the entrance.

Margaret Hilda caught a glimpse of the deflating parachute, a strange, wafting shape of white, like (she thought) a vast wedding veil, over the shoulder of the young soldier energetically if rather inexpertly thrusting away on top of her in the brick street shelter.

The landmine clanked across the floor of the entrance and dropped into the ticket hall, its progress eventually stopped by the combined effect of the rails at the top of the escalator and its own parachute becoming entangled in the stairs behind it. It lay inert for moment. Then, the timer, designed to delay its self-immolation for long enough to cause maximum disruption and concern, malfunctioned. In this last split second of its and his existence, the ticket collector stared at it. The mine exploded.

The immense force of over 1000 lbs of explosive went mainly in two directions. Up into and beyond the ceiling of the ticket hall, and down, down the escalator, magnified by the narrowness of the passageways into and along the underground tunnel.

Margaret Hilda saw the whole tube station and the buildings on three sides lift up, intact, into the air, hesitate there for a split second, and come back to earth as their constituent parts. At the same moment, the shockwave of the explosion hit her and the soldier, a huge impenetrable cloud of dust wiped everything from sight and the noise of the blast obliterated every other sound. The bomb shelter disintegrated – the walls simply were no longer there. Most of the roof spiralled away into the air, except for the jagged chunk of iron beam that was driven into the young soldier's rectum, smashing his pelvis and tearing off most of his penis.

Neither Ted Worthington nor Tommy Robinson had seen the mine descend. They were busy smothering an incendiary that had lodged on the far side of the building. On seeing the incendiary device go out under the combination of water from the stirrup pump and a bucket of sand, they both felt quite pleased with themselves. Ted paused to look over the balustrade at the windows of Martin's Tea Warehouse opposite. He saw flames but could not be sure whether the fire was inside the warehouse and he was seeing it through the windows or whether, as was often the case, he was seeing the reflection of flames of a fire in another building. 'Tommy,' he said, still staring, 'Do you thinks that's a fire?' He tried to lean out far enough to see if there was any sign of flames from his building but couldn't get a good enough view.

For a moment, Tommy thought Ted was making a rare joke; there were fires close all around. Then he noticed where Ted was pointing. 'Dunno. Could be.'

Ted made his way back to the observation station and lifted the receiver of his phone to report the fire just as the mine exploded. A jagged sheet of metal, the Underground sign itself, tore him completely in two. When he was found much later, his hand still gripped the receiver. It was not obvious he was in two pieces until they tried to lift his body and it came apart. It made getting him down from the roof somewhat easier, if less pleasant. Nobody was sure where Tommy was. His corpse turned up a day or two later on the ground on the far side of the warehouse, although whether the blast or the fall killed him was unclear and irrelevant.

Those people on the platform closest to the escalators were simply disintegrated by the force wave or ripped apart by the tsunami of tiles, bricks, pieces of metal and timber that was driven in front of it. Limbs, teeth, heads, and bits of personal effects were added to the storm of shrapnel that hurled in both directions along the tunnel, concentrated by the narrow aperture into which it was forced. Most of the wall tiles were ripped off, the station signs and the billboards flew apart and joined the shredding storm front. Further along the platform people were smashed, flung headlong onto the live rails, or through the air against the ceiling and walls. Bits of bodies collided with whole bodies, smashing bones, wrenching limbs from their sockets. Behind the roar of the force wave and the ripping and shredding of brick, tile and metal, was a dull persistent thunder of the remains of the building raining back to the earth to which they had once held what must have seemed an immovable grasp. To this was added two similar thunderclaps of earth and masonry collapsing somewhere in the tunnel itself, collapsing at that point where the force wave lost most of its lethal power and progressively degenerated into a wind that still rushed on, as if from a more powerful train into stations to either side. Then – an extraordinary moment of seeming absolute silence.

The screaming started. Those who were not already dead, and it was not many, screamed from the pain of their mutilations or from the terror that wrenched at their guts. A few shouted for loved ones of family or friends – possibly not even in the underground station with them in the first place. Others were silenced by shock, and would remain that way until they too died of that shock or of their injuries or a combination of both.

Some flickers of light were discernible. Lamps and touches which had not been blown to bits by the explosion or dropped and broken glimmered fitfully through the all-enveloping dust and smoke. Somehow, some electricity still made its way into the station and one or two lights, miraculously surviving the impact, still burnt. Sparks and flashes came from the rails as bodies and body parts flung onto them twitched and jolted, along with all manner of debris, clothes, bits of masonry, personal items.

Gradually, those few who had survived with minor injuries, cuts and grazes, began to stagger upright and to try and help those closest to them still alive. There were not many of those and several of the survivors had to force themselves, thrashing and gagging, out from a pile of bodies and parts of bodies. More than one, overwhelmed, simply collapsed again and wept.

A sailor, on leave, who had already seen some action at sea and had dealt with men blown apart with high explosives, was the first to gather enough sense of what had happened to make an attempt to take command. He grabbed at one or two others who seemed to be standing and not badly injured. He ordered them to try and sort out the tangle of bodies, telling them to push any who were clearly dead off onto the track. To emphasise his demands, he kicked a number of detached limbs over the edge of the platform. One and then two and then more men eventually obeyed. An attempt, futile as it was to be, was begun to try and separate the dead from the temporarily still living.

The one-legged paper seller was still alive although his crutches were long gone. As was his left eye although he had not yet realised it. The racist adolescent lay on his back, the winding handle from the gramophone embedded in his throat. The Jewish family were a tangled pile of bloody limbs. The back of the spiv's head was smashed to a bloody pulp against the precious bit of wall but he sat against it, still protecting it in death.

At this furthermost end of the platform the explosion had been less universally fatal. Here more lived. Here more were not as mutilated. These survivors rallied and at the sailor's behest, began to work back along the platform, the men separating the living from the dead, the women attempting to provide some assistance to the injured. The further towards the entrance they moved, the more hopeless it became and finally the attempt petered out in the face of what was little other than a pile of ripped bodies and a huge pool of blood that flowed over the edge of the platform. Here no one lived, squirmed or screamed. They were the lucky ones. Beyond this, in any case, ceilings and walls had collapsed into an impenetrable wall of rubble.

It took quite a while for Nick to even figure out where he was when he came to. The blast had thrown him off the end of the platform and into the tunnel and by sheer luck he had landed to the side of the rails and not on them. He opened his eyes to a world of near blackness, broken here and there by odd patches of dim, misty light. Even as he lay in the greasy muck beside the rails he saw, without comprehending, the track side signal lights, still red in the wake of the recently passed train, flicker, dim and go out. The lines and their attendant signals, displays and relays had finally lost their power supply. The walls of the tunnel slightly muffled but did not deaden the screams and moans of the dying back on the platform, and he could hear, even if he could not make sense of, human voices shouting. Gradually he became aware that he could see vague shapes, people, moving about on the platform and dark shapes crashing or rolling off the edge. He rubbed a hand across his face, reacting to the mixture of grit and wetness it touched. Amongst the smell of dust and blood, he became aware of another, more human, more familiar smell close by. Then a hand grabbed at his hair. He screamed.

Grandma screamed back. Her breath was worse than her body odour, and Nick yanked himself from her grip. She seemed in better control of herself than she had any right to be. 'Bloody throwed me right through air.' She almost seemed to be amused. 'Lucky I landed on you.'

'You can sodding get off now,' said Nick and gave her a shove.

'Must have been that spirit stove,' said Granny.

'You didn't land on me. You landed on your head. It was a bloody bomb, you daft old bat.'

'Yairs, I suppose it was,' said Grandma. 'Giz a hand up.'

They staggered to their feet.

'Watch it,' Nick said, 'Step on that rail and you'll fry like one of your chops. Probably serve you right if you did.'

He dragged her to one side and they shuffled the few feet to the edge of the platform. Nick scrambled up.

'Oi,' shouted Gran. 'It took a bomb to get me down here and I sure as hell ain't waiting for another to get me back up again neither.'

Nick was tempted to leave her there but turned and dragged her over the edge.

'Sweet God Almighty,' she croaked. A man lying flat on his back tried to sit up and as he did so his arms remained lying on the ground, torn off. He looked at them stupidly as if wondering who they belonged to. Even in the dim remaining light, the pile of debris and bodies towards the far end of the platform was obvious.

'We ain't never gonna get out that way. We gotta walk out the other way. Back there,' Nick said, pointing back into the tunnel again.

'I ain't going back down there,' Granny said. 'Ain't no way out there.'

'Course there is. Next station, innit?'

'What about that rail? I ain't getting fried on no rail.'

Nick looked at the corpses and body parts strewn over the rails, blown or thrown there. 'It's dead I reckon.' He giggled. 'Like them sods lying on it. Look.'

Granny shuffled her way along the platform.

'Stay then, you old bag. What do I care.' Nick jumped back into the tunnel. He inched his way along. It was much darker here and the floor was uneven with junk, debris and protruding sleepers. He felt an electric cable, sheaved in dusty isolation tape, strung along the wall and he followed this with his right hand loosely wrapped around it. His feet hit something bigger than a sleeper or a joist, and then he hit an obstacle with his head. He held out both hands and felt in front. It was a pile of bricks, mortar, concrete, steel reinforcing. The tunnel had collapsed. Even as he worked his way to both sides and then clambered up the rubble as best he could, he knew it had filled the entire space of the tunnel. He tried removing a few bits and pieces in case it wasn't very thick but other than precipitating further falls, it made no appreciable difference. His mind, tuned by living on his own wits since the war started, began to sort his jumbled thoughts. Despite the screaming – lessening now – the shouting and the unidentified sounds of bits of building still collapsing and the earth itself still settling, he leaned into the pile to try and hear anything beyond it. Nothing. He told himself it was too early yet to hear anyone digging from the other side, but they would. Or from above. Of course they would come. He had seen them all through the Blitz, digging people out of the wreckage of their houses. This wouldn't be any different. He headed back to the platform, scrambled up and moved along it. The armless man had lain back down and, so Nick figured, died. Nick kicked the arms off the platform. Even if he wasn't dead, he wouldn't need them anymore and they were just in the way.

Grandma had shifted along a bit but not in any meaningful way. She peered in the gloom for Nick, forgetting he had gone down the tunnel to try and find a way out. She stopped and stared at the wall a few feet ahead. Behind the ripped off tiles, a large gap in the ground was apparent; loose, moist soil was weeping out onto the platform. Two men had also noticed it. One called to a woman with a torch. She pointed it at the crack. Others joined them.

'What do you reckon?' a man asked.

'Got to be worth a go,' said another.

'We can't stuffin stay here.'

'Maybe it's a ventilator shaft like what them do-gooders are always unblocking.'

'Yeah. Would lead to the top if it's to get air in. Stands to reason.'

'Talking about it ain't getting us out.'

Several men started grabbing at the edges of the gap, pulling away remaining tiles and the bricks behind, digging wherever they felt earth. A whole section of the wall suddenly gave way. The men fell back. In the light of the torch a pile of putrescent, slimy corpses, barely more than skeletons although some retained remnants of skin, tissue and hair, tumbled out, piling up on the platform.

Grandma shrieked, 'I knew them poor diseased devils was down here. You didn't listen. You said I was mad. You know different now, don't you.' She cackled in hysterical delight.

Whether the bigger-than-usual explosion of the mine drew any extra attention to itself among the continuous explosions of lesser high explosions, crash of anti-aircraft guns and roar of fires already blazing was hard to tell. By the time most of the heavier dust had settled, human figures began to arrive at what was, in any case, a rubble-filled shallow crater more than a hundred yards wide, where the underground station and other buildings abutting it had been. In ones and twos, air raid wardens and sundry others with or without authority to be outside during an air raid stared, numbed, at a sight which bore no resemblance to anything with which they had, if they were locals, any familiarity.

Over the noise, those closest to where the flimsy street shelter had once been heard Margaret Hilda's screams. They quickly dug her out by hand, so insubstantial were these pointless shelters. It took longer to separate her from the barely conscious but moaning soldier. Once his weight was from her, Margaret Hilda was able to stand up, lower her dress and found she could move quite freely. Her injuries amounted to little more than scratches and bruises, not all of which may have been caused by the explosion. Even so, her rescuers insisted she sit and wait for the ambulance which they sent a man to summon for the stricken soldier. All attempts to pull his trousers back upon were defeated by chunk of steel protruding through the bloody, mangled mess of his buttocks and pelvis. His missing member would be found and removed from Margaret Hilda when she was eventually examined in a hospital much later that day. It was Margaret Hilda who was among the first to realize what it was that had disappeared in the blast – other than the private's privates. Even then her realization was probably alerted by the weird sight of the girl who had been playing chasey as the crowd entered the station.

The girl appeared out of the smoke and dust from who knows where. The few would-be rescuers were still standing about, although another of their number had been despatched to try and phone for a demolition crew with trucks and equipment. The girl wandered, as if sleep-walking, out of a black alley to one side and drifted across the crater towards the middle. So strange was her appearance and her wraith-like movements that everybody fell silent and simply stood and watched her progress. As she moved far enough for her back to be seen, Margaret Hilda screamed. The girl had no back to her head and very little to her body, simply a bloody raw mess. Almost instantly the girl reached where the top of the stairs to the underground station once were, fell straight onto her face and never moved again. Margaret Hilda's scream became a hysterical shout, 'Mum!' She ran towards the girl's body but ignored it and started tearing at the rubble with her bare hands.

As if released from a spell, all those already there and others who arrived were galvanised. Men rushed to join Margaret Hilda and began digging rubble, shifting debris. A woman removed her coat and laid it over the dead girl. Men commenced to dig around her but made no attempt to remove her body.

Archie Clarke had been made senior air raid warden through the subtle gradations of class. Unlike many of the others, he worked at a job that required a starched collar and tie and seated him at a desk most of the day. As a tally clerk in a warehouse, he was thus considered to be superior in some ways to those other men who had volunteered as air raid wardens – drivers, railway porters, mechanics, men who worked with hands and backs. There had to be some sort of order of command, even at the street-by-street level, and Archie's suit, well-worn as it might be, provided his superiors with a way of elevating him, albeit to no great height, above those of his comrades who ordinarily wore overalls. Ironically, when on duty, they all wore overalls (although Archie wore his over his shirt with the collar and tie). It was pretty much the same everywhere throughout London, except in those rare places that an individual showed leadership qualities that transcended his class position.

Archie returned from phoning for machines to help with the digging. Sid, who actually lived next door to Archie, was the mate with whom Archie drank in the local, went to the West Ham games with but who accepted Archie's seniority without question, looked up and asked him when the crew were likely to turn up, arguing the pointlessness of trying to dig out all this rubble by hand. Archie had to admit that he no clear idea, the raid had been the heaviest known so far in the Blitz and all the Heavy Rescue Squads were fully committed. His mate coughed dust from his throat.

'What's this then? A minor incident. They do know it was direct hit? They do know what's under here?'

'Yeah, I told them, once I figured out for meself what was here. But Buckingham Palace copped one. It's got priority. Stands to reason,' Archie said.

'Bound to,' said Sid, spitting dust from his throat, 'I can see that. Might have woken up the bloody ladies-in-waiting. Probably made Georgie's stutter worse. All have to rush around there and calm their ruffled feathers.'

'Now, now, Sid, no need for that sort of talk...' He broke off as a three-ton army truck, grinding its gears, manoeuvred its way throw the rubble strewn street and stopped. 'Well, now here's something,' he said. Parrington hopped out of the cab, followed by Sergeant Leggett. They started walking through the rubble to where the futile digging was taking place.

'Oh Jesus,' said Sid, 'It's that bloody comic opera major.'

From the opposite direction, a gas-burning car with its grotesque, tumour-like bag on the roof, pulled up at the edge of the crater. Its back door opened and a man in a rather old and worn pin-striped suit stepped out. The all-clear had not sounded although the raid seemed to have moved on, the crump of bombs and the buzz of the engines delivering them seemed rather distant. The man leant back into the car, hesitated over whether to pick up his tin hat, and then placed instead a bowler hat on his head and, amazingly, lifted out a furled umbrella which he proceeded to carry with him as, oozing self-importance, he gingerly stepped across the rubble towards the crater.

'Who's this plonker?' asked Sid.

'Some bugger from the sodding council,' said a third man, looking up from heaving a large piece of timber to one side.

'Right,' said Sid. 'Now give us a hand to get this poor kid out of here at least.'

Several men turned to help remove the corpse.

The 'bugger from the council' was Henry Walpole, who had been just one of many extremely junior clerks (despite his advanced age) at the beginning of the war but who had, as his superiors volunteered, were drafted or shifted sideways to essential war work, risen to a higher level that he may ever have conceived of reaching pre-war. He was accompanied, as befitted his standing, by another civil servant of lesser authority and self-importance, whose hands held an assortment of maps and papers. He scurried after Walpole, tripping on rubble, caught up with him and together they stopped to confer.

More local inhabitants who had been sheltering at home or simply unable or unwilling to go into the underground station began to congregate. Already some women were bringing freshly brewed pots of tea, the perennial working-class response to any emergency big or small. Some were unable to do anything but stand and stare. Even those by now used to the bombing and the destruction of houses could not quite encompass the total loss of buildings this vast empty area surrounding a crater represented. Others tried to assist with the vague digging about in the rubble, not contributing much beyond shifting debris from one place to another in tiny armloads and handfuls. Not a few groups simply stood and wept. A few clambered down into the middle of the crater and helped lift the body of the child to the edge, others took her from there.

Parrington, having made his way across the rubble, barely glanced at the girl's body and those removing it but stood gazing down into the crater. Leggett commenced to roll up the sleeves of his tunic and to walk down into the crater.

'Just a moment, sergeant. We have more important work to do,' said Parrington.

Leggett turned, puzzled. 'Sir?'

'This damned bomb has already gone off, sergeant. With surprising effect, I admit, but it has gone off. Our job is with those that haven't. Yet.' He turned towards the men scratching at the rubble. 'Is anyone alive underneath?'

A young man with an eyepatch looked up at him.

'I heard something. Little while back.'

'No you never,' said an older man, probably his father. 'Rubble collapsing. Makes strange noises. Ain't no human noises that I've heard.'

Sid, returning from placing the girl's corpse outside crater stopped and wiped his face with a dirty scarf. 'Poor bastards are too deep to hear anyways even if any of them was still kicking. The one's near the top all blown to bits.' As if to support his claims another man beyond them picked up part of a leg from the debris and laid it to one side. 'The ones on the platform buried too deep.' he continued.

'Probably all drowned like at Clapham,' said another. 'When the mains all burst.'

The youth with the eye patch insisted they had to keep digging anyway. His father nodded. 'Got to have something to bury, son.' The man with the knowledge of Clapham snorted. 'Them poor fuckers is buried already.' His words were truer than he imagined.

A large truck with a crane mounted on the back crunched its way down the street to the edge of the site. The driver leant out of the cab window as Archie crossed to it.

'Gawd struth!' said the driver, 'What a mess, Where'd you need me, guv'nor?'

'Better back her in. Over there. Up to where the crater starts, near where my blokes are.'

'Right, guv,' said the driver, squinting at the crater and then the general lie of the land.

'But for pity's sake, go easy.' Archie warned. 'We don't know how solid the ground is and how much just come up and down with the blast.'

'Sodding great.' He pulled his head in and engaged his gears, to reverse the truck and turn it.

'Just a moment, my man.' Henry Walpole had walked across quickly and rapped on the side of the truck with his umbrella.

'Here. What's your game?' shouted Archie.

'This truck is not to move,' Walpole said.

'Says who?'

'I do.' He turned back to the driver. 'You can switch off your engine, my man.'

'I ain't your man,' muttered the driver. But he turned the engine off.

Archie, who in ordinary circumstances, would only too easily have submitted to anyone in a bowler hat and pinstripe suit, bristled. He was the senior ARP, no matter who this was. Despite Walpole insisting all work cease and the men come out of the crater, Archie stood on his dignity and his responsibility, and argued the toss. The exchange became heated; it was Parrington who ended it. With the self-confidence and the accent provided by public schooling and a lifetime of dealing, at least at the level of overriding, the lower classes, he simply ordered the machinery moved and the clearing continued. The enraged Walpole was about to argue with this new intrusion until he noticed Parrington's major's crowns on his epaulettes. Ingrained class attitudes and many years as a junior clerk came to the fore. He politely insisted that he speak to Parrington away from Archie and the other men, although his attempt to draw Parrington way by touching his sleeve received a withering look that caused him to withdraw his hand as if burnt.

'You understand, major, I couldn't speak in front of the workmen,' he said apologetically. 'Won't do.' As he spoke he signalled his assistant across.

Parrington was not prepared for this shilly-shalling. 'What won't do? Make sense, man.'

'Of course. Of course. I can tell you, major. Senior officer and all that. Here, you see.' He turned to his assistant. 'Hold the map up, Mason.'

The man named Mason unrolled a large-scale map of the streets and building of the area. 'There. Right here.' Walpole pointed rather excitedly at the map. 'Where the bomb fell.

Where we're standing, major. A cholera burial site.'

'Cholera? What are you on about?' growled Parrington.

Walpole looked around quickly to see if anyone else had heard Parrington's words. 'Not widely known. Obviously,' he said, turning back to Parrington. 'Around the time of the Jubilee. Very nasty but contained, luckily. The victims all placed in a single grave. Right here.'

Parrington wasn't following this too well. Walpole explained. 'We can't have the ground opened up. Just imagine if cholera germs get into the water supply. The systems are all disturbed enough thanks to the bombing. No telling how it could spread or how far.'

'Good god, man, this isn't a graveyard, it's an underground station.'

'Kept totally secret. When they built it. Imagine the hysteria. These people, you know.' He gestured, taking in the area with one motion of contempt for the working class. The implications began to sink in with Parrington. He also had a built-in conviction about the mental capacity as well as the unsanitary practices of the lower orders. Before he could respond, Sergeant Leggett, in company of a police constable wheeling a bicycle, present himself and saluted.

'Sir, this copper, er, constable needs to speak to you.'

The constable seemed breathless and more than a bit confused. He started to explain that his station was presently unmanned and that all phone lines seem to be out.

Archie joined them. He and the constable knew each other and the constable seemed to find support in a familiar face. He addressed himself as much to Archie as to Parrington. 'It's Mick Snow. He's gone off his chump.' It seemed that a local resident, driven mad by the bombing and a legacy of shell shock from the previous war had chopped up his mother-in-law with an axe and had his wife trapped in the attic of their home. Parrington assumed command of this situation as well and told the constable to show him the way. Before leaving the site, he turned to Archie. 'Get your men up out of the hole. And then leave it alone.' He removed his service revolver from its holster and checked it as he, Leggett and the Constable strode away.

Walpole reasserted his authority with Parrington's departure. 'Get your gang up from the crater,' he ordered Archie, 'and get them busy filling it in.'

Then he threw the map, the only one in existence that acknowledged the cholera grave, onto a pile of burning debris.

Shortly afterwards, three streets away, Parrington shot dead the mad Mick Snow. It was only one more insignificant death of that night, although at least this one received the formal dignity of a coroner's report – which found Parrington's actions justified if a bit precipitous.

In the dark below, hours, days, weeks, months passed. The seriously injured died. Those with lesser wounds joined them. Even those without physical injury, in shorter or longer time, died simply of despair, although the conditions were hardly conducive to survival anyway. At first there was some light but eventually all the sources dwindled, flashlight batteries, kerosene lamps, candles, lighters and matches all gave out. For a little while there was some light and heat and capacity to cook what little food there was that needed cooking; there was enough debris and enough burnable belongings to keep some fires going. The smoke accumulated, mingling with the ever-increasing stench of purification. Somehow the smoke managed to find a way out but if it was ever noticed by anyone outside, it was assumed to be just part of that ever-present smoke that lingered after the major fires from the raids had been controlled. Or it mixed with the fogs, the dust and the inevitable London smog.

Before the fires gave out, the food, scrounged from the belongings of the dead gave out. And the living, some of them at least, took to eating the dead, although for a while the more active tried and occasionally caught rats. There was, if anything, more food than could be actually eaten once the inhibitions against cannibalism were overcome; the dead rotted before they could be eaten. And the stink alone drove some survivors to simply die or, more than once, to kill themselves. But the hardiest became immured to the smell, it became simply another aspect of the overall condition of death, burial and darkness. Two of the most successful survivors were Nick and Granny Ricketts. Their status as peripheral members of the community even before the bomb brought them into a form of alliance. Nick became Granny's protector. They kept to themselves as much as possible, maintaining their own small fire, and, most useful of all, using Granny's frying pan to cook flesh stripped from the newly dead. Nick became adept at scuttling, like another larger rat, and deftly cutting chunks of flesh from bodies. But in time, no fresh bodies were available. Even those who had adapted to cannibalism with the least difficulty succumbed to want or to the horror or both. The darkness increased as the last fires faded. And, inevitably, it was Granny's turn to die. At the hands of Nick, of course. There may have remained enough humanity in Nick to at least sense the gruesome irony of cooking bits of Granny in her own frying pan, but humanity, physical and emotional, was fading as completely in Nick as the light in the tunnel. He finished Granny raw; there was nothing left to sustain even the slightest fire. But, somehow, his vision had changed; he saw, if vaguely, even in the dark. And he continued to eat, now putrid flesh and then, remembering Granny's dismissive claim much earlier, marrow from the many bones that littered the space. It was years before he was forced to turn to the slimy remnants of the cholera victims which had oozed from the walls. And he endured. And he waited.

Even during the war, official and popular memory of the Limehouse tube station began to fade. Archie died of a heart attack a week before the first V1 rocket would have brought him back into active serve as an ARP. His mate, Sid, moved to Scotland to be near his daughter who had married a sailor. The constable, whose role in the Mick Snow affair, was less than well-received by his superiors was shifted to Richmond and never received promotion, ending his police career still a uniformed constable, although he was inclined to feel that walking the tow paths along the Thames was not the worst that could have happened to him. Henry Walpole rose inexorably up the ladder of local government, a rise accelerated by wartime contingencies, and took a role in organising the Festival of Britain. Following a hushed-up arrest for gross indecency with a youth in one of the temporary lavatories provided ironically as part of his contribution to the smooth running of the Festival, Walpole retired to Ferring-on-Sea where there may have been a number of public conveniences but the average age of the population served to reduce considerably the chances of another incident. Sergeant Leggett was transferred after the end of the Blitz to a group designed to disarm mines, explosives and booby traps on and after the Allied invasion of Europe. Having survived D-Day, he was killed endeavouring to disarm an unexploded British bomb in the rubble of Caen during Montgomery's delayed advance from the British bridgehead. The area around the station was almost completely obliterated during the Blitz, the survivors moved, were rehoused in other parts of London or beyond, grew old and died. London Transport, in the midst of all the post-war rebuilding above, simply bypassed the spur-line that had connected Limehouse and said nothing about it. Official policy on the secrecy of government documents ensured anything that might have existed about the events of that night was lost in restricted archives.

III

Brighton, October 12, 1984

At 2.54 in the morning the bomb planted by Patrick Magee three weeks earlier in the Grand Hotel exploded. If Mrs Thatcher hadn't been the sort of person who considered that dawdling over answering the call of nature was inefficient and a waste of her precious time, she may well have been blown up with it, as intended. Or perhaps as was hoped as it is far from clear that Magee and his fellow members of the IRA could have had any idea when they set the bomb months before which room Mrs Thatcher was likely to be in. The blast blew a narrow incision down the length of the frontage of the hotel, threw debris as far as into the English Channel opposite and, of course, smashed an inordinate number of windows.

For a moment, before becoming fully awake, Sir Thomas Parrington, as he now was, capitalist developer, large-scale contributor to the Conservative Party, and considerable wheeler-dealer with that same party, imagined that he was back in the war. Responses, behaviours from that period forty-odd years previously rushed to the surface, even as a suddenly familiar smell of explosive and brick dust invaded his senses. The memories were not specific. Indeed, from very soon afterwards, Parrington had very little direct memory of the Limehouse Underground incident. To be fair, this was not simply innate insensitivity (although there was that) but because of the physical and emotional demands made on him throughout the war. No one incident seemed to particularly embed itself in his mind. No doubt, Parrington had been brave; it took a rare sort of courage to deal with high explosives in intimate contact, where the chance of being reduced to constituent molecules in an instant was not the abstract notion of the average soldier in the field, sailor on a warship or even civilian under aerial bombing but a reality. Once the Blitz was effectively over, Parrington's army service became, if anything dull and routine. Promoted to lieutenant-colonel, he in fact spent most of the rest of the war in staff positions, although he did traipse across Europe in the wake of the British army, commanding units whose task was mainly disarming the inevitable booby traps left by the retreating German army. Altogether, Parrington had what was often referred to as 'a good war.'

A curious feeling of nostalgia pervaded Parrington even as he became fully awake, a feeling that was to remain with him throughout the chaotic day that followed but one he never fully identified. He sprang from his bed even as the echoes of the explosion were still fading away and the cacophony of screams, alarms, crashing rubble and shattering glass was growing. It is as well that he did. The front wall of his hotel room had completely disintegrated and his bed had slid across the floor to dangle over the chasm. As he stood, at first a little uncertainly due to the slope the floor now took, the bed itself slipped with an oddly graceful movement over the edge. Parrington snatched his silk dressing gown from the bedpost as it did so, and calmly put it on as the bed, bedclothes billowing, floated down into the street. His slippers lay where he had put them in relation to the bed the night before and he slipped his feet into them, tightened the cord of his dressing gown and crossed to the door. As he pulled at the handle the whole door came away from its hinges. He stepped aside and allowed it to crash into the room, where it landed on the television set.

Outside, the hallway was filled with smoke and plaster

dust. Emergency lighting struggled to illuminate the gloom. A number of people in various degrees of undress staggered about, dazed and confused. A Pakistani maid purposefully pushed her trolley of clean bed lined and cleaning items down the passageway, as if oblivious to the explosion and its immediate after-effect. The trolley fell into the hole several metres wide that now existed in the middle of the corridor. She threw a bottle of toilet cleaner after it, then her feather duster, and stomped off in the direction which she had come, muttering angrily to herself as if this was all some new devilment created by the management to harass her.

Parrington walked calmly along the corridor towards an emergency exit sign glowing dimly through the haze. He stopped on encountering a woman lying face down, covered in dirt and dust. Her dull blonde hair, too tightly lacquered into a wispy back-combed pile to be more than moderately disturbed by the blast, made Parrington pause, for an instant thinking the unthinkable, that this was his beloved Mrs Thatcher brought to her knees. He kneeled and turn her over, but it was not She.

'Lady Muqbuquet,' Parrington said. 'Up you, come, my lady.' He dragged the totally dazed creature to her feet and leant her against the wall.

A door burst open. A hysterical man, his pyjamas in shreds, his grey hair on end, his face bloody, crashed out, shouting. 'Oh God! Oh God! Oh God!'

Parrington let go of Lady Muqbuquet, who slipped slowly down the wall, to sprawl in a highly undignified fashion on the Axminster.

'Get a grip on yourself, man.' he said, grabbing him by both shoulders. 'Remember you are a Conservative. And for god's sake put on a dressing gown. There are ladies present.' The man stared at Parrington for a moment. The Parrington released him and the man went back into his room.

'Dear woman,' said Parrington to Lady Muqbuquet, 'You seem to be down again.' He lifted her to her feet and together they made their way to the exit.

One of the lasting television images of that day, along with the Prime Minister declaring, despite it being a clear *non sequitur*, 'All attempts to destroy democracy by terrorism will fail,' with the images of the bomb damage (usually framed to avoid showing the far greater area of the wedding- cake facade of the hotel that was not damaged), was the shot of Sir Thomas Parrington, complete with a Churchillian cigar (conveniently found in his dressing gown pocket) striding from the front door of the hotel and through the tangled mass of survivors, police, firemen and general onlookers. This image, coupled in latter days with the quickly researched details of his wartime exploits, rivalled that of the Iron Lady herself as the media icon of the bloody but unbowed Conservative Party. It also held him in good stead for receiving government approval for his redevelopment schemes in the East End of London docklands.

ONE

London, March 18, 1985

Sir Thomas Parrington's 'defiant-face-of-Conservatism,' bloody but unbowed and endlessly repeated on television news bites, bore significant fruit almost immediately. When those viewed-by-millions images were added to many years of judicious donations to the Party, his grand, self-aggrandising plans for the whole-scale redevelopment of working-class areas in the largely abandoned docklands on the edges of the Thames were expedited. Not merely expedited but where necessary, (appropriately enough) bulldozed through such tangled webs of bureaucracy and rather less tenacious attempts at community objection as might have delayed the process. Within two years of beginning his enterprise, the first tower block was complete. A modest construction by the standards of his intended next construction and the constructions after that, this new excrescence on the East End skyline was already helping with the cash-flow situation for the larger scale destruction now beginning.

Parrington looked away from the large television screen in his penthouse office. The conviction of Patrick Magee two years after the event prompted television news services to resurrect archive footage of the bombing, and broadcast yet again the image of Parrington stalking through the shocked survivors before pausing to talk to a rather flustered reporter. Parrington muted the sound with the remote control. 'If nothing else, there was a better class of survivor that time around,' he said.

If his personal assistant, Angela Snottym, was a trifle confused by the reference to 'this time,' she was polite enough (or canny enough) not to indicate it. In any case, the implications were there to be inferred as Parrington turned to look out of the windows that occupied one complete side of the office at the panorama of the docklands spread out forty floors below.

Of most immediate interest – in fact, of all-consuming interest (Parrington had no concern with the wonders of the scenery dominated by the winding River Thames) – was the area near the foot of the tower block in which he was perched. Here fresh excavation was taking place on a site recently cleared of whatever houses and businesses had once stood there, those which had been the few survivors of the Blitz and those which had been constructions raised in its aftermath alike. From this height, the activities below were toy-like, the actions of ants burrowing in order to build a nest, a nest not for their kind but offices and apartments for their betters. Contrary to Aesop, delving for the grasshoppers.

Down below, closer to the action, the machines of destruction and the machines of construction were many and huge, even menacing in appearance and purpose. Central to the present work was a monstrous earth-gouging machine which was boring itself into the earth. Close up it was far from ant-like; it was like a giant robotic mole, its sharp steel incisors biting into the ground, dislodging earth and the rubble of previous generations, including, had anyone of the workmen operating the machine or monitoring its progress been interested enough to notice, a rusted piece of an old underground station sign.

Below their very feet, what had once been a boy, Nick,

denizen of East End alleys, now a mutated creature, a hairy, emaciated, scabrous horror, lay in the dark, sucking and chewing desperately on a dry bone. He did not know it and even if he had been vaguely conscious of the changes time and habit had wrought, Nick had become a *wendigo*. Neither he nor anyone else at the time could have named the thing he had become – that came later.

There was nothing remotely edible left on or within the bone the creature held. Its yellow pointed teeth scraped fruitlessly at the surface and its black, warty tongue found nothing within its core. It dropped the bone which bounced onto the railbed. This *Nick-creature* fell back, moaning feebly, its scabby, hairy fingers with long, broken, discoloured claw-like nails scrabbled weakly amongst a pile of similarly sucked-out bones. After all these years, all possible sources of food had finally run out. Even the rats that had been attracted at first and with which Nick (as he had probably still been then) competed for food had become food themselves for the creature he had become, and then rats stopped appearing at all. The long journey from boy of the slums to cannibal monster of the underworld was about to end – but not in the way which seemed most likely: in death.

No truly human emotion remained within the recesses of the Nick-creatures brain to surface with a sense of gratitude for its imminent release. Its claws touched something dull and metallic within the pile of bones. It lifted it up: a silver cigarette case, the case with Parrington's family crest, the long-cherished memento of a previous existence. Did some faint echo of some human sensation tremble briefly in some dying synapse?

The Nick-creature lifted the case in its vile claws and held it in front of its face – and then suddenly, inexplicably, there was a savage shaft of light where no more than the merest hint of light had been for four decades. In the surface of the cigarette case, for a split second, Nick saw for the first time the reflection of the thing he had become. Then the light, like a bolt from Heaven penetrating into Hell, was refracted and shattered by the surface of the cigarette case and bounced around the tunnel. The Nick-creature's scream was lost in the crash and roar of a monster more terrible than itself, a monster of whirling, slashing blades and earth-grabbing, piston-driven arms, an earth-borer breaking through the tunnel roof.

The sudden downward lurch of the borer into a cavern where there should have been solid ground took its operators by total surprise. With the lurch of the machine, a workman standing next to the blades was flung forward and the arm he threw out to try and save himself was torn off. In a spray of arterial blood, the arm dropped into the hole.

The arm bounced, skidded and finally rolled next to the Nick-creature. Despite being nearly blinded by the light, it instinctively grabbed the arm, lifted it to its face, sniffed at it, licked the dripping stump with its pustulant tongue. Although it had existed without noise and light for most of a lifetime and its brain was confused and overwhelmed by both, instinct took over. It shuffled backwards into the further recesses of the tunnel, already savouring its unexpected and life-saving meal.

Initially, chaos reigned on the surface around the machine, the hole and the screaming, mutilated worker. Some sense was restored quickly enough that the machine was shut down when the shouting and gesticulating of those close to the work face made their demands clear to the controller of the machine.

Parrington, having given more than tacit support to Mrs Thatcher's obsession with breaking the unions, whether militant or mild, had of course also taken full advantage of the resulting cowed state of unionism when setting his own capitalistic machinations in motion. Thus the site was so poorly unionised that there was no first aid officer employed on it, no safety officer whose interests might have been those of the workers on the site, indeed no union representatives who might have argued for these things or, following this incident, to have led a walkout. Had not at least one of his workmates had a modicum of good sense, the injured workman might well have bled to death on the spot. As it was, his quick-thinking mate wrapped his trouser belt around the stump of the ripped off arm and succeeded in stemming the pulse of arterial blood until the arrival of an ambulance. At least, somebody had managed to summon this by dashing into the site office and ignoring the protests of the engineers and others there. (He was later sacked for his peremptory behaviour in invading space which he was not entitled to enter.)

As the degree of the accident, both in human and immediate engineering terms became a little clearer to the engineer in charge of the site, he ordered the machine withdrawn and made some attempt to ascertain what exactly had happened when the earth had apparently given way. Peering into the hole only revealed that when the borer had gone to some depth, the ground had broken away into an even deeper and, as far as anyone who had surveyed or was overseeing the work was concerned, unexpected cavern. Some portable lights were hastily located and lowered into the hole but these didn't reveal a lot more. Eventually, and not without some trepidation, and in the face of the demand by the worker who had applied the tourniquet that he should be permitted to try and find Bert's arm in case it might be able be sewed back on, the chief engineer's assistant was lowered by ropes through the hole and into the tunnel.

Swinging on the rope, he flashed a random torch beam about the massive space that was suddenly revealed. The beam may have caught for a fleeting instant the eyes of the Nick-creature but if it did, the man made no particular note of it. He saw nothing of the severed arm, most of which had now been devoured in any case. He was able to report, upon being hauled back to the surface, that they seem to have driven a hole into the London underground. The chief engineer asserted the impossibility of this until his assistant elaborated that he didn't think it was a working part of the present system. As an afterthought, he did mention seeing what looked like a lot of old bones. Being no fool, the chief engineer ordered a solid surround to the hole be built and a steel trapdoor to be placed there. He then scurried away to report to Sir Thomas Parrington, a meeting he did not relish.

He was right not to do look forward to it. The meeting took place, after a delay in which he cooled his heels in an anteroom, in the board room on the same level of Parrington Towers as Sir Thomas's office. This room was about the same size as Parrington's office but seemed smaller because most of its space was taken up with a large conference table. Once the meeting got under way, once Parrington was given the gist of the matter, Angela Snottym settled herself with a proprietorial air at one end of the conference table and opened a note pad. Most of the other space in the board room was occupied with architects' models of tower blocks and other buildings, the past, present and future of the Parrington Corporation. Against one blank wall stood a large draughtman's table on was a detailed map of the docklands.

By now, a fuming Sir Thomas Parrington stood immediately in front of this. He ripped the map off the table and revealed underneath another map of greater detail of a small area of the first map. He ripped this one off as well to reveal another.

Even while shredding both these maps and scattering the pieces, he turned to the chief engineer who wisely had placed the considerable length of board room table between himself and his employer. Sir Thomas's voice was seemingly icy calm in contrast to his physical actions, a technique he had perfected over the years to good advantage in negotiations, business and political.

'And how is it, pray tell, that I ask for and am assured that I have the most detailed, the most accurate maps of the area. Maps going back into the eons of time, I am reliably informed, and not one of them has any mention of a mysterious underground rail line running right through the middle of my property. Property chosen, I may add, on the basis of these maps.' He tore off several more and waved them in the air.

The crestfallen engineer picked at some bits of dried blood on his white lab coat. 'As you can see...' He corrected himself, 'Could see, Sir Thomas, none of those maps show any such tunnel. I don't see how we could see foresee...'

'Obviously not. From these maps,' Parrington said.

'There weren't any others,' said the engineer.

Parrington stepped through the confetti of maps that covered the carpet and walked to the window. He stared out at his demesne. He drew breath. 'I didn't get where I am by relying on guesswork,' he said. He turned back. 'All right, Clive, all right. That will do for now. Just go and see no other fool gets himself hurt because he turns up a hole where no hole is supposed to be.'

'We can't be sure there aren't other tunnels,' the engineer said.

'I know *you* can't. I intend to be. I'll see to this myself.

Now, good afternoon.'

The engineer started to turn to leave but hesitated. 'Ah, Sir Thomas, the bones?'

Parrington turned the full power of his infamous gaze on the engineer. 'I'll see to that too.' The cowed engineer scuttled out.

As the door closed behind the engineer, Parrington turned to Angela.

'Damnation, Ms Snottym. This could be awkward.'

'Not really, Sir Thomas. It's only a common navvie and he's not badly hurt. Only lost an arm.'

'That's why I insisted on non-union labour. No, it's that I should have known there was a tunnel there.'

'The advice you got was the best your money could buy.'

'I ought to have known, personally. I was in this area, during the war, you know. Disabling unexploded bombs. If this gets out, it could be just more ammunition for the damned press.'

'But you were a hero. That would be a real PR plus.'

'Not when they figure out I knew...' He stopped. Now Angela looked confused. Parrington continued.

'The fact is that if this tunnel contains anything to suggest the existence of the station, this could give those damned lefties who are opposed to anything that smacks of progress grounds to kick up a stink. I was perfectly justified my decision in the interests of the health of the rest of London, but they won't make anything of that.'

What station? What decision? Angela was not following this but, confused or not, she was also nothing if not quick to pick up on the essentials, essentials as they applied to her employer, his business and her position in it. For the rest, she had no idea what he was talking about. 'It was wartime, Sir Thomas. I am sure you had to make that decision. It was what you were there for. It was your place.' She was also big on the place of the right people to make decisions, especially those that effected or impacted on the 'wrong' people.

'Quite so,' Parrington agreed. 'Anyway, I'm still faced the prospect that my properties are honeycombed with holes and tunnels and god knows what.'

Angela was already setting about earning her not inconsiderable salary. 'We can perhaps kill two birds with one stone here.'

Parrington's impatience surfaced. 'I am scarcely in the mood for ornithological metaphors, Miss Snottym,' he snapped.

Angela was used to Sir Thomas's abruptness, she expected nothing less from someone of his stature. 'What I am suggesting is that we, – you – employ an outside expert to both find any other unknown tunnels and who could at same time be a useful smoke screen if any evidence from the war turns up.'

'Ah. Yes indeed. Well bowled, Miss Snottym.' Parrington, who had hardly ever held a cricket bat or ball in his life despite nearly a decade of public schooling, was nonetheless fond of spicing his conversation with the occasional cricketing reference. While it may have begun as an affected mannerism to facilitate his dealing with the more flannelled foolish types of ex-schoolboy met in Conservative Party gatherings, it had become an established part of his speech patterns. Parrington was not a complete fool, despite having been to (in fact *sent to*) a public school – albeit not a particularly ancient or famous one. Certainly he had taken on board the class prejudices such an education provided or confirmed. Despite the ruthless streak that had enabled Parrington to reach his present position on the heights of capitalism and party machine, he was not primarily a man who used people in the derogatory sense of the term. Rather, he operated at a more subtle level; he knew which people could be useful - to him of course. This meant that he had a wide range of acquaintances and contacts. He had trodden on toes and faces on his way up but seldom on the foot or face of anyone who could conceivably matter at the time or later. This meant that he could usually find somebody to provide what he wanted, directly or indirectly when the need arose. Like now.

'If you would be as good as to phone Tony Eastlake's office and see if he will meet me at my club, tonight if possible.' A fresh train of thought had begun to roll in Parrington's mind. 'And I think I had better have a word with Erroll Gray.'

'That dreadful man, really Sir Thomas,' said Angela.

'Really, Miss Snottym, really. I think I'd better take care of that myself.' said Parrington who, as usual, had the last word.

Angela went off to phone the Ministry of Transport and Parrington returned his gaze to the now deserted building site and contemplated his options. His prospects he fully expected to take care of themselves.

TWO

That redoubtable Austrian ethnologist, Konrad Lorenz, postulated that the difference in appearance between adult and child humans had real consequences for human behaviour, particularly in the way babyish features bring about feelings of attraction and tenderness. Fine for babies (and probably essential for their survival when life was nasty, brutish and short). Fine too for adults who retain the essential features of the neo-nate: the feelings these engender in others can also (and safely) be sexual.

Proof of this could be found in giggling comments of three teenage girls, well versed, when travelling on the underground, in checking out 'hunks' and talking about them in loud voices. On this occasion, fortunately, these inane (and entirely speculative) comments did not travel over the noise of the carriage hurtling through the tunnel to Marc Sharpe, the object of their appreciation. Not that it would have mattered if he had heard them. Marc was used, from childhood, to most of the world reacting to his beauty. He was one of those all-too rare creatures, a beautiful baby who had grown up to be a beautiful adult. Much of his attractiveness was that his face had retained some of the essential features of the neo-nate – round face, large eyes, pert nose – that Lorenz had pointed out are the physical features that bring about the innate response of humans to babies, human and otherwise (cats owe much of their success with humans to this; so, ironically, for that matter does Mickey Mouse). Marc's babyish facial proportions combined, however, with clear evidence of maturity – his cheek bones were high and slightly prominent – although he looked rather less than his actual twenty-five years. His beauty was not simply that of a baby-like face. His dark hair was thick and shiny and very long. His large, round dark eyes were overarched by dark eyebrows and, as if to offset the babyishness, his olive skin had the slightest hint of a dark beard lurking beneath his cheeks.

Although he was more than used to being stared at – in the parlance of the pub, perved on – he could still be made uncomfortable by it, especially in situations such as this where it was difficult to avoid. If it can be said that anyone gets used to hearing repeated praise and flattery, Marc had got used to the compliments his looks so often brought. (Not that he heard them all, or even most of them. He was an object of conversation in his absence to an extent he could hardly have imagined.) Yet, he could be moved to irritation by the unwanted (if warranted) attention.

Certainly he would not have been interested in any of the girls presently ogling him from the other end of the carriage. Their stares and giggles barely registered with him. He was in too good a mood to allow a gaggle of spottily unattractive teenagers to upset him. He caught a glimpse of himself in the window opposite where he was sitting and grinned slightly. This was not because he was narcissistic – although he was. It was pure pleasure he found in the present circumstances of who and where he was at that particular moment. He was, like James Cagney in that old movie: *on top o' the world, ma*; he was back in his beloved London, a fresh PhD. under his arm (so to speak). Okay, he didn't have a job but that was, in his present mood, a minor matter. He would not have stated it so egotistically but life does favour the beautiful and it had pretty much lived up to the aphorism for Marc until now and he had no reason to assume it would not continue to do so.

The train rattled and screeched to a stop at Leicester Square station and the girls got out, with last glances at Marc. Sometimes he returned such looks with a grin, a smile which if the admirer was not already smitten usually did the trick. Other times such as this, he pretended to be unaware, the age-old game played by the object of the voyeuristic gaze. The girls stared through the carriage windows as the train pulled out, then still giggling and exaggerating their lustful intentions, strolled down the platform.

In a minor way, Marc was thankful. Of course, he didn't know and had no desire to know any of those girls. They were the usual unprepossessing English teenagers, with too much make-up and hair product where they didn't need it and not enough attention to diet and care where they did. But he also knew that had he stood to leave the train before they did, he would have been aware of the result of them seeing him on his feet. It was not that he was a midget or anything but he was below the average height for men. If the girls had been able see past the other legs of the passengers in the carriage, they would have seen his feet, his toes really, only just touched the floor. He knew from old that this would have provoked a set of sniggering comments, less flattering this time. Ironically, his height, or his lack of it, added to the way in which he attracted older women wanting, not to ravish him on the spot but to mother him. That had happened too often. Besides, one mother – his actual mother – was enough.

Tube trains do not have time to get up to full speed on the short distance from Leicester Square to Covent Garden, and this one was pulling up already. Marc hopped to his feet, grabbed his Driza-bone – an oil-skin style of Australian raincoat – from the seat next to him and made his way to the door.

He was in the last carriage by choice. For reasons he had

never understood, underground passengers congregated in the middle of the station platforms irrespective of whether the entrances to the platform were centrally located or not. This meant passengers crowded the carriages in the centre of a train and this usually left sitting room in the carriages at either end. Because he exited from the last carriage of the train, he had to walk most of the length of the platform but he was in no great hurry. Even so, Marc had to break stride and take a couple of sideways skips to get past an elderly woman making her way more slowly than the other passengers who had alighted. As she was in the middle of the platform Marc had the choice of passing on her left and being a bit close to the now-moving train, or her right and dodging the seats against the wall while avoiding brushing into her at the same time. A slight pirouette to the left and Marc was by her. Being small made him light on his feet.

This was one of those stations that had a lift rather than escalators but there was no delay at the lift as Marc, coming from the back of the train, was one of the last to arrive before it was full and headed upwards. Not the very last; the little old lady made it just in time after all.

Once out of the escalator, he walked to the exit on the James Street side of the Covent Garden underground station. It was raining slightly, the London weather had pulled one of its conjuring tricks in the time it had taken him to travel from South Kensington, where the sun had been shining (in a fashion) through high, curtain-thin clouds. The rain was getting a bit heavier even as he left the shelter of the station foyer, enough for him to stop to put on his Driza-bone.

He felt a nudge in his back. The little old lady from the platform, an expression of annoyance on her face, was behind him, making no attempt to step to the side and pass. He moved slightly and she staggered on.

'No consideration,' she muttered, and stepped into the street. Only then did she realise it was raining. She stopped dead in the middle of the footpath and tried to get her umbrella free of the straps of her purse and then to open it. This whole procedure forced passing pedestrians to step around her and into the street until she finally managed to get the umbrella to open, to the danger of passing eyes and ears.

Marc buttoned his Driza-bone and stepped around the old lady again as she was still trying to make up her mind in which hand to hold the umbrella and in which to hold her purse. He grinned and walked on. He didn't care about self-obsessed old ladies or about the rain – he was back in his London and it felt good. He allowed himself to be swallowed by the crowds of off-season tourists and all-season regulars thronging Covent Garden despite the rain.

There is never a time when London is not a tourist Mecca, but in late autumn, when the clocks have returned from daylight saving to Greenwich Mean Time and whatever passes for summer is a fading memory, the numbers fall substantially. Even so, the London Transport Museum in Covent Garden was oddly quiet that morning. So quiet that Marc decided to indulge himself with a short play on the underground train exhibit in the centre of the hall.

He clambered into the driving department of the stranded carriage and imagined for moment that it was not bolted in the middle of a room but sitting at the end of a platform, waiting the touch of the driver's hand to send it in electric-charged motion into the gloom of the tunnel ahead. He grabbed the levers and slammed them as if into action. He imagined the slight lurch and the acceleration, and wondered, not for the first time, under what circumstances he might actually drive one. They would certainly be extraordinary circumstances if they ever transpired. And they were when they did.

A uniformed attendant looked up on hearing the noise of the machinery in the train. Like many a museum attendant, he wasn't happy that kids were allowed to play on the exhibits, even when the exhibits were especially set up to allow them to do just that. Still, it wasn't his museum (even if he sometimes acted like it was). At first he thought it was just a kid playing, although a kid by himself was a bit odd, and therefore needed watching. As he sauntered across, he realised it was not a child but a smallish adult. No law against it, but still, not really to be encouraged. *Bloody trainspotters*, he thought, *They can at least stay outside on platforms where they belong, sad sods.*

'Just a minute,' he said loudly as he crossed the floor.

Marc looked up, his revery broken. He watched the attendant approaching and broke into his winning smile.

'Hello Eric.' He climbed out of the cab and held out his hand.

A moment of hesitation and Eric grasped it. 'Well, hello Marc.' He took Marc's hand and shook it firmly. 'Oh, I suppose it should be doctor Marc now, eh? Congratulations.'

'Thanks Eric,' Marc replied.

'Nearly didn't recognise you for a sec,' said Eric.

'No, well...' said Marc.

Another attendant, Hugh, desperate as all attendants are for anything no matter how slight to break the monotony, wandered across and joined the conversation.

'Well, well, Marc. Ain't you looking first class, then? Good to see you,' he said with genuine pleasure in his voice. 'Our first pee-haitch-dee for the Transport Museum, eh?' He thrust out a nicotine stained hand.

'The first to use our facilities for his dissertation, Hugh,' Eric said.

With Hugh's arrival, Eric's speech became a little more upper class than a moment ago, a little less like Hugh's East End accent. Those fine social distinctions that the English have as almost part of their genetic make-up allowed Eric to consider himself just a touch above Hugh on the social scale. A different suburb to be born in, a different type of school or a year or two more schooling, an immeasurable but inescapable difference in father's or grandfather's occupation – any of these that was all it took to allow Eric (and millions of others) to place himself (and millions of others) in a different plane to other millions of others. A subtlety which had occasionally to be reinforced when circumstances demanded. This was one such.

'Yeah, yeah, I know all that. Surprised you know the word dissertation though, Mr Know-It-All,' Hugh said without rancour, simply extending a long on-going mock hostility. He turned to Marc, who had seen this by-play in action many times before.

'We're all real proud of you, son. You done us proud. Mr Pendleton, he's proudest of all, of course.'

The slam of a door nearby caused them all to turn. Just exiting a door marked 'Staff Only' was an oddly shaped woman of indeterminate age. She grabbed a trolley of equal age and decrepitude she had pushed through the door and then stepped on a surgical bandage which had become unwound from her calf. With a hopping, skipping motion she got her foot off the end of the bandage and flipped it momentarily out her way with her toe.

'One of these days that bandage will put her arse over tip into her own teapot,' said Hugh. 'Oy, Myrtle, see who's here, then?'

With a duck-like gait to avoid the trailing bandage and shoving the trolley which threatened, like all trolleys, to glide off at a tangent, Myrtle shuffled up. 'Course, I can. Not blind, am I? It's Marc.'

'It's Doctor Marc now, Myrtle,' said Eric.

'Oh, very, nice I'm sure,' said Myrtle, 'Here, can you do anything about this then?'

She held up her arm, pulling back the sleeve to reveal a scabby, weeping carbuncle.

'Afraid I'm not that sort of doctor, Myrtle,' he said recoiling from the sight.

'What good are you then?' Myrtle insisted.

'Don't show us up, Myrtle,' said Hugh.

'I'll show you up, Hugh Evans,' she retorted.

There was rather more hostility between these two; Myrtle was lower down the unspoken ladder than Hugh was below Eric: she knew it, Hugh knew it, she knew Hugh knew it. Marc stepped in quickly.

'So, what are you up to now, Myrtle? Deserted your mop and bucket?' he asked.

'Oh, I done real well just now,' she said, pleased with herself. 'Making the tea now. Not only the tea. I make sarnies too.' She wiped a drip from her nose onto the back of her hand.

'We all thought you would still be back in Australia. Not that we're not glad to see you,' said Hugh, 'But you know all that sun and *Neighbours*. Not like here.'

'I only went back to defend my thesis. And strut around at graduation. All that stuff. But I've just got back and have to try and find a job,' replied Marc.

'Go on. Back here for work?' said Eric.

'Why can't you find work at home? Must be something, being a doctor and all, surely,' said Hugh, not to be outdone by Eric.

'Ah, but there are no underground railways in Australia,' Marc replied, amused at the look of distress that crossed the attendants' faces. 'Well, a tiny bit in Melbourne. Just in the middle of town. And Sydney too, I guess.' Like all Melburnians, Marc tended to ignore Sydney whenever possible.

Myrtle shook her head, tutted her sadness at the thought of a land without underground trains. Although familiar with the Australia provided by the new soap operas from that country which had taken British television by storm, she had not noted this crucial absence. But then people in *Coronation Street* didn't travel by train much either. Years of coming to and from work and then working at the London Transport Museum had led to Myrtle believing in the ubiquity of the subway systems.

Hugh took Myrtle carefully by her non-boil infested arm and they walked away, like a music hall act. 'That boy really likes his trains, don't he just? Strange boy. Imagine being made a doctor for knowing about trains. If I'd known that sort of thing was on, I'd have made my Kevin stick to his train spotting,' Myrtle told Hugh as they collected her trolley and he saw her on her way across the hall.

Grinning, Marc turned back to Eric.

'I'll just pop on in and see Norman then.'

'Right you are. Good to see you,' Eric repeated and felt a sort of reflected glory as he watched Marc make his way through the 'Staff Only' door.

Norman Pendleton peered at Marc over the top of his half-frame glasses. His face had his usual slightly peeved look, an expression he adopted whenever somebody entered the documents archive. Pendleton liked to pretend that he fiercely discouraged visitors, but it was an act, although it helped him sort out who was a serious intruder with whom he could then engage in matters of mutual interest, and who was likely to be a waster of his time. In an instant, his grimacing turned into a flash of recognition. *That beautiful hair.*

Pendleton grasped Marc's hand in a handshake that was surprisingly firm. 'How lovely to see you.' His eyes did not leave Marc's hair. He had watched it, longed to run his fingers through it, all those months that Marc had spent researching documents and plans and the like here in the archive.

Pendleton was one of those men who had seemed old even when they were young. His facial features had settled into those of middle age before he had moved much beyond puberty, his deeply set eyes and bone structure giving him the appearance of bags under his eyes and a slightly sunken look to his face at an age when most boys are still relatively plump of cheek. He had always walked with a slight stoop and overall his manners, attitudes and interests had been more those of an older (if not old) man even when at school and then as an undergraduate. However, having achieved maturity so early, he stayed there. If anything, he seemed to be getting younger as if living his life backwards like Merlin in T. H. White's Arthurian saga, *The Once and Future King*, or Benjamin Button. While chronologically he had aged, physically he had not. His face had not wrinkled or sagged any more than it had appeared to do when he was in his teens, his hair, a dark brown, had retained its fullness, its lustre, aided by its careful and frequent cutting at Trumper's in Piccadilly. He dressed simply but well.

Pendleton had come to the position of documents curator of the Transport Museum by way of Cambridge but the pathway had begun, if unnoticeably, long before that in the nursery and with his first train set (subsequently much expanded). His entire life was shaped by the deep effects of snug nursery tea-times, soft and comfortable nannies, and the pleasurable fantasies aroused by his model trains. Even his years in a relatively important English boarding school, with all its attendant horrors, had not overridden or even modified these formative experiences. As it had nothing to do with model trains, he had not discovered, consciously or even subconsciously, his homosexuality at boarding school, where he was nowhere near pretty enough to be of interest, nor later at Cambridge. If he had been aware of it at all, it was not until Marc's rather unexpected arrival with a request to use the resources of the museum for his dissertation on the history of the engineering of the London underground that any homerotic feelings percolated close to the surface.

Then and still, his feelings did not take any sort of physical form, and indeed seldom received any form of expression beyond shy, subtly flirtatious comments, while all the time he longed to bury his face in Marc's flowing, Cavalier-style, raven black hair. Without consciously recalling it, this too was a nursery experience, of a nanny with long hair who would release it from its binding and cover his face with it while she played —in the pretence of bath time drying - with his tiny member.

He finally let go of Marc's hand. 'Now, my boy, bringing a ray of antipodean sunshine into gray old London. Splendid. Let me arouse the venerable Myrtle from her lethargy and get her to provide a pot of tea.'

The venereal Myrtle, thought Marc as Pendleton almost skipped off to a door at the far end of the room.

Marc let his gaze wander around this familiar room. He had spent long hours here, searching for and then examining maps, documents plans and blueprints, memos and reports, some from as far back as the 1860s and the first railways built for the purposes of moving people within the metropolis itself, the embryonic London underground system. Engineering details, parliamentary acts, financial documents, minutes and memos, many maps and plans, all these were grist to the mill of Marc's doctoral dissertation on the engineering history of the London Underground. While occasional researchers were allowed access to this archive, Marc was the only long-term researcher who had ever been permitted the extended, daily access over several years. He had also brought an ability for organisation that often assisted in the arrangement and cataloguing of the mountain of material, assistance that Pendleton had been delighted to receive.

Pendleton walked back in, holding the door open with one hand. Behind him, Myrtle pushed the trolley on which balanced precariously a large porcelain teapot of Victoria vintage, so Victorian in fact that it had painted scenes of the Great Exhibition of 1851 on its rotund sides. It was accompanied by some quite delicate china cups and saucers that matched it and a plate of biscuits. Unless Myrtle's elevation had changed ingrained practises, the latter, Marc knew well enough, were likely to be of a similar vintage as the crockery. But, as he also knew and was thankful for, Pendelton kept his own hidden supply of biscuits of more recent origin.

'Here we are then,' Pendleton said with some enthusiasm. 'Tea. At once a beverage and a poem.' This was how, for almost two years, even in the time of Myrtle's predecessor, Pendleton had introduced morning and afternoon tea in the archive, a line Marc knew came from a British wartime film, *The Demi Paradise*. After being first informed of this, Marc had managed to track down the film on video. It proved an amusing piece of wartime propaganda, both subtly and not-so-subtly giving the ruling classes of England a glowingly positive image while seeming to find them a source of gentle humour. Laurence Olivier as a Soviet *stakhanovite* – he had gone on to play ancient Nazis and even more ancient Nazi hunters in his later years and much more besides, so why not? What amused Marc even more was the resemblance, both physical and in behaviour, of Pendleton to the shipowner who indeed expressed that sentiment about tea. Marc wondered if Pendleton saw himself as like Runalow in the film, seemingly vague and dithering but actually possessing a sharp mind and acute awareness behind the upper-middle-class Englishness.

'Ah here we are then. Let me see.' Pendelton paused and reflected.' An Assam blend. No, no. China. For the morning, north of the Himalayas rather than south, Marc, don't you think?'

Marc gave Myrtle a wink to show he shared her amusement at Pendelton's fussiness. Myrtle set about making the tea, taking the leaves from one of a number of small boxes kept in the lower tray of her trolley. The rest of the staff got Lipton's, whether they liked it or not, but Mr Pendelton had, with great patience over the years, trained her predecessors and now Myrtle to make tea to suit his tastes.

Following Myrtle's display of tea-making skills – the skill was not great but the display was impressive – and she had shuffled off, Pendelton tipped the biscuits she had left into a waste bin, opened a filing cabinet and took out a tin of fancy biscuits -from Harrod's by appointment – and he and Marc settled down for a good old chin wag – and a chance for Pendelton to gaze upon Marc with repressed longing.

THREE

Woman Police Sergeant Joan Frazer was both a beneficiary and a victim of a Metropolitan Police policy designed to improve its image and internal structure through the fast-tracking of women officers. As a beneficiary she reached the rank of sergeant rather more rapidly than she might have done under the old regime of institutionalised patriarchy and so ahead of many of the male officers who joined around the same time as she did. Indeed, her father (who was retired by the time Joan joined) had never achieved promotion beyond senior constable. Joan was not sure, had her father lived long enough into his retirement to see her get her sergeant's stripes, whether he would have been pleased or whether he would have resented having spent all his years in the force as a constable in Richmond. Although he had not talked about it, Joan had somehow gained the impression that something had happened to her father during the second world war, that there was a blot on his copy book somewhere from that time and this accounted for his failure to move up more than one rank. Her dad had not specifically tried to stop her from joining the Metropolitan Police, but he had if anything been ambiguous about it. At first, Joan's progress was as measured as that of any female police officer but, when the so-called 'positive discrimination' was instigated in the wake of feminist pressure both in the force and in society generally, she was quickly promoted, although it must be said from an objective point of view, justifiably, to the rank of Woman Police Sergeant.

Within the bureaucracy of the Metropolitan Police an

inevitable reaction set in once the predominantly male organisation recovered from the initial assaults of the new policies and, so to speak, closed ranks. Discrimination against women now had to be more subtle, less formally institutionalised, but gradually at first and then with increasing confidence, patriarchy reimposed itself throughout the force. Ground had been lost of course and continued occasionally to be ceded; senior positions did become available and were filled by women, but these positions were often 'feminized,' roles within the hierarchy that were 'better suited' to women, and which usually did not allow women officers to occupy positions that had any operational control or responsibility. This permeated down the ranks and had a lot to do with why WPS Joan Frazer was the community police officer for Hackney, an effective sideways shift that kept her well to the periphery of what the 'boys' club' considered real police work. That, and her tendency to allow herself a degree of muted aggression in her dealing with male colleagues, especially those above her in rank, when they annoyed her (which was most of the time).

If she had inherited anything from her father, it was a tendency to accept the way things were perhaps a little readily. Not that this stopped her from nursing her complaints to herself and this in turn may well have accounted for the perceived 'problems with attitude' that figured more than one in her assessment reports. Overall though, Joan only occasionally resented what was, after all, a fairly transparent mechanism used to deny her opportunities for further advancement via 'meaningful' police work and administrative duties. That's how the system worked. On the other hand, even if it was an attempt to marginalise her, she quite enjoyed her role as community copper. It did get her out of the station a lot, a considerable plus given the manner in which the sexual dividing lines had become even more pronounced and turned into resentment by male officers who were willing to accept (or claim to accept) the intent but grudge the effect.

If there was an obvious fly in Joan's ointment, it was ironically self-identifying in terms of that particular cliché: the aptly named Superintendent Russell Flize – quickly renamed, not to his face, by Joan as 'Super-fly.' He too, in an entirely other way, was a beneficiary of the gender policy of the force, promoted above his ability and faster than this would have happened except for the subtle machinations of the male backlash. Fortunately for Joan, Flize was so involved in his own self-importance and, of course, satisfied (because senior male officers had told him so) that community policing was just some pointless sop to the 'chattering classes' (which included politicians who feigned a social conscience) and thus could safely be left to women police officers, effectively getting them out of his hair most of the time.

It was in keeping with her duties as community liaison that Joan parked her police car (a Ford Anglia of the type known as a panda because of its blue-and-white paintwork) just off Dalston Lane and walked the few yards to the Grange Tavern. It was still early evening and there would probably not be anyone of particular interest to her drinking in there yet. One of Joan's stratagems was to be seen early in one or more pubs. This would usually be noted and remarked upon by whoever was there to those who came later. Some of the more simple-minded doubtful characters on her patch would feel a false sense of security – the cops had been and gone and were unlikely to reappear. Until that is, during the busy part of the evening, when engaged on trying to flog a few dodgy cigarettes or a knocked-off video recorder, they would feel a hand on their shoulders and turn to find themselves face-to-face with a sardonically smiling Police Sergeant Joan Frazer.

This time, however, Joan had another reason for calling in before the bar trade picked up. She wanted to check on the regular barmaid, Madge, who had been recently on the receiving end of violence from her husband. Joan had learnt from her father the value of 'old-fashioned' policing, the practice of which was another of the causes of her frequent run-ins with her superiors. She was still a believer in it; if anything, the disapprobation of higher ranks such as Super-fly only confirmed her belief in the superiority of old-time policing. In accordance with this, Joan had paid Madge's husband a visit and convinced him, while sitting on his back and bouncing his face off the floor, that his behaviour was unacceptable to her and she wanted no more of it. Now she just wanted to check the lesson had been learnt, something she could not fully be sure of since Madge's husband was, like many men in the area, something of a slow learner, even given the efficacy of Joan's teaching methods.

As Joan came into the gloomy interior, Madge was doing a bit of tidying behind the bar. One or two men were scattered about but the pub was quiet overall. At a quick glance, Joan could see that Madge had no visible new bruises but it didn't necessarily follow that she didn't have any in less public places, although Madge's typical low cut and high-hemmed dress left not too many places for private damage to be hidden.

'Okay, love?' Joan asked.

'He's been quiet as a lamb,' Madge said. 'Bit of a worry 'cause I ain't used to it.'

'Get used to it, Madge,' Joan said. 'Anything I should know about?'

Joan didn't expect people in her community to be narks and most of them would not be anyway, unless it suited them for some reason. Grassing to the coppers was still taboo in this area. But all communities have their own rules, not all of which fall within the clearly designated law of the land, and Madge knew that was what Joan was asking about. There was a point beyond which a relationship with the police, no matter how friendly would not be taken. On this occasion, Madge wandered close to the boundary of community-sanctioned conduct with her nod towards two men seated in the far corner of the pub. Joan followed her look. She recognised both men and was passingly curious. What, she wondered, was Sir Thomas Parrington doing in The Grange, sitting and drinking with Erroll Gray? Parrington glanced up but his gaze simply drifted across Joan without any sense that he registered her presence let alone her uniform. Ordinary members of the police, particularly the uniformed branch, were beneath his notice and well outside his usual society. Joan watched for a while, wondering slightly if she ought to be worried that Erroll seemed to be on speaking terms with an important figure from well outside his usual criminally inclined milieu.

As Joan watched, Parrington produced a cigar from somewhere, unwrapped it a trifle clumsily. Used to a flunkey offering an already unwrapped one at his Club, Joan thought. Rather obviously, Parrington had not offered a cigar to Gray; he may have only had the one, of course. But Gray noticed it and Joan noticed that Gray noticed it. Parrington lit the cigar with a match rather than a suitably ostentatious lighter as might have been expected. Probably a subscriber to that old bollocks that a match brought out the flavour better than a lighter flame, Joan concluded. Madge distracted her. 'Ta for what you done, sarge.'

'He didn't tell you?'

'Nah. Whatever it was done the trick but,' Marge said. Joan

nodded – maybe for a while.

She left the pub and walked back into the swiftly darkening evening. In her panda, she hesitated before turning the key in the ignition. It was hard to know which of the two men she had just observed she disliked the most. Parrington would have been high on her list simply because of what he was, a member of the ruling classes and a high profile one at that. As 'Parrington-the-Spoiler' he had moved from the general field of upper class to a particular item on her personal list. Even though Joan had been born and raised in Richmond, she had a family and a class-based loyalty to the East End, to which was added a feeling for the past, even if the history of that past, as far as the East End was concerned, needed to be viewed through very thick rose-coloured glasses. Also, it didn't seem to Joan that naked capitalism was a good enough excuse for the wholesale destruction of communities – people and buildings – even if both left a lot to be desired.

Erroll Gray provided a much longer term object of dislike. A dislike that was hardly unique to Joan; not too many coppers throughout the wider area of the Metropolitan Police or the City of London Police for that matter were too keen on Errol Gray. His slow but steady rise from back street spiv to one of the main leaders of crime in the South-East had brought him into frequent contact with the law and, inevitably, to a few periods behind bars. But his progress was only slowed never stopped by these and his ability to evade successful prosecution improved over time and in direct correlation to his growing power and financial condition. He was not untouchable but he was pretty much out of the grasp of an ordinary uniformed copper unless he made some extraordinarily stupid mistake, and that was unlikely. There was, however, still something of the old fashioned East End villain about Errol Gray, despite his rise having been all post-war. As far as Joan knew or had ever heard, Errol did not dabble in the drug trade and although he may have tended to turn a blind eye to it on his patch, provided it did not in any way impinge on his activities, he didn't make any money from it. Pretty much the rest of a full range of usual criminal activities were part of his wide-ranging business – protection, arson, larceny, prostitution, strong-arm tactics and, of course, murder although the latter tended to be of criminal rivals or members of his own world who had crossed him in some way.

So why, Joan thought, were Gray and Parrington sitting in a local pub looking a trifle too chummy. She decided that she would maybe drop around Parrington's development sites and even his office building a bit more often during her patrols in the future. She started the panda, turned into Dalston Lane and then Graham Road, heading east to see what the rest of her shift would provide.

Parrington had renewed his wartime acquaintance with Errol Gray shortly after Parrington had developed a financial interest in the East End. His time at a public school had taught him the value of having contacts with certain members of the lower orders who were willing and able to supply goods and services that may have been outside those prescribed by school authorities. The war had simply confirmed the validity of such occasional contacts where necessary or useful.

Both Parrington and Errol had moved on in their respective spheres after the war, rises to power in distinctly different social milieu but perhaps not that far removed in method. Gray had, occasionally, received less favourable notice in the media but at the same time had often garnered a far greater level of support from his society. His spivdom, germinating in the hothouse condition of the war, had flowered into a fiefdom and there was hardly a criminal activity, barring drugs, in the East End in which he did not have some interest, nowadays at a reasonable level of apparent or at least legal remoteness. There were one or two little problems, minor difficulties, that Parrington had found Gray invaluable in having resolved. To Gray's credit, however, he had declined to be of service to Parrington in helping him shift residents, some of whom proved remarkably recalcitrant, from areas Parrington wished to bulldoze and redevelop. As Gray explained, these were 'his people,' it was his community. It was not entirely disinterested, of course, this refusal to apply methods he used quite willingly in other circumstances (especially in the early days with rivals to his growing influence and activities). He was no fool and knew quite well the extent to which his existence and activities in the East End were due to the degree in which ordinary people tolerated even supported him, indeed saw him as a bastion in the class war which had been waged for centuries in the eastern areas of London. In other matters, difficulties with contractors, suppliers and so forth, Errol had been delighted to be of assistance to Parrington, for a price of course and usually without it becoming too common knowledge to his community support base.

The problem Parrington brought him this time seemed easily within Gray's capacity to deal with. Parrington needed the tunnel his excavations had unexpectedly uncovered cleared of what the engineer had suggested where lots of bones, together with some other detritus, maybe of human origin. Parrington knew what they were (or could make fairly good guess) but more importantly he knew or could calculate the financial consequences, if it became common knowledge.

His development could be held up for years while all sorts of inquiries were undertaken, and even his close relationship with the Thatcher government may not be able to circumvent this if word got out. At the worst, the site might be declared a grave site or a memorial or something and development stopped altogether. He needed Gray to have the tunnel emptied without the knowledge of his work force, let alone a whiff of it getting to the media. Thus, as ever, Errol Gray was a useful man to know. He was one of those men of whom it was said, 'he knows where the bodies are buried.' Truth to tell, he had buried a few of them himself, until, that is, he became important enough (through that very process) to have others do it for him. A few old bones were not going to cause many difficulties and as had ever been the case, even at the beginning with a few black market cigarettes in the war, Sir Thomas-bloody-Parrington would pay over the odds and no questions asked.

In time, Errol, not being a mindless thug like some of his rivals, put two and two together and realised (or guessed) what this odd discovery had once been. And so he guessed too that some bones may well be those of his twin brother Oliver. But, sentimental about family as East End criminals usually are, and Errol was no exception, business and to an extent reality, could overrule sentiment. Besides, there was nothing he or anyone could do now about Oliver. It did cross Errol's mind to have his men collect a representative sample of bones which he could inform his aged mother were Oliver's and even arrange a funeral for them. But Mrs Gray was too far gone to really understand what she was being told and a funeral may raise rather too many awkward questions in that stage. In the end, rather than dispose of the bones collected at night while the site was officially shut down, he had them stored in one of the many warehouses he controlled and in which all manner of items accumulated, some awaiting such time as they were no longer too hot to handle, others placed out of the scrutiny of the law and many that had simply been forgotten or never achieved the sort of financial return that made bothering about them worthwhile. Ironically, Errol could have made even more than Parrington paid him had the tunnel been more open than it was at first. Over time, until the metamorphosis took complete hold, Nick had gathered the few valuables he came across in the dark, mainly wedding rings, which of themselves were not worth much – this was the East End after all – but when accumulated and given the rise in the value of gold after the war would have amounted to a sizeable sum. But Nick (or the wendigo) had stored his valuables the other side of the collapsed central section and they were never discovered. Errol Gray would not have lived to enjoy these spoils anyway. A long festering East End gangland dispute sputtered into brief life soon after – literally through the arson attacks on some of Errol's properties including, ironically, the warehouse in which the bones had been dumped. More valuable things than a few bones were lost and in the resulting tit-for-tat, Errol was murdered. For a while afterwards, some of the disappearances of people which, at the time of Joan Fraser seeing Parrington and Gray in peculiar *tete-e-tete*, had not yet begun to be noticed were attributed to this internecine feuding. This was, however, in the future. Gray's murder was, of course, a CID matter to investigate not Joan's and she didn't miss him anyway.

In The Grange Tavern that evening then, over a pint or two of Charrington's beer, Parrington outlined his requirements and Gray negotiated a price. After Parrington left, with more Charrington ordered and consumed, Gray and his duly-summoned lieutenants discussed the logistics of the task, which was then carried out with a minimum of fuss.

After it was done, it is true that several of Gray's men employed for the job expressed considerable disquiet, not with the disposal of bones (some had disposed of fresher human material than this) but with what they said was a feeling that something was lurking down there – something that should not have been there.

At some times of the day and most times of the night the open garden at the front of Hackney Town Hall as well as the public library steps on the other side of Mare Street were the haunt of and hiring place for rent boys – a cheaper range of rent boys than might be found those few miles away in London's West End. By early evening, with the ordinary commuters from the myriad of businesses in the area having found their way to the trains or the pubs and those who actually lived in the area having drifted to whatever they called home whether it was council flat, pre-war terraced house or one of the few (as yet) gentrified Victorian villas, the rent boys congregated in slowly increasing numbers. There were never all that many, certainly not as many as female prostitutes further north and west at the back of Kings Cross station but enough to satisfy a slightly less overt trade.

At ten minutes past seven, custom was just starting to pick up. At the edge of the curb, an unprepossessing boy in tight jeans, anorak and with long black hair, was negotiating with a man in an oldish-model car. Other boys lolled on the steps and garden benches, taking their time as the evening was just beginning and for some it could well be a long night. One or two were standing in the foot bent back to the wall stance, the *sine qua non* of rent boys the world over. Most smoked. Some chewed gum.

The boy at the car turned away and took a couple of steps back to a punkish redheaded kid squatting on the steps. The redhead raised his eyebrows.

'Cheap prick,' the first boy said. 'He can suck his own dick for ten sods.'

One of the boys against the wall, ragged, greasy and anorexic, took notice and quickly stepped up to the car to catch it before the potential punter could drive away. His need for a fix outweighed any notion of value for service. As he leant down to open window with a hand out for the door, no sense of enquiry and negotiation on his mind, the car pulled away sharply.

'Shit,' he muttered. It was not his wrecked appearance that prevented the transaction, although many cruising men, desperate as they may be, did jibe at placing their precious members no matter how well sheaved in mouths or anuses as ravaged as his. This time, however, the driver had seen a police uniform in his rear vision mirror, and was gone.

Joan walked along the street towards the gathered boys. The disappointed kid turned and watched her approach.

'Oh jeez, Sarge,' he complained.

'Oh jeez. Macaulay,' Joan echoed. 'You look like something the cat refused, son. I'm not sure who I just did the bigger favour to. You or the punter who just took off.'

'The punter,' the red-headed boy said, causing the others to laugh. Joan grinned.

'Why don't you get yourself straight, Macaulay?' she continued.

'Shit, sarge,' Macaulay said, in a tone more of good-humoured exasperation than objection.

'No, off the shit, my son,' she said.

The Town Hall and most of Hackney were part of her community beat – not that it was called a 'beat' anymore by the Metropolitan Police, and very little was done on foot. Joan routinely parked her panda a few streets away and walked up to the Town Hall. She had a soft spot for the boys who plied this distasteful and dangerous trade from this location. If Super-Fly was aware of this relationship he would undoubtedly have insisted the boys were arrested, if sufficient evidence was available, or moved on if it was not. Joan knew that dispersing the boys would not solve anything. They would simply find other spots and probably be placed in even more danger if they had to hang out by themselves or in pairs. She knew well the advantages that accrued to the boys forming a loosely knit cadre. Sometimes there were arguments and fights between some of them, and, of course, in a group, drugs could circulate more easily. And the danger from punters when a boy went off alone was hardly ameliorated. But gathering together did provide some sense of solidarity and security even from the odd gang of mindless skinheads who would be willing to bash a solitary 'poof' but were usually too gutless to take on a group.

Joan's carefully developed relationship, which she would have rationalised as good community policing, was partly driven by a latent mothering instinct. She would have quickly sorted anyone, colleague or other, who suggested any such thing but she felt much more strongly about these boys than she did about the women prostitutes who also formed a part of the community of the area. Not that she didn't get along with most of them as well, although some of the real hard-cases maintained a hostile attitude. This collection of boys, some barely above the legal age, some even below it perhaps, and others who were at the upper end of age acceptability to the punters, were something like a family and something like a sort of youth group. If she judged, she kept her judgements to herself most of the time.

She knew that if Macaulay wanted to take the first steps to kicking his habit then she would direct him, advise him, even drag him along that path, but she wouldn't do it unless she thought he was willing. Otherwise she would wait for that day when she either had to call an ambulance or the morgue. Tonight, he was neither hurting yet nor high yet, so she let it go.

She turned to the others clustered on the steps. Some had shuffled to the back, newer members who had not the time to develop a rapport with this odd copper, boys who maybe had something they should not have had in their pockets, small quantities of drugs for personal use or more likely sale, items shoplifted or of fairly dodgy origin. An officious copper or one with less imagination (Joan would have denied *sensitivity*) might have been able to make a few trivial arrests –always assuming the boys had stood still long enough to be arrested.

Two boys, who were over eighteen – Joan had checked – but didn't look it with their thin bodies, baby faces and boyish hair styles were locked in an intense kiss. They made no move, beyond lips and tongues, as Joan approached.

'Come on, lads. Save it for the punters, eh?' Joan said with mock concern.

They pulled apart and one looked up at her. 'Bloody hell, sarge. We don't kiss them.'

'Fuckin' yucko,' said the other.

This rent boy code of fastidiousness always bemused Joan, given what she knew or imagined these boys did do with grown men and sometimes women. Joan spotted a favourite boy, a smile broke across her face.

'Luke. Pretty Lucien.' The boy grimaced. He hated that she knew – god knows how – his real name. He had got rid of it as soon as he could but she found out all the same. 'That blonde rinse is growing out. Time you got it seen to,' Joan continued as she climbed a couple of the steps.

The boy stood in front of a small group. He was a bit taller and a bit older than most of the others, and he held himself with a greater sense of confidence, a proprietorial air, but then he didn't have a habit to feed so conducted his transactions as business not need. He wore tattered jeans and a faded t-shirt which was tight and emphasised his thin, boyish physique. If Joan called him pretty, it was first impression many had of him because his mop of hair gave him an attractiveness which a closer examination of his face actually belied. His straight hair was untidy although not dirty, long down his neck, flopping over his forehead and across his eyes, the outer six inches dyed blond on the end of a good few inches of dark, mousy roots.

'Nah. Punters like it, don't they?' he replied, pushing a hand through the thick hair falling in front of his face, and squinting up into the strands as they automatically fell back. 'Think they're getting a bit of rough. Not some pretty poof from up the West End. 'S what they want to pay for. So they can kid themselves they ain't irons.'

Although Joan didn't know precisely (but could guess) what went on between Luke and those men who picked him up, she suspected that, unlike many of these boys, Luke both enjoyed the sex but, she figured, enjoyed even more being in control. She wondered why, with his looks and his self-confidence, he didn't in fact move up to the better paying environs of the West End, to be one of the 'pretty poofs' he affected to despise. He would probably even find himself a gay Henry Higgins and enjoy the luxury of being kept for a while at least. What Joan didn't know was that Luke's class-conscious attitude was not quite as rigid as he made it appear, that he did occasionally travel 'up West' and to an up-market clientele –who wanted much the same things, of course, but paid more for it, and had it in more salubrious places to do it in. The present length of the mousy roots were an indication of how long it had been since he had plied his trade in the West End; he usually only renewed the dye-job when he did go up-market for a while. Luke liked the East End and knew how to take care of himself with the punters (indeed had some regulars); overall, he didn't like the upper classes (he shared that with Joan) but he had a few customers among them for whom he was prepared to make exception and, of course, be well-paid for it.

Joan smiled at him, reached up and pushed the floppy hair back from his face. They know each other the longest and small measures of physical intimacy were allowed between them. Her smile faded as she looked over his shoulder into the dark recesses at the back of the portico.

'Who's hiding up here then? Anyone new on my patch? Let's have a look at you.'

Some of boys shuffled back in the dark as Joan approached. Luke walked with Joan the few steps to the gloomy area at the top of the steps. 'Is all right, innit. The sarge is all right. And she don't want nothing from you, not like...' He stopped himself.

Joan looked sharply at him. She didn't want to hear about other coppers. Although she felt protective of these boys, her loyalty to the force and other members of it, deserving or not, was stronger. She remained an old fashioned copper irrespective of whatever new brooms were sweeping through the Metropolitan Police, no matter to what extent the Victorian institution of the police force was attempting to emulate or be made to emulate the new economic rationalist-driven private and public atmosphere of the time. Then there was the inescapable fact that, whatever she felt towards these boys, they were a constantly changing group. Boys came and went all the time, some before she even had time to do more than remember a name or recognise a face. Only the enigmatic Luke was a fixture.

Joan walked up to a boy, hardly more than fifteen or sixteen. He tried to avoid her but she took his face in her hands, turned it towards the light spilling from the street and between the columns of the town hall's facade.

Oh Christ, another child, she thought. Then aloud, 'Gordon Bennett. Just off the train from... Liverpool. No, not a hard enough face for Liverpool. Manchester.'

The boy twisted slightly to try and release his face but Joan's grip was hard, her arms stronger than he thought. He was too scared to attempt to push her off but street-play and a dysfunctional family had given him a toughness.

'St Helen's,' he attempted to growl, although his voice pitched a little higher than he wanted it to. He looked her in the eyes though. No copper in a skirt was going to get the better of him.

'Close enough. Bit of both. No point me telling you to go home, is there?'

His hope of out-staring her was turning out to be misplaced bravado even if her grip on his chin was lessening. Her eyes seemed to be looking into him, through him, to his terraced street next to the railway line in St Helen's. His eyes slid away, to Luke, who stood watching, smiling just behind the sergeant's shoulder. He wasn't laughing at him, more smiling as if this was all okay, all under control, all part of a game of which he had yet learnt the rules. Then Joan let him go.

He gulped air. It seemed to him he hadn't breathed once in the time she held him. Joan sat down on the step and patted the worn stone, indicating for him to sit down. As he did,

Luke and the other boys who had been watching drifted back to the lit area of the street, taking up the casual, meaningful positions of boys for hire.

Joan straightened her skirt and took off her hat.

'Okay, son. What's your name, then?'

If he expected her to pull out a notebook, she again surprised him by just straightening her tunic buttons. He hesitated all the same.

'All right, not a full name if you don't want to. Just a first name. Or make one up if you want.'

'Teddy...Edward,' he stammered.

'Is that Teddy on the way to becoming Edward, or the other way around?'

'Yeah, Edward... now,' he said, confirming his intention to become who he wanted to be, having got away from his family and those individuals who had been his friends but who had become his tormentors when he had stupidly, ignorantly and naively allowed his preferences to surface. Christ knows what his father would have done if the story got back to him and if (big *if*) he was ever sober enough to understand what he heard.

'All right, Edward. I'm not going to try to talk you into going back.' The fat sergeant was still talking at him. 'But I'm going to want to know something about you. And I'm going to lecture you about safe sex, anyway.'

Joan reached into her tunic pocket. Now the notebook, Edward thought. Now the report, the arrest, the return home. Instead Joan pulled out a packet of condoms.

'You got any of these?'

Edward shook his head. He knew what they were. 'I thought not,' Joan continued, handing them to him. 'On your dick and on his, for anything but a hand job. For everything but a hand job, yeah?'

He nodded but Joan could see the blank expression even in the dark.

'Have a word with Luke.' She nodded in the direction of Luke who had, with surprising tact, moved away to the side. 'Not in the open. If you can get him alone. He'll show you, right?' She paused. 'You sure you want to do this, son. Sure you don't me to get you home?'

She felt him tense up, almost smelled his resistance.

'Don't worry,' she said quickly. 'I'm not going to try and get you to do what you don't want to do. But I will help you with some of what you want to do, along as it's not illegal. That's why I don't want to know your age.' She hesitated as if she had more she wanted to say but her attention had been, drawn away to a scene unfolding in the street below.

'Oh shit,' she said quietly and stood up.

While Joan was talking to Edward, a recent model Jaguar had pulled up. None of the rent boys moved. They knew this car too well and knew this wasn't a punter. A flash git got out, camel-hair overcoat draped over his expensive but vulgar suit, gold dripping from necklaces and flashing from rings. He walked around the front of the car and grabbed Macaulay by the neck. The other boys stepped back out of the way.

'I thought I told you to fuck off out of it. You scare off the trade, you hophead.' He tightened his grip on Macaulay's neck.

'Leave him alone, Elias,' said Luke, stepping out from the small knot of boys but not getting close enough to be in reach.

Elias held the struggling Macaulay with ease and turned to Luke.

'You what? Just have my share ready, Luke. When I'm finished with shitface here.' He turned his attention back to Macaulay. 'I've had it with you. The rest of these boys can make nice money out of the perverts if you ain't scaring them off. You look like all their nightmares about disease walking around. They don't like it, see. Makes their dicks shrivel up. When their dicks shrivel, so do their fucking wallets. So why don't you fuck off and die.'

He shifted his grip and hauled back his right hand, tightened into a fist. The amber street lights flashed off several large rings.

Before his arm could swing, it was grabbed in mid-flight. A hand gripped his ponytail and he found himself hauled around to face Joan. There was a split second pause, long enough for recognition but not longer enough for reaction and then Joan head-butted him. Elias fell on his arse on the pavement as McCauley dodged aside and took off. A fine spray of Elias' own blood rained down on him and then it settled into a gush from his nose.

He staggered up, both hands clutching his broken nose – more in attempt to stop it bleeding on his camel-hair overcoat that to staunch the flow. Joan stood in his way as he tried to stumble to the waiting Jag.

'Why don't *you* fuck off and die, Elias? These boys make money on my patch. You don't. Be told... for the last time.'

Elias staggered into the car, pushed it into gear and squealed away.

Now, for the first time, Joan took out her notebook. She scribbled down the registration plate of the retreating Jag.

She looked back up the steps but Edward was gone. Probably not far, she thought, but who knows? Maybe, if she ever saw him again it would be in a hospital, a morgue trolley, or crumpled, like last week's garbage, in some lane or alley. But then he might make it. She turned to the others, to the grinning Luke. 'No point me saying don't do anything I wouldn't do, but go safe, eh?'

'We, well, we owe you, sarge,' Luke said.

Joan pushed the flopping bleached hair off his ear, leant in almost as if she was going to tongue it, and whispered, 'And don't you forget it... Lucien.'

Luke squirmed, look around to see if anyone else had heard her use his hated full name. No, she was having a lend, of course.

Joan smiled sadly – what a waste – and walked back to where she had left the Panda. A ragged chorus followed her: 'Night, sarge.' 'See you, sarge.' 'Bye.'

FOUR

The value of the 'old boy network' of which Parrington was such an adept utiliser was demonstrated through the fact at a little after six Norman Pendleton, MA (Oxon) entered the St Stephen's Club in Queen Anne's Gate, just one street back from St James' Park.

His walk from Covent Garden to St Stephen's via the Strand Square, Trafalgar Square (really the pedestrian tunnels underneath it) and the eastern end of St James' Park had been surprisingly brisk given that his 'stoop' made him look as if he ought have trouble being particularly mobile. In no small way, he often made deliberate use of his posture to make it seem he was slower, physically and by extension, mentally, than he actually was. It may not have been actual dissembling but he had found both at public school and since this had some advantages in dealing with others by causing them to miscalculate his abilities – until too late. Pendelton had enjoyed the walk, despite the crowds of workers hurrying home and gawking tourists idling; he usually went in the opposite direction along the Embankment and across the Thames to London Bridge Station to catch his train home. He was less pleased to have been invited - summoned really – to meet Anthony Eastlake MP at Eastlake's Club.

Not being a member of St Stephen's, Pendleton presented himself to the club porter and subsequently was guided by a steward into the library. Even given the time of day only one or two members were scattered about the room. One of these, a flashy, florid man, stood up from the leather armchair in which he had been sitting and took a few steps towards Pendleton as the steward led him across the room.

'Darkie, old man,' the man said, grasping Pendleton's hand in a two-handed politician's handshake, with about the usual amount of sincerity – very little.

'Hello Blot,' said Pendleton.

The use of nicknames established the two men's common background in the same public school. Pendleton had been known as 'Darkie' not because of anything as obvious as his colouring (only his hair was dark anyway) but because his restrained manner and lack of interest in usual schoolboy tomfoolery had led him to be considered a 'dark horse.' Eastlake's nickname was related to matters best left unspoken although the connection to metaphorical copybooks being 'blotted' was not coincidental.

'Drink, old boy?' Eastlake asked.

'Gin and tonic, thank you,' Pendleton said.

'And a scotch for me, thank you, Attrill,' Eastlake said to the hovering steward. 'Sit, sit,' he instructed Pendleton, gesturing at a chair next to the one he had been occupying.

'You're looking well, I must say,' Eastlake continued. 'Hardly changed from sixth form at all. Better dressed though, eh?'

'Thank you. Of course, the school uniform didn't do anyone any favours.' Pendleton settled into the chair.

'Maybe not but I seem to remember a few bums that looked rather splendid in those tight trousers and short jackets,' Eastlake chuckled.

Pendleton offered a slight smile. *Even so, you preferred to see those bums without the trousers,* he thought.

'Ah well, good times, I suppose. But a long time ago now,' Eastlake continued. 'Ah thank you, Attrill.' The steward placed the drinks from a tray he balanced in his left hand onto a small table between the two chairs. Eastlake watched the steward move silently away before he picked up his glass.

'Chin chin, old chap,' he said and took a sip of whisky. 'Good of you to come at such short notice. Although I suppose that I am in some way your boss, eh?'

Pendleton also sipped his drink and looked at Eastlake over the rim.

'Well, the museum is part of London Transport's operations,' Eastlake went on. 'And I have overview of that in my portfolio, amongst other stuff. A lot of other stuff. And...'

'And I am curator of documents of the museum,' Pendleton said. 'So, I guess that, yes, you are my boss as you put it.'

'Quite. But that's not why I asked you to meet me. That is, not entirely. I mean, really, we're just a couple of old school chums having a drink.' He swept his eyes around the Victorian decor of the room as if the dark panelling and shelves of leather-bound books were his witnesses. He leant forward. 'What I am saying, old man, is that this is, well, sort of informal.'

'Quite.' Pendleton hoped that Eastlake would get to the point. He hadn't especially liked him at school and this gin was distinctly inferior.

'You know Tommy Parrington, of course?' Eastlake said.

'Sir Thomas Parrington. I know of him, naturally.'

'An OH, of course. Was a few years ahead of us, so didn't know him when he was there but got to know him pretty well since, party matters and so forth, y'know. Father was baronet. Oldish family. The Indian connection, of course, like most Old Hamiltonians. Not you I recall but there we are. Not ancient. The baronetcy, I mean, not Parrington, although I suppose he has a few years on the clock, thinking about it.'

Eastlake actually hardly knew Parrington at all although they had met at old boy functions and, slightly more frequently, at Conservative Party functions, both social and formal. While Eastlake was always willing – too willing, many thought – to be impressed by family backgrounds (he had none worth mentioning himself) and wealth (of which he had some), he didn't actually care for Parrington that much, possibly because Parrington had never given any indication that he was impressed in any way by Eastlake. But, still, an old boy was an old boy and besides he knew that Parrington was one of those ruthless capitalists that Mrs Thatcher admired and supported and that as a consequence Parrington had her ear. So when he had unexpectedly made his request, Eastlake was willing to try and oblige.

He carried on. 'He is, of course, very much involved in doing something about the mess in the East End. Getting rid of all that accumulation of squalor and years of neglect and developing it no end. Out with the old, in with the new, eh?'

It clearly didn't occur to Eastlake that these sentiments may not be calculated to appeal to a curator of a museum who may well have a vested interest in retaining and preserving the old. The slight tightening of Pendleton's expression escaped his notice.

'Anyway, it seems old Puddles... that was his name at school, y'know, not sure why. Maybe he wet the bed.' Eastlake chucked, a fruity, modulated and carefully trained politician's chuckle. 'Seems he has a little problem with his latest development that he thinks I can help with.'

'I don't see where I come in, Blot,' said Pendleton.

'Getting to that, Darkie. As best I can understand it, and Puddles wasn't all that forthcoming, is that he seems to have found, that is his workers seem to have found, a whacking great hole in the ground...'

Pendleton interrupted. 'I would rather think that would be the point of his operations, surely?'

'That's as may be, but this one, he thinks may be an underground railway tunnel.'

'He's dug into a tube tunnel?' Pendleton expressed surprise. 'I would have thought that London Transport would know about that pretty quickly.'

'Ah, the thing seems to be that this is not an actually working tunnel, so to speak. In fact, it's not quite clear to Parrington or his people quite what it is. Anyway, the fact of the matter is that he wants to find out but without making a great big song and dance about it. I see his point. Millions at stake. Egg on the face of all sorts of planners.'

'Even so...,' Pendleton began to say but was overridden.

'And, of course, the PM is so dead keen on all this development down in the docklands. Her seal of approval is, well – anyway, the long and short of it, is that at this stage, the whole thing needs to be investigated but not, as I said to him, via any official direction by me to London Transport. Damned bureaucrats, bound to want a whole lot in writing and can't rely on them these days to keep schtum.'

'I really don't see how...,' Pendleton said.

'Well, it occurred to me, quite a brilliant thought actually, I thought of you down there in your little museum and thought who but old Darkie would know all about this sort of thing?'

'But I can't... '

Eastlake cut him off again – the natural prerogative of all politicians. 'Of course, *you* can't, old man. Neither can I really. So, this conversation is just too old school chums chewing the fat. But, you must know somebody who knows all about this sort of thing, old tunnels and stuff, who can figure out what this is and if there are any more. Puddles doesn't want any more unpleasant surprises, believe me.'

'Someone who could do what exactly?' asked Pendleton.

'I don't know exactly. I don't really want to know. But basically Puddles wants some sort of expert he can employ who can suss out what it is he has on his hands, or under his feet, I should say, and get this matter seen to. Obviously I can't really ask around the ministry without... Anyway, that's why I thought of you. I hope you will be able to think of someone.'

Actually Pendleton already had.

An enigmatic telephone call brought Marc back to the London Transport Museum. He was quite used to Pendelton's eccentricities but even so, it was unusual for him to be quite so mysterious. And yet he had sounded quite pleased with himself on the telephone. This time Marc managed to negotiate the foyer without catching the eye of Eric. Pendelton had already negotiated with Myrtle in anticipation of Marc's arrival it seemed. A faintly steaming, faintly aromatic pot of tea was already on Pendelton's desk, the Harrod's finest already out of their hiding place. 'Now, my boy, I have what may prove to be excellent news for you. For your prospects.' Pendleton said.

He waved Marc to a chair and sat himself at his desk. Marc looked a bit puzzled but waited while Pendleton let this remark hang in the air and busied himself pouring the tea. He knew Pendleton would get to the point soon enough.

'I had dinner last night with an old school friend of mine. Anthony Eastlake, Blot we used to call him, you know. As in on the landscape, which I always think he was rather. Never thought he'd amount to much. Probably got that right since he's the Minister of Transport. So, in an indirect way, my boss, I suppose. He was a prefect at school, and I wasn't so, *plus ça change* as they say. But, more importantly, the dinner was at the prompting it would seem of Sir Thomas Parrington. You know who he is, I dare say?'

Marc hesitated. 'Parrington? Something to do with building or construction. I've seen the name on building sites, I think.'

'Quite. Not something to do with, however. Probably the biggest developer in London at the moment. Canary Wharf. Docklands. All that and much more.'

Pendelton took a sip of tea. 'Now it seems,' he continued, 'that Sir Thomas has struck a little problem in his latest development in the East End.'

Marc was still struggling to see what Pendelton was on about.

Pendleton sipped his tea again. 'To come to the point, dear boy, Sir Thomas has need of a consultant. Not to put too fine a point on it, someone with precisely your expertise. I was delighted to recommend you.'

Marc stared back, puzzled. 'My expertise? I don't see what I could have to consult with some builder on. Or rather he with me.'

'Sir Thomas Parrington is hardly some builder, but be that as it may. The nature of his problem is what places the ball in your court. You see, he has discovered, well, stumbled across really what seems to be an underground railway tunnel beneath his latest development site. If he is right, and I have only his word so far, and that second-hand, that it is actually an underground railway tunnel, it is one that nobody knows anything about.'

'How can that be possible?'

'I scarcely know myself. There are innumerable tunnels under London, of course. And this may be nothing of the sort.

I mean an underground railway tunnel. But he needs someone to look at it and tell him.'

'Surely he could figure that out for himself. Or one of his engineers. I assume he does employ engineers.'

'I really don't know. I would rather think so. After all, he is not, well, not a professional man in any vocational sense. But there is rather more and I think this is where you come in, and where you might do rather well for yourself. He needs to know not only what he's got but if there are any more of these things. Even, I suppose, *what* they are. Maybe even what to do about them. And, I should also say, that after the dinner, on our way out of the club, Blot told me that Sir Thomas always pays well for advice and assistance. I'm not quite sure precisely what he implied by that and probably don't want to know. But this could be financially lucrative and an enormous step up for you, Marc my boy. I took the liberty of mentioning your name, and now, if you like I could telephone him and make an appointment.'

'This is all rather sudden,' Marc said. Somewhat overwhelmed, he took a large sip of his tea which was still at a temperature to be sipped rather than gulped. When he managed to recover from the shock, he said, 'I did come back to London wanting to find some work, to find something to do with that PhD other than try to impress people. What have I got to lose?'

'Well, as to that, my dear boy, I am afraid, and I am upset to say it, yes, there is something you should lose.'

'I'm not sure that my integrity is much of a loss.' Marc could already see that there was something of a contract with the devil lurking here somewhere, especially if the whole thing was somehow expected to be 'unofficial.'

It was Pendleton's turn to be puzzled, for a moment. 'No, no. I mean, I'm afraid, that wonderful long hair of yours. I think it may have to go. For someone of Sir Thomas's position and standing, well, a more conservative appearance may be a good idea.'

Marc was wondering what he might be about to let himself in for. 'Surely many young blokes still have long hair. Maybe the heavy metal look is a bit *passe* but a tidy pony tail...'

'Yes, well, you know I wouldn't suggest this for a moment if I didn't think it really mattered. Now, what I suggest is that you make an appointment with Vidal Sassoon in Sloane Square. They'll be able to make a splendid job of it, I'm sure, if it must be done.' He sipped his tea. 'And I'm afraid that it must.'

Norman Pendleton had surprised Marc some more. After the phone call, which had resulted in an almost immediate appointment, he had insisted on accompanying Marc to the Vidal Sassoon salon in Sloane Square. There he supervised Marc's transformation, to the irritation of Adrian the hairdresser. Marc's pony tail was quickly dispensed with. (Beforehand Pendelton managed to slip Adrian a few – quite a few – pounds for that pony tail which he took home with him.) Then Adrian set to work with all the mannerisms of a great artist creating a masterpiece, which, within his limited skill set, he was actually doing.

The result was Marc's hair was staggeringly shorter – at least when compared to what it had been before. It was now slickly gelled and swept back with a mere *soupcon* (Adrian's word of course) of a parting on the left. Very young-business-executive-meets-Ricky Nelson. To Marc's credit, he had hardly blanched at all when the cashier added up the total of the cut and the special products that Adrian recommended (on which he received a commission). Later, Marc figured that since he hadn't had his hair cut in something like ten years, ameliorated over that period, it was not all that much.

While Pendelton regretted the lack of time to visit Savile Row, for which Marc and his bank balance were silently grateful, a trip to Marks and Spencers in Oxford Street provided an off-the-rack suit, dark with a subtle pinstripe, several soft pastel business shirts and a selection of matching ties. Along the way somewhere, Marc thought it was probably in Bond Street, the ear ring he wore in his right ear, fully revealed by the sudden loss of the long hair, was replaced with a subtle gold stud. Pendleton's unexpected eye for appropriate fashion and excellent taste was implicitly confirmed by the manner in which shortly thereafter Parrington seemed to accept Marc at face value although, of course, it came on top of his old-boy 'references' from Pendleton and although this no doubt carried more credibility than appearance, had Marc retained his piratical locks, he might not have got the job.

FIVE

Marc's meeting with Sir Thomas Parrington went very well,
even if Marc found it a little odd. Not least because it was not
so much an interview for a position as Parrington telling Marc
what he expected Marc to do for him. Yet, even though
Parrington was obviously used to telling people what he
wanted and them getting on and doing it, Marc had a feeling
that there was something that Parrington did know even
when claiming he knew little (which was why he wanted
Marc's services in the first place). Parrington had confirmed
what Norman Pendleton had already told Marc: that work on
a development site had uncovered a large tunnel running
beneath the property. Marc had pointed out that London was
riddled with subterranean tunnels and passageways of all
sorts, citing tunnels ancient and modern for such purposes as
moving mail, passageways to facilitate earlier building, or
simply moving underground people and objects from one
place to another for any number of reasons. He had also
emphasised that, if he was an expert in anything, it was an
expert in the underground rail systems, not any and every
tunnel. He had to admit, when pressed by Parrington, that he
had some knowledge of other tunnels, at least to the extent
his research had uncovered information as might have had
some bearing on the building and running of the railways.
Afterwards, Marc thought that Parrington, without saying so,
seemed to know that this was an underground railway tunnel
and not some long-forgotten tunnel for some other purpose.
However, Parrington had clearly made up his mind; he
wanted to employ Marc, and was prepared to do so within

such attractive terms that Marc felt he would be rather stupid to decline.

These conditions included a very generous pay packet, a quasi-executive position within the organisation complete with office and ancillaries. Parrington, a familiar participant in the old boy system, seemed to accept without question that, as Marc came recommended by other old boys, then his suitability for the job at hand was unquestioned. Either that or he assumed that if Marc did not measure up to expectations he could be dispensed with easily enough.

Marc for his part was as much bemused as amused by events and the speed with which this took place contrary to the usual way in which anything was done (in his experience) in England. If there was any sour note to the meeting with Parrington it was one Marc only registered peripherally at the time. It came from Angela Snottym.

To her mind, it was bad enough that Sir Thomas was willing to consider let alone actually employ some *ghastly* Australian, with or without a no-doubt barely even second-rate degree from what she imagined as a 'colonial university' (in her mind's eye located in some dusty windswept Outback location, beset by kangaroos, sheep and feral koalas). Not that Angela herself had been to university; in her family women didn't do that. But if she had it would have been Cambridge or, at a pinch, Oxford. The top girls' public school was good enough for her, if only just. That and daddy's contacts would be all she needed to simply find her appropriate place in life, business and society. The proof was her position as Sir Thomas's personal assistant.

What really got up Angela's inbred aristocratic nose was that her notion and implementation of personal appearance was identical to that she took to be Marc's. Other than the fact that her business suit had a dress and not trousers and that she wore stockings, there was little difference in outward appearance between Marc and she, from the short, wet-look gelled hair to the discrete ear studs (although she had two of these). What made matters worse is that Marc looked so much better in almost every way than she did. The clothes, the hair style seemed to have been designed with Marc in mind whereas Angela still looked, as the lower-order workers in the corporation were known to put it, 'like a dog's bum with a hat on' even when she wasn't wearing a hat. Other expressions such as 'a face like a smacked arse' and 'looking like a boiled shite' had been offered at times – out of her hearing, but with a vulgar poetic accuracy.

So Angela sat and glowered at Marc through most of the meeting, taking notes when directed by Parrington but the rest of the time building up a good head of seething if impotent resentment. It was far from the first time she had been eclipsed by beauty or by ordinary common-or-garden prettiness. Even in a public school full of the exceedingly plain results of English upper-class inbreeding, Angela had been notable for being especially unappealing. Things had not improved when Lady Diana Spencer hove into the view of the tabloids and thence to the notice of the great unwashed of Britain and their betters. A newly revived version of the English Rose ideal of British womanhood was suddenly upon the land. To be fair to Angela – not that any but her closest acquaintances were interested in being fair to Angela – she did at least have a Lady Di slimness but beyond that any comparisons were bound to be of clichéd onerousness.

Angela's ingrained sense of superiority, multiplied by her perception of her importance as Parrington's personal assistant, would in itself have been enough to govern her attitude and actions toward Marc. The inescapable evidence that he was not only more attractive than she but that he had demonstrated it by seemingly mirroring her clothes and hair style added to her need to see he knew his place and was put in to it, in the Parrington organisation at least. She took some comfort that at least he was a shrimp.

Parrington's need to get the matter of the tunnel dealt with was such that it was only two days later that Marc took up his new position. And when Angela attempted to fire the first shots in her anti-Marc campaign.

As she came to the office that had been allocated to Marc, an office with a view towards the Old West India docks, the site of Canary Wharf and to the Thames, an office she could not help but feel he had no right to, she was less than pleased with the way in which Marc seemed to be making himself quite at home, having already set up the personal computer supplied to him and, incredibly, to be playing Pacman on it. He swivelled in his grey executive chair – another particular item of furniture, in the subtle hierarchy of Parrington Corporation, to which Angela felt Marc was not entitled – as she came in and had the temerity to turn that boyish smile on her.

Angela held out a thick Filofax but did not relinquish it for the moment. 'This is the standard company kit,' she said. 'Except for reasons best known to Sir Thomas, for this.'

As if handling a holy relic, she delicately extracted from the Filofax a Gold American Express card, separating it reverently from MasterCard, Visa and Diner's Club cards that were also in the package. She held it in her hand between her thumb and forefinger confident she was showing (and hopefully duly impressing) Marc with an object he had never seen before and, presumably, never considered possessing. Not that she would ever admit it, but even she did not have a *Gold* American Express Card for company business. She didn't understand why Sir Thomas had insisted that Marc should have one. (He hadn't, until after he set eyes on Marc and liked what he saw. Nature, Pendelton and Vidal Sassoon were working well together.)

'You will need to sign it. On the back. With a ballpoint pen. Within the space provided. At once. And all the others,' she instructed.

'With my own name or will an X do, Miss Snottym?' Marc asked, deliberately mispronouncing her name as 'snot-time.'

'Snow-team. And for the sake of my curiosity, Mr Sharpe, how is it you know about matters which English experts do not?' Angela nearly choked on the 'mister.' Like most of the English, she had an ingrained reverence for titles, whether earned or not, and it was only her determination to provide a calculated insult that enabled her to override 'doctor' and force out 'mister.'

Marc held out his hand for the card which was clearly embossed 'Doctor Marc Sharpe.' Angela reluctantly released it.

'*Doctor* Sharpe. Although, I am sure we are going to get on well, so, please, call me Marc. If you feel comfortable with it, of course.' He made a show of finding a ballpoint pen and then signing the card, miming a concern that he was signing it in the right place and manner. 'To answer your question, well, to know that is to know my rule for understanding how England functions. Would you like to hear Sharpe's rule for how England functions, Miss Snot... Miss *Snowteam*?

Angela was not pleased with the way this was going. She had hoped her sarcastic question might be taken as rhetorical and would help in putting Marc in his place. Her raised eyebrow, intended to be an indication of surprise that Marc could have such an insight, only encouraged Marc to explain.

'If there is more than one way of doing a thing, the English will choose the least efficient.' He placed the American Express card in his wallet, not back into the Filofax.

'Really? Is that so?' Angela attempted to recover ground she felt she had just lost. 'You will nonetheless be expected to attend our orientation symposia for new organisational executive management team members.'

'Will I buggery,' Marc said.

'We...Sir Thomas...believes in a total development-progress nexus.'

'I'm a collapsed Unitarian myself. I'm also here to sniff out underground tunnels, not to executively manage. So on both religious and professional grounds I'll probably forego the opportunity of watching Business 101 in action.'

Angela, without being aware of it, began to feel like Lady Bracknell in *The Importance of Being Ernest*. 'You will be expected to attend and I suggest you attend with alacrity.' She lacked any capacity for Wildean wit of course.

'And I suggest you abandon the attempt to serve uncooked crustaceans.'

'I beg your pardon?.' Not only were her efforts at asserting her position coming unstuck, Angela did not even know what this impertinent individual was saying. Marc was pleased to enlighten her.

'Don't come the raw prawn. Now, I've got a mystery tunnel to inspect.' Marc left the room, leaving the Filofax lying untouched on the desk where Angela had placed it with sacramental reverence, and leaving Angela – for once – speechless.

Feeling somewhat sheepish over being a little vulgar towards Angela Snottym, even given her attitude of insufferable English upper-class superiority, and perhaps for behaving in a manner not quite fitting to a new PhD, Marc made his way to the site office. Despite the avalanche of executive *materiel* that had descended on him, and even despite his new sartorial appearance, Marc did not really think this position, if it deserved such a categorisation, within the Parrington Corporation was going to last all that long. Unless, that is, Parrington had a lot of other sites in the vicinity that he was sitting on at the moment. Who cares? This situation at the moment looked set to be interesting at least. He knocked on the door of the site office and went inside.

Marc had been introduced to Clive Strangways, the chief engineer, albeit briefly before Strangways was quickly dismissed from the first meeting with Parrington. Strangways had not had time to form an opinion of the young man to whom he was introduced. Despite or perhaps because of his having worked his way up from humble origins via apprenticeships and night classes to his present professional position, Strangways retained the sense of deference to position that was entrenched in the English psyche. At the same time, however, he tended to reserve his respect for who had proved their worth through professional qualification or dependability within his own view of what mattered. Although Parrington, in introducing Doctor Sharpe, had implied that the young man had expertise that linked him in some way with Strangways' own, Clive had not been immediately impressed. Marc's disarming smile had diverted the engineer from an initial fully negative response but appearance and dress had placed Marc, in the engineer's immediate assessment, in the same circle that Parrington and Miss Snottym occupied in Strangways' categorisation of his fellow creatures. That didn't mean that Strangways was not likely to be overly well-disposed to him.

Marc's knock and entry caused Strangways to look up from a desk piled high with papers of one sort or another. He pushed his reading glasses back onto his broad forehead. 'Ah, Doctor Sharpe. Major Tom barking orders, is he?' The use of Parrington's nickname with the work force was a way of testing the water with this young man.

'Not easy to tell who is worse, him or his assistant. Please call me Marc,' said Marc.

'The bulldog or the pit bull, eh? I think you can safely assume that his nibs only keeps the redoubtable Miss Snottym to bark for him when he doesn't feel the need. Or if a particular barking is below his dignity.' said Strangways. 'And you'd better call me Clive.'

'Fair enough. Now how about we look at this hole of yours,' Marc said.

'Let's do that, son,' Strangways agreed. He lifted himself up from his seat and grabbed a safety helmet from a hook behind him. For a moment, he was tempted to let Marc ruin his clothes in the dank tunnel but the young fellow had reacted well to his humour. 'I don't think that suit or those shoes are going to do well in the tunnel. Pretty damp and dirty down there. Maybe I can find something.' He opened a cupboard and pulled out some overalls and held them up. 'Hmm. Maybe a bit biggish.'

Marc slipped out of his coat and into the overalls. Strangways was not wrong about the size – there was nobody as small as Marc employed on the site. Marc rolled up the legs and sleeves. In the meantime, Strangways had located some Wellington boots. Finally he grabbed a donkey jacket from a hook on the wall and thrust it at Marc.

'Ta.' Marc shrugged the donkey jacket on. It too was on the big side and the end of the sleeves flapped. He rolled them back as well. Fully equipped, Marc was without a vestige of the elegance he had a few minutes earlier.

'More like something for music hall than urban potholing,' he grinned.

'Have to mess your hair a bit too, son,' Strangways said, and handed Marc a safety helmet.

'There's more gel where that came from,' Marc muttered, remembering what he had paid for the quantity foist on him. He did put the helmet on as gently as possible to avoid messing his hair too much – his vanity had taken an enough of a beating with the overalls. 'Lead on, McClive.'

The hole which led into the tunnel was much enlarged now. A small crane stood to one side, suggesting heavy items had been lowered into the excavation. A ladder had been secured in place, leading down from the lip of the hole into the tunnel below and Strangways led the way down.

Marc stepped off the ladder and stared about in wonder at the tunnel. Electric cables had been run down into the tunnel and it was well illuminated by flood lights. At some point while the site had been left idle as a result of Parrington's instructions, Erroll Gray's minions had been down and cleared the bones, as well as anything else that might have indicated human remains. There had been little enough of either. Anything remotely capable of burning had been used up in fires lit by the survivors and maintained by Nick as long as possible all those years before. Any lingering consequences of putrification had long dispersed.

Several workmen, who have been squatting against the wall, drinking tea, scrambled up as Strangways and then Marc appeared at the foot of the ladder and did their best to look busy. One strung out some more electric cable. Two others took up picks and shovels and a barrow and walked towards the rubble that still blocked one end of the tunnel. 'Who's the midget?' muttered one. His mate shrugged.

Marc clambered down from the platform via some steps that had been set up and peered at the dusty and rusty rails as he stepped over them. He crossed to the far wall and looked closely at the cables running along it and rubbed the accumulated grime from a section. 'Wow! Look at this. A blue line. Wide-spaced cross-hatching. Still in place.'

Strangways climbed down from the platform and looked, although the pattern on the wiring didn't mean anything to him.

'This style, this make of cable. It was what used in the nineteen-twenties and nineteen-thirties. Certainly before the war,' said Mark, pulling at, then rubbing, a further length of wiring, which came loose, the pins holding it to the wall having corroded long ago. 'It was all pulled out, oh, starting in the mid-fifties. The whole system was replaced with GEC standard, same as they were putting in the new lines. You know what this means?'

Strangways shrugged. 'That GEC made a bit of money.'

'A shit-load. No, this means this line, whatever it is, hasn't been used since, at least the mid-fifties. And given how close in to the centre of London it is, probably before that. Probably not since the war. Now the question is why not.'

He looked around with further delight.

The foreman who had been overseeing work at the far end of the tunnel made his way along the tracks, stepping a little gingerly along the sleepers.

'Guv,' he addressed Strangways while giving Marc a curious look. 'We're just about to have another go at that pile of rubbish down there. Sid reckons that it ain't too much left and we'll have it all gone in a tick. You want to be there?'

'I think I had better, Mac. Oh, and this is Doctor Sharpe, the expert Major Tom's got in to figure out what this all is.'

'G'day.' Marc smiled and held out his hand. Mac hesitated for a moment then took it.

'Wotcher.'

'We'd better all have a look,' said Strangways, 'You never know what might be on the other side. We've already had one ghastly accident.'

'Go easy. You know what happened when Carter opened King Tutemkhamen's tomb. Let loose a curse on all of them,' Marc said. Mac looked at him for a moment but Marc's wide grin persuaded him it was a joke although a residue of his Celtic origins made him a trifle uneasy about ideas of curses. He felt uneasy about this mysterious hole in the ground and not just because one of his workmen had lost an arm when the hole suddenly appeared. Parrington had been up to something in the days after the accident and before he ordered his workers back to sort it out. Mac's ever-present paranoia about bosses mingled with atavistic Scots superstition.

He led the way to where the other workmen were operating a small front end loader, moving aside the last pile of debris. The rubble came away easily and suddenly the tunnel was open. Despite layers of cobwebs and stalactites of mould, it could be seen to disappear into distant darkness. The three men walked beyond the immediate reach of the lights and Strangways and Mac shone their torches down into the receding blackness. The rail lines disappeared off into the distance, well beyond the reach of their torch beams. The workman turned off the engine of the loader and clambered down joining his mates to stand at the edge of the last of the rubble and squint into the tunnel. Mac shoved aside some of the cobwebs, and rubbed the strands that clung to his fingers on his overalls.

'Seems to open for quite some distance,' said Strangways, 'We'll need more lights before I let anyone go further down, Mac.' He turned to Marc. 'Is this getting more mystifying or less, Doctor Sharpe?'

Marc turned away from staring into the newly revealed part of the tunnel and looked back the other way at the well illuminated platform and tunnel. 'On the whole, if you will pardon the pun, rather less. This is clearly an underground line, maybe a branch or spur, but okay, you would expect it to run from somewhere to somewhere. Now, I reckon when you clear away the crap from the other end, you may well find a train waiting since god knows when.'

'I hate to think what sort of condition the passengers would be in,' Strangways said.

'Bloody pissed off I should think,' said Mac.

'I thought you poms were used to queuing and waiting,' Marc said.

Marc and Strangways turned back and picked their way back to the platform. They walked along it getting almost to the far end before being stopped where the rubble and debris still provided a barrier to whatever lay beyond.

Mac watched them for a while. 'It's funny,' he said to one of the workmen, 'All the cobwebs and stuff hanging off the ceiling in the other bit. There wasn't none of that in here, was there, Fred?'

'Bloody glad there wasn't. I hate cobwebs. Don't mind spiders but. Just hate webs,' Fred said.

'I wanted to know that,' said Mac. 'Now get on and get the last of this out. Tomorrow I reckon we'll get the other end seen to.'

At that other end Marc picked at a bit of the rubble and it came away, a tiny piece but several others slipped out in a tiny cloud of dust. The pile seemed hard packed nonetheless.

'Bit hard to say how much of it there is,' said Strangways. 'Could be a couple of miles of tunnel collapsed.'

'Could be. Unlikely though. Say what you like about the underground system, and most of you poms do nothing but whinge about it, it's well made. Only a few incidences of structural collapse, one near the old Borough station when they were doing some extensions back in, oh, 1923. Guard saw it coming, driver put the herbs on and got the train out of the tunnel in time. Collapse ruptured a gas line but also a water main and one cancelled out the other.'

'Well, this has certainly collapsed. You can see that clearly enough.'

'Yes, but why?' Marc wondered.

Mac had joined them. 'Not like the other bit what was got out easy. We got some work ahead of us before we clear this out. Start in the wrong spot and it might all come down on you.'

Strangways looked thoughtful. Mac continued, never one to miss an opportunity to have a shot at the boss, even obliquely, 'And like the guv says, we don't want no more bits and pieces of blokes coming off unnecessary like.'

A sudden gust of wind blew up the newly opened tunnel behind them. It shot a great cloud of dust up from the floor of the tunnel into the air, dimming the light bulbs for a moment. They were forced to wipe their eyes, sneeze, and clear their throats. They quickly brought their attention back to the recently revealed tunnel.

A workman shouted, 'Strewth, is a train coming?'

'It's the curse of King Tut, innit Doc?' said Mac.

'Either that or a ghost train that we've released,' said Marc. 'No, I think it's more likely it's an ordinary, corporeal train. On the Circle Line. No doubt this line enters the inner London system just down there a bit. I bet that's what it is.'

In his hiding place in the darkest recess of the as-yet untouched platform, below what had once been the escalator which itself lay below a carpet of tiles and panelling from the walls, the Nick-creature felt the same rush of air squeeze through the hole in the rubble and stir the long, greasy hairs on the its arms. It opened an evil eye and sniffed the air.

The workmen began packing up for the evening, and several climbed up out of the tunnel.

'Seen enough for now, son?' Strangways asked.

Marc looked away from some of the masonry that had been exposed on the tunnel walls. 'Mm? Oh yes, I guess so. I'll need to come back and record stuff, look around more later.'

'Not tonight.' Strangways said.

'Oh no. Not tonight. When I've done a little more preliminary research. This certainly looks like an underground train tunnel, well, platform really. But what's it doing here?'

At the surface, Mac the foreman stood waiting for them. 'Is that everyone out then, Mr Strangways?

'Yes, thank you, Mac.'

The foreman shut the big steel door over the hole and rammed a bolt home.

'That's a helluva a door,' Marc said, 'You don't think that's carrying security into the arena of paranoia.'

'I don't want to be the one to give Sir Thomas Bloody Parrington a multi-million pound law suit because some silly fucker falls in when trying to find a place to shag some tart,' Mac said.

As Marc and Strangways made their way over the site, Marc asked the engineer if that was a problem, tart-shagging on the building site.

'That's just Mac,' said Strangways, 'But Major Tom is too

cheap for manned security, so the principle is correct. About not wanting anyone falling in.'

Marc divested himself of the overalls and other gear, thanked Strangways and headed back to Parrington Towers. He was able to check his hair in the glass doors before entering in case he ran into Angela. He had not missed the resemblance in hair-style, could hardly have missed it even given the novelty of his new do, and had not missed Angela's reaction either. He was still getting used to it himself, of course, and the unfamiliarity of his reflection still surprised him.

Angela had, however, left a memo on his desk, informing him Sir Thomas wished to call a news conference the next day to explain about the finding of the tunnel. It further added that she would brief Marc before the conference took place. Marc was taken aback by the speed with which a press conference had been scheduled, especially as he had hardly done anything more than look at and, circumstantially, accept that what he had seen was indeed a long abandoned underground railway tunnel and station. He had already planned that tomorrow he'd visit the Transport Museum and try to find something that might give a clue to an underground line where none was, to his knowledge, supposed to be. He did not know at this point that he was being set up to be the star turn at the press conference.

Far below, in the tunnel a new and disturbing element had been added to the already incomprehensible changes that had taken place to the conditions in which the Nick-creature had existed – barely – for so long. The intrusion of light, noise, men and machines had initially caused all-encompassing terror as it cowered, quivering, in the deepest recess below the long abandoned escalator. Revived at first by the inexplicable arrival of fresh food, so fresh only instinct and ravenous hunger rather than memory had allowed it to recognise it as such, then driven into a paroxysm of terror never previously experienced, the Nick-creature had at first been driven into an almost catatonic state. But slowly deeper rooted memories, instincts, perceptions had forced up from deep within its being. Aspects of its residual humanity rose from its unconscious. Smells and sounds and, as its vision began to accustom itself to light, images began to resolve themselves into some form of distant familiarity. Its essential human condition asserted itself but inchoately, its human reactions were atavistic, belonged to far earlier conditions of humanness than even those of a once-adolescent boy of the middle of the twentieth century, those of earlier human ancestors still lurking in the inconceivably ancient history of its DNA.

The men had gone, the lights had been turned out, the machines silenced; the Nick-creature was aware that shattering changes were taking place because of them. Earlier it had noticed that the bones, shattered, dry and devoid of even the slightest life-supporting possibilities had disappeared. (The Nick-creature had been far too terrified, had been far too deeply hidden in its place of safety to observe the work of Errol Gray's minions.) It had investigated as closely as it dared the machines that had somehow replaced the detritus in which it had existed for so long. It had even noted the residual warmth in the extinguished lights, the silenced engines.

Now, two new aspects aroused both fear and curiosity. The air itself was different. It moved for one thing. And it smelt, tasted, different. To the Nick-creature the air of the underground was fresh – a term few of the millions who used the underground everyday would have used – but it also contained a myriad of different smells, some, the slightest, suggestive of the possibility of food.

In addition to this, was the presence of sound. For decades nothing had penetrated its exile. Once the scampering sounds of rats had ceased, after it had caught and eaten the last to venture into the tunnel, the only sounds were the faintest drips and trickles of water, and those of the Nick-creature itself. Now, the rumble of distant trains shuddered distantly but insistently into the tunnel. That most human of behaviours, curiosity, combined with that most animal of instincts, hunger, drew the Nick-creature from its refuge and onto the platform. It moved shakily, weakly, with a gait that was more animal than human to the place where its domain had once ended, where once had stood an impenetrable barrier of rubble, the boundary to its world. It stopped and sniffed the fresh air and peered uncertainly through the hole into the newly revealed tunnel.

The wind of a passing train a long way down the tunnel blew into its hairy face. Something stirred in its memory, some signal of recognition, some long neglected instinct. It straightened up, alert, then started to move with increasing speed down the tunnel.

On the Circle Line a train slowed and stopped on the tracks, to the annoyance of its passengers, although most were used to the rather-too-frequent hold-ups on this line, the oldest (as Marc could have told them) of the system and the one most in need of upgrading. The second last carriage of the train lay opposite the long abandoned entrance to the spur line, a gap in the tunnel wall which, if many passengers ever noticed, was hardly likely to arouse much curiosity; the underground tunnels were pockmarked with all sorts of holes, indentations and odd structures, most barely seen in the darkness.

The Nick-creature stopped in its scrambling down the tunnel, disturbed by the light from the train, the noise – and the smells. In the arched opening of the tunnel, where two lines once met and trains from the spur entered the system, the lighted windows glowed almost unbearably bright, the sides of the carriage, dimly illuminated by from the windows, grubby and dull to anyone else, seemed to glow. As its eyes adjusted, the Nick-creature began to distinguish objects and shapes within the carriage and as these came into some form of clarity, its attention focussed on a woman sitting with her back to the window directly in line with the abandoned tunnel entrance. She was tall, rather elegant, with a long, bare neck, her hair tied up in a topknot.

The Nick-creature recognised fresh food – memories stirred of fleshly bodies consumed so long ago, long before Nick became the creature it was now (had it been capable of recognising the process of mutation it had undergone). Its eyes and its very being became concentrated on one thing - the back of the woman's neck. Although fashionably slim, it looked exceptionally fleshy and juicy to a being that had spent most of its existence feeding on rotting flesh and bone marrow. The Nick-creature rushed forward, all fear of the unknown overpowered by its overwhelming desire to feed on fresh flesh. It hurled itself, jaws gaping, scrofulous tongue slathering, at the woman's neck. And crashed straight into the window at the same moment as the train lurched into motion.

On the seat opposite the intended victim, another woman, dressed in an army surplus great coat and with a broken Star Trek spaceship on a string around her neck, who had been muttering to herself for most of the journey, caught a glimpse of the creature as its face smashed against the window. She shrieked. Behind the elegant woman, great gobs of spit ran down the window. The closest passengers in the carriage, those who had not already put distance between themselves and the 'crazy woman' pointedly ignored her, a cluster of teenagers laughed.

The Nick-creature was thrown onto its back, stunned by both the physical blow its headlong charge into a glass window had caused and by the shock of the unexpected and invisible barrier between it and its meal, which had then inexplicably fled up another tunnel. For a moment, it lay still, endeavouring to reorganise itself both physically and mentally. Then it shook its head and howled, the first time it had made any sort of vocalisation for decades. If it retained any capacity for human speech, this was not an expression of it; it was pure animal. The howl mixed with and was drowned out as another train approached.

The Nick-creature dodged back out of the glare of the onrushing headlights, and now became more alert, its expression seemingly more calculating. It watched as this train thundered past without stopping, the intermittent lights from its windows reflecting on its eyeballs, tiny pinpricks of red in the gloom unseen by any passenger.

After the train had past, the Nick-creature ventured out into the Circle Line tunnel and stared after the disappearing train. A claw-like toenail touched the live rail. A blue spark. The Nick-creature leapt back but already a plethora of new experiences had become essential lessons, lessons learned. It shuffled cautiously down the tunnel in pursuit of the train even as the train's rear lights reduced to pinpoints and disappeared. As a familiar darkness filled the tunnel, the Nick-creature continued in the same direction along the tunnel; darkness was more friendly than light but already it was losing fear of the light, recognising that where there was light there was potential food.

Another train rushed up from behind and although not

surprised this time, the Nick-creature had to leap out of the way. It crouched back in an alcove in the tunnel wall, and watched all this fresh meat passing tantalisingly close but being delivered somewhere else.

The train it was following stopped at a station further down. The Nick-creature's scurrying down the tunnel was encouraged by the sight of the stationary train. It hustled a little quicker. The train pulled away and the Nick-creature saw now the platform, a platform like the very one he had lived on for all those years, a familiar reassuring sight, and, even better, the people who had got off the train. The last few passengers, save one elderly man, straggled off the platform. The elderly man looked a bit vague, lost and uncertain. He reached into his pocket to get a pair of spectacles to peer at the signs to find his way out.

The Nick-creature's hairy arm reached over the lip of the platform and pulled him down over the edge. The man's false teeth flew out as he was dragged over the lip of the platform. Had there been anyone on the platform to notice this strange event, they would have seen the man disappearing from sight for a long moment, then, his head rearing back up into the light of the platform. His attempt to scream was lost in his desire to scramble up, away from whatever his hauling him down. He gasped as if hyperventilating. He was dragged back and forwards along the track, occasionally rising above the level of the platform and then was hauled back down. Finally, all was silent. The false teeth lay in a small pool of the man's saliva on the platform.

SIX

Although pathology was barely practised and only remotely understood in any forensic sense in the Victorian era, many twentieth-century pathology laboratories still had a strong aura of Victorianism about them. Not those types of laboratories that are dependent on modern technology to examine tiny, even molecular aspects of the human condition; rather those types that occasionally still labour under the less-than-appealing title of 'morgues.' Those places that are used for inspection and investigation of the larger usually whole or near-whole aspects of the recently and not-so-recently deceased – these tend to still carry with them the appearance if not the unmodified function of a Victorian dissecting room. Certainly this was true of the pathology area in Royal London Hospital in Whitechapel Road. Of course, some equipment had been up-dated since the victims of Jack the Ripper had been examined here, for those abruptly-departed a brief penultimate stop before an unmarked pauper's grave. But the architecture of the building overpowered any recent equipment within it, and not all of the latter was all that new in any case.

A human lower leg was waiting on a well-used dissecting table. The leg had a torn, flapping chunk of flesh hanging from the severed end and a worn but cared for leather shoe on the foot at the other. A few other odds bits of viscera, less identifiable as to what parts of human anatomy they may once have been, also sat on the table.

Sir Geoffrey North, the Crown pathologist, his green surgical gown slightly soiled with blood and other less discernible material, took off from the foot the shoe and the sock underneath it. He placed both carefully on a trolley behind him. He fiddled about with the foot, checking the ankle movement and, seemingly satisfied, picked at the foot, between the toes and under the toenails with scalpel and tweezers without finding anything of any particular interest.

On the other side of the table, Ismael, the lab assistant, placed instruments used earlier in a sterilising urn. Sir Geoffrey handed him the scalpel and tweezers. 'All right, Ismael. You can put this away now, thank you.' (Ismael was not the lab assistant's name but whatever Sir Geoffrey called you, that was who you were as far as he was concerned. It was the fault of 'Ismael' for being Pakistani in both appearance and family origin.)

Sir Geoffrey's assistant, Doctor Farley, looked up from where he was leaning on an unused table, making notes on a form, a bit surprised that the examination was over. It seemed he was going to say something but he turned back to his form, checked his watch and made a final notation of time and date.

Sir Geoffrey removed his stained gloves and bloodied coat and without speaking held out his hand for the clipboard that held the form. He took it and Farley's pen and signed the form.

Farley accepted the clipboard and turned away to take off his gloves and surgical gown, glancing at Sir Geoffrey, who pocketed Farley's pen. Ismael noticed the purloining of the pen and smiled slightly before commencing to scrape the leg and the other the bloody remains onto a steel tray.

Joan Frazer, a protective plastic coat flapping over her police sergeant's uniform, pushed in through the door, pulling on a pair of rubber gloves as she did so. 'Have I missed the best bits?' She glanced at the tray of remains as

Ismael passed her on his way to put them in the fridge. She put her hand out to stop him and eyed the remains.

'Went a teensy bit berserk with the bone cutter, Sir Geoff?' she asked, 'You want to cut down on the breakfast coffee, maybe to only six or seven cups. Try decaf.'

Sir Geoffrey turned from stuffing his gown and gloves in a large bin and attempted his famous intimidate-the-interns look on the intruder. 'Sergeant, while it is the right of the investigating authorities to have a representative present at autopsies, it is not necessary to have an active involvement.'

The intimidating look was completely wasted on Joan; if high ranking police officers could not manage this singular event, a high ranking doctor, even a knighted one, was unlikely to succeed. 'I like to muck in. An extra finger on the knot when suturing is always a help.'

She attempted to demonstrate that valuable 'extra finger' by clapping her hands together, the effect spoiled by fingertips waving as the gloves were not fully pulled on.

'When are you whacking this back on the rest of him?' She looked around to try and see the cadaver she anticipated. Ismael attempted to continue to take the tray to the refrigerator but Joan stopped him again. 'This is the lot? My butcher has more meat than this in his window display.'

Sir Geoffrey straightened his expensive silk tie and realising that Ismael was being held up by Joan, had to reach for and put on his own Savile Row coat. 'What happens when somebody falls, or jumps, under several tonnes of speeding train, the wheels, steel wheels, sergeant, cut the body up. And the pieces, torsos, limbs, heads, get caught up and dragged along, sometimes for miles. If we're lucky we get some of what is left. The rest is fresh banquets for the rats.'

Joan waved Ismael on his way. 'So, the direction we're drifting in is?'

'You may tell your superiors that, subject to written confirmation, I find that these remains to be those of an elderly white male, whose extensive injuries suggest he was killed by and most certainly mutilated and dismembered by one or more underground trains They are a human leg cut off by a train wheel, in other words.'

Farley turned abruptly around from the sink he was scrubbing at and looked sharply at Sir Geoffrey. Joan picked up Farley's reaction in the corner of her eye. Sir Geoffrey continued, oblivious to his assistance's expression. 'The precise details will be in my written report to your superior and the coroner.'

'Sounds like I can tell the lads in CID it'll be an ordinary 31T and no frills. Keep that dozy lot happy anyway. They don't like having their poker games interrupted by anything that smacks of actual criminal investigation,' said Joan. 'I'm off for a cuppa and a sausage roll. Mind how you go.'

She walked out, taking off the gloves and coat as she went.

Sir Geoffrey made a final adjustment to his jacket and ran a hand over what was left of his hair, an act of fairly pointless vanity giving the little that still clung desperately to his florid skull. 'Whatever happened to policewomen who would faint at the sight of something like this? That woman brings to mind my nanny. Not something I wish to be reminded of.'

Over her tea and sausage roll, which seemed to come from the same organisation devoted to removing any resemblance to actual food that the police canteen used, Joan fumed over Sir Geoffrey's attitude. 'Upper-class tosser. Let me catch you slumming on my turf on boat race night...' she muttered. 'Sorry, not you, love,' she said to a nurse who was passing the table at the moment.

Joan didn't expect Sir Geoffrey to do anything except by the book; she knew him well enough even if attending postmortems was more usually a CID task than that of a uniformed officer. The trouble was the information, when forwarded through official channels, may not actually trickle down to her. Too many self-important superiors along the way. So she liked to try and get it for herself – hence her being at the post-mortem at all.

Crappy as the sausage roll was, she wasn't going to waste any. Even as she picked up a few flecks of pastry with the tip of her finger, Joan puzzled slightly over that odd reaction Farley had. He obviously didn't accept Sir Geoffrey's assertion although it was unclear whether he had a problem with the identity or description of the victim or with the cause of death. So what the hell was going on? The leg was found on her patch and although it was probably the province of CID, or would be if any foul play was suspected, her patch was her patch and she didn't like legs that may well once have been attached to someone who lived in her patch appearing *sans* the rest of him – if it was a him? Yes, she accepted that, too hairy to be otherwise even though many of the women who lived on her patch were strangers to depilation. The medical profession, like the police, was run by men and closed ranks in the face of outsiders and women and she, of course, was the representative *pro tem* of both. So there probably wasn't anything to be gained from trying to make something of it, not that she knew what that anything could be.

At Aldgate station, a motley throng of what a sociologist would consider fairly representative East Enders – men and women and a few children, belonging with degrees of transparency to different ethnic groups and of different ages – were scattered about the platform. As it was well after the morning rush hour the platform was not crowded and few of the intending passengers seemed especially anxious about catching a train or getting to whatever destination awaited them.

From the far end of the platform an elderly beggar shuffled along. A filthy eyepatch covered one eye. Sam Rooney's moment of importance as an air raid warden during the war had proved to be the high point of a life that had been on the skids ever since. He singled out a young man, the essence of the recent phenomenon, 'Essex man,' a working-class oik dressed in a fashionable but inexpensive suit replete with a tie that resembled cat vomit and a trendy hair cut which would not have looked out of place in Kitchener's army except it would have cost a month's pay of any private in that war. The Essex man turned the page of his *Daily Mail* and tried to pretend he was unaware of Sam's proximity.

'Got any spare change, mate?' Lack of response caused Sam to try again. 'Just a couple of bob. For a cuppa.'

Essex Man turned to look at Sam for the first time. 'Piss off, grandad. Didn't you learn to read when you was at school?' He pointed at an anti-begging warning poster on the wall.

Sam wandered off mumbling incoherently. He went a couple of steps then turned. 'I probably dug your bloody grandmother out of the rubble of her slum, you ungrateful, spotty bastard. I should of bloody left her there. I wouldn't have had to look at you or your bloody tie with me one good eye, if'n I had.'

The Essex Man took a couple of threatening steps towards Sam, who backed away. A few of the other passengers stared, others looked away in embarrassment. Sam, a flicker of long abandoned dignity aroused by a sense of his once having been a figure of some authority, of being a part of the myth of the Blitz, felt a sudden need to confront these people who treated him like shit, who tried to pretend he didn't exist. 'I might as well be bloody dead for all you fuckers care,' he shouted over the top of the sound of a train approaching in the tunnel. 'Yeah, look at the lot of you. You'd like me to jump under the train, wouldn't you?'

'If that'd shut you up,' the Essex Man said, looking around for support for what he felt was a witty putdown, but not getting any.

The unexpected adrenalin rush that Sam was getting made him more mobile than he had been for a long time. He waved his arms, swung around, trying to include all the passengers in his field of anger, those watching and those doing their level best to pretend nothing was happening. He wove near the edge of the platform. 'Shut up, that'd be bleeding right. Fought a fucking war just to...'

He didn't get to finish whatever thought had come into his booze-addled mind. At that moment, the Nick-creature, lurking below the lip of the platform, reached up an arm, grown powerful on its recent diet of fresh meat, and wrenched him off in a single pull. To the few watchers, it looked as if Sam had thrown himself under the train that rushed out of the tunnel a split second later. Some people screamed. Others turned and look accusingly at the Essex Man. The train, already stopping for the station, jerked to sudden halt. Passengers in the carriages staggered, some fell off their seats, several about to alight were knocked to the floor. People on the platform ran up to where the train had stopped short of the end of the platform, clustered at the front of the train and some gingerly peered down. Others who had not seen or heard anything of what was going on stood around, trying to figure out what was happening. From the group peering over the edge a cacophony of shouts:

'I can't see him.' 'He jumped.' 'He fell.' 'He was pissed.' 'Nah. He's just a old fool. Went too close to the edge.'

The train driver, visibly shaken, opened the door of the cab, and stepped out. The guard took a few seconds to realise the train was not going to adjust itself further along the platform despite his end section being still in the tunnel, pulled his head back in and pressed the button to open the doors. Passengers from the train, including quite a number who had not intended getting off at this particular station, now joined the crowd.

'What happened?' 'Some-ones under the train.' 'Call an ambulance.' 'Where?' 'I seen it all.' 'Where'd he go?' 'I can't see nothing.'

Forcing his way through the crowd at the front of the train, the driver carefully lowered himself on to the track, gingerly avoiding the live rail. He looked under the front of the train, peered into the darkness, then checked the front of the carriage. He squatted down and looked again. An underground staff member thrust himself through the crowd. He shoved a large torch at the driver who took it and shone it into the space beneath the carriage, along the rails. 'He's not there!'

Later, following the arrival of someone of sufficient authority in the London Underground to order the train moved, a further inspection only found among the accumulated detritus near the rails an eye patch with the suspicion of blood on it. By which stage many of those who had been present had left, not all giving their particulars to the officers of the Transport Police who had turned up. Essex Man had long gone, not unreasonably figuring that his little disagreement might well be exaggerated by busybodies into something more. The few statements the police were able to get were sufficiently contradictory that it was unclear in the end whether or not someone had actually fallen or been pushed off the platform at all. The absence of any body seemed to suggest that whatever had happened it was not a case of 'a body on the track.' Reports were submitted in due course but no action seemed to be called for or was undertaken beyond the inevitable filing and forgetting of the paperwork.

In the abandoned tunnel, the Nick-creature, considerably bigger now and much stronger, scuttled along, Sam's body hanging over its shoulder. It ignored the platform and continued to the far end where rubble still largely blocked the tunnel some yards from the end of the platform, thus cutting off the original entry to the platform. Hard against the curved wall was a hole, a place that had been like a small cavern, slightly warmer and drier than the main tunnel for years and which then led to an additional small area of security beneath the shattered escalators All of this had become more recently a place of safety beyond the reach of the strange and frightening sounds, lights and men who suddenly started to appear. Not that the creature was frightened of any of these things any more. It had to push aside rubble and enlarge the entrance hole to get itself through. Whether it recognised Sam as a figure from his past is impossible to judge. Easier to assume that he enjoyed eating him, whether he guessed who it was or not. There was no doubt about it. The boy that once was Nick was now a fully-fledged wendigo. It didn't know it was and neither at this time did anyone else. But it was.

SEVEN

The idea of a press conference had come about while Marc had been making his initial investigation of the tunnel and Angela's dislike had continued to simmer. To add to her state of irritation, she had already had to field a call from a journalist who had heard something of the injured worker and was sniffing around to see if anything more could be found out or, if needs be, made up. Whatever information he had was vague but he thought he had detected something that suggested rather more than an industrial accident ordinarily barely worth mentioning. Angela had managed to avoid providing information of any value to the press and hung up reasonably satisfied with herself. Her initial and well-rehearsed reaction had been as always to deny everything or at the very least to never tell a reporter anything of use. Then her mind ticked over in an unexpected direction.

Counter to this well-ingrained response that the press was to be ignored, circumvented or simply lied to was the thought that there may be some mileage, more personal to her than valuable to the Parrington Corporation – although she could make it look the latter – in actually telling the press what had happened, or such of it as was useful – to her. This line of thinking led her to determining to hold a press conference at which Marc would have to face the journalists, few of whom, as Angela knew well enough, were particularly disposed to Parrington and his works. The more she thought about it, the more convinced she was that it would be a trying if not shattering experience for that jumped-up little Australian and one which, when he made a big enough fool of himself, could even lead to him ignominious departure.

Flushed with this scheme but outwardly as business-like as ever, Angela convinced Sir Thomas of the need to hold a press conference as soon as possible. Parrington was far from enthusiastic as his initial thought, once he had guessed what it was that had been uncovered, was to sort the mess out 'in-house,' which basically meant covering up the tunnel metaphorically and literally. Angela countered with a convincing argument that a failure to be appear to be open and up-front early on would lead to greater suspicion and even greater investigation later on by a press always eager to uncover secrets, scandals and conspiracies.

Parrington finally got it. 'Bowl them a wrong un, eh? Very well, go ahead.' In fact, once he grasped the notion, he saw the value if anything went wrong of a stalking horse or even, in a further zoological trope, a scapegoat, in the form of Doctor Marc Sharpe.

Angela's initial hope that Marc would be flung into a state of panic by having to deal with a press conference at short notice and, she presumed, without any experience of doing so, was dashed by Marc's apparent disinclination to be in any way perturbed. Still, Angela waylaid him on his way to his office next morning and insisted that she brief him on the purpose of the press conference and his part in it, which she stated was to provide (and only provide) verifiable facts about what the excavation had uncovered and to avoid speculation as to what this may mean, especially in terms of the operations of the Parrington Corporation. Marc reasonably pointed out he could hardly comment on the latter, since he had not been there long enough to have the faintest idea what these might be, and his comments on the former couldn't reasonably amount to anything much at all.

The latter at least played into Angela's hands as she rather hoped that Marc would be made to look as if he knew nothing because he was not the expert he claimed to be. But she was rather put-out by the fact that Marc didn't seem particularly concerned about the imminent event.

Marc was only too well aware of what Angela was up to. While it smacked of vanity, Marc knew quite well his looks could set off envy-driven behaviour. On not a few occasions in his life, Marc had been on the receiving end of such behaviour and had learnt to recognise it and to take precautions, the most useful of which was to avoid responding to it, to decline to rise to the bait. The easiest thing was not to play Angela's game – after all to do so would be to have to abide by her rules and only she knew what they were.

So, her briefing, such as it was, ended with Angela feeling that she had been out-manoeuvred but not quite knowing how, and with Marc knowing not that much more about what was required of him but being for the most part unfazed. He'd wait and see. He was more interested in what the tunnel actually was, where it had come from, and why it was abandoned and, seemingly, unknown. The press conference was a minor inconvenience that prevented him from pursuing his investigations as soon as he might have liked.

At eleven o'clock, the time for the press conference, the board room in Parrington Towers had lost its air of a site in which calm deliberation took place within an atmosphere and decor of space and wealth. Now, with the director's table thrust to one side, it was awash with a mob of reporters sitting (where there were chairs) and standing, talking, shouting, checking tape recorders, scratching backsides (usually their own) and doing all the sorts of things that are standard preliminaries on the endless round of press conferences to which the journalistic flesh is heir. Interspersed but tending towards the front of the crowd, were photographers, most with an individual array of largely superfluous cameras – their badges of office and self-importance. Behind and to the side several television crews, standing around large news cameras mounted on tripods. The general attention or at least the direction in which the crowd faced was towards the front of the boardroom where there was now set up a podium bestrewn with microphones.

Angela Snottym walked into the room from a door to one side. The cacophony lessened by several decibels and cameramen thrust their eyes into the eyepieces of their cameras and pressed buttons to start recording. The photographers raised cameras but did not shoot any pictures. Most of them knew firstly that Angela was simply Parrington's assistant and not newsworthy in herself and secondly she was hardly attractive enough to worth a few shots for that reason by itself. No page three girl she.

It's doubtful that any really noticed that Angela had made some effort to change and hopefully improve her appearance. In an attempt to try not to look quite as much like Marc, she had added blonde streaks to her hair. The result was, despite the considerable sum she had paid a currently fashionable hair stylist, she now resembled less a weasel as previously than a skunk in a power suit. She took her place behind the podium and gained sufficient attention from the assembled journalists to manage a barely sincere 'thank you for coming' and then announced Sir Thomas Parrington.

Parrington entered by the same door, accompanied by Marc. A few photographic flashes went off as Parrington replaced Angela at the podium. His public face was well in place, a slight smile that did not override or belie a look of serious purpose. Once the photographers paused, he gazed purposefully around the room although not really looking at anyone.

Parrington was at his usual public best. His address to the assembled journalists emphasised the importance of his developments, the support it received from the far-seeing government of the day and its value to the local area in 'removing slums,' offering employment and, he implied, dragging a forgotten Victorian area of London into the excitement of the post-industrial twentieth century. He then touched upon the discovery of an unsuspected underground tunnel and the unfortunate accident this had caused. In order, he asserted, to prevent any such incidents recurring, he had employed the services of Doctor Marc Sharpe, an expert in the subject who would identify this particular tunnel and ascertain if there were any others. He then informed the room that not he but Doctor Sharpe would answer any questions and introduced Marc.

As Marc walked up to the microphones, the photographers aroused themselves to a slightly increased level of snapping. Here was at least a new face, a photogenic one, though it was not immediately clear what if anything could be made of this. Parrington and Angela stepped back, Parrington with a face that now expressed a mixture of pleasure in being able to introduce such an interesting young man and serious interest in what that young man was about to say. Angela was less successful at disguising her recognition that Marc was still prettier than she was and that the photographers and some journalists had already picked up on the fact. Several of the female journalists were showing rather more interest than previously; one or two gay male journalists too were looking at Marc with rather less of the jaundiced look most journalists had most of the time.

No great clamour followed Parrington relinquishing the microphone to Marc; this was not the sort of news that led to cries of 'hold the front page' as the cinema would have it. One reporter, an untidy, scruff-bag of a female reporter, waved her hand. Ash flew off the cigarette she was holding in one hand while waving a large official underground map in the other. The map and a little bit of priming had been provided behind the scenes by Angela for whom Daphne Gratton had a mild attraction. In return for which Daphne, raddled bag as she might be, had offered Angela some fashion advice. 'Get rid of the streaks, darling, you look like a badger or something.'

Gratton asked the first question even before being acknowledged. 'Daphne Gratton, *Express*, Doctor Sharpe. If this is an underground line, perhaps you could tell us why doesn't this line appear on the official, authorised government-sanctioned underground map?'

To Angela's suppressed chagrin, Marc did not seem particularly concerned by the implied challenge the question posed. 'Beck, who designed this map, was a genius, a first-class genius...'

Another reporter interrupted him, shouting, 'Who? Spell that.'

Mark smiled, a smile that as always disarmed practically everyone. 'B. E. C. K. Harry Beck. Only got paid about ten quid or something in 1932 for it and now it is the most famous map in the world. Copied everywhere. New York. Paris. But of course, it's an abstraction.'

'Weaver. *The Times*. What's that supposed to mean?' This journalist, compared to most of his colleagues, was notably well-groomed and trendily dressed and the fact that his long but neat hair was streaked in a similar way to Angela's suggested the use of the same hair stylist. He was already thinking of changing both style and stylist after seeing Angela's new look.

Marc smile widened a little together with a slight nod, as if recognising that this time, further explanation was required unlike the spelling of a four letter name. 'It's not a literal geographic representation of the underground system. It's an idealised abstract metaphor.'

Angela whispered to Parrington, 'I still think we should have got a Cambridge man.'

But her arguments made in support of even holding this conference at all had been too well made for this undermining to have the effect Angela hoped. 'A colonial makes a better stalking horse for this sewer,' Parrington said.

Daphne Gratton was not going to be put off by what seemed like obfuscation, even from such a charming source. 'You trying to tell us that the underground is an work of abstract art?' Someone muttered the name of Picasso and a couple of journalists within hearing chortled. Another countered with Matisse.

Weaver was not prepared to cede his place as the asker of the most probing questions, especially to a bloody old cow like Daphne Gratton (who personally and professionally offended every aesthetic instinct in his body). 'Just a moment,' he shouted over the top of any reply Marc was about to make. He too waved a copy of the underground map.

'West End stations where they ought to be. East End stations right down here where I suppose they ought to be.' (Weaver seldom if ever ventured east of Liverpool Street if he could help it; his being here today was a testament to his editor's dislike of both him and Parrington.) 'No line where you're saying one is,' he continued. 'Are you telling us that London Transport have been secretly digging tunnels?'

Another reporter interjected, 'That's your News of the World headline, Jeff. "Lucan and Presley seen on Secret Underground Line".' It was a standing joke among the reporting fraternity to pretend that Weaver worked for *News of the World*. Given that rag's insistent homophobia, this was unlikely.

Another ripple of laughter ran around the room, although one or two more junior reporters (including the one who actually did work for *News of the World*) scribbled down the *bon mot* just in case. Weaver, without turning to look at the source of the quip, raised his hand in a one-finger salute. The object of the gesture reacted with mock shock, bringing on a smaller laugh amongst those who saw his performance.

Marc ignored the by-play among the journalists and answered the question. 'No need for London Transport to dig secret holes. London is honeycombed with tunnels and underground lines. Not all of them belong to London Transport.'

'Who do they belong to then?' another reporter asked.

'The post office has some. Some are government. Some are private. Some are secret, or supposed to be. There are lines and tunnels that have been abandoned for reasons long since forgotten. During the war, there were all sorts of tunnels...'

Unnoticed, Parrington's face tightened at the mention of the war. For a split second, he thought he might have to intervene, to head the discussion in another direction. He was saved from any such precipitous action by another reporter interrupting Marc.

'McNamara of *The Daily Mirror*. Perhaps you could explain, Doctor Sharpe, why it is that Sir Thomas feels the need to get a dinkum Australian digger...'

Again, there was general laughter. McNamara quickly pretended he had meant the pun, and nodded to his colleagues before continuing. 'An outsider from half a world away to tell him what his English experts don't know?'

'My degree was from the University of Melbourne. My research was done in the London Transport Museum. If I didn't know of it, nobody did.'

'Do you seriously expect us to believe...' challenged Gratton, but Marc decided to assert some authority as the only person here who actually knew what he was talking about. His smile faded - as charmingly it should be said as it had appeared in the first place. It may be that, as the cliché asserts, that beauty is as beauty does, but Marc knew how to 'do beauty.' If it were possible outside of animated cartoons for steam to come out of ears, Angela would have looked like a boiling kettle.

'Logic would dictate there should have been a line,' Marc explained. 'In transport, engineering, economic terms. It makes perfect sense. It's very peculiar that there were no maps to indicate its presence. But I have not yet had a chance to do more than a cursory examination of the tunnel myself. The history of the underground railway system in London reveals many instances of lines, mainly spurs or branches, that were built and then closed, sometimes without being used. There are innumerable stations that have been closed over the hundred plus years of the system. Dover Street in Mayfair. King William Street in the city. That street doesn't exist anymore. Mornington Crescent. If any of you travel by tube, especially the Piccadilly Line, you would probably have noticed a station never used between South Kensington and Knightsbridge. That was Brompton Road. Much of this is due to the fact that for the first fifty years, the railways were all privately owned and operated.'

The reporters were beginning to glaze over. They had no interest in a history lesson. In fact, most had now decided there was not anything much of interest at this press conference at all. If the more canny of them could have been bothered, he or she may have wondered why Parrington had called this press conference. Most, if they wondered at all, assumed it was simply yet another Parrington public relations exercise. One, from a well-known left-wing paper, thought it was an attempt to deflect attention from the injured workman. Most television reporters doubted there was anything for them although they did recognise that Marc made a good visual subject. One female reporter did contemplate the possibility of a puff-piece along the lines of 'the sexy face of underground history' or something like that and considered for a moment whether to ask for a personal interview with Marc. Her personal one-on-one interviews with rock stars in the past had often led to in-depth probing, although usually of a very indifferent nature and then only with very minor rock 'stars' – even Keith Richards had proved immune to her limited charms and blatant suggestions.

Gratton, always niggly no matter what the subject, made an attempt to find some news where little seemed to be. 'Doctor Sharpe. What about this discovery of yours? What is it actually?'

'Well, it isn't actually mine,' Marc replied. 'Neither the tunnel nor the discovery. All I can say is that it appears to be a long abandoned underground rail station, possibly dating from earlier this century, maybe pre-war. World War One that is. My research is continuing.'

At this point, Angela stood up and moved purposefully to the podium, almost nudging Marc out of the way. As she did so, some waiters took this as a signal to place bottles of wine and beer on a table at one side. Their actions caught the attention of quite a number of reporters and immediately they began to head for the table. The movement quickly became a general stampede.

'I think that will conclude this press conference...' Angela started but she was roundly ignored by the reporters rushing for the free alcohol. 'Sir Thomas would like to thank you all for coming,' Angela finished lamely.

Parrington walked across to Marc and placed his hand on his shoulder. 'Well done, my boy. Now it's going to get really ugly in here. Bloody swine.'

He walked quickly from the room, the pressure of his arm on Marc's shoulder ensuring he walked with him. Angela cast a final look the reporters now helping themselves to food and drink, television camera operators hurriedly turning off equipment in order to join the melee. The conference had not gone as well as expected; Marc had stood up to the situation and the reporters – damn their eyes – had not been as aggressive as she had hoped. Her miscalculation, though she would not have seen it as such, was that she assumed that the reporters would be as offended by Marc being Australian, a jumped-up colonial and by definition (Angela's definition) of lower class. Although the knee-jerk objection of the English to Australians might have worked, none of the reporters were sufficiently bothered to make a big deal of it. If Marc had been claiming expertise in something any of them could have given a toss about, like football, beers or darts, even cricket, it may well have gone differently. But this group of reporters, for once typical of their wider readership, shared the Londoners' indifference to the underground, except as a source of complaint when they felt inconvenienced by it. Angela was also less than happy to see Sir Thomas's arm around Marc's shoulder as they left ahead of her.

EIGHT

Despite the confidence he expressed at the press conference that what the excavation had unexpectedly revealed was an underground railway tunnel, Marc was too experienced a researcher to consider his initial, brief examination to be conclusive. In addition to which, his pride was a little shaken, because if this was an underground line of some sort, he had not considered its existence in his PhD dissertation, had not in fact even noticed it in lengthy archival research that went into that dissertation. As he had said (but hardly been able to fully expand upon) at the press conference, there were many tunnels under London built for a multitude of purposes, some long forgotten, some still in use like the post office tunnel to and from the Mount Pleasant sorting office. His research had not included these, although he had been aware of most of them. Had he missed this one? Were the hallmarks of underground railway engineering he had spotted misleading? He phoned Pendelton and returned in the afternoon to the London Transport Museum.

Here he and Pendelton commenced to pour over maps that, ahead of Marc's arrival, Pendelton had pulled from boxes and shelves in the archive storage rooms. They checked and inevitably discarded most as they went. Unseen by either, the ubiquitous and irrepressibly nosy Myrtle wheeled her tea trolley into the room. 'Don't want to interrupt or nothing, but thought how I would ask if you wanted a cuppa at all,' she announced.

'Sorry, Myrtle?' said Pendelton, looking up at the sound of her voice.

'I'm just about off home and I want to see if you wanted a nice hot cuppa before I switch off me little urn like, 'cause this'll be the last of the hot water,' Myrtle said, managing to make an offer of service sound like an ultimatum.

'I'm dry as a wowser picnic, so I'll be in one. Ta,' Marc said. Myrtle was not quite sure what that meant, the allusion escaped her. (If she had known what a 'wowser' was, she would have found the concept of a teetotalling spoilsport incomprehensible in her life experience). It took her a moment to recognise Marc with his unexpectedly short hair – she told herself he was Doctor Sharpe now as well. He was still was bleedin' easy on the eyes but she never could figure him out a lot of the time. Pendelton's response removed her confusion.

'Thank you very much, Myrtle. The Ceylon tea, if you'd be as kind. Yes, Ceylon, eh, Marc, for this time of the day, I think.'

Marc gave Myrtle a wink and she turned and went to work on her trolley.

Marc picked up a large, transparent overlay of the area of the redevelopment on which he had marked Parrington's properties and the line of the tunnel that has just be uncovered. Pendelton laid out 1946 London Transport map of the area and Marc placed the overlay on it. Both examined it. There was no sign of a tunnel on the LT map.

'Hmm. The next comprehensive map was in 1951,' Pendelton said. 'Shall I get that out, do you think? '

'I don't think there's much point. All the rail power and signal cabling I saw show this tunnel has to be pre-war,' Mark said.

Myrtle, who was herself considerably 'pre-war,' stopped making the tea but not for nostalgic reasons - she needed a tissue, because her nose was dripping again.

Pendelton pulled out some map drawers from a large map cabinet. He looked at the contents briefly before closing each drawer and opening another.

'Perhaps we need to find some maps of proposed, even started but never completed lines. If there are any,' said Marc.

Pendelton paused before sliding another drawer shut. 'Difficult that. I mean, certainly the postwar planners had this absurd utopian feudal idea they were going to ring London with ersatz rural villages after the war, and some tunnelling was started, you know, under Atlee.'

Marc nodded. 'I noted that in an appendix. It wasn't germane to my research. But in any case, Atlee got slung out and the conservatives stopped the building.'

'Festival of Britain got priority. The good lord knows what we thought we were celebrating. I was just a nipper, of course, but I remember bits of it.'

'The Skylon,' said Myrtle unexpectedly. 'Stood up all by itself.'

'Of course it did, Myrtle,' Pendelton said.

'No, it done, on its teensy-little point.' Myrtle wasn't conceding the matter. 'Bleedin' wonder of whatsname, it was.' She'd taken her whole tribe of kids to see the Festival. She forgot about the tissue search.

'Still, whatever happened, to the planning for new undergrounds, I mean, those tunnels were nowhere near the centre of London, unlike this one,' Marc said.

Myrtle brought two cups of tea. Unnoticed by any of them, a drip from her nose fell into one.

'Ah, thank you, Myrtle. Could you just pop them on the desk there. Splendid. Thank you,' Pendelton said.

Marc reached out. 'It's okay. I'll take mine. Ta.' He took the cup that had been received Myrtle's post-nasal drip. 'Right now, I'd kill for an Iced Vo-Vo.'

There he goes again, thought Myrtle. *I dunno what he's on about.*

Marc was about to sip from the cup (talk about a poisoned chalice) when he noticed that Myrtle was about to put Pendelton's cup down on top of some maps. Marc hastily put his own cup aside and shifted the maps out of harm's way.

'It's a mystery all right,' said Pendelton, taking the maps from Marc. 'I am wondering whether it is worth checking out the stuff that came across after the GLC was closed down.'

Marc started to reach for his tea. 'GLC?'

'Greater London Council.' Myrtle thought she was being helpful as she swung her trolley about in order to leave.

Marc knew what the GLC was but not why Pendelton had mentioned it but he nodded a mute thanks to Myrtle anyway. She left the room feeling quite pleased with herself for knowing something a doctor didn't, even if he wasn't a real doctor.

Pendelton walked behind the cabinets to where a number of cardboard boxes lay rather untidily abandoned. 'Yes, dear Margaret closed it down. Too left-wing for her, it would seem.'

'Attila the Hun would be too bolshie for her,' said Marc.

'That's as maybe,' said Pendelton, whose days as a boarder at a public school had given him unresolved issues about commanding, matron-like women. 'This material was all sort of dumped on me when they cleared out County Hall. You won't have seen it, dear boy. It must have come, oh, when you were writing up your dissertation.'

'That's the ever-present curse of having to stop and write up your research. Something new comes along all the time,' said Mark.

'You weren't to know, dear boy, and heavens, I haven't looked at this stuff myself let alone set about cataloguing...

Now then. Look at this!' His exclamation stopped Marc from picking up his tea cup.

Pendelton stood up from now open boxes, knocking aside some rolled-up documents which were scattered about in the near vicinity. Marc bent down to help pick them up. 'Tch. Leave them for now,' Pendelton said, anxious to examine his discovery.

Marc stood up, his arms full of maps, but now with nowhere to put them, he put them back on the floor in an untidy heap.

'Now then,' Pendelton repeated. He handed a folded map to Marc who took it across to the map table. He straightened it out and put the plastic overlay on it. Pendelton returned to the boxes. 'That's late forties. So there may be something earlier.'

A quick glance allowed Marc to see there was nothing relevant to their search on this map. 'I hope so. Our tunnel's not here.'

'These are not in order. Very poor. They've obviously just shovelled anything that had London Transport on it into these boxes any old how. But they seem to be maps from some other source. Still, they are labelled by line.' He read the labels. 'Central. Rotherhide, even.'

'Sounds good. Sounds like you're getting close,' Mark said. He let the map he was examining roll itself up again, picked up his tea cup and lifted it to his face.

'I say... Limehouse Line!' Pendelton almost shouted. He brandished a map. Marc put the tea down again on the edge of the desk. They unrolled the map and Marc placed the overlay on top.

'Look.'

Pendelton peered over Marc's shoulder. 'Heavens.'

Marc pulled the overlay to get a closer look at the original map, and knocked the tea off the edge of the desk. 'There's a bloody station. Right there.' The tea cup crashed to the floor in perfect counterpoint.

Academic arguments frequently rage over whether coincidence actually exists other than a cultural shorthand for two or more phenomena that seem to be inexplicably linked. Perhaps Carl Jung was closer to encapsulating the phenomenon with his term 'synchronicity.' It would seem that history or fate or synchronicity were somehow involved, although nobody realised it or had reason to, when the wendigo, barely sated by the unfortunate Sam (who, truth to tell, did not offer much to sate its increasing appetite for human flesh), found its next victim. Coincidence or synchronicity, or given who the victim was and who Nick once was and the geographic location of both then and now, just a statistical possibility, it remains that this next victim too was another person from Nick's past.

Outside Whitechapel Station, a small group of young men in Territorial Army uniforms helped Margaret Hilda, now a blowzy old bag in her early-sixties, her hair artificially the bright red it had been naturally back in the days of the Blitz, to walk the few yards from Mile End Road to Whitechapel Road and to the entrance of the station. Non-existent Jungian synchronicity was working overtime; the station stood opposite the Royal London Hospital where just recently the pedal remains of the creature's first victim had received Sir Geoffrey's scant attention in the mortuary. Not that Margaret Hilda knew anything of that and it is doubtful she would have cared too much. She was tipsy and teetered threateningly in scuffed red patent-leather high heels. But she was happy at least in her befuddled state. Old memories, old behaviours gave her a warm glow that was not entirely gin-induced.

'Always had a thing for lovely men in uniform, din I?' She grinned, looking with less than perfect focus at the group of young men who surrounded her and who largely held her upright. 'And soldiers always had a thing for me.'

'Who could resist you, love?' one of the soldiers laughed. 'Those lovely big-bags under your eyes.'

Margaret Hilda wasn't too far gone not to register a joke at her expense, but she didn't really care. 'Another bit of the blackout, darling, and you wouldn't be worried about a little wrinkle or two.'

A second soldier entered into the spirit of the occasion. 'Yeah, you'd soon take the wrinkle out of mine, eh sweetie?'

Margaret Hilda was slipping off into her own world, a world of the past, a world that she returned to in her mind more and more easily – with less and less gin these days. 'Shelters. Girl's best friend, they was. You'd be surprised what a shelter and an army great coat could provide a soldier and his girl.'

'A dose, I reckon,' the first soldier said, looking over her head at his mates.

'Jesus, her crabs'd died of old age long ago, mate,' one of them retorted.

'Not nice, you cheeky sod,' Margaret objected. 'Soldiers used to be nice.'

'And you was nice to them and all, eh, ma?' the second soldier asked.

The group halted at the entrance to the station.

'Here we are. My station. You come along with me and I'll show you how to have a good time.' Margaret said.

The first soldier disentangled Margaret's arm from his. 'Another time, eh?'

'Yeah, when you're out with your daughter, eh?' The second soldier stepped away.

'With her grand-daughter, you mean,' added his mate.

Margaret Hilda swayed for second or two then, from many years practice, she got her balance. She looked at each of the soldiers in turn. 'You young people today don't know how to have a good time. You should a seen what I got up to in the war.'

Two of the soldiers spoke together. 'Which war?' 'You mean who got up you.'

'Cheeky devils.' Margaret giggled, prepared to be forgiving. 'Oh well, you're not bad boys. Ta for the drink and the fish and chips, boys.' She walked with a stiff attempt at some sort of dignity into the station.

As they turned away, the second soldier asked, 'Sweet Jesus. Can you really imagine fucking that old trout?'

'For gawd's sake, no. Be like poking your johnny in a sack of rancid chicken's guts.'

'Do you mind?

'Pack it in. She's just old nellie who likes to remember what it was like.'

'Come on, youse blokes, before I forget what beer tastes like.'

Margaret Hilda passed out of their existence as easily as she had come into it a hour or so earlier in a pub near Stepney Green. Since there was no particular attention given by the police to Margaret Hilda's subsequent disappearance although the community officer Joan Fraser was advised of it, the soldiers had no occasion to remember the encounter. As things were to turn out, Joan was to solve the mystery without knowing it, and too late for Margaret Hilda. She was, after a long delay, a victim of the Blitz after all.

In the foyer of the underground station, Margaret Hilda put her fish and chips on top of the ticket machine and fumbled in her purse for change. With a degree of difficulty brought on by the boozy if enjoyable afternoon she managed to insert sufficient coins to get a ticket. After a couple of attempts she inserted it into the ticket barrier.

Margaret Hilda wandered unsteadily out on the platform. A couple of younger women, already sitting and waiting, stared at her and giggled. She looked at them, turning over in her mind whether to take issue with giggles which she was fairly sure were directed at her but then decided to ignore them.

'Sod it.' She suddenly remembered that she had left her fish and chips back on the ticket machine. She walked back to the foyer as quickly as her legs, not inclined to be particularly responsive, would let her, muttering to herself. 'Somebody will have seen off me nice bit of cod by now. You can be sure of it round here.'

In the passage leading back to the foyer, she stared accusingly at a man walking in the opposite direction. Satisfied that he didn't seem to have her fish and chips, she waved him on. No sooner had the man turned the corner than the wendigo reached from a ventilation hole in the wall and with one powerful sweep of its arm, wrenched Margaret Hilda off her feet and, grasping her ankles, pulled her into the shaft.

If the man she had passed heard any of the slight noises of Margaret Hilda's short and futile struggle he undoubtedly thought it was just that appalling-looking drunken tart making some sort of fuss. He kept on walking. And, as with the soldiers, the situation never arose that he was required to remember seeing her at all.

NINE

Oddly enough, Margaret Hilda was actually missed and reported missing. Margaret Hilda was a creature of habit, even if some of those habits were unsavoury ones she developed back in the Blitz, and her husband phoned Limehouse Police station in the morning after her fatal meeting with the wendigo (not that anyone knew about that at the time).

Turning from West India Dock Road, Joan Fraser drove her panda into the yard of the station. A couple of police cars, rather newer and more stylish than her old panda, past her on the way out as she parked against the back wall. She extracted herself from the front seat, feeling a little pissed off that a couple of wet-behind-the-ears PCs got to hack about the borough in flashy vehicles while she was stuck with the dated panda. Or stuck in, she thought, when as usual she had to engage in considerable squirming to simply extract herself from the front seat. She was tempted to slam the door but knew well enough that all that would do was cause it to bounce back at her. Instead she pushed and lifted at the same time and the door managed to actually click shut.

As she turned away, a paddy wagon pulled up opposite the caged back entrance of the station. Two young uniformed constables manhandled an unwilling suspect out of the back. Joan's mood immediately improved. It was Elias; his nose still looked swollen and had taken on interesting deep magenta shade. The constables struggled to get Elias out of the wagon and into the station. Joan stepped in front of them. Elias looked up. She straightened her cap. 'Now that didn't take too long.' She pulled her notebook from her tunic pocket and pretended to read a page. 'Naughty. Not your car after all it would seem. Dear me.'

Elias struggled, almost breaking out of the constables' grip. 'You...,' he began. Joan gave him a withering look and flexed a meaty fist. The effect cowed him immediately. She stepped up closer and he flinched back.

'Nice coat that. Camel hair is it? Lots of unexpected pockets and things I'll bet.' Joan reached into the lining of his coat, inside the lapel and pulled out a plastic bag. She held it up in front of him.

'Oh dear. Not your day really. Not your year even. You scallywag.'

She stood aside to let the coppers take him inside.

'She hit me,' whined Elias.

'Never did. You'd have known all about if she had.' One young constable turned back to Joan. 'Oh, Sarge. Super-Fly hisself wants a word with you. Sharpish, he said.'

'That's Superintendent Flize to you. Constable Lewis,' she corrected. 'Hell's bells. Haven't even had time to grab a cuppa before the brass are screaming their tits off.'

As the constables and prisoner went through the wire door into the station, she considered for a moment whether the hand that was itching to punch Elias in the face might instead give young Lewis a pat on his rather nice bum. His face was nice too but Joan knew too well that although it would be unlikely Lewis would complain, if it did get back to her superiors it would provide them with just more of the ammunition they were constantly looking for. As she reached the door, it burst open and an another young constable charged out.

'Whoa. Sorry, Sarge,' he apologised.

'What's your rush, Buckmaster?' Joan said, fending him off.

'Something tasty in Leicester Square, Sarge.'

'All you'll get in Leicester Square, Buck, is something lasting.' She pushed past him as he stood holding the door. The door closed behind her.

Not too many minutes later, Joan stood in the middle of Superintendent Sidney 'Superfly' Flize's office and waited while the man himself fiddled with a fax machine on a table to one side of his unnecessarily large and suspiciously uncluttered desk. On the other side of the room, on a piece of furniture that in a domestic situation might have been called a dresser, a Marks and Spencer's china teapot steamed quietly, pluming a slight odour of bergamot into the air (so it was not real Earl Grey, which contains *Citrus bergamia*, not some herb). Even so, Joan eyed the teapot enviously, thinking of the delay to her getting a rather less expensive but equally as satisfying cup of tea in the police canteen if and when Flize finished faffing about and got around to her.

'I have been trying to send this return to the Yard most of today.' Flize pushed a sheet of paper into the machine and pressed a number of buttons, to Joan's eyes not with any sense of organised purpose. 'This machine doesn't seem to want to accept it.'

'Quite, sir. The Police Manual does emphasise the need, or is it the duty, for the modern policeman to be fully conversant and up-to-date with modern technology. For the efficient running of today's complex policing activities.'

Any implied sarcasm went over Flize head. 'Absolutely essential. Couldn't possibly hold a station like this together, under today's pressures, without the help of technology.'

'Still, if the particular piece of modern technology is not working, sir... Of course, the police manual may well have something to cover this situation.'

Flize looked up at Joan for the first time since she had knocked and, as usual, entered his office without waiting for a response. He occurred to him she might be taking the piss. She looked impishly innocent. He tried again, punching buttons on the fax machine with rather more force but with no greater success.

From the desk Joan picked up an old-fashioned truncheon, which was mounted like a trophy. 'Then again, the old fashioned percussive persuasion might work.' She slapped it into her palm a couple of times. 'Worked on villains before modern technology. Might work on modern technology.'

Flize gave her a harder look. She put the truncheon back in its place of honour.

'If I could... you did ask to see me, sir,' Joan said.

'I know I did, sergeant. And Scotland Yard asked for our weekly crime return.' He messed around a bit longer with the fax. He hit the buttons harder.

Joan took a couple of steps closer and bent down to turn the machine on at the power point.

Flize glowered as the fax machine lit up, pinged and basically came alive. Joan gazed back at him as if butter wouldn't melt in her mouth. Flize abandoned the fax machine and shuffled behind his desk in an attempt to reassert his authority. He sat down, rather more abruptly than he had intended which rather detracted from the intention.

The fax machine suddenly burst into life and spewed out a message. Before Flize could get to his feet, Joan grabbed the single page that coughed out. 'Allow me, sir.' She handed it to him.

Stupidly, Flize read it out aloud. '"You bald-headed old pisspot. Conzinc at fifteen hundred. Rendezvous at the Briar Rose as usual. Thank your mother for the rat traps". What on earth? Who is this from? Totally irregular to omit division and section. Is this in code?'

Joan was barely able to hold it in. 'I think you'll find it's just been sent to a wrong number, sir,' she spluttered.

'Wrong number. Ridiculous. This is a dedicated police number.'

'To send a fax, sir,' said Joan grinning like the Cheshire Cat despite her best endeavour to keep a straight face, 'You just dial a number, like a phone. This mug dialled the wrong one. Just like a wrong number on the phone.'

'You mean if I, er, the machine misdialled, my police messages could end up somewhere unauthorised?' Flize was almost shouting.

'Absolutely. Modern technology, modern cock-ups,' said Joan. 'No doubt that is why the Police Manual...'

Flize managed to get a grip on himself. He screwed up the offending fax and threw it, unsuccessfully, in the direction of his waste paper basket. 'Right. Thank you, sergeant. And speaking of cock-ups, perhaps you can explain to me just what is going on. You are community liaison officer and the people of your community are disappearing and you don't seem to know when, why or where to.'

'I don't exactly tuck them into their beds and give them a good night kiss each night, sir.'

'No, you don't, do you? Four people have been reported missing. In one small bit of London, your small bit of London, Sergeant, in one week. Don't you find that a bit disturbing, liaison-wise?'

'I only know of three, sir. And yes, I do...'

'If instead of worrying about electronic devices that are not your concern, sergeant, and kept up to date,' Flize interrupted, on a roll, 'You'd know that a Dennis Holloway has reported his wife missing. That's four.'

Joan reacted with feigned exaggerated surprise. 'I'm staggered... that Holloway would even notice Margaret Hilda missing.'

Flize, having felt he had regained the upper hand, poured himself a cup of tea.

'Unless he's run out of his dole money to put on the horses and couldn't find her handbag.' Joan continued. 'I wouldn't put much credence in anything Denny Holloway...'

'Since you are so enamoured of old-fashioned policing, Sergeant, perhaps you'd like to get out there and do some.' He put his cup and saucer carefully in the centre of his blotter. 'Start with Holloway and see if you can't get some idea of what is going on. The old-fashioned way. Out on the ground, sergeant.'

'Sir. Anything else?' Joan turned to leave. Flize waved his hand dismissively and sipped his tea. 'This tea's gone cold.'

Joan smiled in satisfaction and stepped outside, deliberately leaving the door open behind her.

In the board room of Parrington Towers, Angela Snottym finally finished a carefully prepared and staggeringly condescending presentation to a collection of eager junior executives. Each of these was a clone of the others and all were only too obviously members of that growing sub-culture of Essex Men. Angela made sure the recruits to the organisation – or those she was able to have her say over (she glared at Marc, who was doodling on the company-supplied writing pad in front of him) – were all, in her terms, members of the lower orders. This lot fitted her bill: trendy suits, a range of ties bright enough to start a wildebeest stampede if their shirts were not able to do the job by themselves. They all had military hair styles of course and right twats they looked. It made Marc nauseous just to look at them – so he didn't.

Behind Angela, a projected slide provided an image of coloured graphs and pie-charts. 'The overall management structure is thus reflected in the dynamics of the responsibility devolution mitigated by the decision making and policy operative protocols,' she concluded. And added without any conviction. 'Thank you.'

The words were barely out of her mouth than Marc leapt to his feet and made for the door, pushing past some of the junior executives who were still making notes.

'Mr Sharpe.' Angela demanded. When Marc did not stop, 'I mean, Doctor Sharpe. Just a moment, please.'

Marc turned to see what she wanted but Angela was in no hurry. She pretended to be fully engaged with turning off the slide projector and gathering her papers. She waited long enough for the homogenous flock of Essex Men to leave the room.

'You didn't seem very interested in the presentation, Doctor Sharpe,' Angela said.

'I don't know why I have been here, sitting on my backside all day. I have other, important stuff to do.'

'We all have to make sacrifices for the good of the company.'

'Some sacrifices are too great. This is one.'

'I went to considerable trouble...'

'Somehow, I just bet you did.'

'Considerable trouble to make sure you were included in our introductory symposium for our organizational executive management team players.'

'Maybe. But I'm not one of what you just said.' Marc paused. 'Introductory? There are more of these?'

'We believe in a total development-progress nexus. Yes, there are more. So I suggest you attend with a little more alacrity.'

'And I suggest you manoeuvre so as to insert your cranium in the rectal cavity of extinct member of the family Uriade.'

'I beg yours?'

'Go shove your head up a dead bear's bum,' said Marc.

The courtyard of the Richard Owen estate, a tower block of flats close to the gas works at Bromley, was empty, save for one or two cars that looked as if they had been understandably abandoned rather than simply parked there. Two pre-teen boys – one fat as butter, the other scrawny as a beanpole – watched as Joan pulled the panda car into the car park. They slipped behind a broken picket fence and peered back, their wary old-before-their-time eyes on the police car. Joan got out of the car and walked towards the block of flats. As she disappeared out of their sight beyond a brick wall uselessly shielding an array of festering garbage bins, the two boys sidled out from behind the fence, carrying cans of spray paint. They approached the police car, shaking the cans, trying not to giggle in anticipation.

'I know you, Elton Butcher.' Joan's voice behind made them jump. They swung around to find her standing right behind them. They tried to hide the spray paint behind their backs. 'If I come back and there is one spot, one tiny molecule of unauthorised, non-Metropolitan Police-approved paint on that car, your mum'll have to sell you to the Sheik of Kuwait.'

'You what?' spluttered the fat kid, seemingly the aforementioned Elton.

Dawn pinched his fleshy cheek. 'What do they teach you at school these days? You tell him what I'm on about, handsome,' she said to the other boy. She turned and walked back towards the entrance to the flats.

'I don't go to school, do I?' Elton called to her.

'I'm not surprised. You're too thick, you stupid herbert,' Joan muttered.

The scrawny kid enlightened his mate. 'I think she meant she'd have your bollocks off.'

Joan walked across the weed-infested and rubbish-strewn area in front of the entrance to the flats. A couple of shadowy figures scuttled away from a dark area at the far side of garbage bins. Dawn watched them go, touching her truncheon for reassurance. When she got to the front doors, she loosened her truncheon from her belt and pushed the doors open with it, peering in before entering. The foyer was dark and most of the lights, despite being caged behind metal bars, had long been vandalised; it looked safe enough despite the gloom.

She stepped across the foyer, her police boots sticking slightly on the surface. Joan didn't stop to consider what it was on the floor but hoped it wasn't blood because if it was and if there was enough it would undoubtedly mean that at some time she would be back again. The barely maintained lift descended reluctantly in response to her whacking the button, or the place where the button had once been, with her truncheon. As she waited for the lift to come down, she touched a 'tag' graffitied on the lift door. The paint was still fresh. 'Elton, you little prick.'

The lift ground to a halt and the doors shakily opened in protest at being summoned at all. Joan reacted to the stink of urine and god-knows-what-else that lurked within, reluctant to even drift or dribble out. She got in anyway, offered a short prayer to a god she didn't believe in and hit the button for a high-level floor. Despite her lack of faith, the lift doors actually closed and the lift itself grumbled into vertical motion.

Twenty or so floors up, the light from the lift doors creaking open fell on a group of punkish teenagers leaning against the walls and the balustrade of the walkway that led to a series of scabby front doors. They looked threatening with their shaved or mohawked heads, cheap jewellery attached to or inserted into every available orifice or floppy bit of their anatomies – and into some bits that are not all that available. Those with hair patch-worked with bits of scalp shaved into some arcane aesthetic of their own, had coloured that hair a rainbowesque variety of hues. They all watched impassively as Joan stepped out of the lift and walked towards them. She stepped through the group until she was about to pass an obviously pregnant girl, who despite her appearance-altering (she would probably consider, enhancing) efforts, didn't look to be much more than about 15 years-old.

'It ought to be just about time it popped out to see all that it has been missing, isn't it, Sheila?' Joan said, pausing to look at the girl's swollen tummy.

'Go right back in, if it does,' retorted a male punk, who may or may not have been the father. Sheila seemed distinctly uninterested in either prospect; she probably hadn't been a lot more interested at the time of the conception. Not that any of these boys would have been likely to make the event in anyway memorable, Joan thought. She carried on walking. 'Tell your Mum to let me know, all right?' She didn't expect a reply but Sheila did offer a shy smile even so. As punks, these kids didn't have anything against coppers anyway and Joan was, as Sheila's mum and indeed most of the mums (few had fathers in the immediately vicinity, that they knew about anyway) would say, 'a good 'un.'

Joan knocked on the door of a flat at the far end of the walkway. She glanced back at the punks. *What chance have they got around here, let alone any kids they have?* The door was opened slowly and Dennis Holloway stood there – a slob incarnate in a dirty vest, four or five day's whiskers, greasy hair hanging down. And that much was obvious in a bad light. Joan hoped he wouldn't turn the light on.

'Oh, it's you, is it?' he said.

'No, Denny, it's Mary Whitehouse.' A pointless sally that went over his head.

'About time. The Old Bill is quick enough when you're up to something. Last time you was around here before I even had time to set the clock on me new video.'

'You might have forgotten the difference in the sexes, Denny, but I'm not a 'bill'. Nor that old either.' Joan pushed past him into a living room which resembled a tip that not even a retarded seagull would touch with a barge pole. She pushed aside accumulated crisp wrappers, beer cans, greasy take-out wrapping, and other detritus she didn't even try to identify. She sat on the edge of a sofa. 'I see you've stopped beating up Margaret Hilda long enough to clean the place up a bit.'

'Hang about. I'll have you know I never belted her hard enough to have her run from her home, if that's what you are thinking,' Dennis retorted with, for him, an unusual level of animation.

'Well, you reported her missing, Denny. And if she didn't suddenly wake up to herself and finally just leave to get away from you and her beautiful bijou residence, what do you think has happened to her?'

His rare display of spirit had evaporated as quickly as it

had appeared. 'No need to be rude, y'know,' Dennis muttered, slumping back into the remains of an easy chair. 'Tuesdays is the day she goes to visit her old Auntie Nance in Rotherhide.'

'Maybe she stayed a bit longer with her auntie then?'

'Don't talk daft. Her auntie lost her marbles years ago but she still can't stand Margaret Hilda. Nobody much can. 'Cept me.'

'I've noticed that,' Joan said. 'All the bruises are a right give away. Maybe she stopped for a drink with a friend.'

'I know she's a old slag but Margaret Hilda don't stay out after dark these days, not since she got really jobbed over that time a couple of years back. You remember that.'

Joan sighed. It sounded right. Margaret Hilda had been upset by the mugging, more than might have been expected from someone born and raised in this very neighbourhood and who might have well seen it all at one time or another, and to have done quite a bit of it too. 'Okay, Denny. I'm convinced. How's she get to and from Rotherhide?'

'She goes by the tube, don't she. She don't like it much but. She's always had bad luck with the tube. She goes on about how her mum copped it in the tube in the war. And she got beat up in the tube that time I'm talking about. But she goes anyway. Silly cow. What other choice she got? What choice any of us down here got?'

It was quite a speech for Dennis and it indicated the degree of his concern; he probably hadn't spoken that much in one utterance or even one day to Margaret Hilda in twenty years.

'So I guess she'd change at Whitechapel for Mile End...' Joan suggested.

Denny interrupted, 'Yeah but she usually got out at Whitechapel. She liked to get fish-n-chips from the old place, you know the one's the Jews used to own. She lived down that way during the war.'

'They weren't Jews, Denny, but I know the one you mean. I guess she might have had couple in the Marquis too eh?'

'Yeah well, blimey, she likes a drink, does Margaret Hilda. I never minded but.' Denny looked almost as if he was about to cry. It was hard to figure relationships, Joan thought. 'I'll check down there first but if I didn't find her then we may have to do the cemetery and that'll have to be done in daylight.'

'She wouldn't have gone there. She hated the place, always, 'cause her mum, never got to be buried there, y'know.'

'Yeah, I know, but she may not have gone there, she may have been taken.'

'Oh gawd, you don't think...'

'I don't think anything, Denny. Not yet anyway.' Which wasn't quite true as she didn't put much faith in Denny's word although the emotion the old man displayed was worrying.

Joan wrote a couple of quick notes into her notebook and stood up. She brushed her uniform. 'If I find that you have been bashing her, Denny, or messing me about, you'll be joining mad Auntie Nance in the incapacitated ward.'

'Straight up, Sarge. She may be an old slag, but she's my old slag.' Denny's last words were as good an epigraph as Margaret Hilda might have received had she ever been found, or more accurately had any remains of her been identified and buried.

TEN

It was around early evening, about the time that Joan Fraser had finished her not terribly helpful interview with Margaret Hilda's husband (her widower if either of them had known it), that Marc left Parrington Towers and made his way across the excavation site. With the fading light, he stepped even more gingerly than he might ordinarily have done, trying to avoid the piles of equipment, rubble, muddy pools and the usual spoilage of a building site. He had read and written about this sort of thing for his thesis, had studied many early and late photographs of underground tunnel and railway construction sites, but staggering about in something like it was a different matter. Being who he was, Marc hated to be even slightly dirty, hated to wear clothes that were not clean, even it was just the odd smudge, felt uncomfortable if the merest speck of grime got under his fingernails, or a strand or two of his hair was out of place. So all this mud and muck was a major yuck. He carried a torch and checked the batteries as he approached the hole leading to the tunnel. He was a little surprised to find the hole still open and shone the torch into it.

'Who the fuck's that?' The foreman's head popped up from the hole. 'Oh, it's you Doctor Sharpe.'

'Sorry, Mac. I've been wanting to get across all day but I got held up in some incredibly stupid organisation and methods seminar.' Marc refrained from adding, *organised by Angela Snottym, of course, who thought it was wonderful, informative and actually had some practical purpose.*

'Who'd be an executive, eh?' Mac muttered, clambering up from the hole and standing, or rather towering over Marc.

'Not me. And I'm not. So what the hell was I doing... Anyway, I'm going down for another look-see. Fresh info.' Mark said.

'The lads have all gone and I was out to knock off meself like.'

'She's apples. I'll just be a little while and, it's okay, I'll lock up good and tight when I come up.'

Mac would have been inclined to argue but was stopped by the fact that it had quickly got about (or been put about) that Marc was 'Sir Tom's Golden-haired Boy.'

'Oh aye,' he said and then as Marc clambered into the hole, 'We've got overhead lighting in the place now. You'll no need your torch once you're down there. Just give the cord a tug when you come off the ladder to your right. If you finish up in time, I'll be taking a jar in The Arms,' he added, reckoning Marc was a nice lad despite being so tight under Parrington's wing as gossip suggested.

'Right. I'll see. Ta,' Marc said and disappeared out of sight below ground level.

Marc stepped off the bottom of the ladder and shone his torch around in the gloom. He located the hanging cord. The lights strung out along the ceiling of the tunnel flickered into light, creating some bright pools but leaving black patches of shadow where the coverage of the individual lamps did not overlap.

He moved onto the platform and towards the other end, still blocked by uncleared rubble. He looked at the pile, trying to guess how thick it was, how much effort would be required to shift it. It was then that he noticed the hole against the wall. He lowered himself carefully off the platform onto the trackway and shone his torch into the hole.

Clearly the rubble pile was not all that deep, certainly not covering the whole length of the rest of the platform, there was some sort of open space apparent beyond it. Gingerly he started to climb into the hole. His hand pressed down painfully onto a sharp rock. 'Ow, bugger.' He pulled the rock out of the hole and was about to discard it, when he noticed a tuft of hair clinging to it. He looked at it, puzzled, for a moment, then dropping it, he clambered into the hole.

Behind him, a train rumbled past the tunnel in the distance, reminding him of how close this mystery tunnel was to the existing, working underground. It was a puzzle he was determined to figure out. According to the map he and Pendleton had found there was an underground line hereabouts and a station too. Surely this was it.

Marc clambered awkwardly through the hole and out into the space beyond. He brushed dirt from his hands, his coat and his hair and stood upright, shining his torch to see where he has fetched up. To his delight, he was just below the rest of the long-abandoned platform. The torch beam revealed the platform and the tunnel stretching away in front of him but the beam stopped abruptly rather than petering out into the darkness.

Puzzled, Marc walked forward and realised he was looking at a solid concrete wall. This made no sense. Even if this was the termination of the spur line he suspected this was or had been, it would not have finished so close to the end of the platform. He wondered what would have happened if a train failed to stop with this concrete wall in place. He knew of one station, Moorgate on the southern end of the Northern Line, where the tunnel ended too soon beyond the platform, or so it had seemed after the 1975 Moorgate disaster when a train driver seemed to deliberately drive at high speed into the end of the tunnel. Even at Moorgate, there was a 60ft space at the platform's end, much more than here, and a 15 yard sand drag (which would hardly slow down a train at 40 miles an hour and hadn't). There was no evidence of a sand drag or even any buffers – just this concrete wall. Then it struck him what he was looking at. It was a moveable barrier, inserted in a few tunnels during the war because of the fear that tunnels ruptured by bombing would allow the system, or the deep central parts at least, to flood. These barriers were designed to drop down, closing the tunnels, if such an event occurred. But why was this one down, in place, and looking as if it had been for a long time? This line, once, had to have run somewhere quite close to the river or, as Marc considered the topography of the area above and the map he had seen at the museum, possibly the Regent's canal and Limehouse Cut, both of which if breached would certainly flood it.

Clearly there was no getting through this barrier, so he turned to the platform and scrambled up on to it.

Unlike the section previously revealed, this area had not been visited by Errol Gray's gang and far from being devoid of detritus, this was a virtual treasure trove. Although Marc could have no way of knowing it, Nick, even as he slowly transmogrified into the wendigo, had brought to this, his inner sanctum, various items, which if initially useful in some way had, over time, become mere keepsakes. In the beam of his torch, Marc saw Granny Rickett's spirit stove, the gramophone, ragged remnants of bedding and clothes, even broken and faded books. Everything was corroded, decayed and covered in dust and cobwebs.

There were, however, no bodies, skeletons or human remains. Whatever and wherever Nick had eaten over the years, he had disposed of whatever scraps even he could not digest outside his lair. On the walls, there were tattered and peeling World War Two posters, which the drier air in this small area had helped to preserve.

Towards the end of the platform, stood the gaping hole of a collapsed section of the entrance to the platform. Marc levered himself back onto the platform and approached this. He shone his torch inside. In the depths there was a glimpse of metal and wood beneath rubble; the bottom of the escalator. The way seemed largely choked with rubble, less tightly packed than the rubble that blocked the tunnel but still looking very much as if it would require some considerable effort to remove. Marc felt that once it was removed there was a strong possibility that there would be escalators leading towards the surface. But the puzzle remained – when and, more importantly, why had this tunnel and station been abandoned and having been abandoned, why had there been such devastating collapses?

Maybe, he thought, that was the reason. Someone had detected the instability of the construction and, for once, prophesies had been acted upon before they had come about. Had the closure of the flood barrier then been deliberate or part of whatever had triggered the collapse? Further examination of what may still exist above platform level would have to wait until the rubble both here and in the tunnel was removed.

He backed slowly away from the platform entrance, in his concentration on looking about stepping perilously close, to the edge of the platform.

His arrival, the first person to penetrate the wendigo's special place in forty years, had not gone unnoticed. The wendigo, for all its solitary isolation for so long, had called upon deeply immured atavistic instincts to arouse a strong sense of self-preservation. While Marc pondered over the significance of the concrete barrier, it had slipped from its place beneath the wrecked escalator and through a small passageway to beneath the lip of the platform's end. Once Marc was up on the platform, it shifted silently into the darkness below the platform and watched the movement of the light of the torch and occasionally of Marc himself when he stepped close enough to the edge. No longer starving, it was now wary of this presence within its own sanctum.

Suddenly Marc felt as if he was being watched – another atavistic instinct from as far back as the wendigo's more developed one. He turned and shone his torch onto the tracks. There was nothing unexpected there. Or at least, no *thing*, Marc thought. Why should there be? He swung his torch away onto a sign hanging crookedly from the ceiling. Still visible through the cobwebs and filth, it read 'Way Out to White Horse Road.'

Having ducked back under the lip of the platform, the wendigo moved slightly when Marc's torch probed the tracks momentarily. It moved forward again when the beam passed. A claw scrapped against a loose cable running along the platform wall.

Marc, startled, flashed the torch beam around the platform and tunnel but again nothing new was caught in its beam until it lit up a thin trickle of fresh dirt falling from a crack in the ceiling opened by the recent tremors of machinery in the other part of the tunnel. He grinned in relief, slightly surprised at the fear he felt nonetheless. *Great. Promising career snuffed out when young PhD buried in old underground station.* All the same, he felt sufficiently uneasy to decide to curtail this solo exploration. He walked back along the platform and then lowered himself over the edge when he reached the rubble pile. In the dark, hugging the foundations of the platform, the creature started to follow.

It didn't take too many enquiries by Joan to confirm that Margaret Hilda had indeed bought fish and chips at the place the *Armenians* used to own (now a family of Chinese), that she was with a group of soldiers when she came into the shop and, as Joan quickly confirmed, she had been drinking with them next door at *The Marquis* before that. The unidentified and unidentifiable soldiers were long gone and nobody could definitely confirm Margaret Hilda did go to the tube station.

Joan meandered around in her police car for a while, checking spots that a group of soldiers and Margaret Hilda might go to, although Joan didn't really believe that Margaret Hilda was much interested in sex with soldiers any more (she had cut a swathe, she heard, through servicemen during the war and national servicemen after it). Nor did she think it likely the soldiers would want to have sex with Margaret Hilda. Okay, there were sick types around but any soldier could get a better bit of sex from younger prostitutes in a number of places in the area.

Her prowling took her near the Parrington excavation site; maybe it was worth checking. Joan had heard about the accident and there was a remote chance someone like a drunken Margaret Hilda could come to grief in a place like that. She parked the car and hopped out, reaching back for her torch. She walked along the street, next to the razor wire-topped fence that surrounded the site passing a sign that proclaimed, in addition to the involvement of Parrington Corporation, that the improvements taking place were for all Londoners and represented the future. Joan was remarkably unconvinced by either assertion. She tested the gates. They were loose, unlocked.

Marc pulled himself into the hole and crawled through. Although once again covered by dust from the hole, Marc did not stop to brush himself down but flicked at the filth on his clothes, face and hair as he walked. One part of his mind said that it was just his imagination that was creating his growing sense of unease, another part said to hell with that, just get a move on.

The wendigo followed but its recent growth spurt caused it to have real difficulties pushing through the hole.

The rational side of Marc's mind had just about won the war of conflicting responses when the faint sounds of the wendigo pushing through the hole added a further frisson of fear. He reached the end of the ladder and started up, then realising he had left the lights on, stopped. Before he had a chance to consider going back down, the wendigo itself grabbed the dangling switch and, whether by design or accident, plunged the whole area into darkness. For split second, Marc remained staring back but he could see nothing in the blackness. With renewed purpose, with a mind running rapidly through all sorts of reasons why the lights might go out – timer? fuses? – he climbed faster.

Part way up, he felt he ladder began to shake – as the wendigo climbed onto it. Marc stopped. The ladder continued to shake. Marc climbed faster, reached the top, grabbed the edge with both hands and almost gymnastically swung himself over the lip.

A torch beam struck him full in the face the moment he appeared, like a genie from a bottle, in front of Joan. 'Okay, Sunshine. Come on out of there. What do you think you're playing at?'

Marc staggered and almost fell back into the hole. He righted himself and looked back at the ladder. It was still shaking as if being climbed from below.

'Come on out of it. Now.' Joan grabbed him and pulled him, none too gently, out of the shallow depression around the hole entrance even as Marc continued to look back into the hole – it was too dark to see anything down there.

'I'm talking to you.' Joan did not relinquish her grip even though this emerging troglodyte did not seem to be paying her much attention.

Marc looked away from the hole and into the full glare of Joan's torch. 'You're also blinding me.'

Joan scanned the torch slowly down Marc's face and body. She noted the gelled hair, pretty face and particularly of the way he was dressed. As the torch came all the way down, the beam shone down the hole, blinding the wendigo lurking just below the surface. It stopped its awkward climbing and held a clawed hand across its eyes, nearly losing its step on the ladder.

'Oh, it's a wonderful British bobby,' Marc said, his own vision returning once the beam had shifted from his face. 'It's all right, constable. I work for Sir Thomas Parrington.'

'You might think it's all right to work for Parrington the Barbarian. And by the way, it's sergeant wonderful British bobby.' She shone her torch on her stripes. 'Now convince me you're an agent of the great destroyer himself.'

Marc turned away and lowered the steel door over the hole and locked it shut.

'Closing a door and locking it behind you doesn't prove that you should have opened it in the first place,' said Joan, irritated that her suspect didn't seem particularly concerned with her questions.

'How could I have opened it in the first place unless I had a key?' Marc stood up, satisfied that the lock was truly closed. 'And if I had a key, that proves I work for Sir Thomas

171

Parrington. This is his land. This is his door. This is his lock. Got you there.'

'No, you haven't. Get over here where I can get a good look at you.' Joan reapplied her grip to his arm and pushed him across to where the site lights were brighter.

'Ease up on the strong-arm tactics, Sergeant, I'm not a striking miner,' Marc protested although too outweighed to provide viable physical resistance.

'You're the cleanest one I've seen, if you are.' Joan looked him over again in the better light. 'Prettiest, too.'

'If you're going to come the heavy brigade, I'll have to fess up...' Marc eased himself from Joan's grip and brushed at his coat sleeve. 'You've caught the head of an international gang of tunnel thieves. If you hadn't caught me when you did, London Transport would not have had a hole to their name in the morning.'

Even if slightly disarmed by Marc's looks, Joan wasn't taking any cheek. 'Let's just see if you can lay your hands on some ID as quickly as you can exercise what passes for wit where you obviously come from.'

Marc reached into his coat pocket, pulled out his wallet and offered his Australian drivers licence. Joan took it and shone her torch on it. 'Marc Sharpe. How poetic. Marc with a C, Sharpe with an E. This won't keep you out of the nick this fine night. This doesn't prove you're one of Parrington's flunkeys. Almost the reverse. Parrington isn't into pretty exteriors.' To make her point, she waved her arms in an expensive gesture that took in the whole demolition sight. 'Or colonials, I would guess.'

'If I'd known that the might of Scotland Yard was going to descend on me while stealing tunnels to smuggle back to the tunnel-deprived *colonies*...' Marc checked his wallet. 'Hang on. Look here. This ought to prove something.'

Behind them, unnoticed by either the door over the hole moved slightly as it was pushed from below.

Marc pulled out the gold American Express card, waved it at her.

'Well, in that case you *are* nicked.' She reached out a hand but not to take hold this time. 'And you've got a bit of crud in your hair'

She removed a piece of plaster clinging to his hair behind his left ear. And if her fingers stayed on his hair a bit longer than necessary, well, what harm was there in that?

She took the American Express Card. She tapped the card a couple of times as a thought came to her.

ELEVEN

Joan and Marc sat at a table in a none-too-flash Indian restaurant in the oddly named Artillery Passage, a very narrow lane in the tangle of short streets and alleys east of Liverpool Street Station. Joan, being clearly familiar with both this cuisine and this particular restaurant, had done all the ordering without consulting Marc. In turn, Marc thought what was being brought in a procession to their table was rather a lot of dishes, all of which overflowed with extraordinarily coloured things, things that Marc was fairly certain he had never seen before in his life or if he had, he had not realised that were actually edible.

During the ride in the panda and while awaiting the arrival of the exotic comestibles currently lying rather threateningly on the table, Marc had managed to grasp the opportunity to disavow Joan's assumption that he was a closely integrated member of Parrington's business and, by extension and (more importantly it seemed to him) Parrington's class. In so doing, he also had managed to convey his own amazement that, being actually not much more (or less) than an unemployed academic, he found himself as a paid consultant to Parrington. He explained that his present situation was a matter of his expertise in the underground rail system and that he had no background in capitalistic development beyond the study of it as it pertained to the development and growth of that very system. In the light of Joan's clear hostile attitude to what she called 'Sir Thomas Bloody Parrington and all his works,' Marc had tried to distance himself from any of that and to emphasise his skills as a (innocent) researcher.

Now he looked suspiciously at the plates of iridescent Indian food with which a turbaned waiter, who Joan addressed as Nabil, had completely filled the small table. Joan placed some on Marc's plate and loaded a good plateful for herself. She tucked in, while Marc unenthusiastically pushed at his with a fork.

'Get it in you. Go on. Try it.' she said between mouthfuls. 'You'll love it. It's not that hot. It's just spicy.'

'That's always said by people who routinely cauterise their taste buds with this stuff.' Marc had been a victim before of this inexplicable love of the English for highly spiced Asian food, so completely at odds with the bland nothingness of 'traditional' English cuisine. Did this seemingly insane embracing of curries, vindaloos and other, barely pronounceable items of shimmering, odiferous mystery somehow provide them with a culinary connection with an Empire long gone and for which the working class should have had no reasonable nostalgia anyway?

'Don't be a big girl's blouse. Try it.' Joan commanded.

Marc plunged his fork into the smallest and least threatening item on his plate. 'I thought condemned prisoners got a choice of their last meal. Even if they weren't paying, they got to choose.'

He gingerly placed the food in his mouth and chewed before quickly swallowing. He reached for the carafe of water. Joan moved it out of his reach and slowly poured a glass. Marc watched as the clear water gurgled hypnotically into the glass. Then she swallowed it.

'If some bloke with four nostrils can take your word you'll pay, with a gold-plated card no less, the Metropolitan Police can.' She shovelled into her mouth another large forkful of something a frightening green colour. Then relented and pushed the carafe of water to him. His desperate gulps didn't help much. 'Four nostrils?' For a moment he thought she was referring to something on one of the dishes.

Joan pushed her nose flat with her spare hand. 'Karl Malden. Enjoy yourself. Is this the way you wine and dine a member of the fairer sex down under?'

'In Australia, wining and dining the fair sex or any sex doesn't include dragging innocent victims out his legal employer's hole in the ground and torturing him with Indian food.'

'A member of the fair sex who happens to be the community liaison copper for this area. You're on my patch. I'm liaisoning.' She attacked the curry with renewed gusto.

'Does community liaison include arresting completely innocent Australians?'

'No such thing as a completely innocent Australian,' Joan retorted. Or right, fair do. I'm a bit more toey than usual because people have been disappearing on my patch.'

'If you take them here for supper as part of your duties, I'm not surprised,' Marc thought he scored with that. But picking up from her tone, he continued, 'From what I can see, the whole East End is disappearing with this development. What's a few people one way or the other?'

Joan looked up sharply. She dropped her fork back onto her plate, causing a splatter of curry onto the table cloth. 'That's callous, even for an Australian. Still, it explains the gold-plated American Express card.'

'It's just gold coloured.' The sudden vehemence of Joan's accusation caused him to back track a little. 'But I didn't mean it like... it's just that Sir Thomas's plans, and I've seen them, mean there won't be an East End before long. Maybe people are just moving out... and not leaving a forwarding address.'

'Yeah, right, and Jack the Ripper's victims were just indulging in a little DIY surgery on themselves.'

The shift in the focus of the conversation confused Marc. 'How'd Jack the Ripper get invited to this little soiree?'

'Just who's happy hunting ground do you think this is out there?' Joan waved a sauce-stained napkin at the window. Marc glanced in that direction, but there was little to be seen beyond the garish artificiality of the *faux* Indian decorations dustily adorning the window.

Joan suddenly stood up and pushed her ample frame back from the table causing a few unconsumed dishes to slop their technicolour sauces on to what was, fortunately, a paper table cloth. 'Come on. Settle up with the management. Don't hang about.'

While not unhappy that he was no longer expected to sit there and try to eat this muck, Marc was surprised by Joan's sudden eagerness to depart. Nabil hurried across with the bill. Joan grabbed her police greatcoat from the coat rack by the door as Marc, barely glancing at the bill, offered his American Express card to the manager behind the till. The manager shook his head and hands the card back. 'I am sorry, sir, we cannot accept this card.'

Marc looked across at Joan as she opened the door to leave. 'They don't take American Express here, smarty,' he said in an attempt to remind her whose idea it was to come here in the first place and what the inspiration for that idea was: her overreaction to his possessing a gold American Express Card. Joan turned back just as she went through the door. 'Then pay cash.'

'That's the woman I want to be mother of my children,' Marc said to the bemused manager. 'I just don't want to have to father them.'

Outside, Joan waited for Marc on the corner of Middlesex Street and then led him off, away from the restaurant, which turned off its lights as they walked away. 'Where are we going now?' Marc asked. It was turning out to be a very odd night indeed and not one that Marc, for all his attempts at cheerful repartee, was enjoying that much.

'I haven't started telling you about Jack yet. And you're special, you're getting the guided tour. Free.'

'Except for a dinner. And they didn't take American Express.'

'You said that,' said Joan, as she led around a corner into Wentworth Street. Like Artillery Passage, this street was really dark and the very few street lights didn't help much. Everything was wet. The street was grubby, the buildings, whatever their purpose, now or in the past, were suffering from terminal neglect. They turned again into Gunthorpe Street but had not walked far when Joan stopped.

'This is near where he did his first victim, a prostitute by the name of Mary Anne Nicholls. The actual street, Buck's Row, is long gone.'

'I think you're a bit late to hope for an arrest,' was all Marc could think to say.

'Imagine this like it was a hundred years ago. No electric light. Hardly any light at all, just a few feeble gas lamps. They couldn't pay for nice, bright ones in this part of London.'

'Still can't by the look of things.' Marc certainly felt that even if it was darker in Jack's day, it was still plenty dark enough now.

'Yeah. Right. Now shut up a tic. This was a right mix of slum houses, grimy pubs and factories, smiths, breweries, even slaughter houses. Yeah, right in where people lived. Charlie Chaplin grew up next to a slaughter house. You didn't know that. Not here but. Other side of the river. Still, same open drains. Blood running in the gutters. Piss and crap and not only the animals. The whole bit.'

'Come home, Charles Dickens, all is forgiven.'

'No laughing matter if you'd had to live and die here.'

'Okay. Sorry. I wouldn't be laughing my box off if I had to live here now.'

'Some of us do, but for how much longer? Sure it has changed but no thanks to enlightened politicians or the welfare state. It's a combination of Hitler and money-grubbers like your Sir Thomas Parrington. Come on.' Dawn bustled on down the street.

'I can quite see me dying here though.' Marc continued his thought. 'Hey. Hold on.'

Joan led him out into the brighter confusion at the junction of the concatenation of roads where Whitechapel and Commercial Road commenced their separate journeys eastwards.

'Whoa,' said Marc after dodging across the intersection in Joan's wake. 'You like to explain the connection between Hitler and Sir Thomas?' Marc felt a slight loyalty to his employer, who was at least paying him a sizeable sum even if it wasn't to buy his loyalty only his knowledge and, though Marc didn't know it, his potential as a scapegoat.

'Jack the Ripper and Parrington. That's the comparison I'm making,' Joan said.

'I don't see the connection.'

'You wouldn't. Jack the Ripper tore the hearts out of some six East End women. Thomas Parrington is tearing the heart out of the East End.'

'And you reckon my name is poetic. That's a nice bit of poetic rhetoric but I don't think you can make...'

Joan didn't let him finish. 'Let me tell you about the class system in Britain. The upper classes, those who have names and those who have money, one hundred years ago and today in the nineteen-eighties, they all think the working class don't belong here, are some sort of aliens, like migrants. It's not their England. That's what the upper class reckon. So they can do what they like with the lower orders. Or to them.'

She abruptly turned left into Greenfield Road, causing Marc to do a quick stagger-step to stop, turn and catch up. It was, as Marc quickly noted, another dark, wet, empty street.

'Hang on,' Marc said, 'I seem to recall it was Marx who said the workers had no country.'

'Well, he was wrong, wasn't he? The establishment, though, it exists all right. You're part of it,' Joan went on.

'Hardly.' Marc didn't see why he should add, *I'm not even English.*

'You take their coin. And I know what you're going to say. So do I. What's more I protect the bastards and their precious property. You're right. But that's not all I do.' Joan stopped and pointed at a house, clearly a long way off from any imminent gentrifying. 'You know what this is? This is the one house that the Ripper actually murdered one of his victims in. All the rest were out in the street. Right out in the open. But the last one, Mary Kelly her name was, was done in, right in there.'

'Jesus. In there? How about that?' Marc impressed now.

'In this very house Mary Kelly, thirty-five, prostitute, was nicely dissected. Into all sorts of pieces, mind you but not hacked about. Not chopped up at random. Nose, eyebrows, ears sliced off. He took his bloody time. Surgically slaughtered. While she was alive, note. He didn't kill 'em first then mutilate them.'

'Fair crack of the whip,' said Marc. The image Joan was painting hardly added to his troubled attempts to digest the Indian meal, or that little of it he had eaten. Joan went on anyway. 'Like Parrington doesn't ask first. He just moves in and dissects living communities a bit at a time.'

Marc protested. 'Oh, for Christ's sake.' It was not clear whether he was referring to the defamation of the upper-classes or the description of Jack's *modus operandi*

'All right. Okay. But that bastard, Jack that is, Jack-the-bastard not Sir Thomas-the-bastard, okay? Jack knew about anatomy. That's clear. And to know about anatomy, you had to be educated, and to be educated you had to be...'

'Let me guess. Upper class.'

'Top of the form. Anyway, Mary Kelly had been gutted like a fish. It was all clinical, delicate and professional. He wasn't an animal. He didn't rip her up, despite the nickname.'

Like many brought up on the legends of Jack the Ripper and not the facts, such as they were, Joan didn't know there was nothing in the least professionally clinical about the rending of those unfortunate women's bodies. That was just one of the prevailing myths. That didn't stop her from charging on. 'The wounds were all precise and the establishment knew that. Who were the pathologists and surgeons then? Same as they are now.'

'Oh sure. And Son of Sam was a Harvard medical school graduate. Serial killing isn't the invention of the upper classes. Maybe Jack just liked a bit of fresh meat in his diet.'

Joan thoughts were not on food but the crack about medical school, set off a sudden thought. 'Oh shit!'

She turned and quickly, for a big woman in police boots, ran back the way they had come. Taken by surprise, Marc stood and watched her go. He looked around the street. And at the Ripper murder house. It looked distinctly more sinister than before. He ran after the rapidly disappearing police sergeant.

Joan, by taking a short cut and retracing her earlier steps arrived back at where she had parked the panda in Bell Lane. She started the car and was about to drive off as Marc ran up and planted himself in front of the car. He managed to gather his breath. 'Don't leave me here.'

Joan opened the passenger door and Marc clambered in. Joan revved the engine and did a tyre-squealing and no doubt illegal U-turn. Marc, between gasps for air, wondered if he might have been better off not getting in, a thought which gained merit as the panda did a couple of quick turns that brought it into Shadwell High Street and then into Kingsland Road. From there for the next, lord knows how long, Joan negotiated across London via a series of side roads in a manner that would have done proud any London taxi cab driver demonstrating 'the Knowledge.' During a rare moment that the car stayed in one street for small length of time, Marc did manage to ask where they were going.

'To see Doctor Farley,' was the enigmatic and only reply. His attempt at humour – 'I did try to tell you about Indian food' – did not elicit so much as a grunt (let alone a smile). At one point, he thought he heard Joan mutter, 'The bastard knows something he wasn't saying.' But since this didn't seem to be aimed at Marc and he had no idea what it meant, he let it go and simply held on for the ride.

Marc would not have been able to recreate that journey even under hypnosis. All he could be sure of was that, eventually, somehow, they finished up in Flask Walk, Hampstead. And he only knew that from a street sign set in the front wall of a corner house, glimpsed as they hurtled around that very corner. He thought he saw an underground sign for Hampstead tube station as they screeched out of Hampstead High Street. The thought occurred to him he could at least figure out how to get home from here if he had to – and he might have to if Joan's habit of leaping into her car and zooming off was exercised again.

Joan pulled the car to a stop and nudged it into a space on the only side of the road cars could park, between several considerably more highly priced models. She looked at a renovated and obviously expensive Victorian house on the uphill side of the street. She got out of the car and started towards an small iron front gate in a low brick wall at the front of the house.

Marc, still in the passenger seat, wound down the window. 'He must have, what's its...consulting hours. You can't just call around any old time.'

Joan's reply was as much to herself as to Marc: 'It's still early. And besides I'm a big grown-up police woman, with a warrant card and all. I can do what I like.' She reached the front gate and turned back to Marc.

'Stay in the car then. This is nice, middle-class Hampstead. Nothing nasty can possibly happen here.' As her hand touched the gate, a large, slathering-at-the-chops mastiff leapt at her, barking loudly. Joan performed an equally athletic leap backwards. Marc laughed and got out of the car.

'I'd better come and look after you. You're clearly out of your depths in nice middle-class suburbia.'

As the barking continued, the front door to the house opened and light spilt out into the front garden. The dog shut up but stayed glaring over the gate on which its front paws rested. Farley stood in the doorway, looking out. 'What's going on out there? Come here, you dog Heseltine.' Which, amazingly, it did.

With the dog Heseltine safely negotiated, a clear case of a dog's bark and his appearance being worse than his bite (or so Joan and Marc assumed since the dog Heseltine did not bite either of them), once Farley had recognised Joan, he ushered them into what was obviously his study.

'Please come on in, Sergeant and...?' he said, looking at Marc enquiringly. Too short, too pretty to be a policeman.

'Thank you. This is Doctor Sharpe.' Joan said.

Farley raised a quizzical eyebrow. Marc held out a hand. 'Of the strictly mechanical not human engineering, Doctor.' Farley, reassured, shook Marc's hand briefly (and noted the lack of a masonic grip, of course).

'Ah. Ah. Please sit down,' he said, crossing to the television set, which was showing *Spitting Images* –with, at that exact Jungian moment, a Thatcher puppet beating a fawning Michael Heseltine puppet around its rubber cranium. Marc looked from the television to the dog that had followed them in but before the question could form, Joan spoke up. 'I apologise for disturbing you this late at night.'

'Not at all,' Farley responded with upper-class politeness, which probably translated in his mind as *bloody cheek if you ask me*. 'Weren't you at the post mortem the other day?' he continued.

The dog Heseltine started to take an intense, canine interest in Marc's crutch.

'That's what I want to talk to you about,' Joan said.

'Oh?' said Farley, looking at the dog with its nose sniffing Marc's crutch. 'Behave yourself, you dog Heseltine.'

'As I left, the post-mortem that is, I got the idea, well, the strong impression that you did not agree with the findings of Sir Geoffrey,' Joan said. 'I'm not asking you to publicly dispute with your senior, and whatever is said here is off the record. I'm not even sure I should be here and it may be that I'm not. But something is troubling me and I suspect that it is something that was troubling you too at the post mortem.'

'Where is this leading, sergeant?'

'Beats me, but if I'm not out of my tree altogether, I reckon you were not too sure that the wounds on the remains were caused by a train wheel. Or wheels.'

'Ah.' Farley thought for a moment. 'Now as I have your assurance that this is strictly off the record, and I will probably deny this took place if the situation arises, but yes, I felt that some of the wounds, the major ones, were caused by teeth.'

Marc was not following the conversation at this point, being more concerned in trying, politely, to stop the dog Heseltine's salvia from ruining his pinstriped trousers, particularly around the crutch area. Or providing a stain difficult to explain away.

'Teeth?' Dawn echoed.

'Bite marks.'

Marc reacted to Farley's mentions of bite marks – especially as the dog now had his muzzle in even closer and even more unfortunate juxtaposition to Marc's serge-covered genitalia. Serge seemed unlikely to offer much protection, Marc thought, even Marks and Spencers serge. He tried to discourage the Dog Heseltine without risking some bite marks of his own.

'Can you tell something like that?' Joan asked. 'From a few scrag-ends of some poor bugger?'

'Oh, certainly. Let me show you.' Farley stood up and started to head out of the room. 'Come along with me. Doctor Sharpe, bring the dog Heseltine with you, if you will.' He went out. Dawn looked at Marc and followed.

'Do you want me to bring him hanging off me, or will he walk on his own four legs?' Marc muttered. That attempted piece of drollery was quickly answered by the dog Heseltine himself. Marc carefully got up without getting the dog too excited, or more excited than it already was, and walked to the door as casually as one can with a dog in front of one, backing up, its nose in one's groin. At least, there was no question that the dog Heseltine would follow its owner as requested, if backwards.

In the kitchen Joan and Marc watched as Farley removed a large steak from the refrigerator. 'Bite marks are quite different from those caused by metal objects. Even jagged metal, which a train wheel is not. Let me show you. Here you dog Heseltine.'

He held up the steak and the dog, at the sight of a piece of meat not guarded by Marks and Spencer's suit, jumped up and bit off a chuck with comparative ease. It swallowed it and stayed on the *qui vivre*, hoping for some more, food overriding whatever its doggie brain had previously been occupied with in relation to Marc's crutch.

'You see the end? Where Heseltine bit it?' Farley held the steak out to Joan and then to Marc. Of course, they saw the end – so what?

Farley selected a meat cleaver from a rack next to the wall. He placed the steak on a cutting board on the bench top and chopped it. 'There. See. Nice, clean. Practically no tearing of the fibrous muscular tissue. This isn't visceral tissue of course but even so, the tear is, to the human eye, quite regular.'

He held it out for Joan and Marc to see. The dog Heseltine watched with keen interest too this time but Farley was holding the meat just too high, so it looked as if the dog too was examining the cut with scientific curiosity or maybe the sexual curiosity he had previously focussed on Marc. Farley turned it over to look at the bitten end.

'Here though you can detect just how irregular a bite mark is and...' He stopped and looked closer. 'I must say, that's odd.'

'What's odd?' asked Joan, who was getting a bit fed-up with this classroom tone. 'Other than you've stuffed your chances of a nice nosh unless you like dog saliva on your filet mignon?'

'Nothing a quick casseroling and a touch of Gravox wouldn't fix,' Marc said, and wished he hadn't.

'We have a quite different type of bite mark on this steak. I mean different from the remains,' Farley said.

'Sorry. Are you now saying that those weren't bite marks you saw?' Joan asked.

'Oh no, they were bite marks alright, but they were not animal bite marks.'

'Come on. Have to be. Rats.'

'The teeth of animals like the dog Heseltine here, even rats on a smaller scale, tend to puncture deeply before they tear flesh. That is they penetrate, tearing tissue, like a large pair of scissors but of course ragged and uneven as I've said. Human teeth tend to give a blunt bite, to abrade flesh rather than cut or tear it. Quite different. And the bite shape is different too. Human bites are ovoid. The dog Heseltine, as you can see, has made a sort of V-shaped bite.'

The Wodehouse-type references to the dog were starting to annoy Joan more than a little, although Farley presumably didn't know he was doing it. 'Let me get this right,' Joan said, a slight aggressiveness creeping into her tone, 'You're saying the victim was torn apart by human teeth. Is that possible?' She paused for a thought. 'So where's the rest of him then?'

There was a moment's silence, even the Dog Heseltine seemed to pause its slobbery panting. They all looked at each other as the possibility of where the rest of the victim ended up dawned on them.

'I feel sick, and I don't think it's only that vindaloo,' Marc said.

'We could all use a drink. I can, and I thought I was used to most things,' Farley said.

Back in his study, Farley, without even asking, poured whisky into a couple of shot glasses and handed one each to Joan and Marc. Joan knocked her's back in one gulp. Marc sipped his tentatively – he was not a whisky drinker, not even a drinker at all, truth to tell. He managed to give an impression of swallowing some but surreptitiously put the glass down on a paper-strewn desk. He was more grateful that the dog Heseltine had managed to get itself stuck in the kitchen when they had all returned to the study than he was in need of a restorative, even though the notion that something or rather somebody had *eaten* some person whose death Joan seemed to be investigating was rather repellent. It was all a bit unclear still and the disquisition of Jack the Ripper that had led Joan to this present discussion didn't help his sense of unease. Joan, on the other hand, seemed to be putting some matters together although hardly to her satisfaction.

'Jesus. I can't go around trying to tell my superiors that some mad man, some cannibal is loose in the London underground,' she said, holding out her glass for another dash of whisky.

'I'm out of my depth here, I'm afraid,' Farley admitted. 'I'm pretty new to forensic pathology. I don't know if this sort of thing...' He topped up Joan's glass and offered to do the same for Marc, who shook his head.

'I can just see me fronting the Super-fly and telling him someone is eating the residents of my patch. That'll impress the hell out of him about community liaison,' Joan went on.

'I don't know about your colleagues, Sergeant, not much about police procedures at all yet. Sir Geoffrey, well, he's not exactly terribly forthcoming. Nor is he likely to appreciate me offering him this, er, insight.'

'Shit, no,' said Joan, who knew Sir Geoffrey rather better. 'Not without knowing a damn sight more. Same with Super-fly.'

Farley was beginning to recognise the potential problems if he got any further entangled in this situation, whatever it was. 'I really don't think I can be involved, in any official way, I mean. But if I could maybe offer a suggestion? I think you need to know a bit more about this before taking it to your superiors, sergeant.'

'I can't really go asking to see the bits again. Sir G would be onto my bosses...' Joan said.

'God no, I wasn't suggesting that for a moment. Heaven forbid.' Farley could see his own career going down the sewer before it even started. If he wanted to become a Home Office pathologist, he couldn't upset Sir Geoffrey nor, as importantly, any top brass in the police.

'For the moment, it seems to me you need to find out a bit more information about, um, human flesh-eating, a bit of scientific credibility is what is wanted. I could maybe help. Maybe you should talk to my old mentor at Cambridge, Doctor Solti. It's a hobby, well, sort of obsession of hers, cannibalism. Afternoon tea in her rooms was an interesting if far from appetising event. If anyone knows she does.'

'I knew I should have stayed home with the bunyips,' said Marc.

That wrapped up the meeting with Doctor Farley except for his extracting from Joan an undertaking not to bring his name into things if she did take matters further. Then he showed them out.

At first, the drive back to the East End was, to Marc's gratitude, a less fraught affair although this time it came with conversation and that was not actually all that settling. Joan filled him on the post-mortem which had sent her to Farley and also mentioned the recent spate of disappearances, most of which were connected to the underground in some way. Then Marc opened his mouth without fully thinking and set Joan off tearing through the streets like a rally driver again. All he said, and he thought it was relatively innocuous, was that a bit of research would be helpful. As an scholar, it wasn't surprising he would think along those lines. The real problem was that when Joan challenged him as to how that could be achieved, he responded to the effect that's what libraries were for.

In front of the Hackney Public Library and across the road at the Town Hall, the rent boys were out in larger numbers. The later hour when punters were more likely to be on the prowl, together with the slowly improving weather, brought two or three who might not have been as eager or hurting as much as some others on to the steps. Some of the early ones had already done or trick or two and were back waiting for another customer – only rarely was the sort of trade these boys did in this part of town likely to be an all-night job with the largish cash payment that brought with it. In addition to the usual traffic in Mare Street, a number of cars were cruising, the drivers getting up the courage or checking the merchandise on offer this night or making sure they were not going to be seen. It was all part of the game and some of the boys amused themselves with guessing how long one particular driver would take until he finally crawled up to the kerb.

It was, however, Joan and not a punter who pulled her car up at the kerb. She jumped out, barely paying attention to the traffic. Marc, bemused as he seemed to be most of the time in Joan's company, with even less sense of where he was this time, and only a slightly better sense of why he was there (or he would have when he realised this was a library), climbed out of the passenger side.

The abrupt nature of Joan's arrival and her sudden charge into their midst, contrary to her usual approach, had the effect of scaring off some of the boys who did not know her well or who had never trusted her that much. A couple darted off quickly. One or two others affected to wander off casually, but made themselves scarce nonetheless.

Luke, as usual, detached himself from the knot of boys on the steps. His eyes quickly fell on Marc. Although his clients, if they deserved such a dignified term, were always men, they were seldom young and never attractive in even the most generous use of the concept. Even as he spoke to Joan, his eyes drank in the young man closing the door to the police car.

'Sarge, Don't leave the chariot there. The punters'll be off like a week-old tandori.' Most of them already had, the cruising cars having found a turn of speed and their drivers a need to be elsewhere almost as soon the panda hove into view.

Joan was already striding quickly and purposefully up the steps and seemed to pay him no attention. Marc, however, looked at the boy who has spoken. He hesitated slightly. The young man in front of him was exactly the sort of guy who could be guaranteed to hold a magnetic attraction for Marc – long, faintly sardonic face, the cupid's bow lips, and especially the ruthlessly untidy streaked blond hair. Marc felt a rush of blood or, more strictly speaking, hormones. His eyes met Luke's.

Joan swung around to see where Marc had got to. So fixed was she on the purpose she had to come there, she didn't notice the electric exchange between Marc and Luke. She took the moment to answer Luke's complaint. 'What about "we owe you, sarge"? Have an early night, Luke. Or watch me car, eh?'

One of the by-standing rent boys piped up. 'Do you want us to mind your friend as well? No charge for him.'

Luke turned to face the boy, an instant surge of jealousy, and equally as instantly saw the kid was simply making a joke.

With the moment broken, Marc smiled wanly and started to follow Joan up the steps. He still didn't know what was going on or why he was there, but he realised quickly enough who or what these boys were and so what the blond-streaked boy probably was as well. That only made him more interesting.

Joan paused outside the only brightly lit doors under the portico, doors clearly marked 'Public Library.' Then she plunged in and Marc followed.

Inside the library a small mixture of readers variously wandered the stacks or sat in chairs or at the one or two tables. Some were clearly regulars, elderly for the most part and searching for something, anything, they had not read previously to help stave off the long hours of retirement or widowhood. There were one or two teenagers, students undertaking, with greater or lesser degrees of enthusiasm, research for school assignments. They were joined for similar purposes by older individuals, probably undertaking adult education or even polytechnic courses part-time.

During the brief journey from Hampstead to library, Joan had grasped the implications of Marc's remark and asserted that she needed Marc's skills as a researcher. Now that they were in the library, Marc moved quickly to a cabinet that contained the library catalogue. There weren't many drawers. 'You sure this is what you want to check? I mean...'

'Right. Try and get something on cannibals,' said Joan..

'Along the lines of, who does it? Why? Where? That sort of thing. I take it,' Marc said.

'You're the researcher here but that sounds like it. If I know it even happens, I might be able to do some sort of search for any cases in the police files. But I don't quite know how I could explain...' Joan stopped. Maybe she was jumping to all sorts of crazy conclusions.

Marc flicked through various cards, open and shut a few drawers. 'There's not much. Still, something. Bit hard to know quite what subject it'd be under.' He made a note of a reference on a piece of paper from a box provided by the library. 'See, mother, I knew that PhD would pay for itself some day.' He turned to Joan. 'Well, I suppose it has already, thanks to your bosom buddy, Sir Thomas...'

'My bosom is the second last part of my anatomy that is ever likely to come close to Sir Thomas-bloody-Parrington,' Joan retorted.

A quick search among the shelves located a number of books, several of which were largish reference books, but only a couple that seemed specialist tomes to do with the field.

'Who's a clever boy then?' said Joan, although she was actually quite impressed. Having never wanted to become a detective, books, files and suchlike sources of information were not something she had much working familiarity with. They piled them up on a large, empty table. Marc checked indices, contents and, in the case of encyclopaedia, individual entries. Joan flicked through various books. A particularly gruesome illustration in one of them caught her attention. She held it up for Marc to see but he simply glanced at it, nodded his head, and went back to checking a thicker reference work.

Joan closed the book and gazed at Marc bent over the book in front of him. He really was ravishing but would he respond to an offer to be ravished, she wondered.

'This is all rather bloody vague.' Marc pushed the book away and rubbed his eyes. 'There's stuff here about China but it says it's probably some folktale to do with yetis.'

Joan dismissed her salacious thoughts. 'Bloody brilliant. I can just see me going to Inspector Flize and telling him that a yeti is riding around in the underground eating the ratepayers of London.'

Mark tapped the entry in the book in front of him. 'There is something else here. A Canadian Algonquin - that's American Indians to you, sergeant - an Algonquin legend apparently.'

'Give me strength. Yetis. Red Indians. This is bloody London, not the tampa.'

'Tundra.'

'Okay, professor. What does it say?'

'There's only this one paragraph: "A North American Indian myth, persistent but difficult to quantify. Evidence is difficult to obtain and so far impossible to verify. The process is not understood or at least not revealed and the links with eating human flesh so far not established." And that's it. And that's it for this particular library too.'

'Two important questions immediately leap to mind.' Joan leant back and held up two fingers, then quickly reversed her hand to palm outward instead of inward. 'Sorry. Churchill did that once, during the war, there's newsreel footage of him giving a two-figured salute instead of the V for Victory...'

'Fascinating,' Marc interrupted, 'But your two questions, unless they have to do with Churchill. Although I believe there is a Churchill on Hudson's Bay in Canada, so...'

'Smart arse. Anyway, question the one, where the hell are we going to find a North American Indian to ask?'

'I can answer that. Maybe. Indirectly. The author of this article is, guess who?'

'How the hell would I know, sunshine?'

'None other than Doctor Solti.'

'Farley's old mate.'

'I imagine so. Locate her and you can apply your well known interrogation techniques.'

'Rubber hose, phone book or curry powder?'

'I bow to your superior knowledge of what is likely to be most effective. For me, even the merest threat of another Indian meal and I would tell you anything.' He flicked to the front of the book and checked the list of contributors. 'Bingo. The esteemed Doctor Solti just happens to be still teaching at Cambridge University.'

Joan raised an amused eyebrow. 'Bingo?'

'I didn't feel it was worthy of a eureka, or should that be *an* eureka. And your second question is?'

'For fifty points, do you fancy being locked in here all night?'

Marc looked up and followed Joan's gaze to see the librarian standing by the door, rather obviously playing with a large set of keys. 'Better than being locked up in your nick, I should think. At least here there's something interesting to read.'

'You haven't seen the walls at the nick.'

They pushed back their chairs and made their way across to the door. Marc's *good night* to the librarian only caused a grunted response. As the door closed behind them and the click of the lock echoed in the marble foyer, Marc asked, 'Do you think her polite farewell was increased or lessened by your uniform?'

'Nah. It's all that silver fish poo that gets into their lungs. Let's get out of here before it gets into ours.'

As Joan and Marc walked down the hall towards the outside. They passed a sign indicating that a special exhibition of photographs of 'London People' was currently being held inside the hall. Sadly neither paid any attention, because if they had, they may have saved themselves some more trouble and even saved a few lives. Instead they would have to come back again.

'Listen, thanks for the help.' Joan pushed the front doors open and let Marc through. 'Not that it has been much help, you know. But thanks anyway. I'll drop you at the train station. My shift's pretty much up. I'll need to check in.'

Business for the boys on the steps had been, as they had predicted, reduced to practically nothing thanks to the glaringly obvious police car in the street. Some had moved on across the road to the Town Hall, which being set back from the road was less public but also less accessible to the kerb-crawling punter. Others had given up or shifted to other known pick-up points. A few, including Luke, were seated further back, waiting for Joan to eventually come out and leave. Luke had considered moving to a spot he actually preferred, the Limehouse Town Hall, although it had the disadvantage of being rather too close to the Limehouse Police Station and tended to attract only the bravest or most desperate punters. It also had the advantage of being almost next to the abandoned Limehouse Basin, which was a convenient spot to take the punters. But he had hung around, hoping for another glimpse of the guy with Joan. Most of those left were smoking, except Luke; all outward appearances to the contrary, he was actually considerably health-conscious and did not smoke. He stood as Marc and then Joan came out of the foyer. 'Leaving, Sarge? Please.'

'Yeah. Okay. You ought to realise I'm doing you a favour, leaving the car there.'

'We all appreciate it, don't we?' Luke turned to the few remaining boys, none of who shared quite the easy, even affectionate, relationship he had with Joan. But then none had shared a night in Joan's bed as Luke had, a one-off both had thoroughly enjoyed but Joan had not offered to repeat. On his own time, Luke was a bit more sexually eclectic than his professional activities might have implied.

Joan located her car keys and continued down the steps. Unnoticed by her, Marc and Luke exchanged a look that each understood.

TWELVE

Parrington's Bentley Mulsanne glided into the forecourt of the Parrington Corporation tower block, each – the tower block and the Bentley – reflected each other in their respective windows in a display of materialistic self-regard. The two reflections shivered, shimmered and settled in mutual admiration as the car purred to a gentle stop. A uniformed chauffeur, tightly encased in a dark blue suit, in choreographed moves turned off the engine, slipped from behind the wheel, placed his cap beneath his arm and with his spare hand, swiftly opened the back door, his face fixed in a blank expression that still managed the demanded degree of obsequiousness.

While this job-saving servility was taking place, an elderly Morris Minor drove into the forecourt and also stopped, in this case far enough to the rear of the Bentley that the highly polished glass surrounding the revolving door to Parrington Towers was spared the insult of reflecting such a plebeian object. Joan, in what she called 'civvies,' basically a bulky and none-too-new sweater in a vaguely pea-soup green and matching pants that might well have served as combat fatigues in the army, hopped out and kicked the door shut.

Angela allowed a carefully measured second or two to elapse to impress the chauffeur and for anyone who might be observing (no one was) to register her insouciance even when obviously no more than a slightly important cog in the Parrington machinery. She then slithered rather than stepped from the limousine. She paused and carefully straightened her tailored suit while the chauffeur reached into the car and retrieved Angela's brief case. He stood holding the case and waited until Angela had finished making sure her attire was correct before she accepted it from him without acknowledgement. She walked sedately up the steps towards the revolving door, unaware of the discreet double-fingered gesture the chauffeur made to her back before he closed the door of the car.

Joan saw and approved the 'salute' as she charged up the steps and pushed into the revolving door just ahead of Angela. Angela glowered as she stepped into the door but her attempt at a measured (and she felt appropriately dignified) entrance was disrupted when she had to step faster than anticipated because of Joan pushing the door forcibly in the panel ahead. Angela half-stumbled out of the door into lobby and was forced to take several quick, staggering steps to retain her balance.

While Angela was attempting to restore a *gravitas* only she thought she had, Joan walked across to where a uniformed security guard sat sleepily behind his desk in the foyer. Angela crossed the foyer behind her, still trying to recover her dignity. Joan stopped at the desk. 'Could you tell me where I find Dr Sharpe, please?'

Unexpectedly, the security guard stood up. 'I'm not the queen. There's no need,' said Joan.

The security guard ignored Joan and touched his cap in the direction of Angela. 'Good afternoon, Ms Snottym.'

Joan turned and looked at Angela. Angela did not even look in the guard's direction but raised a hand in what may have been a dismissive acknowledgment of some sort and continued walking towards a pair of lifts at the far side of the foyer.

Joan turned back to the security guard, with an expression on her face that registered plainly that she thought he was a first-class suck. She waited for him to acknowledge her presence. 'Doctor Sharpe?'

Joan's expression had not gone unnoticed and the security guard, rather transparently, given his job did not call for nor his natural abilities allow for a great deal of thinking, considered whether to answer. Joan's next expression suggested he'd bloody-well better.

'Fortieth floor,' he said grumpily.

'There now. That didn't hurt.' Joan walked towards the lifts where Angela stood after summoning a lift. The lift arrived, the doors slid apart and Angela entered.

'Ooh, ooh. Hold the lift.' Joan called across the foyer.

Inside the lift, Angela pushed the 'Close' button even as Joan bustled up. The doors closed. And then opened again. Joan had stuck her boot in the gap. Angela looked decidedly miffed and moved to one side of the lift as it began to ascend.

Joan began to sniff with little rabbit-like twitches of her nose and mouth. Angela watched Joan's reflection in the mirror on the lift wall. Joan noticed Angela noticing. 'You really must tell me where you get that perfume.'

'If you don't know, you can't afford it.' Angela forced herself to respond but pleased that she managed a put-down.

'I don't want to buy it, I just want to keep well away from any place that sells it,' Joan said, adding in a low mutter, 'And in future anyone who wears it.'

The lift continued to rise while the temperature inside plummeted. Joan, it seemed, had become fascinated by Angela's hair, which was now fully blond (Daphne Gratton's advice had been followed) but even more plastered with wet-look gel, none of which noticeably added to Angela's limited appeal. Joan had an irresistible urge to touch Angela's hair – to find out what it felt like: greasy? slippery? set like a rock or a slab of toffee? In the mirror, Angela watched the finger inching closer. Against her will, she swivelled and looked at Joan's raised finger. Joan looked at it as well as if equally amazed to find it pointing at the back of Angela's head. She sniffed her finger and wiped it on the wall as if she had a gob of snot on it. Angela turned away again. Joan joined in with the lift's Muzak, singing along with 'Don't Sleep in the Subway, Darling.'

Angela's forced, public school trained *savoire faire* threatened to crumble but was saved (she hoped) by the arrival of the left at the fortieth floor. The lift doors opened to reveal Marc standing there, obviously waiting for the lift. Angela made sure she stepped out in front of Joan.

'Oh no. After you. I insist.' Joan made a slight bow of her head and a gesture with her hand.

'I have been waiting to see Sir Thomas all day,' Marc said, staring at Angela's hair.

'Thank you for sharing that with me,' said Angela. It was just as well she wasn't wanting an approving look at her new hair from Marc; she didn't get one. (She wouldn't get too many from anyone else either.)

As she stepped out of the lift, Joan smiled at Marc but he only gave her an off-hand nod.

'Sir Thomas isn't with you?' Mark persisted.

'We have been having luncheon at Number Ten with the PM,' Angela was pained to have to reply let alone provide information but she continued anyway since it did at least enable her in to demonstrate her importance. 'Sir Thomas has remained to attend the reception for the Crown Prince. Whereas I had to pop off to get fitted at Liberty's for my new fox hunting outfit.'

'Foxes, another great English import to Australia. And just for hunting,' Mark said. 'It is essential that I speak to Sir Thomas.'

'I think, Doctor Sharpe, that as Sir Thomas's Personal Assistant, you can discuss anything you consider to be important with me.'

'Never happened, you know,' Mark said.

'What never happened?' Angela asked before her mind had a chance to tell her not to.

'All the requisite yoicks tally ho. Foxes buggered off into the bush. Ate the native wild life. Never played up and played the game. Funny that.'

'Hilarious. Now, what do you have to say to Sit Thomas?'

'Fair enough then. I have discovered that not only is there a tunnel below the ground here but there is a station, an actual station.'

'How simply riveting. I'm sure Sir Thomas would desert his place at a state function for visiting royalty if he only knew.'

'Sir Thomas might find this more interesting than you imagine.'

Angela stiffened and looked at Marc rather sharply. Joan, rather put out at being ignored, watched from the sidelines and her honed police instincts picked up on Angela's change.

Marc continued, 'What we have here is a genuine, untouched, one-owner, pre-war underground station. In original condition. No others exist.'

Angela seemed to relax a bit but retained her hauteur. 'If this gets out we'll have the National Trust, or even worse, the Prince of Wales, coming around and insisting this be preserved for posterity. Sir Thomas will not be pleased.'

'I don't see why not. This is unchanged from the war.'

'Next I suppose you will be wanting to turn it into a war memorial for all those wretched poor people who were killed down there during the war.' Marc looked at her oddly. 'Sir Thomas has told me about it,' she added quickly.

Before Marc could ask what it was Sir Thomas had told Angela about, Joan felt the moment had come to interrupt proceedings. The interchange between Marc and Angela had afforded the time to recall why Angela seemed familiar. 'Now I know where I know you from. I had to save you from the hunt saboteurs last season.'

Angela looked at Joan abruptly. 'I don't think so. We don't need any protection from that rabble.'

'That's not what you said when they had you arse over tit in a ditch.'

'I was simply unseated in the heat of the chase.'

'Got you there. It was you.' Joan smirked in satisfaction.

'Look, just who are you?' Angela was barely holding it in now. Marc stepped in to prevent something, he wasn't sure what, happening. 'I'm sorry. This is Sergeant Frazer of the Metropolitan Police.'

Angela visibly blanched, an interesting trick not even she knew she could do. 'What have the police to do with this? You haven't called them in because you've found a missing station?'

'What? No,' Marc said, startled.

Joan was now bored with this. Baiting the upper classes was fun but only momentarily. 'You coming or what?'

'Where?' Marc asked.

'Just get in the lift.' Joan pushed the button and the lift doors opened. She took Marc's arm and pulled him in. Angela stared after them, then, when the doors closed hurried towards Sir Thomas's office. This might well necessitate calling him away from the regal reception. He would be angry if she did, but he may well be even more angry if she didn't.

If not the actual car itself then certainly the model of Joan's Morris Minor predated England's motorways. It certainly was not built to take advantage of them. Joan had bought the car from a police auction not long after she joined the force. It was an ex-panda but she had it spray-painted cheaply – even in the early days of her being a policewoman, she had developed relationships with individuals on her beat who operated in that vast penumbric world that was best summed up by the useful term 'dodgy.' The job, in British racing green, possibly the legacy of a fell-off-the-back-of-a-truck deal, was done in a railway arch workshop just off Cable Street. Joan paid for the work – there was no suggestion of favours being done, although the price was more than reasonable.

The mismatch between car and motorway became readily apparent when Joan got onto the M11 to Cambridge from the A406, a thoroughfare that undergoes so many name changes as it runs through north-east London that even Joan wasn't sure what it was called at that point. There is some claim among motor-car enthusiasts (and one had to be mightily enthusiastic to enthuse over the Morris Minor 1000) that the car was capable of 77 miles-per-hour. While this may have been true of the model in general, it didn't apply to Joan's particular car, which to be fair, was well into its second decade. It struggled gamely up to about 60mph – eventually. And stayed there most of the time of the trip, mainly because the majority of the trip, once beyond somewhere around Harlow, was through the flat fen country of East Anglia.

After Joan told him all that she could about the body (or the remains) taken from the underground track, the increasing number of missing persons from the area, and now her growing sense that whatever was going on, somehow cannibalism was involved, the conversation had rather dried up, except for a couple of accurately disparaging remarks about Angela Snottym.

Although he was not about to say so, Marc thought the cannibal bit was pretty much a load of bollocks. But he was actually enjoying his involvement in whatever this was – an investigation? If so, it was hardly an official one and rather obviously not sanctioned by whoever Joan's superiors were. And, oddly, he found himself also enjoying being in Joan's company and thought, despite Joan's less than bouncy sociability, that she enjoyed his in some way.

To Marc's surprise, Joan did not take the first exit to Cambridge from the M11 nor indeed the next but turned off at Junction 13 and approached Cambridge via Madingley Road. But then Marc, in all the times he had been to Cambridge, mainly in connection with his research, had travelled by rail and thus approached the centre of the city from the south-east and by foot from the station. For a short space of time, before the first built-up area impinged, there was some open countryside still.

Joan suddenly broke the silence, 'Cow.'

For a moment, Marc thought she was back onto the subject of Angela Snottym, then he realised she was pointing at an animal in a field on the side of the road. He looked at the cow and then at Joan.

'Tree,' Joan followed up, pointing. Marc just looked at Joan this time.

'House,' Another point. Marc pointed at her.

'Nana,' he said.

'Nana?'

'Nana.'

They were still laughing as Joan turned right into Queens Road and the towers and spires of the various colleges came into view over the Backs and the River Cam. By good luck, a car pulled out of a parking spot just ahead of them and Joan deftly manoeuvred the Morris into it.

However, it took skill of a different sort – it took Marc's title (and his knowledge of the ingrained deference to it), personal appearance and familiarity with the system – to avoid a confrontation between Joan and the porter at Gonville and Cauis College and to have the porter direct them to Professor Solti's rooms.

These rooms seemed to be a deliberate attempt at the cliché of a Cambridge don's study: piles of books, ancient and modern; essay papers yet (or never) to be marked in heaps or stuffed into corners or peeking out of cabinet drawers; bust of some old philosopher-type (actually for no clear reason the Eighteenth-century Astronomer-Royal Maskelyne, whose arena of science had nothing to do with that of Doctor Solti); a notice board with several generations of papers yellowing under rusty pins; and odd things in bottles.

Professor Solti was an owlish woman of untidy appearance and an indeterminate age between seventy and death who was doing her utmost to complement the room or vice-versa. Once introductions had been effected, Solti poured tea into a fine bone china cups rather the worse-for-wear, so possibly dating from Maskelyne's time. Whether the tea had been made in anticipation of their arrival (Joan had made an appointment and despite the idiosyncrasies of her car and her driving, they had arrived punctually) or whether Solti had tea on the brew practically all the time was not clear. She handed a cup to Joan and waved vaguely in the direction of milk and sugar.

'And how is young Johnny Farley then?' she asked, pouring another cup.

'Couldn't really say. Hardly know him,' Joan replied.

'I can vouch for his dog being in good mettle,' Marc said.

'Positively wretched animal,' said Solti, handing Marc his tea. 'Didn't know he had one. I thought...Well anyway.'

'With or without canine companion,' Joan said, looking rather pointedly at Marc, 'He led us to believe that you are an expert in cannibalism.'

Solti poured a third cup for herself and sat down in a well-worn easy chair, facing Marc and Joan. 'Not as a matter of personal practice,' she said. 'Please help yourself to a sandwich. Fish paste, so safe in that respect at least. Unless you subscribe to the evolutionary principle that we are descended from fishes.'

The sandwiches didn't look safe in any respect but Marc took one in the interests of politeness and a foreknowledge of the ubiquity of fish paste sandwiches at Cambridge teas.

'Still as my good friend, Stephen Jay Gould once claimed, there is no such thing as fish. God knows what he thought he was talking about. But then he is American,' Solti said. 'Well, yes, it's not my academic line of course, cannibalism that is not ichthyology, but I do have a passing interest. Perhaps you are familiar with my book on the subject?'

Without having to move from her chair, Solti reached to a nearby shelf full of copies of the same book – *Eating Each Other: An Historical Survey of Cannibalism* by Imogene Solti. She took one down and placed it in front of Joan and Marc. Joan hardly noticed it. Marc picked it up and flicked through it.

'We were hoping you could lead us directly to what we want to know,' Joan said.

'Which is what exactly? It's a complex area.'

'Mm. Well, my problem is that I have some human remains that seem to have been chewed on by another human or humans.'

'Ah, I see. I'm not a forensic scientist, you know. And I'm not that sure I could recognise, I mean positively identify such a thing if I even saw, well... '

'No, I'm not asking...rather, just assuming that the evidence suggests something like cannibalism. What I really need to know is, is it likely at all.'

'Goodness, I shouldn't have thought...' Solti took a sip of tea to allow herself a moment of consideration. 'Background, that's what you want.' She sipped again before launching forth

'To put it simply, over-simply, cannibalism is defined by two major types or activities. One is endocannibalism in which the remains of relatives or other members of the group or tribe are eaten. The other is exocannibalism in which the remains of one's enemies are consumed. It's a matter of reverence in the first case. That is what is also referred to as mortuary cannibalism. On the other hand, exocannibalism is ritualized vengeance, anger or disdain for enemies. Both of course a form of institutionalized cannibalism. In both it's a matter although a varying matter, of absorbing so to speak the qualities of the person being eaten.'

Marc looked from the sandwich he had picked up but not tasted to a specimen jar on a shelf directly in his line of sight on the other side of the study. He put the sandwich down the side of the cushion on the sofa.

'And they don't eat people for food?' Joan asked.

'Nutrition has little or nothing to do with cannibalism.'

Marc asked, 'What about survivors on life rafts or plane crashes in the Andes?'

'Or the frozen tundra of the Arctic Circle, eh? This too has a name, slightly less academic perhaps but usefully called lifeboat cannibalism for fairly obvious reasons. Exceptional circumstances. Very much the exception. Very rare overall in any case, at least in the twentieth century. Cannibalism of any or all of these types was much more widespread in prehistoric times but in some parts of the world, probably yes, it still takes place although credible evidence is becoming harder to find all the time.'

'We are talking about the London underground,' Marc said, glancing at Joan, but she didn't seem perturbed by Marc venturing this piece of information.

'Dear lord. I can believe almost anything of the London underground but cannibalism, not even in Brixton,' said Solti, possibly not quite meaning to be as racialist as that sounded given her credentials as an anthropologist (or perhaps on that score she knew exactly what she was saying).

Joan ploughed on: 'So what you are saying is that these remains are not the result of cannibalism?'

'Bit hard to imagine the circumstances for lifeboat cannibalism in the London underground. One may get lost but trapped and starving? Cult cannibalism for religion or ritual? I suppose not entirely impossible but taking place in the underground? That surely stretches credulity to breaking point.'

'We have the bits. Or some bits,' Joan insisted.

'If we were talking prehistory in south-east England, well then, there is some controversial evidence that neolithic cave dwellers near Salisbury may have engaged in cannibalism but I'm talking of two or three thousand years BC. I take it these are recent remains. What are these remains exactly? '

'Exactly? A chewed over and probably spat out foot. A foot and a bit of calf of the human leg type, not bovine.'

'Ah, well this certainly isn't cannibalism as I have described it. Oh no. In ritual cannibalism one only eats certain organs, brains, hearts and one or two other bits. It varies a bit from place to place but it follows much the same design. Key magical organs. Organs the culture attributes certain properties to.'

Joan put down her cup. 'I'm not sure where this leaves us. Doctor Farley was pretty sure.'

'Oh, I trust Johnny Farley.'

Marc was more used than Joan to considering the complexity of matters. He tried a different tack 'And there is no other explanation? I mean, no other types of cannibalism? '

Solti turned her attention to him. *There's more than a pretty face here*, she thought. 'In strictly anthropological or scientific terms, there isn't.'

Joan leapt in with less regard to academic niceties: 'But?'

'There is a whole body of work, nonscientific work, that exists on this matter in one form or another. I devote a chapter to it. Hard to prove or disprove but cannibalism persists in the myths of many cultures. The Tung-chin of the mountain regions of China, a version of the *yeti*. Others in South America. The most persistent are the Algonquin of Northern Canada. Very much still alive there, I mean the stories. Not quaint parts of a mythical history. They speak of a wendigo, a human monster that eats flesh.'

'Yes, I've heard that one. Heard *of* that one,' Joan interrupted.

'Have you now? Anyway, personally I think it is also a version of sasquash. Much the same type of legend. Except sasquash is in the forest of the west coast and the wendigo is in further north closer to the Arctic, so maybe that's an insupportable hypothesis. Wouldn't be my first.'

'Ah, well, it all doesn't sound too likely, does it?' Joan was disappointed; this didn't seem remotely relevant. She was certainly coming to conclusion that her feeling that dealing with academics was usually a waste of time was being confirmed. And the tea was not all that much superior to the police and hospital canteen quality.

'Especially not in the London underground,' Solti agreed. 'More tea?'

'No thank you. I appreciate your time, professor,' said Joan, who did nothing of the sort. She rose from her seat.

'Not at all,' said Solti, 'Shall I sign my book for you? Yes.'

She took the book from Marc and found a pen with considerable ease despite the clutter. She signed with a flourish and handed the book to Joan. 'There you are. That will be, shall we say, twelve pounds? A little cheaper than Heffers, but I don't like to undercut them, and they don't lecture in anthropology.' She laughed, a surprisingly masculine chortle given her size and physique.

Joan looked at Marc. He had to hunt around in his pockets to find the money.

'Give my best to Johnny,' Solti ushered them to the door. 'So kind of you to drop by.' She allowed Joan get a little ahead and out of the door before whispering to Marc. 'I would have loved to invite you to college high tea, old chap, but out of the question when you're with this little police person, of course. Another time perhaps.' She closed the behind him. 'What a peculiar couple,' she said as she returned to pour herself some more tea. (The sandwiches she disposed of in the trash.)

Outside the college gate, Joan turned to Marc and waved the book at him. 'Crafty old sod. But what's this about it costing less than a heifer? I should hope a book cost less than a cow.'

Marc laughed. 'Not heifer. Heffer's. The bookshop. Look. Over there.' He pointed across Trinity Street at the facade of Heffer's Bookshop.

'Shut up, smart-arse. How'm I supposed to know?' Joan retorted. They turned right and walked back along King's Parade and into King's College, towards the river.

'Why did I have to pay for this book? It's your investigation,' complained Marc.

'You're the one with the gold American Express Card you're so proud of.'

'Again with the American Express Card. A lot of good it's done me. You may have noticed she didn't take it either. Heffer's might have done if we'd bought her book there.'

As they walked through the grounds of the college, Marc took the book back from Joan and flicked through it, looking for the chapter Solti had mentioned. Instead of crossing King's Bridge they strolled along the path on the east side of the River, past gawking tourists and a few undergraduates, crossing at Garret Hostel lane and then following the towpath on the other side towards the bridge behind Trinity College.

'This has been a monumental sodding waste of time,' said Joan, breaking the silence.

'I think this book is a monumental waste of money, my sodding money,' Marc said. 'For one thing, from the bits of one victim and the fact that others, if there are others, have nothing left of them, means that this isn't cannibalism. At least not anthropologically as the learned professor explains it.'

'You can read that while you're walking?' said Joan.

'Better if I wasn't,' Marc said. And plopped down on a wooden bench set back a pace or two from the path. He continued reading. Joan watched him for a moment then stared across the river at the colleges, beginning to glow various shades of gold in the sinking sun.

'I'm trying to find those other explanations. This is all bloody vague,' Marc said without looking up.

'Bloody brilliant. I can just see me going to Super-Flize and telling him some flesh-eating monster from outer Mongolia is having lunch in the underground.'

'China. What it says about the Tung-chin people of the Chinese mountains is, and I quote, "despite the persistence of indications of myths or at least notions of a human-like cannibal figure in Tung-chin culture, anthropologists have been unable to find definite evidence of cannibalism within that culture itself. There is equally no archeological evidence. Travis (1956) has linked these remnants of folk-lore with the neighbouring Tibetan legend of the Yeti. But Tibetan myths do not indicate clearly that the Yeti is human, although it is generally conceded that it eats human flesh. Recent discussion of the residual Tung-chin myths suggest that the stories are probably related to the worship of the Giant Panda, and the notions of flesh-eating may well have been confirmed by the recent discovery, to the astonishment of Western zoologists, that the Giant panda eats flesh, usually carrion." End quote.' Marc checked the index further. He leafed through the pages again.

'Bloody marvellous for my career prospects,' said Joan, 'Excuse me, Inspector sir, but I think that the Abominable Snowman or maybe just a giant panda is riding around in the underground eating the ratepayers of London. I'm just popping up to the London Zoo on the off-chance that in their economic rationalisation they let Chi-Chi loose at Camden station.'

'Chi-chi's deady-deady. We do keep coming across one term though, wendigo.'

'Maybe just maybe Chi-chi's alive-alive and has a season ticket on the Circle Line.'

'What a rip-off,' said Marc, not paying attention to Joan.

'Rip-off? If I told Inspector Flize that I'd be out giving parking tickets on Hackney Marsh.'

'No. This book. There's only one entry for wendigoes. That's what she said. It's here in the index. But, *voila*, it's a footnote.'

Joan looked back at Marc, engrossed in the book. An odd ray of the slanting sun broke through the trees behind them glinting gold off the shining perfection of his gelled hair.

'What are you on about?' Joan had a sudden urge to touch that shiny hair, a different urge altogether from wanting to touch Angela's earlier; whereas Angela's looked like a melted plastic hood, Marc's hair looked soft, like silk. It certainly exuded a faint and arousing fragrance. She slowly raised her hand, extended a finger, contemplated running her whole hand over his hair.

Marc, oblivious, continued. 'Solti mentioned wendigoes back there and there was that stuff in the library the other night. There's only this one footnote.' He read it out loud: '"A North American Indian myth, persistent but difficult to quantify as the Algonquin people are disinclined to discuss it with Western anthropologists. What can be gleaned is that wendigoes rather than being member of a species capable of reproduction in its own right come into existence so to speak by the mutation of individual human beings. The process is not understood or at least not revealed and the links with eating human flesh are so far not definitively established. The persistence of the belief and the strength with which it is held is oddly persuasive." And that's it. Practically word for word her entry in the encyclopedia we looked at.'

Joan's finger touched Marc's hair, then stroked it; it *was* silky. His head shifted minutely as if to lean back into beginning of the caress – then a splash and scream caused them both to jump and look in the direction of the river.

A young woman in a punt had screamed when a young man, no doubt trying to impress her with skills he did not have, had taken a header into the river. Within seconds, as his dripping head, long hair hanging over his face, surfaced, the young woman was laughing instead of screaming. Almost as quickly a small body of students and others ran up to the bank, and another punt, more expertly guided, rescued the floating punt pole. The young man struggled back into the punt, causing a few screams (of thankfully lesser decibels) when it wobbled threatening as he did so.

Marc and Joan sat and watched the small (but no doubt regular) drama unfold and finish as punts and crowd dispersed. It was now getting into twilight. The last rays of the setting sun struck the western facade of King's College Chapel. The crowds of tourists had wandered off and as the boaters drift away, a quietness fell on the quad, save for the cawing of rooks coming to roost. The evening was sharp and clear and more than a little tinged with romantic possibilities. But now Joan was rather less clear of what she thought had been Marc's reaction to her touch and in turn less certain might happen or what she might want to happen if his reaction had lasted longer or been less ambiguous.

'This is beautiful,' Marc said suddenly.

'It's always beautiful but especially at this time of day.'

'You've spent a lot of time here?' Marc was surprised. And it sounded in his voice.

'Why are you surprised at that? Do you think England, home and beauty only belongs to the upper classes?'

'It's just that... I don't know, I would have thought you'd be the last person to admire all this privilege, the halls of the elite.'

'Bugger them. They're just the soft centres. I like the picture on the box.'

'Ah, that's more like the police sergeant I know and love,' Marc laughed.

'You don't have to like religion to enjoy the hallelujah chorus,' Joan said.

'Hallelujah to that,' Marc said. He paused, then: 'You really think that I'm one of the soft centres, don't you? '

Joan didn't know how to answer that. She turned and looked at Marc, lingeringly. He was still looking at the scene. He turned and looked at her quizzically.

'There really is a question I must ask,' he said.

Joan waited, oddly anticipatory.

'Where the hell are we going to find a North American Indian to ask about wendigoes?' he asked.

THIRTEEN

The journey back to London was as uneventful as the journey to Cambridge had been. Every other vehicle on the motorway passed them at speed. For the first few miles from Cambridge, their conversation revolved around the notion of whether or not to investigate this seemingly bizarre notion of wendigoes. Joan was downcast and inclined to maybe forget the whole thing. Marc, on the other hand, despite the apparent dead-end, was keen to continue for a little while at least. His experiences as a student, particularly as a postgraduate researcher, meant he was far less willing to give up any line of enquiry before every avenue had been explored and, if possible, exhausted. Even so, the matter remained unresolved and since, as Joan cogently pointed out, the next step was not merely unclear but conspicuously absent, there it seemed it would have to rest.

The countryside, never all that absorbing in daylight, in the dimming twilight held less interest for Marc and once the conversation dried up he dozed most of the way along the motorway. Joan pushed her car to its limited limits, not because she was pissed-off by all the other vehicles constantly overtaking her (although she was) but because she had to make sure she got back to the police station in time to commence the late shift, and it looked like it could be a close run thing.

Marc came back to life once they hit the streets of the metropolis. As ever, Joan seemed to have a special knowledge of every possible short cut or way of avoiding crowded main streets. By some legerdemain, Joan navigated the car down the last stretch of Salmon Lane and thus, with a few minutes to spare, idled at the lights at the junction of Commercial Road. Marc stared at the impressive facade of The Mission, sitting ponderously in the angle at which Salmon Lane met and entered Commercial Road. He was about to ask Joan about this building when he glanced across the junction at the rather dismal front of the Limehouse Town Hall diagonally opposite. Although it hardly made any difference to its engrimed, soot-blackened facade, the area was bathed in that oddly futuristic dimension-denying glow of amber from the sodium vapour lighting of London's main thoroughfares. Inside that shadowless amber arena, a metallic flash of blond hair caught Marc's eye when somebody standing on the footpath in front of the town hall moved his head.

The lights changed. Joan pulled away. Marc stared across the road and recognised the boy Luke from outside the library. He hardly heard Joan telling him she would have to drop him at the police station gates but since this wasn't far from Parrington Towers, he would know what bus to catch.

'I said, is that okay?' Joan asked him.

'Huh, oh sure.'

He didn't want to turn too far and look back at the town hall but he found his heart was thumping oddly.

Joan pulled the car into the gateway on the far side of the station. 'Look I can't stop. Got to change and clock on. But, thanks. I mean...'

Marc opened the door. 'No, it's fine. I enjoyed myself. Really. See you.'

He didn't even watch as Joan engaged gears and pulled into the yard. Given how close he was to the front door of the police station, Mark thought it would be prudent to cross Commercial Road by the zebra crossing a few yards down where it met West India Docks Road. He didn't want to get nicked by one of Joan's colleagues. This meant walking away from the direction he wanted to go in, left instead of right, but only for a few yards. As he waited for the lights to change, he impulsively reached up and checked his hair.

He wasn't clear in his mind what he thought or hoped would happen as he walked back up Commercial Road, turned the slight curve that momentarily hid from view the front of Limehouse Town Hall – and saw Luke. Even though he had only seen Luke close-up once on the evening of the rushed visit to Hackney Library, his short glimpse of him from Joan's car had been enough (when added to whatever the exchanged glances had implied) to bring on this overwhelming desire to go and speak to him – and what? As he passed the tall wrought-iron fence around St Anne's church, he slowed his pace, apprehension crowding desire. Almost up to the town hall now, he spotted Luke again and stopped, considered turning around and going back the other way.

Luke was partly leaning on a car stopped at the kerb. It was, of course, the bleached lengths of his hair that glowed iridescent under the sodium lights. As Marc hesitated Luke looked up from the car window and straight at him. As usual, Luke's fringe flopped across his eyes. He pushed it back a bit with the hand that had been leaning on the car, glanced at Marc and turned back to the window. 'Fuck off,' he said and stepped away from the car. Even before he had taken the two or three steps to where Marc stood, the car had driven away, not that he or Marc took any notice of that.

Luke's grin widened even as the curtain of hair slid slowly back over his eyes. Marc felt his face breaking into a grin just as broad.

'Wotcha,' Luke said, his eyes, such as could be seen under that fringe, seeming to be drinking in Marc.

'Hey,' Marc replied.

Without hesitation and without seeming the need for further salutation, Luke walked past Marc the few steps to a side gate leading into St Anne's churchyard. 'C'mon,' he said. Marc fell into step beside him.

St Anne's stood out, its white walls, despite the desecrations of soot and diesel-laden air, glowing a faint beige in the sodium lamps of Commercial Road. The churchyard itself was a maze of bright patches of light and fragmented shadows thrown by the tall beech and chestnut trees and the scattered tombstones. A single lamp illuminated the steps to the front door but the interior of the church itself was dark.

Having entered what was a side gate although it was on the main road, Luke led Marc towards the front gates that opened from Newell Street. They passed a large, curious pyramid-shaped tombstone (or perhaps it was a mausoleum), grey and mossy, between a shaggy sycamore and a lamp on a tall pole. The lamp was clearly vandalised and its electrical wires dangled from its decapitated trunk. On the side of the pyramid away from the street, a man leant back along the slope, his head thrown back, eyes closed, groaning. Between his spread legs, another man – or boy more likely – kneeled, his face lost in the man's groin, his greasy, long, dark ringlets swaying as he moved his mouth forward and back. Marc felt himself becoming aroused. He looked away to see Luke glancing, Marc felt sure, at his crutch.

Without speaking, Luke took, and Marc surrendered, his hand and they began to almost run out of the gates to the church and into Newell Street which ran down from the Commercial Road towards the river. Ordinarily Luke would lead, or more likely, get his punters to drive back along the Commercial Road slightly, over the stagnant waters of the

Limehouse Cut, under the railway and into the derelict grounds around Regent's Canal Dock (or Limehouse Basin as it was becoming more regularly called). There he would enact whatever business was required, either giving or receiving as the punter wanted and usually in the punter's car – the ground was too rough and littered with all manner of debris for alfresco sex. But this time, he and Marc hurried south, turning unexpectedly (to Marc at least) into Oak Lane. By now they were running, hand-in-hand, like giddy school children. At the end of Oak Lane, just before they might otherwise have plunged into the Cut, Luke pulled them to a halt. Without releasing Marc's hand, with his free hand, he pulled a key from his jeans pocket and unlocked the door to an unprepossessing terrace house at the end of the small row that occupied the lefthand side of the street.

Luke's flat was on the second floor, at the top of the terrace, reached by stairs that ran past flats on each of the lower floors. A light operated by a spring-loaded button at the bottom provided a feeble illumination and flicked off almost as soon as they reached the top, even though they practically ran upon the two flights. Luke unlocked his door by habit and almost dragged Marc inside.

At first the only light was from the window. Oak Lane was not important enough run to sodium street lighting and this light was the duller glow of fluorescent lamps. The room in which Marc found himself was the living room. It was surprisingly large given the size of the house and faced on one side the street and the other Limehouse Cut glinting oily below. The room was actually L-shaped and at the Cut end was a sort of kitchen alcove. A door opened out of the wall which, as Marc would soon discover, led to the bedroom. It was this into which Luke, finally relinquishing Marc's hand, disappeared. 'Hold on a tick,' he said as the door closed behind him.

Marc looked around him. Contrary to the 'rough trade' appearance that Luke adopted when plying his trade, the flat was clean and tidy, furnished cheaply but simply and yet with taste. The walls were painted rather than wall-papered in the preferred English fashion. They were, moreover, adorned with a number of framed black-and-white photographs that proved, when Marc examined them to be all pictures of Luke, nude. Yet there was nothing pornographic about these photographs, probably they should be described as sensual, but the poses all involved postures that were oddly distorted, almost tortured in some indefinable way. Luke looked younger in these, probably early teens if Marc had to guess. His body was that of a pubescent boy, thin, undeveloped. His hair was not even partially blonde, but what Marc assumed was its natural colour, really a rather nondescript dark shade and considerably longer than Luke's' hair was even now. In one, taken slightly from behind, which emphasised the narrowness of his shoulders, Luke crouched on one knee, like a naked knight making obeisance to a king, leaning forward, head bowed his hair falling down either side of his face. In this shot, unlike all the others, his genitals were clearly apparent even if not the primary focus of the shot – or so the photographer had made it seem. His face was barely glimpsed because of angle or shadow.

'I'm not sure what Freud would make of them.' Luke had come back into the room while Marc looked at the photographs, studied them really. 'I don't mean the photos themselves. I mean the fact that I display them to myself. She's pretty famous now. The photographer, that is. Not because of these.'

'They're great. Sexy and not. At the same time.'

'I was just a kid. But she took my virginity. As well as my picture.'

'Took?'

'Well, I gave it up without too much of a struggle. She was a devil with a dildo.' Luke wrenched his tee-shirt over his head in a swift movement. His body seemed to have changed little despite whatever years (how many it was impossible for Marc to judge) of post-puberty and adolescence. He was still skinny with little or no muscle tone, save a slight suggestion of the ridges of his abdomen, his skin white (as might well be expected from any sun-denied Englishman). His jeans descended with practised ease and he stepped out of them and his underpants. Marc lunged towards him, quickly, eagerly.

'Hold up, son,' Luke said. 'Fair's fair.' He slipped Marc's jacket off his shoulders, unbuttoned his shirt. Marc was tempted to say what was 'unfair' was that he hadn't got to undress Luke, but it let it go. Although he had hardly spoken to Luke or Luke to him, Marc did notice that Luke's accent was rather less 'rough,' less working class than previously. 'Well, hello,' was all Luke said when he swiftly finished undressing Marc totally; although whether he was saluting the revelation of Marc's olive-skinned, well-developed body or his exposed genitals was not clear.

'God I love this,' said Luke. Marc thought he was referring to being naked with him (or maybe just another man) but looking up he realised that Luke was talking about Marc's hair, his fingers already sliding smoothly across the gelled stands.

'Your's is better,' Marc responded. He had to reach up and pull Luke's head down in order to run his hands over the straight locks falling down across Luke's face.

Luke shifted his face further down, right in front of Marc's and then gently but firmly his mouth met Marc's, his tongue pushed past his teeth. A line that had stuck in Marc's mind from reading Raymond Chandler suddenly surfaced even as he pushed himself hard against Luke: 'There could only be one ending,' Chandler had written.

Chandler was wrong or at least inapposite this time. As the night progressed, there was more than one ending.

Despite the energetic and time-consuming night that they had, and that it could barely still be called night when the fun finally slowed down and stopped, neither Marc nor Luke seemed especially interested in sleeping late. Following an encore of one of the variations indulged in the previous night, they shared a shower. Luke insisted there wouldn't be enough hot water for two separate showers, even though it was a bit tricky, even risky, in the old-fashioned bath tub to which a curious piece of British plumbing had provided a sort of shower attachment. After fits of mutual giggling and the occasional gasp as the loofah, changing hands frequently, scrubbed areas not usually scrubbed – 'hygienic and erotic,' Luke observed – and conversation became possible, naturally the question arose of why Marc was with the sarge at Hackney the night they had seen each other for the first time.

'How do you know I'm not a copper?' Marc asked. And then laughed at the ridiculousness of the suggestion. Luke laughed but tactfully did not point out that no one of Marc's size, or lack thereof, got to be a police officer.

'I reckon I know a cop when I see one,' he said. 'And feel one,' he added ambiguously. 'Not that I've felt one *that* way,' he said in response to Marc's quizzical look. 'Not that I know of, anyway. This way.' Luke made a fist and gestured being hit in the face.

'Bloody hell,' Marc said.

Luke shrugged. 'So what were you and the sarge up to? Seemed a hell of a hurry whatever it was.'

As he meticulously groomed his hair, Marc proceeded to tell him about the strange investigation he was involved in with Joan. Luke, despite the fact that he did not seem to pay much attention to his own grooming, was able to supply some surprisingly expensive salon product. Marc finished his hair and his story at the same time. He concluded by saying that the immediate puzzle was how to locate a native American in London, Luke burst out laughing. Instead of explaining why he thought this was so funny, he changed to subject, declaring bluntly that he was 'fucking starving.' Marc agreed that he 'could eat a horse and root the jockey'; Luke insisted they go to a place he knew for breakfast. Marc, although not keen to have to put on the clothes he was wearing the night before, agreed to do that before heading home.

Managing to keep their hands off each other for the moment, they wandered out to meet a new and rather different day. Neither man had shaved. Luke didn't need to; Marc did. He hoped that, if they were outside, it might be assumed he was going in for what he had recently read in a fashion magazine (at the hair salon in Sloane Square) was being referred to as 'designer stubble.'

Marc assumed that they would find somewhere local to have breakfast but Luke insisted they catch a bus, which deposited them outside the Hackney Empire in Mare Road. Luke grabbed Marc's hand again briefly as they dodged the traffic – a very pleasant alternative, Marc thought, to Joan's abandoning him to negotiate the Whitechapel Road traffic by himself the other night. Luke's choice of café turned out to be an establishment somewhere along a culinary evolutionary journey from a traditional greasy spoon to a quasi-trendy coffee shop. That the journey was not complete was made obvious when Luke ordered and received without undue delay what Marc referred to when he saw it, as 'a fried horror-show,' in other words a 'traditional English breakfast,' while he was able to order and get muesli and yoghurt. Once the mutual expressions of mock disgust at each other's idea of what constituted breakfast had been made, they demolished their respective choices with almost (but not quite) the same gusto as they had enjoyed each other's bodies the night before.

As each slowed down to drink but hardly savour what passed as coffee (the café wasn't *that* far into its transition), Luke prompted Marc to go over again some of the aspects of the story of the cannibal (Marc stressed 'maybe' cannibal) in the underground. Luke, paying perhaps more attention (being less distracted by Marc's naked grooming this time), mentioned that he had heard of some odd things, disappearances, including a new kid, Teddy, although he admitted, street kids, whether rent boys or not, appeared and disappeared all the time; most of them were 'missing' in the legal sense in the first place. In telling the story again, and this time at Luke's prompting, Marc provided details about himself, without any intention of boasting, mainly to try and explain how it came about that he was messing around in old underground tunnels in the first place.

In return, Luke seemed quite happy to talk about himself. In fact, it might have been difficult to stop him. Marc, who previously had no reason to develop any opinions about rent boys had not been especially surprised by the things like the number of books Luke had in his flat, even by the fact that Luke had a flat, let alone a rather nice one. To most of his punters, of course, Luke was barely a person at all, just hands, lips, a mouth, an arse and a cock. By the same token, his tricks were hardly even that much to him. He had a few regulars but very little in the way of a personal rapport truly developed with them – intimacy, obviously, but nothing personal. Once or twice, when he became what he called 'a fully fledged flashy blonde' he actually had a few women clients, nearly always better-off women, slumming, who took him back to their places. Once or twice there were suggestions he might like to consider a more stable position as a 'toy boy,' although, as he put it (to Marc's embarrassment although the few customers in the café didn't seem to be paying any attention) his sexual techniques weren't as well developed for women as for men, so he knew such a situation would be short-term.

Of more interest, and of less embarrassment, to Marc were the details that Luke provided of his background. He had been born locally. Most of his small family had been killed in a single night in the Blitz – his grandparents, an uncle and aunt, and there was, he understood, a cousin who was said to have survived the bomb but later 'disappeared.' His father had been spared because he had been evacuated and spent four years with a middle-class family, an experience which had led him to, in Luke's terms 'have ambitions above his station, for me.' Luke had been sent to a very minor public school (he emphasised the minor); his father had set himself up in business and prospered by conducting it with an eye firmly fixed on 'the main chance.' Luke denied Marc's tactful attempt to ask if the public school experience had led to his current 'occupation.' He had left school a virgin. 'But made up for it since.'

'Amen to that,' Marc said.

Eventually Marc asked the question that was uppermost on his mind: 'Why the hell did we have to come all the way to have breakfast here?'

'Ah.' Luke brushed his fringe out of his eyes, pointlessly as it immediately crept back. 'The culinary excellence and the ambiance not to your liking?'

'If this place had either...' Marc looked around and let the remark go unfinished.

'Well, the staff then.' Luke grinned.

Marc had been vaguely aware that the waiter (if that wasn't too elegant a term) had spent most of his time, leaning on the counter, watching them both. Looking up, Marc saw he still was and had been joined by what Marc assumed was the cook. Then he got it; they were both gay and enjoying the sight of two attractive young men.

As if in response, Luke grabbed Marc's wrist, but he only wanted to check the time on Marc's wristwatch.

'Right. Time to go,' he said.

'Go where?'

'Ah, my dear Watson, I am about to solve all your problems.' This in a mock upper-class accent. 'Well, one of them at least.' Luke stood up and headed for the door. 'Pay the nice man.'

'Bloody hell, you too?' Marc muttered.

By the time he had paid for the breakfast – the waiter took a little while to add the bill and get change, probably to allow the cook to get a close up look – Luke was slowly walking up Mare Street, waiting for Marc to catch up. Without saying anything, he led Marc to the Hackney Public Library, the very spot that he and Joan had visited and where he and Luke had first seen each other.

'Been here. Done that,' Marc said.

'Been here, yes. Done that, obviously not,' Luke replied. They went up the steps, into the foyer, and towards the desk set at the back. Luke stopped abruptly, so suddenly that Marc walked into him. Luke was staring at, on the wall, a large, framed photograph, a portrait – of a North American Indian in full feather headdress.

'Ta ra,' said Luke, grinning fit to bust. Even then Marc didn't get it, not until Luke pointed out that the photograph was one of a collection that adorned the walls of the library foyer, a special exhibition of 'London Faces.' Incredibly, to Marc and probably to anyone who viewed it, this North American Indian was an inhabitant of London; somewhere out there among the millions of London faces was one which, even without the feathers, would have been unmistakably that of a native American.

Marc gathered a pamphlet relating to the exhibition from the reception desk. It didn't have much information, certainly nothing as convenient as a name and address for the portrait's subject but it did of course identify the photographer. Back on track now, whatever that track was, Marc figured Joan could manage the presumably minimal detective work to get the rest.

He returned to the photograph, staring as if willing it to be an image of someone who knew about wendigoes. He hardly considered the possibility that even if he, or rather they, found this man they may simply make complete idiots of themselves, hardly considered that the idea that a wendigo was living (if wendigoes lived at all, were not, say, undead like vampires or zombies) beneath the streets of Limehouse, nor really reflected that it was a flimsy set of circumstantial evidence and meagre research that had led to Joan and he deciding on the that possibility. But he did decide he needed to tell Joan as soon as possible. But his heightened sense of self-esteem was strong enough that he needed to get home and get into fresh clothes as first priority and shave.

He left Luke on the steps of the Library, uncertain whether he should kiss him or shake his hand. Luke solved that problem by mischievously ruffling loose some locks of Marc's perfect hair. 'There's your bus,' was all he said by way of farewell, pointing to a bus approaching down Mare Street. Marc scurried off to the bus stop. Luke pushed back his incorrigible fringe and watched him go.

Marc arrived home to his flat in Mecklenburgh Square on the edge of Bloomsbury after a bus trip and a couple short rides on the underground from Liverpool Street to Russell Square. It was only while he changed his shirt that he noticed the number of love bites obvious even against a skin still suntanned from an Australian summer. There were probably more where he couldn't see. The memory of how Luke's long fringe brushed against his skin as he inflicted the love bites excited him but not enough to deflect him from the need to tell Joan about the Indian in the photograph. He suddenly realised that he didn't have a telephone number for her or even know where she lived. He knew of course she was on late shift, so she probably wouldn't be at the police station at this time. All he could do was to find the number of the police station and leave a message for her to call him.

After putting down the phone, he flopped face-down on to his bed and instantly fell asleep. He didn't wake until the phone rang shortly after Joan had come on duty that night.

Joan received Marc's message when she turned up for her shift, early as usual as she liked to grab a cuppa and something greasy in the canteen before hitting her beat. Constable Buckmaster waved a note at her as she passed the front counter. He looked concerned, too concerned to be genuine.

'You okay, sarge? I mean in yourself?'

'Never better, Berry.' Joan replied.

'Not caught something nasty?'

'This concern is touching... and therefore puzzling,' Joan said.

'So, a message to contact a doctor is...,' he paused for effect. '...a secret admirer then, sarge,' he said with an exaggerated leer.

'Down, boy,' Joan replied. 'You'll have to join the back of the queue.' She grabbed the note and turned away.

'As if,' Buckmaster muttered.

'I heard that, Berry,' Joan said.

The nickname was one Joan had bestowed, derived from Queensberry, as in the Marquis of Queensberry, the famous homophobe who had been Oscar Wilde's nemesis. The nickname came about because Joan had found cause to stomp on a trio of young constables who had been hassling the rent boys of the district – until Joan put a stop to it. She had a quiet, informal word – more informal than quiet – and more than adequately got her word across, that she would not tolerate gay-bashing on her patch. Although she doubted that she had cured Buckmaster of his homophobia, there were no more outward demonstrations of it, and they had actually developed a friendly if spiky working relationship. He wasn't a bad kid, she thought, and ironically good-looking enough to be gay himself. And she was pretty sure he didn't know what her nickname for him really referred to. Still, he had a cheeky boyish grin that saved him from trouble – or deeper trouble – on not a few occasions, and he flashed that now.

'And Superfly, er, Superintended Flize...' he started and paused until he saw Joan's face turn sour, 'Doesn't want to talk to you tonight. Strange, you must be doing something right, eh, Sarge.'

'You could try it yourself sometime, *Constable* Buckmaster.' Joan continued on her way to the canteen. Over a cup of what the canteen called, apparently in all seriousness, tea and a bacon sandwich, Joan contemplated the note, which was on the surface, uncomplicated: 'Doctor Sharp' (she guessed Marc had not bothered to tell whoever took the call about the 'e') and a phone number and time. It could only be something about the thing and the trip to Cambridge – although for a brief moment, it flashed into Joan's imagination that Marc had, like herself, felt that vague sexual electricity while on the banks of the Cam, but she quickly dismissed that. She needed to think about whether or not she wasn't making a wally out of herself. Cannibals! And worse, some sort of fairy-tale monster that was a cannibal to boot. She could imagine without difficulty at all what Super-fly would say about that, let alone colleagues like young Buckmaster. She had in fact screwed up the paper and was about to dispose of it, together with the crust from her bacon sarnie, to the waste bin before changing her mind – about the message not the crusts.

After logging on and setting out in her panda for the first of that night's beats through the area, Joan phoned Marc. He told her about the photograph in the Hackney Library. She thanked Marc for the information but really didn't think that it was of much interest. She had pretty much decided, after the largely pointless trip to Cambridge that all this Red Indian fairy-tale stuff about cannibalism and so forth was bollocks and certainly had nothing to do with either the corpse she had seen in post-mortem or to do with the unconnected (so she told herself) disappearances of a few local individuals. Even so, when her patrol took her along Mare Street, she did stop, go into the Hackney Public Library, and see the bizarre image of a fully headed-dressed Red Indian staring at her

232

from an all-too-obvious South London background. She took a brochure with the photographer's details and left.

Marc had picked up that Joan seemed not very excited by his news that a recent photograph of a red Indian, an inhabitant of London, was hanging in the foyer of the Hackney Public Library. He wondered at his reluctance to tell her that Luke had shown it to him. He wasn't quite sure why unless he felt ashamed that he had been with a rent boy. He didn't think he was, he knew he hadn't been, not professionally speaking, but would anyone else think of it that way? Did Luke, in fact? Even so, since it was obvious from that first night on the library steps that Joan knew Luke rather well, Marc decided not to volunteer any further enlightenment. He had kept the conversation to the fact of a native American who, on the basis of no evidence at all, he tried to convince Joan would know about 'wendigoes.' Joan had finished the conversation with an indication she might look into it while she was still out on patrol and maybe, just maybe, then try and track down the photographer and, if that succeeded and the photograph *was* of the genuine article, then see if this miraculous Red Indian could be found.

Marc was left wondering whether Joan's rather distant tone was due to her feeling this whole wendigo theory had more than a touch of bollocks about it. The bottom line remained that none of this was much to do with him. Other, that is, that there was something odd in the very underground tunnel he was supposed to be investigating for Parrington. Now he thought about it, he didn't even know that was true. After all, he simply had been caught up – dragged into, really – Joan's assumption that there was a cannibal or something lurking, maybe, in the underground and everything had snowballed from there. Okay, it was the case that he had come up with the wendigo theory, found the vague library reference anyway, and for some reason had allowed himself to be shanghaied to Cambridge instead of pursuing Parrington's business. And thinking of Parrington reminded him that the whole day had gone by without him turning up at Parrington Towers. It didn't matter all that much, he supposed. After all, as far as anyone was concerned, by which he meant Angela Snottym, he may well have been actually down the tunnel or researching somewhere.

It was not until later when, having been told by his body that he hadn't fed it since breakfast with Luke hours ago, he was working his way through a large plate of *fettucini carbonara* at the *Mille Pinne* in Queen Square that it suddenly occurred to him that he had leapt to a conclusion that there was a connection between Joan's 'cannibal' and his getting spooked in the tunnel the other night. Why should there be? Was it just the coincidence of Joan appearing out of nowhere as Marc scrambled out the tunnel hole? Given the speed with which everything – what everything? – had happened with Joan thereafter, his mind just seemed to make connections regardless of logic.

Over his coffee, Marc tried to recall what he had said to Luke. He didn't think he had made any such supposed connection about what he and Joan were up to and Parrington's tunnel, so it must have been his subconscious mind sifting the many new experiences of the last couple of days while he was sleeping. But, there was no reason why there should be a connection. Well, there was the fact that Joan's victim was apparently found in the underground but he didn't know where, so again, why did he think the two were related? When he finished up, paid for the meal, and wandered down Great Ormond Street and his way back to Mecklenburgh Square, Marc decided when or if he heard from Joan again, he would tell her it was all nothing to do with him and he saw no reason to continue to be involved.

He didn't, of course.

Crossing Guildford Road in front of Coram's Fields, Marc thought instead of turning right and heading back to his flat, he would go left, walk to Russell Square tube station and make his way back to Limehouse and see Luke. It was only as he walked past the concrete brutalism of Brunswick Centre that he wondered whether this was a good idea. Yes, last night had been fantastic, but was he kidding himself there was anything more between them, or likely to be any more between them, than one night of rampant, animalistic sex? What, any case, was the etiquette of such a situation? After all, it was obvious that Luke earned his living doing sexual favours for men (and maybe women too, Marc didn't know whether women kerb-crawled for rent boys). Okay, last night had not been a commercial transaction; the possibility had not arisen with either of them seemingly. Would this still be the case if Marc turned up again?

He turned around in the tube station foyer and retraced his steps to his flat where, it must be said, he spent the next bit of the evening thinking about Luke. Eventually, thinking about Luke was only too obviously a long way short of what he imagined would happen if he actually was with him. This time, he made it all the way to the tube station and onto a train. A couple of line changes and a bus ride later, he rang the bell to Luke's flat. There was no answer. He berated himself, this time of night, of course not. But Luke wasn't outside the nearby Limehouse Town Hall either. He dawned on him that Luke was probably with a pick-up; for a moment he felt physically sick. Marc headed home, torturing himself all the way with images of Luke servicing strangers.

FOURTEEN

A weekend intervened and Marc fund himself strangely feeling the absence of both Joan and Luke, although it was thoughts of Luke that intruded most and left the most lingering sense of a void. He tried to tell himself that because Luke was a rent boy his sexual interactions with men were based on detachment. Yet he also felt that what they had together, even if it was only one night and one morning after, was more genuine, more deeply personal than a simple sexual encounter. Marc was certain that was true for him. Was it true for Luke and even if it was – so what? Like so many in the first throes of love, Marc wavered between action and inaction, going back to the East End in hope of seeing Luke and not doing anything of the sort for fear he was creating hopes and dreams from emotional turmoil. In the end, it was Joan who reappeared to, as it were, take charge and to further compilicate Marc's emotional state – even if that is not what she intended. Then again perhaps subconsciously she did.

Whether or not, Joan had been, in an entirely different way, wrestling with conflicting thoughts. She had eventually acted on the brief information Marc had left about the unexpected revelation of a native American in London, had visited the Hackney Library to see for herself and even tracked down the photographer. No great detective work there, the photographer's name and address was freely available in the catalogue for the exhibition. So Joan didn't think a move to CIB would follow as a result of this sub-Holmesian investigatory activity. From the photographer,

Joan gained a name – John Stillwaters – and access to electoral rolls soon provided an address. On Monday evening, she gathered Marc from near Parrington Towers. He felt another visit by Joan to the Parrington offices would be less than diplomatic and, besides, he was starting to share Joan's concern about keeping the notion of cannibals to themselves. So meeting around the corner seemed a more tactful stratagem.

It is difficult to catch the Thames-side streets of Southwark at their best as they have no best. Dingy in Dickens' day, the erosion and eradication of the grimy industries since had not brought about a vast improvement. Once even a passing glimpse of the Thames had disappeared from view, Marc was completely lost. Even Joan seemed a bit uncertain but to be fair, it wasn't her patch; the Thames was a bureaucratic barrier for the Metropolitan Police as well as a physical one and a psychological one for many Londoners

The faded green door to which Joan had eventually led them, after checking with her notebook a number of times, would have been considered nondescript had it not had, in the centre and rather inexpertly attached, a huge door knocker in the unmistakable shape of Elvis Presley.

'I didn't think you actually bought this wendigo crap. I am the one who comes from a land that believes in bunyips, remember,' said Marc.

'I'm not doing this officially. This side of the river isn't even my beat. If they find out back at the station, I'll be a right laughing stock or get a right bollocking or both,' said Joan. She reached out and grabbed the door knocker. It was sculptured in such a way that her grip was obliged to embrace its brass groin. Design fault or native American humour? 'Ooh, sorry Elvis...' She paused, 'Let's not do this.'

'We've come this far. Can't hurt. He can only laugh at us,' Marc said.

'Or maybe scalp us.' Joan rapped on the door.

'Or eat us,' said Marc as the door opened.

A small, dark man, whose jet-black hair was contradicted by a face of many wrinkles, pushed the door back and peered out at them. He paused, looked worried and then smiled. 'Ah, the paleface sheriff.'

'Mr Stillwaters?' asked Joan.

'S'right,' His grin broadened. 'Enter my lodge, eh?'

He stood aside and ushered them in.

The inside of the flat was expressively ordinary, no different from thousands of such flats all over London. Stillwaters led them into the small living room and switched off the television set that sat on a tea trolley in one corner. He waved them to a sofa and sat down in a well-used armchair.

'I'm not quite sure what this is all about.' He looked quizzically at Marc.

'This is Doctor Sharpe. He's...' Joan decided it really was too complicated and probably irrelevant who Marc was. She wasn't entirely sure what this was all about either. 'As I said on the phone, I, we, saw your portrait in a photographic exhibition.'

Stillwaters laughed. 'That photograph. Everyone around here's seen it. Then again, everyone around here's in that exhibition. It's fake anyway.'

'Fake?' echoed Joan.

'In a way. I mean, it *is* me but we don't wear feather head dresses. I mean. My people, the Algonquins, don't. That's plains indians, Commanche, Kiowa, Cherokee and that lot. The Hollywood injuns of choice. I was having a lend.'

'You borrowed the head dress?' said Marc, feeling vaguely cheated.

This amused Stillwaters. 'Well, yes, but what I meant, son, was I was having a lend of the photographer. She was so excited about finding a real *red Indian* as she called me, I decided to play it up. Red indian, be buggered. Do I look red to you?'

He pointed at a photograph on the mantlepiece.

'There's me in another fancy dress costume.' It was a formal studio portrait of himself in World War Two soldier's uniform, very much as he looked the night he had been with Margaret Hilda, the night the bomb struck the station.

Joan glanced at the photograph. She had no way of knowing just how close to what in another context might be called the epicentre of events Stillwaters and then her own father had been. 'Not everyone else around here is a red... native...'

Stillwaters interrupted, corrected. 'Algonquin, and I'm a British citizen. I've been here since the war.'

Somewhere quite close a British Rail train screeched past on its way to London Bridge Station, drowning out any attempt at conversation for a few seconds.

'Since the war,' Stillwaters repeated. 'And I still can't stand those bloody trains. I just don't understand why the trains have to be above the ground on this side of the river and not nice and quiet and under the ground.'

Marc fielded that one: 'It's a matter of demographics, Victorian demographics that is. South of the river nobody had enough clout to stop the railways coming right up to the river. North, they were made to stop short of crossing areas where the well-to-do lived...'

Joan interrupted. 'Save it, Doc. We haven't come here to talk trains...'

On cue, another train rumbled past.

'I got in touch with you, as I said, because you are a... an Algonquin. And the only one we could find. I mean, locally.' She paused, not certain whether even as this late stage she wanted to go through with this. She deflected, 'So Algonquins don't wear feathered headdress?'

Stillwaters laughed. 'A fair cop. I'm guilty. As I said, I was sending up that twat of a photographer. But you didn't come to nick me for impersonating a Cherokee with malice aforethought, did you?'

'No. It's more unlikely...' Joan paused. Marc looked at her puzzled – this wasn't the tough-as-old-boots copper he was used to. Joan read his expression. 'This is all rather strange and it may be that you cannot help us because it doesn't necessarily follow that just because you are a native American you will know what we want to know. After all, just because I am English doesn't mean that... Well...' She ran out, realising she was rambling but reluctant to actually say what was on her mind. It suddenly seemed even more rather than less stupid now she was face-to-face with Stillwaters.

Stillwaters watched, waited, but uncertain.

Marc spoke up suddenly. 'What do you know about wendigoes?'

Stillwaters switched his look from Joan to Marc and stared.

'Yes, okay. That's what I was coming to,' said Joan. 'We, I need to know about wendigoes.'

'Wendigoes? Why would you want to know about wendigoes? Is this a joke?' Even six decades and a continent and an ocean away, Johnny Stillwaters, war veteran of Southwark, felt a frisson, an echo of that fear first felt as a child.

'Yeah, probably. I don't know. Let's just say, it may be important.'

'If you say so, sergeant.' Stillwaters leant back in his chair. 'Goddamn, I haven't really thought about them much and not for years if ever. Still, my grandmother, she had a thing for them. Y'know. Back in Canada. When I was born, we, well, we were still tribal, that is. At least, we still lived like we were. And the old ones, well of course they still thought like they were.'

Joan and Marc waited for Stillwaters to go on but he stood up. 'I need to get me mind around this. Gather me thoughts. How about a cuppa?' Without waiting for an answer, he shuffled into the kitchen.

Joan turned to Marc. 'What do you reckon, then? I still feel a bit of a prat.'

'He knows the name at least,' said Marc. 'Okay he could have got that from a book too, or tall stories in bars, but I think we ought to hang around and see what he comes up with.'

'Other than of pot of Mazawattee,' said Joan.

'Hopefully as well as a pot of Mazawattee,' said Marc.

The tea that Johnny provided was much better than Tesco grade Mazawattee, a fine Ceylon tea from Twinings in the Strand. The story he told Joan and Marc was equally as authentic but rather more difficult to digest. He told them what his grandmother had told him a more than fifty years ago but which he had no reason to think about or speak about for maybe forty of those years. And what he told them was his memory of the event when he was five or six years old.

'And that,' said Johnny Stillwaters, 'Is what wendigoes are. Or were.'

'Ah, well,' said Joan. 'But do you really believe in them?'

'Granny Stillwaters was a shaman, a sort of holy woman, or a spiritual leader. And she sure did,' said Johnny.

It was Marc who asked the obvious question. 'But what do they look like?'

'No bloody idea,' said Stillwaters.

If Lady Muqbuquet had survived her meeting with the Docklands wendigo, she could have told them. But then she didn't.

As if in some supernatural way linked with these discoveries of his name and nature, the wendigo began to prowl far more widely in the underground system. Since food was so readily available, it was now as much curiosity and the exhilaration of freedom as the bloodlust imprinted on its brain by the very circumstances that brought it into existence in the first place. A foray well into the West End enlarged its horizons considerably, it was further afield when it wandered out near South Kensington Station than it had ever been when it was still Nick the urchin from the slums of Shoreditch.

Above the ground, above the wendigo's head, Lady Muqbuquet walked out of Harrod's, ignoring the Commissionaire who held the door open for her. She turned left and made her way forcefully along the Brompton Road. *Really*, she thought, *Harrod's was going downhill. All these what are plainly tourists thronging the place.* As she progressed, she developed a theme composed of unhappy thoughts about the way her privileges were being threatened, even disappearing one by one. What did that Thatcher woman think she was playing at? It was alright giving a few wogs in the South Atlantic a touch of gunboat diplomacy when they got uppity, but what about uppity lower orders at home? Still that Thatcher woman was a grocer's daughter and from somewhere in the North so what could the country expect? Her cogitations on class behaviour were further compounded by what she saw on the platform of South Kensington station.

The punks from the Richard Owen Housing Estate, bored presumably with standing about vacantly on breeze ways, had made one of their occasional forays to the King's Road. Sheila was with them, seemingly having not yet taken Joan's hint as she held a baby in her arms. But looking as if she ought. They all looked at Lady Muqbuquet as she walked disdainfully past.

Sheila, who had an eye (if not an income) for such things, peered at Lady Muqubuquet's ostentatious jewellery. 'Nice gear, darling.'

Lady Muqbuquet walked on with as much dignity as she could muster (which after a lifetime of practise was plenty) to the very end of the platform. Sheila turned to her fellow punks. 'I was only complimenting her. Them ear rings are really fab.'

Having got about as far down the platform as she could get, Lady Muqbuquet turned to look disdainfully back at the punks just as the wendigo's arm reached out from the tunnel and swiped at her. Lady Muqbuquet's distasteful glance back saved her life – for the moment. The wendigo's claws missed and tore off her wig off instead – revealing Lady Muqbuquet to be a man in drag.

Not surprisingly, the sudden snatching of her (his) wig grabbed Lady Muqbuquet's attention. He turned to find himself face-to-face with the wendigo, hardly a sight for a Lady (even one who was no lady). It snarled. She screamed hoarsely. The wendigo hesitated, startled. Lady Muqbuquet grabbed his wig from its startled grasp. As he put it back on, the wendigo pulled him off the platform by his fox stole.

'D'you see that then?' Sheila asked.

'Radical, man,' said the punk with the greenest hair.

The train arrived. The punks inside the train and the Wendigo outside on foot commenced separate but basically the same journeys back across London. The punks did not stop at St James' Station to snatch an Ex-Army type in a cavalry twill overcoat and homburg off the platform; the Wendigo did. The Army-type's umbrella, ripped to shreds, a bare skeleton of wire and a mangled horse-head handle was flung back onto the platform.

Joan's expression and silence made it quite clear to Marc that, as they wound their way from Stillwater's flat, she was in no mood for chit-chat. Beyond Stillwater's willingness to accept the existence of wendigoes, nothing that remotely suggested even circumstantial evidence had come out of this afternoon's visit south of the river. Marc too was thoughtful, although his thoughts drifted rather easily away from the farrago of wendigo nonsense to the rather more physically provable existence of Luke, of his flat, his bed and, especially his body. It was as they strolled across Tower Bridge that Joan stopped and stared out at the Thames stretching off to the west. As if she had made up her mind, she turned to Marc. 'Okay so wendigoes may exist in Canada. I maybe, a big maybe, can accept that but what's it got to do with us?'

'Us?' echoed Marc.

'Okay, me, but you've got yourself into this.'

'No, you got me into this, if memory serves. You pulled me out of a hole in the ground when...' He stopped as he recollected just why he was in such a hurry to get out of the tunnel the night he met Joan.

'True enough, sunshine. It hasn't got anything to do with you,' Joan conceded.

'No.'

'No what?'

'No. It has. Or maybe it has.'

' I don't see how. I'm grateful for your help. I suppose I am. I wouldn't have got on to wendigoes without your help but beyond that, I repeat, it hasn't anything to do with you.' Joan turned to walk on.

'I think I know where your wendigo is,' Marc said and as Joan stopped and stared back at him, 'But buggered if I know how it got there.'

Marc explained to Joan for the first time what he actually did for Parrington Corporation and why. After she took it in, she had only one response.

'We'd better go and have a look,' she said.

Once again, the lower orders, or such of them who were clinging onto their homes and communities were registering their objections, objections to the destruction of both and to their re-development as buildings designed to celebrate the post-industrial future money was creating. In short, a rowdy public demonstration was taking place outside the Parrington Corporation Tower Block. It was a swirling, seething sea of angry faces, raised fists, and shaking bodies. Some of the demonstrators carried placards which read, amongst other slogans, 'Piss Off Parrington', 'No More Development', 'East End for East Enders', and 'Upper Class Vandals'.

From his eerie on high, the unruly scene was looked down upon by Sir Thomas Parrington. Angela Snottym stood to one side of Parrington, also looking down, almost leaning on the window pane. Parrington glanced at her, wondering what had got into her, with the sudden bright yellow colour added to her excessively gelled hair. 'Don't make a greasy mark on my window, Miss Snottym.'

Angela flushed and turned away. She thought of protesting that gel only looked greasy but wasn't, just shiny, that was the point. But she thought better of it. Unfair that the annoying little Australian could use wet-look gel without untoward comments from Sir Thomas.

Parrington turned away from the panoramic if elevated view of the demonstration that now threatened to move from the street, through the fences and onto his development site or to skirt the police and security guards and spill onto the forecourt of Parrington Towers. He changed his attention to watching the demonstration in close-up on security camera images on monitors that lined one wall of the office. 'I wish now I had made this more like Rupert did at Fortress Wapping. That was a good job of work.'

'They won't get in here, Sir Thomas,' said Angela, building bridges while still smarting from the unexpected personal remark.

'They were happy enough when I came around and risked my life defusing bombs and saving their wretched hovels during the war,' said Parrington.

'Typical working class ingratitude, Sir Thomas,' said Angela who would have expressed her hatred of the lower orders more strongly if she was a bit more certain of Sir Thomas's mood, which sounded oddly nostalgic rather than angry.

'Ironic when I think about it,' Parrington continued as if he hadn't heard her. 'Had I not defused bombs but let them explode and blow up their precious bloody East End I wouldn't have half the trouble clearing my sites.'

'They are your sites, after all. You bought them from the landlords,' said Angela, who, when it suited her, placed great store in the rights of possession, provided the right class was doing the possessing.

But Parrington wasn't listening. 'I should have shot more of them then, you know, not just the mad ones,' he said in a moment of precise recollection.

Angela didn't understand the reference but felt that she needed to assert herself. 'I'll get rid of them.' She picked up a telephone on the desk and punched in a number. 'Superintendent, I think we, that is Sir Thomas has had enough of this. Please remove that rabble.'

Superintendent Flize took Angela's call on a radio-phone where he was standing in a small group of uniformed officers amongst a gaggle of police cars and vans. He handed the phone to a WPC and paused, to pointlessly give the impression he was giving thought to the situation and not simply reacting to instructions from his betters. He turned to a sergeant leaning against the bonnet of a police car. 'All right, sergeant. Let's re-establish a bit of law and order here. Make the streets safe for those who have legitimate business in them.'

'Yes sir,' said the sergeant, thinking to himself, '*Pompous git*.' He walked with a mixture of purpose and casualness to the entrance of a narrow street at one side of the gathering of police cars. Here, out of sight of the demonstrators, stood serried ranks of policemen. As he approached, most straightened up slightly, several quickly dropped cigarettes they had been puffing.

'Okay lads. Up and at 'em,' said the sergeant, stepping out of the way as the officers formed a rough but tight line and marched out of the lane and into the back of the crowd.

Before even the closest of the demonstrators had realized what was going on and what was about to happen, several coppers grabbed hold of one individual demonstrator. But in their haste or in their arrogance, they tackled the wrong one, a youngish man who proved to be a bit handy and who fought back, shouting and flailing, putting one copper flat on his back before two more piled onto top of him.

Slowly at first and then more rapidly, the crowd became aware of what was going on at the back. In a ripple effect, they turned to face the encroaching ranks of the police which fragmented into small groups and single individuals as scuffles broke out all over the place. Police batons were flailed about indiscriminately and, where space allowed sufficient room to swing, with bloody effect. The more aggressive demonstrators began to use placards as clubs or simply as shields.

In the primitive arousal of the flight or fight response, some people tried to run while others fought back, the latter because they were actually being hit or kicked or, sometimes, because they were enraged and aroused enough to attack first. The police officers, their training and discipline working in their favour, waded in left and right, dragged people out, kicking and hitting them, and threw the cowed, beaten or dazed ones into the back of waiting paddy wagons that pulled out from hiding places in narrow nearby streets or from abandoned factories and warehouses.

In typical fashion, the demonstrators were forced into ad hoc sections, those in the melee of fists, boots and batons, those pushing away from this, those on the periphery seeking escape routes and a large contingent, unable or unwilling to get into the fray, reduced to watching, as it were, from the sidelines. The chanting changed to shouts of anger, 'Bastards. Bastards.' 'Who's side are you on?' 'Class traitors!' 'Get out of it, stinking copper! '

A little old lady, who would never have heard of the Soviet film *Battleship Potemkin*, nevertheless perfectly reproduced one of that film's most memorable images as she staggered away having been struck in the eye by a police baton. The irony of the resemblance of circumstance and appearance seemed to occur to no one at the time or even afterwards; there were no film scholars present on either side.

Parrington turned away from the bank of monitors and back to the window, from where the melee below resembled not much more than might have followed from kicking over an ant's nest. Behind him Angela continued to survey the riot being presented in many different views on the security monitors. She was taking no little sexual pleasure from the monitor images. Panting and perspiring slightly, she switched between cameras, trying to get the best close up of bits of violence.

The demonstrators were mainly by now trying to get the hell out of it, running hither and thither. Many tried climbing the fences into other adjoining building sites, the fitter (or the more panicked) succeeding despite barbed wire and other deterrents. A lot of older members fell or were pushed over by desperate demonstrators whose sense of common cohesion and purpose had been easily subsumed by a more ancient instinct for self-preservation.

From his vantage point, Parrington could see more police arriving on launches via the Thames. As the melee spread out and away from the immediate vicinity of the Parrington Towers forecourt, some desperate demonstrators leapt into the river and were pulled out by the police, and given a few slaps and punches as well.

Angela's face was glowing strangely and covered with beads of perspiration. Some fronds of her otherwise immovably gelled hair had come adrift and hung lankly over her face.

Parrington looked at her with distaste which, in her concentration on the monitors, she did not see. Had she done so, if she had been capable of reading it if she had, her immediate future might have segued into a longer term one than was to prove to be the case.

Parrington poured himself a single malt whisky and lost whatever passing interest he may have had in the demonstrators and in his aroused personal assistant but not in the fact of the demonstration itself and what it implied about the continued opposition to his attempts to raze this area and to then bring it into the twentieth century via his developments and to the considerable enlargement of his bank accounts.

FIFTEEN

Marc and Joan made their way across the construction site, the place where the demonstration had taken place a few hours before. Evidence of the riot lay strewn about: broken placards, odd bits of clothing, broken police helmets, some blood stains on the asphalt, abandoned possessions, spilled bags of groceries. Joan surveyed the detritus of democratic protest and authoritarian suppression. 'Really helps me with community liaison when Flize has had every local copper but me beating the crap out of the locals.'

She kicked at a tin of baked beans, a supper some pensioner was not going to have tonight. 'Just as well it was my day off. I might've got stuck in, on the wrong side.'

Marc looked at her but decided not to respond to that. Instead, he took a key from his pocket and unlocked the door. He swung the door up and open. 'You sure you want to do this?'

'No but I don't see what else I can do.'

'You don't think this wendigo stuff is a crock?'

'Jesus, sunshine, I sure hope so.'

'Okay but remember I only said I thought there was something down there that night. But nobody else has said anything. That I've heard anyway. And workmen have been in and out.'

'It's all I have got. Bits of a body in the underground. This unknown bit of the underground. The coincidence of both.'

'And wendigoes.'

'And maybe wendigoes. Still I need to look. To satisfy myself.'

'Yeah, but satisfy yourself of what?'

'That this is all just bollocks.'

Joan looked into the blackness of the hole. 'After you.'

Marc lowered himself onto the ladder and Joan watched as his gleaming hair descended into the gloom. She took a deep breath and followed. When she was about halfway down, the lights came on. Marc waited by the light switch, one hand steadying the ladder, until Joan stepped off the last rung. She looked in amazement in both directions.

A rumble and screech from the near distance reverberated down the tunnel. 'Train. On the Circle Line, about a half a mile that way,' said Marc. 'It's okay, they don't come up here. Didn't I tell you this was fantastic. Look at this.'

He led the way along the tunnel to the platform. 'Cop an optic. Pre-war. Mint condition.'

Joan glanced around. 'This is mint condition?'

'Well, okay. Bit time worn maybe, but this stuff doesn't exist anymore. Except here. And maybe some other long lost tunnels. Who knows.' He scrambled up onto the platform and turned to help Joan up. She shrugged off his hand.

By now, the items of the 1940s removed by Gray's minions had been replaced by workman's tools, lumber, bits of cables and the flotsam and jetsam that inevitably accumulates by accident and design around industrial work sites, some of which is never taken away (so that archeologists centuries hence will have something to spend their grants on – always assuming archeologists and grants are still around centuries hence).

Marc pointed to where shreds of old wartime posters still clung to parts of the walls of the platform. 'Do you believe it? I mean, do you bloody believe it? How do you like the squander bug, eh?' He brushed dirt and cobwebs off a poster on which was still visible a cartoon creature with a grotesque hairy body and slathering, fang-toothed face, part of a wartime propaganda imperative against waste in the face of rationing. Joan laughed. 'Maybe that's our wendigo.'

'Come on,' said Marc and continued to lead the way along the platform to the blocked exit to Whitehorse Lane. 'This is as far as I got last time.' He looked through the arch. It was pitch dark in there. 'Bugger, they haven't got around to putting the lights in here yet.' He turned to Joan. 'Got a torch?'

'Uh, nup.'

From the tools lying about, he picked up a primus lamp. 'We can use this. Got a match?'

'A good copper has everything,' said Joan.

'Except a torch.'

'I have got one,' Joan retorted. 'Just not right here, right now.' She produced a box of matches and lit the lamp.

'Okay. Off we go,' Marc grinned. 'This is bloody exciting.'

'I may wet myself,' muttered Joan. She followed Marc through the arched entrance into an area from where a great deal of the rubble had been removed. They walked carefully in the pool of light thrown by the primus lamp.

'This ought to lead to an escalator,' said Marc. 'Come on.'

'Eager little beaver, ain't you,' Joan said. She sniffed lightly. 'It doesn't half pong down here.'

In the darker, as yet unlit, recesses of the far end of the tunnel the wendigo emerged from where it had been sleeping off its most recent meal. Bold, confident now, it howled.

Marc and Joan froze.

'What the fuck was that?' Joan looked around but beyond the light from the primus and the glow from the lights behind them, framed by the entrance they came through, there was nothing to be seen, nothing living anyway.

'Another train. Maybe the wind.' He adopted a stage-Shakespearean tone. 'Who knows what strange pathways the wind flows through down here?'

'More noises like that and it won't be just wind flowing through me, mate,' said Joan.

'Big brave wozzer.' Marc laughed.

Joan's her feet skidded slightly. 'It's very slippery down here,' she said rather redundantly.

'Fifty yonks of moisture running down the walls and no Myrtle around to mop it up. Or bring a cuppa, thank god.' Marc pushed on.

Joan followed, 'What the hell are you taking about?'

'Just someone I know.'

Joan's boots skidding on moisture caused her to try and tread a bit more carefully. She didn't succeed.

'Doesn't matter. I can't believe that all these years...' Marc stopped as Joan slipped and fell on her bum. He laughed.

'It's not funny, you callous bastard,' said Joan, as she tried to push herself upright. 'This doesn't feel like water. Give me a hand up.' She reached up to where in the gloom she thought she saw Marc's hand in front of her. She grasped instead the hand of a corpse hanging unseen from the ceiling. 'God, your hand's cold and clammy.'

'What?' Marc asked. 'You haven't got my hand.'

Before Joan could make sense of this, her attempt to lift herself up pulled down the corpse and a whole lot of other corpses in various states of putrefaction from where they have been hanging from exposed ceiling supports. The bodies, whole and in parts, showered on top of both Marc and Joan, knocking them to the floor. Understandably, forgivably, they panicked, they flailed, they yelled, they got covered in blood, viscera and rotting matter. Thrashing about managed to get them clear of the bodies and bits of rotting flesh.

'Well that sort of confirms the theory. Let's...' Joan did not get a chance to complete her rather obvious thought because as Marc swung around, holding up the lamp to shine the way out the wendigo's face was revealed a few feet away, red eyes, yellow teeth, greasy, crenellated skin glowing in the gas light. Marc yelled, rather redundantly.

For a moment, nothing moved. Marc's shout echoed and faded. Historian, cop and mutant monster stared at each other. Then, without a word or a gesture passing between them, Marc and Joan both started to run, stumbling over the bodies and bits in their sheer panic, deeper into the unexplored interior of the old station.

They burst out into a space at the bottom of a cobwebby escalator that disappeared into absolute pitch blackness at the top. They hesitated, looking up.

'Up. Up.' Marc shouted. Joan started to run up the escalator. Marc followed close behind. As they ran up, the escalator actually started to move down. The shriek of the tortured, rusted machinery merged into the howl of the wendigo as its hands pulled at the rubber belts on either side of the escalator. Marc and Joan raced upwards whatever the escalator was doing. Then the steps stopped moving.

They were almost at the top when Marc was grabbed by the wendigo. He flailed with the gas lamp which burst against the wendigo's face. Marc lost his grip on the lamp which continued in its arc and crashed against the wall and exploded, spewing flaming liquid all over the top of the escalator. The wendigo screamed in pain and tumbled backwards down the escalator.

The flames spread rapidly and easily through the old rotten timbers and decayed fittings of what was once the ticket foyer. As Marc and Joan ran into the ticket hall, wood and glass exploded, suddenly heated by flames after years of cold. Here, as no one had penetrated since the opening of the tunnel, there were scattered bones and a few skeletons lying about. One of these was the skeleton of a baby, still in the rotted and rusted remains of a 1940s pram. Old yellowed and tattered posters, timetables and notices, on the walls burst into flames.

'Where to now? There's no way out,' Joan shouted. What had once been the entrance from street level, seen in the light of the spreading flames, was blocked by piles of rubble.

'There has to be a down escalator,' said Marc.

'How do you know that wasn't the down escalator?'

Marc stared at Joan. 'What possible difference could that make? When an escalator isn't being used, it's just like stairs. You can walk up them. You can walk down them.'

'How about we bleeding run down them,' said Joan.

Marc pointed to one side where there was the top of another escalator. 'Over there!'

Burning timbers fell from the roof as they leapt through flames to get onto the escalator. As they rushed down the steps, the flames rushed along in pursuit, igniting the rubber belts at the side. Then the wooden sides to the escalator steps burst into flames behind them. They crashed off the end of the escalator and ran through another cobweb-infested archway and out onto the platform.

The fire spread back through the hallways and the platform itself was now alight. The old posters burst into flames. Lumber and items of construction burnt. The electric lights exploded. Smoke and flames threatened to engulf the whole tunnel.

Marc and Joan fought their way through the smoke and scrambled off the end of the platform, running like the clappers down the tunnel while a string of exploding lights went off behind them.

As explosions rocked the tunnel and flames shot along it, Marc pushed Joan up the ladder and followed. Ungainly as Joan may have looked coming out of the hole, she was fast enough not to obstruct the smaller and livelier (and frankly more frightened) Marc. Even so, their respective exits were conducted with more haste than dignity, more desperation than grace. Which was just as well as a burst of flames, the legacy of bottles of gas and other inflammable items left as part of whatever Parrington's workers were doing below, exploded up out of the hole, nearly catching them.

They fell to the ground, out of the way of the flames.

Marc dragged himself up and tried to shut the steel trap door. Joan ran off. He stared after her, surprised that she should demonstrate such fear, then managed to slam the door down on top of the hole, despite the flames shooting up it.

Joan ran to her panda parked just inside the yard. She flung open the door, leant in and grabbed the radio. 'Two-forty one to CD, receiving.'

The voice of the bored officer at the communications centre came back to her. 'Go ahead, Joan.'

'I need fire services and all available assistance at the development site, Salmon Lane. This is priority A1. Now. No. Sooner than now. Okay CD?'

'Understood. Calling fire services. All available to assist. Salmon Lane development...' Joan leant against the car, radio still in hand, looking back across the site area where Marc had managed to slam the steel trap door over the hole. The radio officer returned to Joan. 'Fire services on way, Joan. All mobiles in vicinity responding. What is going on?'

Marc jogged across to the car. 'I managed to shut the door.'

An explosion blew the door sky high, and flames gushed out again. The ladder shot up out of the hole like a rocket. The lid crashed to the ground near them. The ladder cartwheeled down out of the sky. Marc dodged around the rear of the car and Joan dodged around the front to avoid it when it came down – on the roof of the police car.

'Really good, Marc,' said Joan, looking at the ladder see-sawing across the dented roof of her beloved panda. 'Terrific. I could have told you that was going to happen.'

The radio squawked, rather indistinctly now the car's aerial was bent double. 'Are you okay, sergeant? Are you receiving, two-forty?'

Joan, surprised she had instinctively thrown her microphone into the car before dodging the ladder, picked it up again. 'Yes, CD. I'm okay. A few fireworks here though. You ought to be able to see them from where you are, CD.'

Marc stared at the flames shooting up out of the hole, like a mini-oil well fire.

Joan flicked the microphone back into the car and looked at Marc. She started to giggle and then laughed out loud.

Marc turned away from the dying flames and stared at her. 'Don't get hysterical on me now.'

Joan struggled to control her laughter. 'If you were thinking of slapping my face, sunshine, just forget it. I've got my bovver boots on.'

'Well, what's so funny then?'

'You spend your time doing a bloody great impersonation of an adman's wet dream and now look at you. You're covered from ear to arse in glunk.'

Marc looked down at himself. His immaculate yuppie clothes were ruined, his hair and face a mess of blood, body fluids and god-knows-what. He looked back up at Joan. 'You should take a quick shufti at yourself, mate.'

Suddenly he grabbed Joan's head between his hands and kissed her deeply. Joan responded with enthusiasm. They eventually came up for breath.

'It's usually considered polite to give a lady warning before commencing to hoover her tonsils,' Joan said.

'I've been waiting to do that, since Cambridge,' Marc said.

'I almost...' Joan started but Marc's mouth got in the way again. And then the sounds of police and fire engine sirens, getting closer – rescue service spoil-sports. 'The cavalry arriveth,' Joan said.

'I'm going off to get cleaned up, 'said Marc.

'You vain little egotist,' Joan said.

'Little maybe. Anyway, to use the local vernacular, get knotted.'

Fire engines and police cars screamed into the construction site as Marc dodged his way out past them. 'It's all right. I'll explain everything,' Joan shouted at his retreating back. 'As if I could,' she concluded to herself. She leant back against the car, swinging the ladder off as she did so, and waving, traffic control-style, the fire engines across to the smoking hole.

People from the nearby houses and flats, attracted by the flames and by the sounds, started to appear to stand and stare.

The fire brigade leapt into action and an organised chaos of hoses, running men, pumps and all the paraphernalia of modern fire-fighting took over.

In the underground car park of Parrington Tower the noise of the activities on the building site hardly penetrated through the concrete foundations. Parrington and Angela walked the few steps from where his Bentley had drawn up near the elevator. The chauffeur, having called the elevator, opened both doors (Parrington's first of course), closed both doors after the passengers alighted, stepped back to the car and slipped into the driver's seat to wait. If His Nibs and Snotty weren't interested in all the flashing lights and fire trucks and so on that had roared past them as they approached Parrington Towers, he wasn't going to draw their attention to them. He wasn't all that interested himself come to that. He turned on the radio to listen to the results from the dogs.

'Did the PM have any ideas on how to shift the last stayfasts, Sir Thomas?' Angela asked as the elevator doors closed.

'Maggie and I are eyeball to eyeball on this one,' Parrington said. 'These hangers-on have no right to interfere with the development of the docklands. Holding the country to ransom, is how she put it in her inimitable way. But, damn it all, her hands are tied because of the bolshie legislation left over from the blasted Labour governments and especially the ruddy GLC.'

'But the PM got rid of the GLC.'

'Damn sight easier to get rid of the GLC than all the stupid, bolshie regulations it put in place. But Maggie's working on...'

Unexpectedly, the elevator stopped at the ground floor. The doors opened to reveal Marc covered in goo and dripping nasty stuff onto the floor. He stepped inside.

Parrington and Angela barely acknowledged his presence, maintaining tried and true British *sang-froid* in the face of embarrassing circumstances. Angela stepped into the conversational hiatus.

'It really is too, too tiresome, the way go-ahead forward-looking planners like yourself, Sir Thomas, have their hands tied by outmoded and senseless social legislation,' said Angela.

'Ah yes, well, skinning cats cannot only be done one way. But some careful thinking needs to be done. Very careful,' said Parrington.

'I shall make it my number one priority, Sir Thomas.'

Unable to maintain the pretend-he-isn't-there any longer, Angela turned to Marc. 'Is there a reason you are dripping all over the berber in the executive lift, Doctor Sharpe?'

All looked down at where blood and other stuff too hideous to identify was dripping in great splodges onto the white carpet.

'For god's sake man, what is the matter with you?' Parrington demanded.

'Well, you may not quite believe this but Joan, that is Sergeant Frazer of the Tower Hamlets police, thought...'

The elevator doors closed on the rest of Marc's explanation, which (as the lift rose) included a reference to events in the tunnel and the presence of what he seemed to be claiming was a mutant cannibalistic monster residing there. A monster that was feeding on underground travellers.

The elevator arrived at its destination, the fortieth floor. The bell pinged. The doors opened. Marc stepped out. 'And that in a nutshell is what happened really.'

Parrington and Angela stared at him in blank astonishment and then at each other, as if mutely conveying the same thought, *This man is mad*.

Marc looked at the two of them, unmoving in the lift. The moment dragged out. 'Yes, well, I'll just pop along to... to clean up. Change my clothes and sort of maybe shower 'n' stuff.' He smiled in what he hoped was an ingratiating yet concerned manner.

Parrington and Angela looked back at him. Marc continued, 'I'll just pop off then. Get cleaned up. All right. I'll do that then.' He walked away, still oozing slightly.

The last police car and fire vehicle pulled out from the building site and drove off down the street. The site was an even bigger mess than in the aftermath of the riot, water still draining in some places and large pools of water and puddles of mud spread about.

As the last vehicle left, Parrington and Angela left the front entrance of Parrington Towers and made their way across the site. Parrington held his wartime service revolver, kept all these years never far from his person. Angela held a torch. If she felt any surprise when Parrington opened his office safe and took out the revolver, she had kept it to herself. She walked gingerly, trying to avoid stepping in mud and slush.

They got to the opening of the hole. 'Never mind about your shoes,' said Parrington. 'Shine that torch down here.'

Angela did as she was told even though it meant stepping up to her lumpy ankle in a puddle. 'That's rather deep, don't you think? I don't see how we could possibly get down there, Sir Thomas.'

Parrington spotted the ladder, somewhat buckled but still in one piece, lying where it fell from the sky to earth via Joan's panda roof. He thrust it down the hole. 'Hold the torch steady and down I go.'

He climbed in and disappeared from sight. 'Come along then, Ms Snottym,' his voice barked from the hole.

Angela, with rather less bravado, clambered in after him. Seen from above, the light from the flashlight flicked about and then slowly faded from view. The hole sat yawning open but difficult to distinguish in the general disarray of the surrounding ground. Somewhere nearby a dog barked pointlessly.

Parrington and Angela stood at the bottom of the ladder, in the tunnel. Angela swung the flashlight around. Water still dripped from the efforts of the firemen and pools of it had formed between the rails. Smoke hung in the air. The abandoned station and platform could be obscurely discerned in the torch light.

'This way I think. Come along now,' said Parrington.

They made their way carefully towards the platform, Angela growing increasingly nervous.

'Hold the torch steady, woman,' ordered Parrington. 'Here we are.' He clambered up onto the platform. Angela waited for him to help her up. 'Sir Thomas.'

Parrington turned back to her. 'Mm? Oh, right. Ups-a-daisy. Hell of a time to suddenly become a delicate blossom, Ms Snottym.' He pulled her up. 'This really is quite fascinating. Have you ever been in the underground before, Ms Snottym?'

'Of course, Sir Thomas.'

'Really? You never ceased to astonish me, my dear. So where are we now?'

'This is the platform. The trains pull in and stop here. People get on and off.'

'Oh really?'

The wendigo, skulking as ever in the further recesses of the tunnel, heard the echoing of their voices and roused itself. After the initial terror, it was now more than a little pissed off at the sequence of, first, easy meat that had escaped, then fire and explosions, followed by hordes of firemen squirting water everywhere.

Parrington and Angela worked their way along the platform.

'I wonder where this thing is, then?' he asked.

Angela stopped and Parrington realised she was no longer at his side. He turned to see what has happened.

'I don't care for this one little bit. Can we go now?' said Angela.

'Odd's teeth, woman. If this was wartime, you'd follow your superior officers orders, to the letter, to the letter. Do you have any idea what happens if orders are not obeyed in wartime, Ms Snottym?'

'Sir Thomas, really, I must say.'

'I would be perfectly within my rights to shoot you on the spot. In fact it would be my duty. Insubordination. And the perpetrators get shot. That's what happens in war, Ms Snottym.'

Hidden just inside the entrance to the ticket hall, the wendigo listened. In some deep recess of its mind, it recognised, remembered, this sentiment, these very words, and what may well have been a tear rolled from its eye. It slid out the cigarette case out through the arch; it skidded down the platform.

The scraping noise caused Angela to swing the torch beam onto the case as it stopped against Parrington's foot. There was a still, timeless moment as the cigarette case lay shining in the beam of light. Then Parrington picked it up and turned it over in his hand, recognising it as his, unseen for forty years. Angela stared at the case and then at Parrington as if she suddenly found herself in the middle of some miraculous but explicable happening.

Parrington exclaimed. 'Good god.' He paused. 'Shine that torch over here.'

Angela followed the direction of his raised arm and shone the torch towards the entrance of the ticket hall. The wendigo's eyes and teeth gleamed in the light. It shuffled back out of the torch beam, but not before Parrington and Angela had glimpsed its frightful appearance.

'Great Scott. Sharpe was right after all.' exclaimed Parrington. 'What did he say this... this thing is?'

Angela prided herself on her ability to comprehend and memorise. 'A wendigo, was what he said. I'm not sure how it's spelled but...' Parrington's sharp glance shut her up. Whatever else he was, he too was not slow on the uptake. He already had made two and two into four. Boggling as it was, it dawned on Parrington what the sum came to.

'Is that you, Nick?' Parrington exclaimed. The urchin's name had come back to him without bidding. 'I'm sorry, old chap. Very rude. Shining a light in your face. Point that thing away, Ms Snottym.'

Angela turned the torch away. She felt there was some plot-losing going on and it was she that was losing it; Sir Thomas seemed to be talking to an old friend. Maybe there was marble-losing going on as well but that it was Sir Thomas not her in this regard.

'Come on now, old fellow. No-one's going to hurt you. You know me, your old guv'nor, Major Tom,' said Parrington.

The wendigo slowly shuffled out into the half-light. At his first full sight of the wendigo, Parrington staggered back a few steps. Angela almost collapsed and turned to flee. Parrington grabbed her by the arm. 'Steady the buffs. Remember, we're Conservatives.'

The wendigo watched them, like a fawning dog uncertain of whether it is to be patted or kicked, and yet half-slyly, calculating. Its eyes shone with a malevolent intelligence. It licked its lips with the supple tip of its scabrous tongue.

'Well, Nick, old man, I suppose that some people would think this was something of a miracle,' said Parrington. 'But I must say, you have been a bit naughty. Just because you have been buried down here for, what is it, forty years or more is no reason to start devouring the customers of London Transport, you know. Don't know how you managed to survive, but there it is. Still damned bad form, scoffing paying passengers.'

The wendigo shuffled forward slightly. Angela gasped and moved back. 'Sir Thomas. Please.'

Parrington turned sharply to her. 'Shut up.'

He turned his attention back to the wendigo. 'There. There. It's all right now. No one is here to hurt you. Just to do what has to be done. You can see that, old chap. Remember the war, Nick? Remember the bombs and all that? Course you do. And you remember my old revolver. Remember how you liked me to show it to you. Yes? Well, I still have it, Nick. And I'm going to show it to you again. Look, now, I'm taking it out. Nice and slowly. Look, here it comes. Easy now. Easy.'

He slowly removed the revolver from his overcoat pocket and held it loosely, away from the wendigo. The wendigo's expression became harder, more canny, more sly.

'Now listen to me, old man. All these ruddy tunnels are just a nuisance. Home to you maybe but no good to old Major Tom at all. Absolute blight, old boy. Got to be filled in. Concreted over. Sorry, but that's just the way it is. So you can see the bind, old man, nowhere for you to go, I'm afraid. Whole area, up top, I mean, totally altered, totally changed since your day. Since the old days when we fought old Adolf together, eh, Nicky? Different type of person wandering about up there now. Not your sort at all. Hardly fit in, could you now? Let's face it. Especially given from what I gather of your eating habits. Just not on, you know, not on at all.'

Parrington raised the revolver and aimed it.

Angela, suddenly, 'No. Sir Thomas. Stop.'

'No insubordination now, Ms Snottym. This between old comrades in arms.'

Angela grabbed his arm. He looked at her hand on his arm. She dropped her hand. 'I just don't think you should be too hasty, Sir Thomas,' she whispered. 'Skinning cats and all that.'

'Cats? This is no bloody cat. What on earth are you jabbering about, woman?'

'I have thought of a use for this, this *wendigo*.'

'Are you losing your grip, Ms Snottym? Because if...'

'We, you can use this thing, Sir Thomas. It's already working for you.'

'Working for me? Good god, woman, you're raving.'

'Getting rid of the local riff-raff. We can get it to go on... eating them I mean. And those it doesn't eat, well, it will scare them off rather sharpish I should think.'

'Have you lost your senses?'

'It's perfect economic-rationalisation logic. Little outlay. No legal responsibility. Think of the rabble at that demonstration. They won't stop making trouble once their injuries have healed. My word, no. And the PM, well, I am sure she would be appreciative, very appreciative.'

The wendigo, unperturbed by the gun, paid close attention to the exchange, its almost colourless eyes peering from one to the other through the matted, greasy hair that fell over its face.

'Dear god, I think you're right on the ball, Ms Snottym,' said Parrington, cottoning on. 'But, will we get away with it? I mean to say...'

'What do you mean, we? It's him. Hasn't he already gotten away with it?'

'So far, certainly. But will he go for it?'

'Ask him.'

Parrington laughed at the suggestion then, looking back at where the wendigo had squatted on its haunches, taking in the conversation with an unexpectedly intelligent look on such of its features as could be seen. Parrington noticed for the first time that the wendigo was paying attention to what is going on, that maybe there was an intelligence behind the monstrous appearance.

Parrington stopped chuckling and started thinking. 'Nick, old fellow. Here's the set up. I think you'll find it is to your taste, shall we say. Now I'll be frank, old man, I was all set to pop your clogs. Nothing personal, just good business. But I'll tell you what. I want you to stay here and carry on. Know what I mean? Just keep picnicking on the local people you find about the place.'

He waved his hand, the one with the revolver in it, in the vaguely general sense of above.

The wendigo shook its head. Parrington was taken aback. He was well used to getting his own way in all things, including (if for the first time) ordering mutants about. 'What's the problem here? I'm commuting your sentence. You get that? And all you have to do is to eat a few people. Which I gather is not a problem for you. And, naturally, not get seen. But you've managed that too. Mostly. So I don't see the difficulty.'

The wendigo looked away from Parrington towards Angela. It stretched itself up to its full and frightening height and reached out a hand towards her. Angela recoiled.

Parrington paused, puzzled, and then understood. He turned towards Angela. 'A token of good faith. We must all make sacrifices for the good of the corporation, Ms Snottym.'

He shot her once.

From that distance he couldn't miss, even after years without practise. She fell to the platform, twitching and bleeding. 'There, Nicky. Take this in lieu of a written contract. And let's hear no more about it.'

The wendigo stepped over Angela's body. Parrington patted the wendigo's hairy arm and reacted to the repulsive feel of its greasy, matted hair. He turned on his heels and walked away, taking out a white silk handkerchief and wiping his hands. Then turning, he slid the cigarette case back along the platform. The case stopped next to Angela's bleeding body. The wendigo picked up Angela's body, hoist her over its shoulder, bent for the cigarette case and carried both back into the darkness.

As Parrington walked away, he heard Angela's terminal scream. He muttered, 'I used to be a damned sight better shot than that.' A sudden thought occurred to him. *I'd better get rid of that damned colonial. Shame. Rather fancied him. Still, don't suppose I have to actually shoot him.*

That damned colonial, freshly showered, changed, powdered and preened, was at that moment engaging in mutual fancying with Luke, whom he had dragged, without any sign of reluctance whatsoever, from his post at the Limehouse town hall and into Luke's flat and into Luke's bed. That too would not have been a shooting offense in Parrington's book – even if he had known about it.

SIXTEEN

The report which Super-fly was brandishing in his carefully manicured fingers had been written by Joan only because she had to, had to produce the requisite paperwork which explained how and why a large number of police officers and an even larger number of emergency services personnel had been summoned on her say-so to the Parrington building site. And when there, had to deal with a fire in an underground tunnel. Fortunately, for all concerned – Flize and his budget, Joan and her career – the fire had surprisingly not turned out to be particularly intense, just spectacular at first because of the venting effect of the entrance hole, nor involved much damage of what, in any case, was not especially valuable property at least according to Parrington's chief engineer, a Mr Strangways.

If the event itself caused Flize to choke, Joan's explanation caused him to nearly froth at the mouth. All lessons learnt or at least taken down to be repeated parrot-fashion at advanced management classes at Hendon Police College about calm and assured leadership behaviour seemed to have been forgotten. Instead of sitting calmly but with stern determination at his desk in Hendon-approved fashion, Flize was standing, almost dancing a jig, and waving the offending pages.

'You cannot seriously expect me to fax this report of yours to headquarters,' he said with as much control as he could muster, which wasn't much.

Joan stood on the other side of the desk, trying to do so as casually as she thought she could get away with, without setting Super-fly off even more. 'I do not seriously expect your fax to be working,' she replied.

Flize was not to be easily diverted although he did slip from the point at little. 'You know what happens with faxes? Some people read them.'

'Some of the people read some of the faxes some of the time...' She let the thought peter out.

'Utter preposterous nonsense. You seriously expect me to use my fax to send a load of balls about some hairy wild man of Borneo or something to Scotland Yard. And tell them that this thing is eating people, eating people in the underground.'

'Yep.'

'Shut up. You didn't have permission or a warrant or anything to go down there in the first place. God knows if Sir Thomas Parrington decides to get legal...'

Joan interrupted, 'Being Sir Thomas-bloody-Parrington ought to be illegal in itself. Besides the London Underground is public space. I didn't need a warrant.'

'I said to shut up. Sir Thomas is really jacked off. You don't seem to realise how many ears high up he has access to.'

'Ears he can piss into. People are still disappearing...'

'I won't tell you again, sergeant. It's none of your business. You're a community copper, not CID.' He paused to allow that telling assertion to take effect (it didn't). 'So get out around to Abdullah's Halal grocery and see who has been nicking the tampons. That what community coppers do. Now sod off.'

'Sir.' Joan turned to leave the office. Flize had the last word; Hendon lecturers would have approved. 'And stay away from underground stations, sergeant.'

As Joan wandered through the corridors of the Mile End Underground station, she was still smarting from the scene with Superintendent Flize even though, as she had typed the report, she knew quite well how it would be received. Nonetheless, the innate stupidity of her superiors rankled. She muttered to herself, 'I'll decide whether to stay out of underground stations, you bald-headed prat.' And received a dirty look from a small, bald-headed man who entered the corridor just as she spoke. The coincidence lightened her mood and she grinned. The bald man did not smile back.

She passed a steel access door set into the corridor wall without paying it any more mind than the thousands of paying customers who passed it every day and continued down the corridor and turned the corner. The door, which lead to a service shaft, started to open outwards. The wendigo pushed its hairy way out, sniffing the air.

Joan continued to walk along the corridors that were, at least between trains, deserted and quiet. She turned another corner. A busker, a hirsute youth in denim, leant against the wall, raised a mouth organ to his lips and blew it. The music, if it was such, mingled with a howl from the wendigo in such a way that neither was truly distinguishable from the other.

The busker stopped and watched uneasily as Joan walked up. She paused, looked down at his hat with its pitifully few coins in it on the floor in front of him. Her look indicated quite clearly she knew he had put the coins in to encourage others – and that she was not in the least surprised he had to. She did not contribute to the self-generated largesse.

The busker watched her go out of sight around the next corner. He mouthed 'bitch' once he was sure she was out of sight.

The station platform was quite deserted when Joan walked out on to it. Behind her, in the corridor, the busker started up again. Joan wondered whether he was soft in the head or whether he was on something of dubious provenance. There was nobody about at this time of day to toss any money in his hat even if they had felt the urge – which could only be pity, not appreciation. The comparison did occur to her that she was engaged in an equally pointless pursuit. If this wendigo thing actually existed – a fleeting view of something nasty, not in the woodshed, but in the underground, and some exiled American Indian's yarn hardly added up to proof positive. Why would it conveniently pop up in any underground station she happened to be prowling about it?

Even as the ludicrous nature of her being in the station crossed her mind, Joan walked along the platform and peered up the tunnel. It was dark beyond the lights of the platform although a few, well-separated lamps on the tunnel walls provided pinpoints of light until the tracks curved out of sight in the gloom.

'No bloody wendigoes,' muttered Joan. 'And I'm bloody talking to myself. Or maybe you, you cow.' She looked with distaste at a conservative party poster with a large image of Margaret Thatcher on it. 'Come down here and let a wendigo get you, why don't you?'

Suddenly the busker's weird music was cut off in mid-chord. Joan turned abruptly and stared back towards the corridor entrance. Then she sprinted down the platform towards the corridor.

The busker had gone. His hat lay on the ground as before. His mouth organ lay near it, some gobs of bloody salvia hanging off it.

'Shit! Shit! Shit!' There was no way she could think of to make any sort of report that would remotely get her off the hook for being where she was let alone provide any grounds for her explanation being more acceptable than a simple acceptance that somebody had just left these things there. After all, any underground employee could come up with an inexhaustible list of weirder things found in stations, platforms and corridors. It was clear now, even if it wasn't before, that she would have to locate this thing herself. More than that, she guessed, she would have to catch or kill it. Could she count on that delectable little Australian to further help? The thought of the kiss amongst the chaos of the fire excited her. And helped make up her mind.

Marc stood in the bedroom of his small flat in Mecklenburgh Square. He was completely naked and was inspecting his body in the full length mirror behind the door. One lot of love bites, the first, had begun to fade before last night had added a new collection. The buzzer of the front intercom startled him. For a fleeting second he thought it might be Luke but then equally as quickly realized that Luke didn't know where he lived. The intercom buzzed again. He went to the intercom by the front door. 'Hello.'

Joan's voice came back scratchily. 'Let us in, digger.'

'Yeah, right.' He hesitated, then pressed the button to release the door and in the time it took Joan to get up the stairs, dived into the bathroom and grabbed a towel to wrap around his waist. He tightened the towel as the Joan's knuckles rapped on the door.

Marc pulled the door open. Joan stood in the passageway, holding a huge bunch of flowers, and a bottle of champagne. Marc grabbed the champagne from Joan's hand and before she could react, or even start to speak, he slammed the door in her face. Joan had hardly even time to register anything beyond the most atavistic of responses at the sight of his semi-naked appearance when Marc flung open the door again, grabbed her by her coat and dragged her inside. She fell on top of him, and he kicked the door closed as they descended floorwards.

The champagne bottle flew out of Joan's hands, crashed into the skirting board and proved it *was* the stuff racing car drivers bought (as the assistant at the off-licence had said) by unilaterally popping its cork and showering the hallway and its recumbent occupants with alcoholic froth. On the other hand the bunch of flowers flew upwards and burst asunder as it reached its apogee, then flowers drifted down in a spreading formless pattern. As they both lay on the floor, Joan's lips sought Marc's and clamped themselves on while her hands simultaneously loosened the towel.

The neighbour, Mrs Tully, an elderly lady, who had popped her head out of the door to see what that nice young man next door was up to with all this slamming of doors, was too late to see anything but certainly heard the pop of a champagne cork, splashing of wine, what sounded like that young man giving a sudden yelp and then two voices, male and female, in a gush of giggling. Followed by, if her memory was not failing her, the sounds of sexual activity of a particularly vigorous kind. She stepped back into her flat, thinking she may have revise her initial impression about the niceness of that young man. Perhaps he wasn't one of those ever-so-pretty 'lavender boys' she had known in her flapper days, so decorative at a dinner party and wonderful dancers, all of them, but totally useless for anything else. To Mrs Tully's ancient ears, that 'anything else' was certainly being provided behind the door to Flat 4. Rather wistfully, she went back into her own flat and closed the door, gently.

An instinct, equally as ancient, equally as powerful, was driving the wendigo. It too sought other humans – despite all the inexplicable changes that had been wrought to it – not to slake a sexual appetite but one for blood and flesh. Now, revived and revitalized, a greater cunning but also a greater daring entered its hunting forays. Disturbed as it had been by the sudden reappearance of Parrington into its life, the physical reminder of its previous existence may have also reconfirmed that it was, no matter how mutated, human and had a human brain. Much stronger as well, the wendigo now realised instead of being reduced to shambling about the dark tunnels by foot, it could hitch a ride on the back of the trains themselves; the rear was nearly always still in the tunnel while the train itself was in the station.

So, while Joan and Marc were playing their own version of 'mind-the-gap' – having progressed mainly by hands and knees (and bums and backs) across the champagne and flower-strewn hall floor to the bedroom – at Bank Underground Station, a train pulled in and unloaded and loaded passengers, most of whom were clearly, by manner and dress, city 'gents.' The late peak hour was still in effect although the earlier crush of junior staff and lesser employees had largely dissipated, and the carriages tended to have fewer standing travellers. One carriage towards the end of the train was almost exclusively occupied by city gents in their pin-striped suits and sensible shoes. Nearly all were reading the *Financial Times*; no one was looking through the windows on either side. What could be seen that they had not seen many times before? Platform on one side, wall on the other. The train pulled out of the station, the last carriage disappeared into the tunnel and still no-one saw the wendigo, teeth and eyes agleam, in a recess in the tunnel wall just behind the train. It stepped out and loped after the train, avoiding the third rail in a manner that showed that it knew well enough what it was. This time, it wasn't interested in riding the train.

The next train overtook the wendigo but it had been avoiding oncoming trains for some time now and knew how and where to duck out of the way without being hit. Whether anyone in any carriage who may have been idly and pointless staring out a window ever caught a fleeting glimpse of something – some *thing* – lurking in the tunnel is impossible to say, and if they had, it would have been equally as impossible for them to say what it was they thought they saw.

The train lingered as a few passengers alighted and rather more clambered on board. Just as it was about to leave, a city type, to his annoyance delayed by the small but pushy mob thrusting out the wrong exit (by right and fiat, an *entrance* to the platform) strode out and stepped towards the last carriage. A Rastafarian-styled Caribbean youth pushed past him and leapt into the carriage just in time. The doors slammed shut in the city gent's face. And the West Indian guard, leaning out of the side window in the end of the train, grinned at him as the train pulled away.

The city gent watched the train disappear, already composing in his head a letter to *The Times*. He became aware of a shadow falling from behind him and he turned to voice his complaint to what he thought was a fellow commuter who had also been deliberately left behind by the train. He found himself staring into the face of the wendigo. Before he could even shout or scream (let alone modify his mental letter to *The Times*), his face was ripped open by one swipe of the wendigo's claws. His bowler hat spun down the platform, blood flying off it like sparks off a catherine wheel. Eventually it lay still, dripping blood. Its late owner was already being carried away down the tunnel but in the wrong direction to which he had been intending to travel. And in a totally unexpected condition – dead.

The champagne bottle lay in a pool of its own contents on the passageway floor. A trail of scattered flowers led from this into the bedroom, and then spread as if exploded (again) around the room, mingling with an assortment of female clothing.

Joan lay back in the bed – or rather on the bed as all the clothes were heaped at the end – her make-up smeared, her hair a mare's nest, and a look of not inconsiderable satisfaction on her face, her right hand lay across Marc's bare chest. He looked to be in a slightly better condition although his gelled hair was scattered in every direction including up. An impish smile crossed his face and he sat up. Joan's hand attempted to restrain him but he wasn't getting off the bed. He simply bent forward and grasped the end of the duvet with both hands. In one quick movement, he pulled the duvet up and over Joan's face. And farted loudly. He held the duvet over Joan's head while she thrashed about underneath the sheets and then finally struggled out. She wafted the now-relinquished duvet wildly to dispel the lingering effect Marc's flatulence. Marc was helpless with laughter.

'You dirty little Australian bugger,' Joan said.

She flung the duvet aside and slid a hand down his body. Marc's laughter was replaced with a momentary flash of fear but when he felt what that hand was doing, he relaxed and lay back.

Joan, leaning on one elbow, gazed down at Marc. Marc opened those huge eyes – god, they were dark –looked at her for a moment, grinned, and closed them again. Now Joan noticed the faint marks of three, no four, no more love bites on Marc's olive skin; Joan was pretty sure she hadn't put them there. Her finger tips traced several of them softly – but not softly enough: it tickled. Marc came back to life, grabbed Joan, rolled her over beneath him, and it was on again for young and old (or young and older, which is probably all Joan would admit to).

It was only after a rather high degree of mutual satiation was achieved and recovered from that Joan mentioned the second thing that had been on her mind when she rang his bell.

Johnny Stillwaters opened the door to his Southwark flat to Joan and Marc. Joan was out of uniform this time but both she and Marc had, of course, managed to sort out their various items of clothing from the bomb-site that was Marc's bedroom and dressed themselves or, actually, each other with the requisite amount of giggling and general fooling about.

'Oh, It's you two again. Come on in,' Johnny said.

In the living room, a board game was set up on a card table. Marc recognised it at once.

'Round London! My favourite game,' he exclaimed. Joan looked at him, not understanding.

'Know this game, do you?' Johnny asked. 'I have a couple of oppos around every week to play.' He glanced quickly at Joan. 'Not for money or nothing.'

'I don't think you can bet on Round London. Or not in a way that would make any sense. But it's a fantastic game,' Marc said. He caught Joan looking at him rather quizzically. 'No, it is. Really. I know the guy who invented it. Met him during my research. We ought to have a go sometime.'

Looking at the places set at the table, Joan realised Johnny was expecting company. 'Do you mind if I get to the point of us being here before your friends arrive?'

'Oh they won't mind. They've had occasion to meet quite a lot of policemen in their time,' Johnny said.

Marc started to riffle through the cards and check the pieces, and set up for the game.

'I'm not sure how to do this but...' Joan hesitated, then ploughed on. 'Oh hell, we think there is a wendigo in the underground.'

'Go on. You don't. Pull the other one,' Johnny said although he didn't seem especially fazed.

'Straight up. And what we want to know from you is how we get rid of it.'

'Get rid of it?'

'Well, get rid of wendigoes generally speaking,' Marc interjected while still sorting out the game.

Johnny looked sage, pulled his bottom lip in thought, 'Well...stuffed if I know'.

There was distinctively patterned knock on front door. 'That'll be my old mate, Buffalo Tom,' said Johnny quickly.

'Perhaps he'll know,' Joan said. Johnny, already on the way to the door, looked back at her oddly.

As he opened the door, a tiny middle-aged man in a cardigan and well-worn suit trousers and with a startlingly unconvincing comb-over bounced in. 'Wotcher, Johnny. How's yer mother's ducks?' he shouted to Johnny. Without missing a stride or a beat, he beamed at Joan and Marc. 'How you going? Sod of a day.'

'He's not a Red Indian,' said Joan.

'No,' said Johnny.

'Then why do you call him Buffalo Tom?' Joan demanded.

'Cause he's full of shit,' Johnny said.

'Charming as ever,' Tom said. 'Excuse me, darling.' He pushed past to the card table. 'You joining us, mate?' he asked Marc.

Marc looked at Joan but she gave him a stern, we-are-here-to-do-a-job look in return. Marc shrugged and raised his eyebrows to Tom who sat down and searched among the tokens. He grabbed the purple one. 'This is me,' he said.

'Always purple. Emperor's colour. Caesar and all that shower.'

'So how do I find out how to get shot of wendigoes?' Joan asked Johnny.

Johnny rubbed the tip of his nose. 'My granny'd know,' he decided. He crossed the room and picked up the telephone.

In the Canadian North-West, in a tepee attached to a mobile home, a telephone rang. Granny Stillwaters (understandably much older now than Johnny's childhood memories) picked it up. In the corner, though, an equally older Grandfather Stillwaters was still sleeping.

'Hello... Johnny darling, how lovely.' Granny glanced across at Grandfather and clearly decided she wasn't going to bother waking him, dozy old bugger. 'No, I'm just fine. I just got back from Aunty Bearclaw's yesterday... The annual potlatch... No, of course I didn't... What? Wendigoes, my son... Get rid of them?'

She pulled back an animal skin curtain across a window (a hole really) in the tepee and looked out. 'If I knew how to do that, I do it myself.'

She picked up a native carving from the table (an unwanted memento of the potlach), looked at it, and threw it out the window. 'Get away from here, you horrible hairy wendigoes,' she yelled.

From outside there came the thump of the carving hitting flesh; an injured animal howled.

Grandfather opened a sleepy eye. 'By the spirit of the Great Raven, wendigoes can only die by eating their own flesh,' he said. 'Now stop throwing things at Willie Elkhorn's dog, woman.' And he went straight back to sleep.

Granny looked at him. 'I hate that dog. Who keeps a poodle as a hunting dog anyway. And it looks like a wendigo anyway,' she muttered. Into the phone, she said, 'Did you hear your grandfather, Johnnie?... Now you know as much as I do.'

Following some declarations of affection and a totally untruthful assurance he was getting plenty of deer meat to eat, Johnny said goodbye to his grandmother and put down the phone. He turned to Joan, an expression on his face of knowing something others don't. Joan looked back, expectantly. Marc and Tom played with the Round London board.

There was another knock at door.

'I got it,' said Tom, bounced up in what seemed his normal elfish manner, and skipped (it looked like) to the door.

Johnny pretty much ignored this. 'She says that wendigoes can only die by eating their own flesh,' he announced.

A rotund Pakistani, dressed in a mixture of tradition garb and oddly formal English clothes, strode into the room. 'Eating flesh. Oh no. Not good at all. Fills the body with toxins.'

He beamed around at all of the others in the room. 'Oh good. Some more people to play. We need some new faces. Come. Sit down. Sit down. Let us not delay.'

'Don't I know you?' Joan asked.

'I am Doctor Satyajit Bungah. I put myself about a bit,' the new arrival replied.

'I've seen you on my patch,' Joan persisted.

'I look like a lot of people. I look like my twin brother. He doesn't look much like me, though. Come. Highest dice starts. Deal the cards, my dear Johnny.'

Other games were also commencing elsewhere in London that night.

In a London Transport Train Depot, out-of-service carriages lined the rail spurs and barns in the yard. Whether waiting for service in the next peak hour, for repairs and engineering attention, or just for the final journey to the scrapyard, these carriages were all closed, silent and empty.

The chain-link fence around the yard swayed and rattled. A group of boys climbed over it where the barbed wire had collapsed or been pulled away. Each kid carried several spray cans of paint. They made their way across the lines to the carriages and spread out slightly.

Elton, the fat tagger-king of the Richard Owen Estate started to tag a carriage. His inevitable side-kick, the scrawny kid, watched Elton with a look of hero-worship and then moved along the row of carriages to start his own tagging.

A dark presence – the wendigo – watched from one of the sheds, his newly discovered ability to ride the back of underground trains had greatly expanded his travels, although he hadn't quite planned to come this far out, beyond the end of his preferred tunnels and into the open air. He was feeling rather insecure about this and was, as much as his damaged brain would let him, trying to work out whether to attempt to scuttle back down the line to the tunnel entrance (not actually all that far) or perhaps try and find another train on which to ride back to safety when the sounds of the boys arriving drove him into the shadows.

In Johnny's flat, Joan picked up a card from a special pack face down on the Round London board. 'I'm changing lines.'

'Here we go. This'll stuff us up. You watch,' Marc said.

Joan read the card out loud: '*It is your birthday. Send all other players to buy presents for you at Petticoat Lane market* – cheap bastards – *Station: Aldgate East.*'

Johnny groaned. Tom gathered up all the pieces but Joan's and moved them to the Aldgate East station position on the board.

'Jack the Ripper territory,' Joan said.

'Wendigo territory now,' said Marc.

'What please is this wendigo?' asked Bungah.

'You're a vet, Bungah. Maybe you can help here,' Johnny said.

'You're a vet?' Joan said.

'I have that privilege. But I do not treat goldfish. What is the problem you are having?'

Tom, being more interested in the game – until the unfortunate if predictable outcome of Joan changing lines he was close to completing his various 'visits' and turning for his home station – threw the dice. 'Six. I never get a bleeding six when I want to open a station.' He started to move his token.

'I won't bother with the whole bit. It's too... ' Joan tried to explain. 'Well, anyway. What I need to know, doctor, is... this sounds really dumb. But...'

'Yes?' Bungah had to wait until Marc had his throw. He looked at Joan.

'Okay, look, how can you get an animal to eat itself, I mean, eat its own flesh?'

'Goodness. How strange. Of course, any carnivore will eat almost any meat, if you serve it up. Or if it finds it lying about.'

'Your turn, Joan,' Marc said. He picked up the conversation. 'I think what Joan means is to get something to eat its own flesh, literally. To eat itself.'

'Oh no. I have never heard of such a thing,' Bungah protested.

'Sure. When I was a kid. Out trapping. We'd get foxes that'd bite their legs off to get out of a trap,' Johnny said.

'There is that of course,' Bungah conceded.

Tom appeared to have been listening after all. 'I heard of a bloke who woke up next to this woman who was so ugly that...'

Now she had got back to the point of their visit, Joan tried to keep the conversation on track: 'We've all heard that one.'

'Wait,' Bungah had a thought. 'I don't quite understand what this is about but back home in Pakistan, well, in Bangladesh actually, not part of Pakistan any more. But they have enormous trouble with rats eating the rice crops. Oh yes, they lose up to forty percent of the rice yield. But they have come up with a novel way of getting rid of rats. They capture some and don't kill them, no. Do you know what they do?'

This was a game stopper, and all were now listening to Bungah. 'This you will not believe. But it's true. They...' He held up an imaginary rat by its imaginary tail. 'They sew up its rectum. And then let it go.'

'Adds a new wrinkle to the idea of being stitched up, eh,' Tom said, with a meaningful look at Joan.

Bungah continued: 'And the rats get very frustrated at being unable to defecate.'

Tom interrupted again. 'Me too. Out in the desert, in the last war, yeah? Only had bully beef for weeks on end. Didn't half bung yer up.'

'And they become very aggressive. It is the toxins. They stimulate the hypothalmus. Releases serotonin which heightens aggression,' Bungah said.

Tom interrupted again. 'That's how we beat Rommel. It weren't Monty and the Eighth Army. It was seri-whatsit.'

'You weren't kidding with his name being Buffalo because he's full of...' Joan said.

'If I might be permitted,' Bungah insisted. 'And they fight and kill other rats. And other rats, the ones that are not killed yet, you understand, they get aggressive too and kill more rats.' He sat back, looking pleased with himself despite Tom's interruptions.

'I don't see how this helps,' Joan said. Bungah realised he hadn't actually got to the point. 'No, please, wait. I have read that some rats so treated become so aggressive and hostile they eat themselves to try and relieve their frustrations.'

'I'll be goddamned,' said Johnny. 'You ever try that in the desert, Tom?'

'Eat themselves out of frustration?' Marc wanted to be clear.

'Indeed it is so,' Bungah declared with an air of Solomonic judgement.

It was at this point, they all started to laugh, tried to stop, saw each other laughing, and started again. Eventually they were all helpless with laughter.

Although not as helpless with laughter as the adults in Southwark but still enjoying themselves, Elton, his scrawny side-kick and the five or six others kids who had clambered into the railway yard with them worked away between two rows of carriages, tagging for all they were worth.

Elton sprayed a long, wavy line along the side of a carriage. He came to the end of the carriage but didn't take his finger off the nozzle straight away. His paint spurted onto the hairy body of the wendigo standing between the carriages. For a moment, Elton stared, gob-smacked, up at the wendigo and then backed away. The wendigo followed.

The other kids somehow – a sort of gang-telepathy – become aware something was wrong. There followed an even longer moment of frozen tableau encompassing the whole yard. Paint cans fizzled into silence. Then Elton sprayed paint in the wendigo's face. It stumbled back and the kids took off as one. Elton and the scrawny kid ran together until the scrawny kid stumbled and fell, dragging Elton down with him. They turned over from where they sprawled, face down in the dirt, looked up at the wendigo standing over them, slathering.

The scrawny kid instantly lost any lingering hero-worship he felt for Elton; he had seen quite a few movies despite his young years and he knew the appropriate movie cliché. 'Take him! He's fat! Take him! Eat him! He's fat! He's fat!' he screamed.

A train rumbled through on the outer line, it's the lights strobing on the kids and the wendigo. Elton lay, frightened shitless (unlike a Bangladeshi rat), hearing his friend and unable to move, unable to scream although his mouth opened to do so. He closed his eyes tight. A great splash of hot blood shot across Elton's face. He opened his eyes, started to scrambled away onto all fours, crawled out between the wendigo's legs. The wendigo held up the scrawny kid's struggling body. The kid's legs kicked feebly and blood ran down them in a steady stream.

Elton tried not to hear the crunching noises or look at the blood pouring down, a lot of it onto him, as he struggled past the wendigo and to his feet. He ran.

Through the whole yard in all directions to the horizons were running kids, yelling for their mummies.

The wendigo hurled the skinny kid's body into the windscreen of another passing train – it had dawned on him that he had grabbed the wrong one. He was long gone before the train stopped and the hysteria started. The consensus eventually was that the kid had jumped, although no one was sure from where, the best (and hopelessly inaccurate guess) was from the roof of one of the parked carriages. Nobody ever asked Elton directly and he never told anyone of his own volition.

Joan and Marc walked along the path on the south bank of the Thames. Tower Bridge loomed up in its gothic Victorian vastness in front of them. The moon shone silver off the river, or as much of the river that could be seen beyond the bulk of HMS *Belfast*, an incongruous warlike presence in the Pool of London. A faint breeze stirred the water. Romance was palpably in the air, despite the silhouette of guns on the decks of the warship or perhaps *because* of their phallic symbolism. Marc and Joan stopped once they were past the stern of the ship and leant on the balustrade, looked over the river at the Tower of London in the moonlight.

'Do you know what I am thinking?' asked Joan.

'No, what are you thinking?'

'I am thinking...' she hesitated.

'Yes?'

'I am thinking...' she began again, 'How they hell are we going to sew up some monster's poo chute?'

Although they were not that far from where Shakespeare's Globe Theatre had once stood, Joan's turn of phrase was hardly Bardic; it was, unlike most Shakespeare, to the point.

'I was thinking the same thing,' Marc said.

'It is going to have to be us, isn't it?'

'I reckon.'

'I mean, Flize isn't going to do anything. He doesn't believe... he won't believe in this wendigo until it bites him on the bum. I should be so lucky.'

'All this talk of bums and biting, it's getting me really excited,' Marc said. And it was.

Freud himself could probably have explained Joan's thought processes that followed, although it may have been too obvious even for him, even if it was subconscious for Joan. She asked without thinking (even if her subconscious guessed at the answer already): 'I've been meaning to ask, just how did you know to find that photograph of Johnny?'

Marc, innocent fool, replied, 'Oh, I didn't. Luke did.'

And that, Joan thought, explains the love bites. She didn't have time to follow that line of thought for the moment.

'You can sew, I take it?' Marc asked.

'Shit no,' Joan replied, rather more abruptly than seemed reasonable. Marc thought for a moment he had offended her by being sexist. Sex was certainly part of his offence, but not in the sense he imagined. She refused to let him hold her hand as they walked back along the river's edge. Marc was no fool; he soon figured out the cause of the change of mood, he could have kicked himself for the stupid references to being excited by bums and biting. At the same time, he was no less excited despite his *faux pas*.

And since Joan decided to go off and brood for a while, when they parted Marc went and found Luke in his usual place, went home with him again, and indulged in quite a bit of activity than did indeed involve biting, bums and a few other parts of their respective anatomies as well.

Joan, whatever else could and had been said about her, was a pragmatist. She had learnt that much from her father, and from her years in the police force dealing not so much with the criminal classes but the entrenched structures of male power. Her brooding only led her to conclude that she was bloody lucky to even get the attention let alone the attentions *plural* of somebody as desirable as Marc, and she could hardly dismiss *their* night of rampant how's-your-father is an aberration. It took her a day or two of indecision to make up her mind. The notion of a wendigo preying on Londoners preyed on Joan's mind and it was with the intention of getting Marc's help with that – mainly – that she visited him again a couple of days later.

She knocked on his flat door again (watched, of course, through her peep-hole by Mrs Tully), Marc let her in. Things were a little awkward until Joan addressed the situation – the personal situation, not the wendigo one –- by an enigmatic reference to *Cabaret* which she then explained was an allusion to the scene where Brian shouts at Sally, 'Oh screw Maximilian' and she retorts, 'I do' to which he responds in turn, 'So do I.' In the circumstances, Marc thought it was quite astute of Joan to mention it, although his immediate response was 'Ah, right, get you.' Even so, the great wendigo destruction campaign was put off until the following morning. The question of sewing up wendigo rectums was thus put on hold.

In another Square across London, a collection of what Joan would considered complete arses were heading towards what they hoped would be a fun-filled night. At Sloane Square Tube Station, a party of 'Hooray Henries,' dressed in their finery, clattered in a milling herd onto the platform, forming a shifting and rowdy group halfway along. Some were draped with streamers. One blew a party whistle. Another let off an exploding streamer. A balloon burst somewhere in their midst.

A Princess Di wannabe guffawed nasally and struggled to set off her own exploding streamer. She had trouble even holding it so of course she dropped it.

'Are you sure we should be going to drop in on the old Squiffy?' asked one Henry. 'S'awfully late,' he pointed out – to whom was not clear.

'Don't worry about Squiff. He'll be burning the midnight,' a clone of the first Henry replied. 'It may be that he couldn't make Marianne's bash because the New York exchange was still open and that rather restricts the old social but it's still the pater's firm so he won't have to get up in the AM.'

Princess Di had somehow managed to retrieve her streamer. 'Can't get this to go off. Nigel, darling...' she said. As the train pulled in and the Henries piled on board, Princess Di was still fumbling with her party favour.

The one who seemed to be the Nigel she addressed urged her onto the train. 'Come along, Sarah. You'll miss the bus.' This was too much new information for the one now identified as Sarah. The streamer occupied what little cognitive attention she could muster. 'I can't get this to go pop.'

The train doors closed, leaving the other Henries staring out at Sarah, little knowing – how could they? – they resembled almost exactly the upper-class group that passed through the Limehouse underground platform in 1941, just before the bomb hit and set in motion the inexorable set of conditions that led to the wendigo – who was presently watching them from the darkness, his colourless eyes glinting,.

It finally penetrated the tiny mind that lurked, under-exercised, beneath the carefully dyed, heavily sprayed Princess Di-styled sweep of Sarah's hair, that the train was leaving. 'Oh. Wait for me at the next station, okay, yah?' she shouted, although it was pretty unlikely that any of her friends heard her over the rumble of the train. It quickly disappeared down the tunnel, leaving Sarah giggling to herself. She went back to fiddling with the streamer – watched by the wendigo. Her struggles and her tipsy state, exacerbated by the high-heeled shoes she was wearing, brought her as if in a modern interpretive ballet move to the end of the platform where by a sudden piece of dexterity, she managed to get the party favour to burst.

It shot out over the edge of the platform into the wendigo's face. Sarah looked to see where the streamer had gone and found herself face-to-face with something truly ghastly. Before she could react, the wendigo pulled her over the edge.

From the platform all that was heard (had there been anyone to hear) of Sarah's abrupt departure from the mad social whirl she had only just left school to join were horrible crunching sounds. Followed by a resounding belch. Then, a stream of pearls was spewed up onto the platform. They rolled all over the place and it was a member of the late night cleaning staff after the station closed who noticed one of these round white objects was an eyeball.

SEVENTEEN

Marc, unselfconsciously stark naked, leaned against the bedhead and attempted to fold a pillow in half. He looked at it, trying to gauge the effect of whether, so squeezed, it actually resembled the cheeks of an arse, the hollow in the centre of the fold an anus.

Joan sat on the edge of the bed, slightly more dressed, at least to bra and underwear, her back to Marc, bent over and tense, her body contorted. She grunted as if there was something rather wrong with her. A few more grunts and she straightened up and held up a sewing needle into which she had singularly failed to thread some cotton.

'This is bloody impossible. No wonder you can't get a sodding camel through one of these. I can't get a tiny bit of cotton through.'

Marc laughed. 'It's a rich man.'

'What?' Joan barked.

'Surely, it is a rich man you can't get through the eye of a needle.'

'Oh yeah, and a camel can't go to heaven? Stick to engineering.'

'Let me do it,' Marc said. 'You make the dates.' He handed her the scrunched-up pillow, which, bent and twisted hard enough, did bear a passing resemblance to an arse. Until, that is, Joan let it go when taking it from Marc and it sprang back into just being a slightly rumpled pillow.

In the absence of an alternative, Joan had decided that Doctor Bungah's suggestion would be her plan of action, her *only* plan of action. One of the flaws in that decision was, as

Marc had pointed out, neither he or Joan could sew. When she broached the notion in the early hours of the morning, Marc had helpfully pointed out that expertise was hardly called for, neatness not an essential requirement. Since Joan had arrived at Marc's flat prepared – for sewing practice at least – she brought needles and thread. After the energetic preliminaries had been dispensed with and recovered from, they set about trying out the bum-suturing scheme.

Marc squinted at the sewing needle as he succeeded finally in threading it.

'Got you, you bastard. See that?' Mark held aloft the threaded needle.

'Very good, you capable little bushman, you,' Joan said. 'Now get on with it.' She held the pillow bent tightly into two while Marc sewed with big, awkward strokes its 'cheeks' together; not, however, without tangling the thread, and sticking the needle into himself. 'Ow. shit. That ought to do it.' He sat back.

Joan held up the pillow. Instead of staying folded together, the pillow fell out of the slip and Joan was left dangling a clumsily sewed-in-half pillow slip.

'We may need to think of something else,' Marc said.

'No? You think so?' Joan picked up the slip-less pillow and hit Marc in the face with it. Sewing up animal arses was forgotten for a while. Indeed, until over the very late breakfast they were hungrily devouring, when Marc had a better idea.

Unlike 'Old Bill' of the famous World War One *Punch* cartoon, Marc had a 'better 'ole' in mind (barring all the Freudian implications and possible *double entendre*). It took the form of a junk shop in Portabello Road. It was here after actually getting the attention of the owner (who was one of that indomitable breed of second-hand dealers who seemed more interested in accumulating stock than actually selling it), that Marc showed keen interest in a stuffed aardvark gathering dust in a crowded corner.

Having been roused to the possibilities of showing off what he had rather than to the actually selling of something, anything, the owner then proceeded to produce from deep within hidden depths of accumulated auction room detritus several other old, moth-eaten stuffed animals to show Marc.

Marc examined the bums of each – if this surprised the owner, he made no sign of it. Marc rejected a once-pet dog but took the others: a feline of some sort (possibly once an ocelot, now rather more like a moth motel), a badger and a mongoose. He produced his American Express Card but the owner wasn't having any of that – that would not do nicely, it seemed, or do at all. Like light itself, the twentieth-century had barely penetrated the dust-engrimed windows of the shop and anything other than coin of the realm (or its paper equivalent, modern times had made that much of an ingress at least) would suffice. Marc paid cash and staggered out of the shop with his arms loaded with ratty animals. It was probably just his imagination, but out in open, the various animals seemed to look to be as surprised by the daylight as passers-by were by the sight of the creatures themselves held in Marc's embrace. Under the circumstances, Marc wisely caught a cab back to Mecklenburgh Square. It also turned out to be fortuitous in another way: the wendigo visited Notting Hill Gate station that day, although the thronging tourist crowds inhibited his activities and he did not obtain a fresh victim. Having been successful gorging himself for some time now, the wendigo was not particularly hungry anyway and in the end chose to go home and sleep. He was seen on the back of a Central Line train by a few passengers, of whom only a couple could be bothered to try reporting it, and then no London Transport staff member was willing to try and pass on the garbled accounts to anyone in authority.

Over the next few days and nights, Marc's 'better idea' resulted in a pin-cushion full of bent needles of practically every kind not excluding huge carpet-sewing needles. So far not one bum was successfully sewn shut. More forceful methods were called for.

The surprised expression of the face of the stuffed mongoose Joan was holding was probably frozen there in its last moment of life (perhaps that is what surprised it) or maybe imparted by a taxidermist with either a small amount of skill or large sense of humour. By design of by accident, it was a particularly pertinent expression at that moment. The mongoose vibrated violently, belying its long-maintained immobility. With one hand, Joan clasped it by its neck, with her other she twisted its tail up as far as its internal wire frame would allow. Marc attempted to drill into its bum with a power drill. The bit caught in the mongoose which then whirled like a fan blade and Joan lost her grip. The mongoose circled wildly on the end of the drill until Marc managed to extract the drill by main force.

Marc dropped the mongoose to the floor where it joined the small pile of its much-abused brethren. Joan and Marc looked at each and shook their heads in mutual defeat and despair.

From a toy shop in Commercial Road, a sheepish looking Joan, in uniform (so obviously on duty) emerged carrying a huge rag doll. She hurried across to her police car, parked in a bus stop. She pushed the doll into the back seat, next to an unhappy-looking felon she arrested a little earlier in Petticoat

Lane. 'Company for you, Sid.' She slammed the door and climbed into the front seat.

Sid, never one to ignore an opportunity for a little bit of perversion on the side (which accounted in part for his presence in the car), started to 'feel up' the doll. Joan turned and glared at him. Sid withdrew his hand.

That evening, the doll received a rather more rough feeling-up than Sid would have given it. Watched by Marc and an amazed Mrs Tully, Joan forced the doll's backside through a sewing machine. Mrs Tully supplied the sewing machine. For an elderly lady of seemingly refined demeanour, she had not been overly flustered by Marc knocking on her door and making what ought to have been a very odd request. Having established to her own satisfaction and minor disappointment that Marc was not a 'lavender boy' (she would have to revise that when Luke came calling on Marc, but for now she had only seen and heard Joan – especially heard), Mrs Tully was intrigued as to what Marc would want with a sewing machine. Maybe he was that way after all. She managed to insist she accompany it. While never a blushing flower, Mrs Tully had not seen or heard of anything quite like this in her young days in the social whirl that existed between the wars, nor since in her slightly quieter years as Mr Tully's wife. Still it was bit of fun (she supposed) and nice to get out of her flat for a while. And she certainly noticed that whatever else was going on, the police sergeant she now knew as Joan was in love with that dazzling boy; she wondered if he knew.

The doll came out the other side of the sewing machine. Dawn held it up. Sawdust poured out its backside.

In the Prime Minister's office in No.10 Downing Street, Mrs Thatcher rested her blue power-suited arm on a formidable pile of documents in official-looking files. She reached out her hand and shook the ash off the huge cigar she held into a large ash tray with a Houses of Parliament crest. 'You told me, Parrington,' she took a fresh pull on the cigar, 'that it was only unfortunate persons of a bad class who would be taken by this thing of yours.'

Parrington sat on the other side of the desk. He watched Thatcher like a mouse watching a snake.

'Is that not so?' The Prime Minister sent out a forceful jet of cigar smoke. 'And now it seems it is showing less than a fine degree of discrimination in its eating habits. The *Belgrano* business only concerned a bunch of dagoes and look at the trouble that caused me. What do you think is going to happen now that conservative voters are being whatever they are being?'

Parrington opened his mouth to speak and thought better of it. He turned instead and looked longingly at the drinks cabinet. Dennis Thatcher was already standing at it. He raised a large gin and winked at Parrington then subsided when he saw his wife looking at him with less than tender affection.

'Have you the least notion of how my cabinet are going to react to this?' She continued to address Parrington while putting a wealth of unspoken eloquence in her gaze at her husband. 'They are all jelly fish, the whole useless lot.' She turned a gimlet eye back on Parrington. 'No, you don't have to concern yourself with such things. I do. Now, listen to me, Parrington, you must go and do something about this right away. Do make myself clear?'

Whether she did or not, Parrington was only to grateful to be dismissed. He may have been awarded medals for bravery in the war, for dealing with unexploded devices, but he was far from keen in seeing this device explode. Although, irreverently, he did wonder if such an explosion would even disturb a single hair in that frighteningly sculptured coiffure. He bid the Prime Minister good evening and only just managed to stop himself backing out of the room, all the while feeling that Mrs Thatcher would probably have preferred that he did.

The London Zoo at Camden was a popular spot for courting couples, as the keeper in charge of the elephants described them. In keeping with the animals for which he had a duty of care, Old Simon was a dignified man of late middle age who had taken on, by some sort of Darwinian osmosis, the characteristics and, truth to tell, some of the appearances of his beloved pachyderms. Even so, he could not help but find a bit odd the couple at present paying rather close attention to the several elephants out in the open enclosure. As he would tell his wife over supper that night, at first he thought they were mother and son.

'And what changed your mind, dear,' his wife said, popping a piece of haddock on his plate and smothering it with that entirely English and entirely revolting invention, white sauce.

'Well,' Old Simon explained, 'Two things really. One, they didn't look much alike. He was, well, quite, um, beautiful really.' (He was surprised to find himself saying that about a man but it seemed the only appropriate term to use). 'And she was a horse's-bum-with-a-hat on.'

'Stranger things have happened with parents and kids,' his wife interrupted. 'My Uncle Ted's and Aunt Marie's boy...'

Old Simon already had his own unspoken opinion on that, an opinion that ruled Uncle Ted out of the equation and explained why their boy was good-looking and consequently did not remotely resemble the said Uncle Ted. 'But it was that they was way too, um, what's the word, affectionate with each other.'

Old Simon's story that night, long-winded as always, went on to describe how the young man was so keen on photographing one of the elephants. The woman had waved at him, got Simon to move the elephant for the photograph. Old Simon was so involved in moving the elephant ('Patricia, it were. Always the most obliging one') that he didn't notice (so he said) until it was all over, that the elephant had been manoeuvred in such a way that any photograph was of the elephants rear end. 'Me and Patricia didn't half give each other a funny look when we realised,' he concluded. 'Why would anyone want to take a picture of an elephant's arse?'

'Language, dear,' said his wife, who had hardly heard a word he had said until that one.

For once, Parrington was thankful that 'those interring bolshies,' the unions, had shown a bit of spine in their dealings with the Parrington Corporation, made some demands felt and, in this case, there was no work on his site on Sundays. Ordinarily this was a further matter of extreme irritation towards the 'layabout working class' but now it enabled him to enter that damned trouble-making tunnel unseen.

Having negotiated the ladder and the length of exposed tunnel, he clambered into the remains of the booking hall. The wendigo – Nick as he actually thought of it – had obviously been busy, too busy as Parrington knew only too well. Or rather not busy in quite the required way. He had to avoid bits of human anatomy which hung from the walls and ceiling. He forced his way towards where he thought he could hear muffled sounds emanating. In the half-light, he stumbled over a body. At first he was going to ignore it but there was something familiar about the corpse. He stopped and bent down, looked more closely. It was Lady Muqbuquet, he (or she) with both legs torn off. Despite the liberal amount of perfume, she (or he) had used when living, she (or he) was smelling rather rank. He turned his face away and was shocked even more. For a horrible, truly horrible, moment he thought that was Lady Diana Spencer lying next to Lady Muqbuquet. He recovered enough to realise it wasn't. Thank god. Maggie would torn his testicles off if it had been. Parrington straightened up. Mrs Thatcher was right – as always. Nicky was clearly exceeding his orders.

Nearby, the wendigo sat at its ease and sucked the marrow from one of Lady Muqbuquet's torn-off legs. It had heard Parrington coming ever since Sir Thomas scrambled off the end of the ladder – in fact the light that burst in when Parrington opened the trapdoor had alerted it. But it did not look up at Parrington until he was standing in front of it, and then it did once, quickly, and returned to its meal.

Parrington stood looking at the wendigo, uncomfortable at being ignored; he wasn't used to it. 'Look here. I know you're eating and all but this is the very thing I have come to pick a...' An unfortunate metaphor nearly used but quickly prevented.'... to speak to you about.'

The wendigo continued to ignore him. Parrington pointed at Lady Muqbuquet. 'This is just the very thing I am talking about. You just can't eat quality. That's not what I told you to do. Not remotely what I ordered you to do. This is rank insubordination.'

Now the wendigo looked up at him, swallowed a mouthful and dropped the bone.

Parrington blustered on. 'This is may not be wartime but the rules still apply. You follow your superior officers orders... to the letter, to the letter. Do you have any idea what happens if orders are not obeyed in wartime, Nicky?' He pulled out his revolver, brandished it. 'I would be perfectly within my rights to shoot you on the spot.'

He put the revolver back into his pocket. 'Now look here. I don't like having to talk you in this way, old chap. It's just that I know what's best. I know what has to be done. And what is not to be done. After all, you have just been living in this unspeakable way. Not getting things done at all. Not taking charge. No perspective on the big picture at all. You weren't born and bred to it.'

The wendigo unhurriedly lifted its hairy frame to its feet.

'You know what I mean. Not your fault. Just unlucky. Wrong parents. Barely submersible gene pool.' Parrington blundered on. 'And then old Adolf playing silly buggers, dropping one of his bombs on the station. One that went off that time. Bad luck. Nobody's fault that we had to just fill up the hole. Nobody to know you were still down here. You see what I mean. I had to give that order because it was my place to give that order.'

The wendigo stretched to its full height and growled. Parrington was taken aback by the size it now was. But he had been used to having and getting his own way for too long. 'Don't use that tone of voice to me. I am giving the orders. I did then, I am now. Some things don't change.'

The wendigo moved menacingly towards Parrington. It pushed back the hair dangling over its face. For the first time, Parrington saw those terrible eyes, pale to the extent of being almost colourless. He had a sudden image of the boy Nick, yes, his eyes had been like that but they had never held the sheer animal power these had. The courage that Parrington had during the war did not desert him now, but in a terrible sense of flashback, he did feel that gut-churning fear he had felt every time he moved into the close proximity of an unexploded bomb.

'Right, Nick or wendigo, whatever you call yourself. That's all the rope I am giving you.' He reached into his pocket for his revolver. Before he could level it and fire, the wendigo tore off his arm with one sweep of its razor-sharp claws. The arm fell to the ground and the finger tightened on the trigger – too late.

Before Parrington's brain could register the pain but not before it could register the sight of his arm lying on the ground in front of him, he shouted, 'You can't do that. It's anarchy.'

The gun went off with a deafening report.

Finally it dawned on Parrington that he was not in charge after all. He turned and ran, ignoring the blood streaming from his severed arm, delaying the shock, adrenaline released by fear overrid the pain. He stumbled over bodies and bits of anatomy, ran head first into other corpses, flailing with his remaining arm at the viscera that dropped on to him.

The wendigo pursued him steadily, playing with him, catching up and tripping him, not grabbing him firmly before letting him get up and run on. All down the tunnel they went, cat-and-mouse. Parrington staggered out into the junction with the Circle Line and looked up just in time for a Circle Line train to bear down on him. As it approached, a flicking paw sent him tumbling for the last time.

He fell on the line, lay across the outer rail. And was decapitated.

The train disappeared out of sight.

Parrington's corpse was dragged by the wendigo back into the tunnel. His head the wendigo booted like a football ahead of himself as he went.

EIGHTEEN

The day at the zoo did result in a faintly questionable collection of photographs of far more animal bums than just the elephants Old Simon knew about. The notion behind all this anal photography, if there was one, was something along the lines of 'know thy enemy' although neither Joan nor Marc were able to recall taking any particular notice of the wendigo's bum the only time they had actually set eyes on him. (They didn't know it was a 'him' either although Joan tended to argue it was as its manners – leaving aside eating people or maybe including that – were distinctly male, although she may have been a trifle prejudiced in the matter.) So, they didn't really know whether its bum was hairy like a yak (they had several shots of one of those) or a basically bald like chimpanzees (who were less co-operative in posing but with backsides like that, they could hardly be blamed).

These and quite a number of others now plastered the walls of Marc's flat. Even so, neither Marc nor Joan could quite remember which belonged to which species. Marc asserted that Joan was the police officer and should therefore have taken notes at the time without having to have it pointed out to her. She retorted to the effect that it hardly mattered for their purposes, which Marc had to admit was fair enough. In view of the seriousness with which Joan was now taking the matter, he tactfully refrained from pointing out that having studied all these mammalian posteriors, while it had provided a good measure of revulsion, had not given him much idea how such a familiarity was going to help with 'sorting out' (as Joan put it) the wendigo. He trusted Joan had some notions that she had not bothered to vouchsafe to him. All the more so, since she insisted they were now ready and would be heading off to put those notions into effect immediately.

The gallery of photos, albeit stuck on the wall rather than framed and assembled, resembled a surreal pornographic exhibition, so Mrs Tully said and she ought to know as she had known one or two surrealist artists and even a few pornographers back in the 'thirties until Mr Tully had put a stop to that side of her social existence. Mrs Tully, who insisted on being called Esme (which was odd as her name was Florence) had appointed herself purveyor of steaming pots of tea while the display was being assembled. She did not quite know what was going on but she hadn't had so much fun since, oh, well, since she married Mr Tully. He had been, as she put it, a good provider but hardly much of a live wire – she was vague as to how they had even managed to meet let alone consummate a courtship. Oddly, he had worked in the Patents Office although as Esme put it 'he was no Einstein.' She was delighted to report that one arse-portrait, it was possibly an eland, did bear a striking resemblance to the late Mr Tully's. Tea duty performed, Mrs Tully retired from the fray and went off to have a quiet lie-down in the hope she could shake loose the mental image of the late Mr Tully's backside.

When Marc returned after carrying the tea things back next door for Mrs Tully, Joan was sitting on the sofa and pulling on a pair of enormous rubber Wellington boots. He took his Driza-bone coat from the closet next to the front door. He looked at Joan, struggling with the boots. 'What are they for? '

'I'm not stumbling around in the dark onto a live rail and becoming new oven-crisp copper,' Joan said.

'And I am?'

'You're not a copper. But to stop you becoming oven-crisp, I got you some too. They're over there.' She pointed to a pair of pink rubber boots standing behind the door. Marc looked at them, then back at Joan, aghast.

'They were in the lost property. Nobody had claimed them. Nobody'll miss them,' Joan said.

'Why doesn't that surprise me?' Marc exclaimed. 'I'm not wearing those.'

'Do they offend your manhood?'

'They offend my aesthetic sensibilities.'

Joan, having succeeded in planting both feet into her boots, leapt up, stamped her feet a couple of times and picked up a large case from the floor. She opened it and took out a tranquillizer-dart rifle.

'No need to get violent. All right. All right. I'll wear them,' said Marc, kicking off his shoes and sitting down on the floor.

'I got this from the dog squad,' Joan said, squinting along the barrel. 'Well, that is, I didn't tell them but...'

'You sure you know how to use that thing?'

Joan opened the chamber. 'Of course I do. I'm a trained professional, aren't I?' She slammed the chamber shut with a flourish. It went off and a dart thudded into a photograph of a gorilla's bum.

'Geez. I already said I'd wear them,' Marc said.

Joan pulled the dart out of the wall. 'It'll be dark. No one will see you.'

Joan eased her police car to a halt next to the wire fence surrounding Parrington's construction site. Parking was no problem at night, not since Parrington's developments had successfully got rid of any residents in the immediate vicinity. The street and the site itself were quiet as the grave, an unencouraging metaphor had it occurred to either Marc or Joan. A few miserable drops of rain spattered on the windscreen and pock-marked the oily puddles in the potholed road. A slicing wind cut across the waste ground, creating faint moans and whistles as it blew through earth-moving equipment and piles of building materials.

Marc stepped out of the car, carrying a flashlight. The pink rubber boots protruded from beneath his Driza-bone and, despite the darkness, glowed rather obviously.

Joan leant across and locked the passenger door behind him, then reached over the back seat to grab the rifle. Without warning, a chanting horde of West Ham football supporters crowded around the corner and poured down the street towards the car. Joan hesitated about pulling out the rifle until they were past. Marc grabbed the door handle and tried to open the door. 'Let me in. Let me in. They'll see me in these things. Let me in.'

He pulled desperately on the door. Joan laughed and got out the other side. The fans surged around and past Marc, Joan and the car. The boots could hardly go unnoticed and as the mob swirled past Marc endured a few appreciative comments: 'Lovely boots, mate.' 'Show us your legs, darling.' And a few that managed to suggest the possibility of a match between the boots and Marc's genitals. Marc certainly felt his face probably matched even if his member didn't. Then the crowd was gone, an echo of 'I'm forever blowing bubbles' from their spontaneous chorus of the West Ham theme song rolling out behind them.

Joan opened the back door and grabbed the rifle.

'Come on, you great girl's blouse.'

'Scarred for life. Traumatised. If I turn into a serial killer, you know whose fault it's going to be.'

'Why not try turning into a wendigo killer first, eh?'

She led the way into the site. The tunnel entrance was still open from Parrington's earlier and terminal visit. Although they had no idea about this, the fact it *was* open gave them pause. Finally, Marc lowered himself on all fours and stuck his head into the hole. There was no light to be seen, nor sound to be heard, other than a low modulated moaning of wind in the tunnel. He scrambled back up, brushing the mud and slime from his coat. 'I guess it's alright. Don't know why the door's open. Maybe they don't bother any more after the other night.'

'Hmm. Maybe,' said Joan. 'Down we go anyway.' She handed Marc the rifle, climbed onto the ladder and quickly disappeared below ground level.

'Oh right, Bwana. I'll carry the gun, shall I? And the torch as well.' Mark pushed the torch into a coat pocket and, rather more awkwardly, climbed down the ladder.

Joan waited at the foot of the ladder and retrieved the rifle from Marc. He removed the torch from his pocket and flicked it on as they proceeded along the tunnel. With the lighting destroyed in the fire, the tunnel was much darker than at any other time Marc had been in it. The torch beam wandered about the cavernous interior as they worked their way towards the platform. To Marc's further chagrin, the pink boots proved to have the property of glowing in the dark. 'Who the bloody hell manufactures glowing pink boots?' Marc asked.

'Who the bloody hell buys them?' Joan echoed.

Marc started to laugh.

'What?' demanded Joan.

'Just occurred to me,' Marc said. 'You made me wear these bloody things, to protect me from the dreaded live rail. And there is no live rail down here. Hasn't been for forty bloody years.'

'I just wanted see to you wear them. Soon as I saw them, I wanted you to wear them. You and your refined yuppie dress sense. I know the line's not alive.'

'You know?'

'I know. How many times do you think I touched it running like the bejesus out of here the other night? Look.' She bent down and slapped her hands in a bongo-drumming riff on the rail. 'Look. See.'

Marc shone the torch down to where Dawn was hitting the rail. Parrington's head, rather the worse for wear but still rather too obviously his, lay in the grime right next to Joan's hands.

'Shit!' She stood upright in a hurry.

Her voice carried down to the tunnel – to the ears of the wendigo. It stopped and listened. It shuffled forward to where it could see the platform – and Joan and Marc, silhouetted in the limited glow of the flashlight. It howled – once.

Marc and Dawn looked up sharply from gazing at Parrington's death mask. As the howl echoed down the tunnel, they stared at each other. Joan released the safety catch on the gun. A moment or two of mental girding of loins, although Marc was sure he was close to needing something of a more absorbent nature physically girding his loins. He tugged his Driza-bone about himself more tightly and nodded to Joan. They recommenced walking purposefully down the tunnel until they reached the end of the platform.

Marc scrambled up onto the platform and again took the proffered rifle from Joan while she climbed up. He returned the rifle and they walked together, maybe a little like a couple of members of the Wild Bunch striding out to confront the whole Mexican Army, down the platform. Here and there lay bits of bodies. They stepped with revulsion over or around these. The sight and smell increased their intention to destroy the creature and, simultaneously, fuelled an instinctive desire to turn and flee. Joan kicked a piece of body over the edge of the platform.

It landed quite near the wendigo, which had crept below the lip of the platform. Its pale eyes watched them through its hanging hair. It let them pass and then climbed up and followed them, surprisingly silently for its size.

But perhaps not silently enough. Or perhaps its size simply radiated some sort of feeling, some sort of disturbance in the air. Whatever the reason, at the same moment both Joan and Marc became aware that something was behind them and equally realised the range of options available to the identity of that something were pretty limited. Each glanced at the other and then, as one, they swung around.

The wendigo was caught in the beam of the torch. Joan swung the rifle up and around, and in her haste pulled the trigger too soon.

The dart struck the charred remnants of a wartime poster, the same one which had used the stylised cartoon monster, the 'Squander Bug.' The dart embedded itself right between the Squander Bug's eyes.

The wendigo pushed back its greasy fringe and looked at the dart quivering in the poster. And then back at Marc and Joan.

Marc and Joan looked at each other, then at the wendigo.

There was one of those still, silent moments which, while lasting mere seconds, the mind insists has lasted far longer. During that hiatus the only thing that seemed to be moving was the still-quivering dart. On the other hand, Marc could have sworn he felt every beat of his heart like a hammer blow. And was absurdly surprised his whole torso was not visibly reverberating with each beat.

The wendigo's eyes swivelled down to look at the rifle. It was like a movie cliché (Marc thought afterwards) with Joan following the wendigo's gaze to the rifle, staring at it herself as if surprised to find herself holding it and the wendigo raising its eyes again to look at Joan, then back at the rifle. Its fringe flopped back over his eyes. To Marc there was something very familiar about the way the hair flopped over the eyes, another thought which did not really fully form until later. In any case, before any such recognition could register, the wendigo swiped at the rifle.

Joan, instinctively following the implications of the wendigo's gaze, pulled it away at the same second. The wendigo grabbed the rifle but failed to simultaneously grab Joan's arm. The force of the wendigo's swing pulled the rifle from Joan's grasp but the momentum flung her over the edge of the platform.

Without thinking, Marc jumped down after her, grabbed her, pulled her to her feet. The wendigo flung the rifle away, up the tunnel where it catherine-wheeled into the wall and smashed into bits. The wendigo leapt down from the platform, cutting off any possibility of Marc and Joan escaping back the way they had come.

Marc and Joan ran into the further part of the tunnel. Long formed instincts and atavistic evolutionary behaviours drove them into flight but even as they did, Marc knew that there was no escape – the tunnel was blocked at this end. He would have paused and scrambled up on to the platform and into the wreckage of the ticket foyer except that Joan didn't slow down and, judging by the sounds and smell of foul breath, the wendigo was rather close behind them. They scrambled (since the sleepers and rails hardly allowed for an Olympic running track smoothness) past the end of the platform. Miraculously, Marc still held the torch although the beam was all over the place and only intermittently of any use until instead of bouncing back from the concrete finality of the tunnel barrier the shaft of light fragmented over a pile of rubble.

The heat and explosions of the other night had caused the long-immovable barrier to collapse. Not that Marc stopped long enough to examine, even consider, the cause; he and Joan scrambled up and over the results. The wendigo followed, even though it had not been this way previously. Nobody and nothing had, bar generations of spiders, whose unchallenged kingdom this had become in the decades that trains had ceased to hurtle through it.

Marc and Jane had to fight their way through thick, entangled, uncountable generations of cobwebs. They slid in the slime that had been dripping from ceiling and walls for as long as the cobwebs had been accumulating.

A glimmer of light flickered around a bend in the tunnel and then they burst through a final cascade of cobwebs into another, functioning line, just where, as Marc surmised (in what seemed like another lifetime – this one seemed to have only and entirely consisted of rushing around in sheer terror), the 'lost' line had joined another line as a spur line. (He figured to congratulate himself on his insights later – if he survived.) The spur connection was only a short distance from the platform of a Central Line station.

A train stood at the platform, facing along the tunnel into which they now emerged. The station's public address system was announcing this train was 'out of service,' the last train from this station that night, even as Joan and Marc scrambled up onto the platform, dived into the first door and onto the first seat of the first carriage.

Collapsing, they tried to drag air into their lungs and frantically to wipe slime and cobwebs off themselves and each other.

The driver had missed their sudden, dramatic appearance for the simple reason that at the precise moment he had been bent down in his cab, returning his tea thermos and cup to his carry-all bag. Wiping his lips on the back of his hand as he stood up, he glanced up at the convex mirror on the wall that showed the platform behind him empty and reached for the driving handle to start the train.

The wendigo suddenly leapt up from the tracks and grabbed at the front window frame of the cab. The driver froze, then – quite reasonably under the circumstances – panicked. He scrambled out of the compartment and started to flee along the platform.

Marc and Joan sat, oblivious, in the carriage wiping the intensely sticky cobwebs from eyes, hands, face and hair.

'This isn't exactly going to plan,' Joan said, as she reached up to remove a large gob of cobweb from Marc's hair, which, in a testament to his chosen hair product, had hardly a strand out of place – until then.

'This train is exactly going either,' Marc observed.

Cobweb and hair gel proved to have a chemical affinity that in Jane's still shaking fingers caused a large chunk of Marc's hair to come tumbling down over his face.

With their backs to the windows and their preoccupation with cobwebs they did not see the driver as he started to run along the platform nor his being suddenly pulled down below the level of the window. A great gout of blood splashed across the panes.

'Oops,' Jane said, pulling harder to loose the cobwebs from the locks of hair. As Joan made matters worse, Marc said, 'Maybe leave it, eh?' pointlessly. Ignoring his directions and actually getting some free, she tried wiping the webby mess off her hands onto the seat cover.

'But I get so aroused by your hair,' Joan insisted.

'Isn't getting nearly killed by some bloody great hairy monster arousal enough for you?'

'His yucky hair is no turn-on,' Joan shot back, rubbing her fingers harder on the seat.

'I wasn't suggesting it was. Why isn't this train moving? But that hairy face, it reminded me of...'

Atavistic instinct cut in again. Marc suddenly looked at the blood-dripping window. The driver's face, spewing blood, shot up against the window. As one, Marc and Joan leapt up, ran down the carriage and out the far door. On the platform, a distant exit sign beckoned, a better prospect of escape than a train – especially one that was clearly not going anywhere soon. They hared towards it.

The wendigo was no longer hunting for food or driven by the bloodlust that its metamorphosis had caused. It recognised, as a result of its final and terminal meeting with Parrington, that Marc and Joan represented further danger to its very existence. It pursued them not as prey but as mortal enemies. This was personal. It dropped the driver's bloody body and ran after them.

That cosmic perversity, timing, was not on Marc and Joan's side. Unbeknownst to them a row of monitors in a room at the back of the station which were set up to show various parts of the station were being switched off at that very moment by a tired security guard whose shift ended when the station closed. Strictly speaking, he was not supposed to stop watching until the last train had left the station but he had never seen a train not leave the station and had no reason to assume this one wouldn't. So what did a minute or two matter? Just as the last monitor faded to black, Marc and Joan appeared fleetingly at the bottom of an escalator in that monitor's screen. The security guard did not see them. He switched out the lights, stepped out the back door into a lane behind the station and waited for his mate, who was closing down the station, to join him.

Marc and Joan ran on to the escalator and charged up. About halfway up, the escalator stopped and in accordance to Newton's Law, which they would have had occasion to curse if the urgency of their situation had not mitigated against them bringing it to mind just then, they fell in a heap.

'Shit. *Deja vu*. Again,' said Joan, pushing Marc off her. They struggled back up as the lights started going out one by one.

Marc shouted: 'Hey! Hey! We're here!'

Joan joined in: 'Wait! Hey! Hey!'

Despite their shouting they still heard the clang of metal gates closing. In the dark, they struggled up the rest of the escalator. They dashed through the foyer, up to the automatic barriers. The barriers had been turned off like everything else. They climbed over these. And ran up the last few steps to the entrance. It was closed and locked tight. The street outside was deserted.

'Cooee! Where are you? This is bloody London.' Marc shouted. His cry dissipated into the damp and cold night. In the silence that followed they heard only too plainly behind them the sounds of the wendigo climbing the escalator.

'We got to go back down,' Marc said.

'Don't be bloody daft. We'd only get trapped down there,' Joan retorted.

Marc rattled the gates. 'We're bloody trapped up here. Down there, we can drive the train out of here.'

'We can, can we? Where to? This line is closed down. We couldn't get out. This bloody country. Everyone goes to bed and the public transport stops running. Or vice versa.'

But, by and large, there is nothing like a bit of adrenaline to get the mind working overtime. And Marc's mind pretty well had the schema of the underground system stored in it. 'The Piccadilly Line. That's still running,' he said. 'Runs out to Heathrow, so it goes late. This line connects with the Piccadilly Line. Come on.'

He grabbed Joan's arm and pulled her with him. They ran back and hurdled the barriers.

'Can you drive an underground train?' Joan asked as her own brain fell back into gear.

'Easy peasy.' Marc had a thought, 'As long as the power is still on in the tracks, of course.'

The carriages were still lit up even if the platform wasn't when Marc and Joan cautiously peered out from an entrance to the platform, so the power was still in the track system. On a telepathic count of one-two-three, they charged out of the entrance and into the driving compartment of the train. Joan slammed the door behind them.

Marc gripped the controls. 'Here we go.'

He pushed the control handle and the train lurched forward. 'This is great. The one in the museum never moved. Well, it wouldn't really. '

'Move, you bastard,' Joan shouted. Marc looked at her. 'Not you, the train,' she explained.

'Take it easy. It'll pick up. Relax and enjoy the ride,' Marc said and in response the train's speed did noticeably pick up. Joan looked at Marc. He looked more like a big kid than he usually did. His usually immaculate hair was flopping over his face, his mouth was grinning fit to bust. 'Jeez, I love you,' Joan said, not realizing she had said it out loud. Whether Marc heard or not, Joan reached across, pushed his hair out of his eyes and planted a kiss on his mouth.

'Hey, take it easy. I'm driving here,' Marc said.

As the train pulled away down the platform, the wendigo took a flying jump at the back of the train. Recent practice had perfected its technique and it hung on as the train disappeared into the tunnel.

In the driving compartment, Marc relaxed slightly his hold on the driving handle, trying to get a sense of how much grip it required. 'This is great. This is really great. Isn't this great?'

Joan, to whom reality was returning a bit quicker now, looked at him in amazement. 'Getting chased by a great big hairy man-eating beastie is great?'

'Well, no, not that bit obviously. But I'm driving a train. I'm actually driving a London Underground train. I've always wanted to be at the front of one of these things.'

'Boys and their toys,' Joan said with no small touch of exasperation. 'On which subject, I wish I still had the gun.'

'It's back there. We're here.'

'We're where?'

'Here,' Marc said just as the train thundered into the next station. Marc eased off on the control. The train juddered to a halt, just too far past the end of the platform.

'Hang on. I'll back her up a bit. So I can read the sign,' Marc said. He fiddled with the controls; the train backed up. He fiddled some more. The train went forward, and then back, as Marc tried to line up the front with the exact stopping spot.

While this mindless shunting backwards and forwards went on, the wendigo scrambled up onto the roof and tried to make its way forward. The sudden jerking movements of the train threatened to dislodge it but it hung on each time.

Joan was finding the shuffling equally as irritating as she bounced around the cab.

'I'll get this in the right place so's we can get off,' he explained.

Taking swift advantage of a moment of stability, Joan rapped him on the forehead. 'Hello, what the fuck are you playing at?'

'What?' Marc stopped fiddling with the controls.

'There is nobody on this train. What does it matter where it stops?'

There was somebody *on* the train: the wendigo crawled along the roof towards the front of the train.

'Okay. Sorry. It's just...' Marc said. 'Well, this is the first time I have actually driven a real live moving train.'

'D'you think it's safe to get off?'

'Oh sure,' Marc said. 'Do you?'

Joan lowered the window in the driver's cab. Marc peered out the front window at the closed circuit monitors attached to the wall at the front of the platform. They were all blank.

'The surveillance monitors are off. This bit's closed for the night. The other platform will still be open though... if we are where I think we are.'

'So, you're sure the other line's running?' Joan asked.

'Of course,' Marc said, rapidly trying to figure out in his head which way the train was actually facing when they hijacked it. 'You going to look or what?'

Joan hesitated, then stuck her head out the window, peering down the dimly lit platform. Marc pushed up behind her and tried to look out as well.

The wendigo, moving silently, shuffled carefully closer to the front of the train.

'I can't see anything. I don't think there's anything,' Joan said as she pulled her head back inside. 'The buggers are saving electricity. It's not too bright down there.' She started to open the door.

'Hang on. It's probably better if we wait, wait until we hear the Piccadilly Line train at the other platform, and then we run like the clappers through,' Marc cautioned.

'I don't know. If that thing comes up the tunnel while we are hanging about in here...'

'I don't think it can go as fast as this train. Not the way I drive, baby. So it'll be way back. If it followed us at all.'

Joan stuck her head out again for another look. 'Seems to me it had its mind fixed on getting us. So...' She left that thought as better unspoken.

The wendigo had managed to work itself into a position almost directly above where Joan's head stuck out the window. She pulled her head back in.

'Why would it pick on us? I mean why keeping chasing us when...' Marc's rationalisation was cut short as the wendigo jumped off the roof in front of the train. In a single movement, it smashed the front window with a paw, grabbed Marc, pulled him out through the window onto the track, and, dropping him, pulled itself into the cab through the shattered window.

Joan sprawled backwards as the wendigo hurtled in. The door from the driving compartment into the carriage fell open at the weight of her crashing against it and she fell through onto her back. Reflexively, she kicked the door closed in the face of the wendigo. The door locked itself.

The blow of the door slamming into its face caused the wendigo to stagger back onto the driving controls. A hairy, clawed hand gripped the handle.

The train started to move forward. Marc, staggering to his feet, leapt onto the front of the train and held on for dear life as it gathered speed down the tunnel. His shadow suddenly appeared in front of him on the metal front of the carriage and he realized in a flash he was caught in the headlights of an oncoming train down the tunnel. He turned as best he could and stared in frozen horror as the two trains rushed towards each other. Seconds before an inevitable impact, the trained veered off at a fork in the tunnel, each down different line. *Of course they would,* Marc thought. *Trains don't run in opposite directions on the same tracks. I know that.*

He scrambled up onto the ledge of the broken window and then up onto the roof. Once there, he had to lie flat to avoid being wiped off by the low ceiling in the tunnel. This much was vaguely instinctual or maybe just adrenalin driven, but what the hell did he do next, he wondered. And came up with no immediate answer – adrenalin can only do so much. Beneath him, he could hear the wendigo pounding on something. Where was Joan? And why was the wendigo driving the train? It was all he could do to hang on; the train was picking up speed.

The wendigo could not have answered if Marc had been able to ask it why it hung onto the control handle (if it could speak at all – it was far from clear whether the supernatural process of mutation from boy to beast had robbed the creature of human speech; Nick had not had any reason to speak long before the manifestations of that mutation had become apparent). It probably didn't even realise it was gripping the control handle; its attention, if only one of its hands, was occupied with trying to beat down the door to the carriage beyond. Certainly that prevented it from seeing – even if it could understand what it meant – the light on the panel in the driving compartment that warned whoever was able to heed it, that the train was reaching a dangerous speed.

The speed was now such that the train was bouncing enough to bash against the tunnel wall. The movement may have been the reason the wendigo held on so tight. Even its bulk would not have prevented itself from falling over with each thump and rebound. It simply did not connect the rocketing, ratcheting movement with its cause – its leaning on the control handle.

Marc tried to move further down the train while also holding on for dear life as the ride he was having started to resemble the roller-coaster at Luna Park in St Kilda in Melbourne. He hadn't really cared for *that* as a kid then, he cared less for *this* now.

Inside the carriage, Joan lay on her back in the passageway. At first she had been partly stunned by her fall, the breath knocked out of her. Illogically she thought this is what footballers feel like when they were described as being 'winded,' usually by a power-driven football in the solar plexis. As she gradually regained some semblance of ability to order her limbs to obey her brain's commands, the shaking of the train made it even more difficult to get to her feet. Besides which she was transfixed by the sight of the door to the driving compartment starting to splinter. With a supreme effort (as she thought of it) she scrambled to her feet sufficiently to stagger back along the carriage and to hoist herself up by the pole near the door. In what may or may not have been an inspired moment, she grabbed the emergency brake handle and, literally, swung off it. For once the cosmos acquiesced in the timing. The brakes jammed on just as the driver's compartment door fell into the carriage.

The train screeched and screamed to a halt, sparks flying from all its wheels, threatened for a moment to start a somersault but settled down and stopped with its nose just into the next station. For some automated reason or other, the station public announcement system felt obliged to offer the warning to 'Mind the Gap.'

The halt to the train's momentum had several effects beyond activating electronic devices: Marc commenced an unstoppable slide along the roof at the same time as the wendigo was hurled bodily out of the front window. Marc, a second or two later, was thrown off the roof on top of the recumbent wendigo.

Having had the decidedly softer landing, even if face down into a pile of tangled, greasy and appallingly odiferous hair, Marc recovered first. He struggled to get up, pulling out handfuls of repulsive fur in his mad scramble to get off and then away from the wendigo. The wendigo, though stunned, tried to hold onto him.

A hopelessly one-sided wrestling began, with Marc's only slight advantage being that he was both smaller and more agile. And, it must be admitted, in a condition that had exceeded shit-scared by a mathematical factor too great to calculate. Adrenalin decided it still had a role to perform afterall and upped the ante on its secretion.

If the wendigo could not hold Marc, it could – and did – try to bite him. It opened its hideous jaws – its breath by itself nearly did for Marc – and sank its fangs into the folds of Marc's Driza-bone coat.

Joan, having been spared the effects of Newton's Law for the second time that night by dint of hanging onto the emergency brake handle staggered through from the carriage. She grabbed the driving handle and pushed it forward. What she had in mind was not clear; maybe in her peripheral vision she had seen the wendigo make its spectacular exit out the front window and figured that she could run it over. It is reasonable to assume that she didn't know Marc was there in front of the train – after all she was in love with him, and, since love conquers all, reasonable doubt can be applied to the notion that in order to save her own life she was willing to risk ending his.

The net effect was to add an even greater impetus – if one was really needed – for Marc to free himself from the hold the wendigo's teeth had on him, or actually on his coat. He wrenched himself sideways, the wendigo's teeth tearing a huge chunk out of his coat. The train lurched at them. (Thank British engineering genius for the low acceleration ratio of London Transport engines.) Marc pushed the wendigo with enough force to free himself but in trying to leap to the side of the tracks only managed to fall precisely between them.

The combination of Marc suddenly becoming free by adrenalin-powered push and his coat tearing caused the wendigo to fall backwards over the rails onto the tunnel wall. Even as it did so, it reached again for Marc and managed to grab hold of his trailing coat tails. The train wheel cut off the wendigo's arm. It screamed in agony.

Joan let go the driving handle go, a second too late, after seeing Marc emerge from behind the wendigo. The train lurched to a stop. Joan leapt out, fell to all fours, peered into the gloom at the front of the train. From the darkness below the front of the train, she heard Marc's voice. 'I didn't know you could actually do that.'

He emerged, pulling himself out from underneath the train. 'Actually lie between the tracks and have a train go over the top of you,' he explained.

He climbed a little shakily on to the platform. Joan grabbed his arm and pulled him up the rest of the way and into her arms. She held him off the ground, his toes not even touching and whirled them both around in a mad pirouette of relief, joy and passion. The momentum carried them into the carriage and they collapsed on the floor in a heap, hugging each other in speechless relief to find each other still alive. Finally they separated and leant back, catching their breath, neither knowing whether to laugh or cry.

'Oh, you bloody fool,' Joan said for no reason she clearly understood.

'Me? Who started the train again?' Marc retorted.

If Joan had an retort about to spring to her lips, it froze on the passage from brain to mouth when she saw the wendigo, blood gushing from the stump of its arm, crawling up onto the platform. She leapt to her feet and dragged Marc up as well. She pulled desperately at the door on the tunnel side. Marc, realising in time, slammed the platform side door in the wendigo's face. Together, they leap out into the tunnel.

They shuffled along between the train and the tunnel wall, trying to avoid the live rail. Marc accidentally just touched it slightly with his foot and it sparked and hissed.

'I told you you'd need those boots,' Joan said. Marc felt sick at the thought he had moments before been wrestling with the wendigo almost on top of the same rail.

The wendigo beat on the carriage door and tried to open it with its remaining hand.

As Joan reached the front of the train, the wendigo's detached arm lying on the track grabbed her ankle. She screamed (although later she asserted that she did nothing of the sort but admitted she may have shouted something like 'Fucking hell!'). Together they tried to get her free of the arm. With a superhuman pull Marc wrenched it free.

The wendigo forced the door to the carriage, crossed the carriage in a single bound and leapt out the far side. It pushed itself along between the train and the tunnel. It raised itself to its full height and gave a blood curdling howl. And threw itself, jaws agape, onto Marc.

Marc raised his arm in his coat in an instinctive if seemingly futile and fatal attempt to fend off the beast.

The wendigo's massive fangs sank deep into Marc's coat. It tossed its head and the sleeve and what it contained came away from the coat. The wendigo bit savagely down onto the arm.

It was not Marc's arm inside the sleeve.

The wendigo bit on its own severed arm. It didn't realise at first and then the effect smashed through its whole being. It went into throes of agony, howling, thrashing about, until it fell against a Conservative Party election poster pasted to the tunnel wall. It vomited a huge quantity of revolting matter from the depths of its bowels over the face of the prime minister.

The wendigo fell onto the live rail, burned, twisted, screamed. Then lay still.

'Pick the bones out of that,' Joan said.

Neither Joan nor Marc spoke again for what seemed like an eternity. Then Marc cleared his throat. 'Can we get out of here, please.'

They started to walk up the tunnel. Joan took Marc's hand – the one where there was no longer a sleeve. 'That's enough to put you off your dinner,' she said.

'How can you even think of eating after seeing all that?'

They walked into the darkness of the tunnel where it forked after leaving the station. Their voices carried back.

'I don't know. I just thought a nice curry,' Joan said.

'Curry. After what that just brought up? You don't see a passing similarity?' Marc was disgusted.

'I don't know. All this excitement makes you kind of hungry.'

'Gold American Express card or any colour, we are not having curry ever again.'

'No. Go on. Oh well, sushi then?'

'For pity's sake, woman...'

'I'm joking. Your hair's a mess. Spaghetti bolognaise then?'

Their voices faded as they disappeared into the gloom of the tunnel. Behind them, the wendigo, in a reversing of the process that had changed it forty long, lonely years ago, transformed back into Nick. If Grandpa Stillwaters had known this was the consequence of a wendigo dying as a result of eating its own flesh, he had not said so at the time of the all-important telephone conversation. Of course, he was more than half asleep when he had overheard Grandma Stillwaters talking on the telephone to Johnny and it is likely he inadvertently gave away what was secret knowledge that only initiated men of the tribe should know. When he woke later, he had a vague memory of doing so and was thankful that he had not revealed the other secret that a wendigo, as it dies, reverts to the human form it once was. That this was a secret for men only was because it was felt that to see the lost loved one 'return' was usually distressing, more so than ordinary death as many would know what the loved one had been up to while a wendigo. No doubt Joan and Marc would have experienced a considerable degree of distress had they witnessed the wendigo transmogrify back into a teenage boy. It had all been horrific enough without that.

POSTSCRIPT

London Transport, for all that it is a multi-levelled and unwieldy bureaucracy, did miss the train that Joan and Marc had left stranded in the tunnel. They probably would have found it quickly enough but an anonymous phone call alerted them to its location anyway. The staff sent to investigate called the Transport Police upon finding the naked body of a teenage boy, with a severed arm, lying beside the tracks in front of the train. And the inexplicably shattered front window and driver's cab door. No-one could make any connection between the two. Nor the later discovery, a station back, of the mutilated remains of the train's driver. Memos flew. Meetings were minuted. No conclusions were reached. Ironically, in due time, all the paper work found its way to the archives at the London Transport Museum.

Details of the body of the boy were circulated to police stations both in the area and wider but no missing persons reports were found to coincide with the description of the anonymous corpse. Joan, who had hoped that the finding of the wendigo's body would be mystifying enough to deflect any investigations that may have led to her unauthorised part in its demise, was herself mystified when the reports of the finding of a boy's body but not of animal of an unidentifiable species came to her attention.

The curious series of disappearances of individuals in the inner London area, most of which seemed at some point to connect with the underground – the individuals were variously reported to be understood to be going to use the tube or in some cases were actually seen entering or in a tube station – ceased about the same time that the body was found. Again, no obvious connection suggested itself – or was suggested by Joan.

Joan had braced herself for a tabloid field day when *The News of the World* and its kith and kin got hold of the news a fantastic dead monster in the underground. But, of course, the newspapers never did, because there was no longer any monster to be found. She and Marc were unable to make sense of the lack of a report of finding the wendigo nor able to make any better sense of the report of the body of a naked teenager. Joan was inclined to believe that the discovery of the wendigo was probably covered up and that the boy, whoever he was, may well have been the wendigo's last victim, although neither she nor Marc could explain when the wendigo may have killed him; it would hardly have had time while chasing them. And why was he naked?

A photograph of the boy was circulated and Joan, as community liaison officer, carried it with her, asking around her patch. She of course showed it to the rent boys and street kids in the area. Certainly both she and Luke, when she showed it to him, noted the remarkable similarity that the boy's eyes had to Luke's but Nick's corpse had been cleaned up in the morgue in order to be photographed and the wendigo's hairy fringe that had sparked a vague sense of familiarity in Marc had disappeared along with the other aspects of his metamorphosis, so this matter did not arise to make any further link. Luke had no close relatives of that age, and no relatives that he knew of who were recently missing, so he and Joan wrote off the eye resemblance as mere coincidence.

Parrington's disappearance was noted almost immediately and much public and private speculation followed. Among the many idle speculations (some of which led to investigation of his finances without reaching any unusual revelations) his disappearance was given a passing hint of intrigue when it was mooted abroad that he had been seen not that long before in an intimate *tête-à-tête* in St Stephen's Club with the Minister of Transport and some journalists tried to make some connection of the fact that Eastlake was an Old Hamiltonian as was Parrington. But not even the most wretched tabloid conspiracy theorist could make anything of that. The newspapers, for once, did not find out about the meeting between Parrington and Erroll Gray Joan had witnessed. In-built class attitudes probably prevented any reporter from even considering the possibility that Parrington would set foot in a Hackney public house.

Then, rather less urgently, Angela Snottym was also rumoured to be missing. Daphne Gratton got onto that one but even she could not really bring herself to a tabloid conclusion that Parrington and Angela may have debunked together. Although Daphne could just (with a shiver) imagine Angela wanting to take off with Parrington, she could not for a moment imagine Parrington wanting to elope or something with Angela.

For a while Daphne, having a certain attitude about ex-public school men, had headed the tabloid pack in the hunt for scandal to associate, no matter how tenuously, with Parrington. When the pack had left in pursuit of other quarry, she had tried to keep the story alive but, all-in-all, although once or twice ill-informed speculation flared up around alleged sightings in unlikely places in far flung regions of the world, it soon enough became yesterday's news.

Truth to tell, no one missed either of them all that much. If the Prime Minister made any connection between Parrington's disappearance and their discussion about the creature in the underground, she made no mention or note of it. In all likelihood, she forgot about their meeting soon after it took place; she, no doubt, had other mere males to bully at the time. All work ceased on the building site and years of untangling of legal matters followed. Many years after that concrete was poured into the tunnel following London Transport quietly sealing off the ends of the spur. Whatever remains it may still have held simply became part of the foundations of a new high-rise office tower. Whether Parrington would have seen this as being in any way ironic would be impossible to determine. Joan, however, would have enjoyed the irony, had she known about the original burying of the station that started it all.

It is possible that Joan had some fairly good ideas on the disappearance of Parrington after all, she had briefly held his disembodied head in her hands. Whatever thoughts she may have had about that and about Angela Snottym, she didn't express them formally to her superiors nor even note them in any report she may have filed nor even raised them with Marc, of whom she saw rather less, partly for prudence sake lest, unlikely as it seemed, someone in the force noticed them together and arrived at some awkward questions if not unwelcome conclusions. Joan also recognised that, much as they had fun having sex together, Marc's attentions in that direction were well and truly focussed on Luke. *Fair enough too*, she thought. And was grateful for the rather energetic moments they had enjoyed.

Given what she knew about the disappearances, not only about Parrington (she was inclined to feel he deserved all that had happened to him) but about other people, including, she guessed, Margaret Hilda and Elton's scrawny friend, Joan decided she no longer wanted to be stationed at Limehouse. Superintendent Flize was only too glad to recommend her transfer; he was receiving enough heat from all directions about the Parrington affair and Joan's intransigence was not helping. In due course, and by the sort of irony the cosmos seems to enjoy, she found herself at Richmond, her father's old patch. There was, however, a compensation. Constable Buckmaster had also been transferred there – the warning Joan had given him about Leicester Square assignations had been ignored and a certain (if minor) indiscretion had blotted his copy book. Joan was not displeased to take him in hand, professionally and personally, to help him to get his career back on track, to ridding him of his homophobia and to introducing him to the delights of the experienced woman. In all these causes she was extremely successful.

Marc too knew about Parrington but even without a warning from Joan, he would have been disinclined to mention it. This did require a little bit of dissembling at first but sooner rather than later no-one was any longer employed by Parrington Corporation – the eventual legal wash-up however netted him a nice little sum. He let his hair grow back, at Luke's insistence. And Mrs Tully was in no way dismayed to discover her initial assessment of Marc was an accurate one after Luke moved in with him. If anything, she preferred this arrangement; they were both, in her terms, 'lovely boys and so kind to me.' She felt the clock had been unexpectedly but delightfully wound back on those occasions when she was taken out to dinner, now with a tall blonde boy taking one arm and a short dark one the other. Just like those halcyon days after the Great War and she had to admit these boys today with their long hair – unthinkable for a young man when she was a gal – were even more decorative than the lavender boys of her flapper days. And it was she who talked Luke into going back to being Lucien. Even Marc, after he stopped laughing, admitted he like it better as well.

Since he never heard anything more about it, Johnny

Stillwaters just filed away his grandmother's story in his mental collection of Algonquin folklore. And over an inevitable game of *Round London*, Doctor Bungah admitted he had no first-hand knowledge of the use and efficacy of induced rat constipation.

AUTHOR'S NOTE

Most of the places mentioned in this book actually exist or did at one time – with one exception. The exception is, of course, Limehouse underground station. There was not a Limehouse Station on the London underground network – to the best of my knowledge. The present day Limehouse Station is on a branch of the Docklands Light Railway (DLR) which, for most of its distance, is *elevated*; Limehouse Station is well above street level. The Docklands Light Railway did not exist at the time the purported events in this book took place. (A previous mainline railway had used a station called Stepney at the site until 1926; the track way was incorporated into the DLR in 1987 and a new station, Limehouse, constructed in 1987.)

Some historical personages are mentioned in the book but any actions attributed to them are totally imaginary. All other characters and all events depicted are fictional. While it is a matter of historical record that some deaths occurred in underground stations struck during the Blitz (curiously all starting with 'B': Bank, Balham and Bounds Green - with the further coincidence of the most deaths occurring, not as a result of bombing per se, in a crowd crushing into Bethnal Green tube station. If that was not bizarre enough, most of the nineteen killed at Bounds Green were *B*elgian refugees), the actions I depict here in no way drawn on those events and no disrespect is intended to the memory of those who lost their lives on those occasions or in the Blitz more generally.

Here I must also express my appreciation to William J. Lyon and Neil Rattigan who allowed me to use aspects of their unproduced screenplay, *Winatou*, which I understand to have been written about the time that these fictional events are set.

ABOUT THE AUTHOR

Clarke Buvelot was born in Co. Roscommon, Ireland into a family descended from Huguenots who fled France in the sixteenth century. He read Arts at the University of Bristol and Education at the University of London, worked on oil rigs in Bass Strait, Australia and now breeds exotic fish in Melbourne, Australia.